He put an arm around her shoulders and gave her a shake. "Hold on, Jenny. Don't go to pieces on me now. I'd really prefer that you keep on needling me. Remember what you were just saying. Tears aren't your style." He brushed a vagrant drop of water off her cheek, then bent over to kiss the spot tenderly. It was no journey at all from there to her lips.

A spontaneous antidote to the harrowing experience that they'd been through. But, for whatever reason, they found themselves kissing— passionately, ardently, frantically, desperately, lengthily. . . .

—from *A Season for Scandal*

By Marian Devon
Published by Fawcett Books:

GEORGIANA
MISS ARMSTEAD WEARS BLACK GLOVES
MISS ROMNEY FLIES TOO HIGH
M'LADY RIDES FOR A FALL
SCANDAL BROTH
SIR SHAM
A QUESTION OF CLASS
ESCAPADE
FORTUNES OF THE HEART
MISS OSBORNE MISBEHAVES
LADY HARRIET TAKES CHARGE
MISTLETOE AND FOLLY
A SEASON FOR SCANDAL
A HEART ON HIS SLEEVE
AN UNCIVIL SERVANT
DEFIANT MISTRESS
THE WIDOW OF BATH
THE ROGUE'S LADY
DECK THE HALLS
MISS KENDAL SETS HER CAP
ON THE WAY TO GRETNA GREEN

SIR SHAM

♥

A SEASON
FOR
SCANDAL

Marian Devon

FAWCETT CREST • NEW YORK

A Fawcett Crest Book
Published by The Ballantine Publishing Group
Sir Sham copyright © 1988 by Marian Pope Rettke
A Season for Scandal copyright © 1992 by Marian Pope Rettke

www.randomhouse.com

Library of Congress Catalog Card Number: 98-93116

ISBN 0-449-00440-6

Manufactured in the United States of America

First Edition: December 1998

10 9 8 7 6 5 4 3 2 1

Contents

Sir Sham   1

A Season for Scandal   153

Sir Sham

Chapter
One

"OH BLAST!"

"Lucy! Your language! What would Papa think?" The vicar of Waring's youngest daughter turned a shocked gaze upon her next-older sister.

"Well, he ought to think I've shown remarkable restraint. My skirt's caught on this blasted thorn hedge."

The hedge was possibly serving as a prickly retribution. It had been Lucinda Haydon's dawdling that had made them late, her choice to take the shortcut to the hall.

"Wait, let me undo it!" Camilla's entreaty came too late. There was a sudden rending sound, followed by an even more heartfelt "Oh blast!" Both sisters stared aghast at the lilac sprigged muslin. Even in the fading twilight there was no mistaking the large, right-angled tear halfway between the ribbon bow, tied just beneath the shoulder blades, and the bottom ruffle of the evening round dress. It flopped limply open to reveal the petticoat beneath.

"Oh Lucy!" Camilla's tone was as censorious as it ever got, an echo of one of their father's mild reproofs. "I did say we should have gone round through the gate. Now we'll have to go back so you can change, which will make us twice as late than if we'd gone the proper way in the first place. And what our aunt Tilney will have to say doesn't bear thinking on. You know how she values punctuality. I wouldn't put it past her to write Mama all about it."

"Well, if she was all that eager for our presence, she could have asked us to dinner instead of having us show up afterward like common hired musicians." The hedge might have served as a substitute Lady Tilney, judging from Lucy's glare.

"But Aunt explained all that." Steeped in Papa's Christian charity, Camilla shed the kindest possible light upon Lady Tilney's snub. "There weren't enough gentlemen to go round. Besides, it would have looked most odd for us to be there without Papa, and our aunt knows how much he hates to go out socially without Mama along to carry the conversation. Oh, do quit staring at that poor hedge as though it were to blame. Come on. We must hurry."

Lucy ignored the entreaty but stuck to her train of thought as she almost absentmindedly began to break off some of the longest, sharpest thorns. "Fustian! Our aunt Tilney would not have invited us this evening at all if she hadn't thought the gossipmongers would spread it all over the neighborhood that she was afraid you'd cast poor Ada in the shade. Not that Mr. More's going to be smitten by our cousin anyway, but with only antidotes invited and us glued to our instruments in the corner, she can always hope. Pity the hall doesn't boast a musician's gallery that she could stick us in." She broke off a final thorn with an emphatic snap.

In the interest of time Camilla abandoned the homily on cattishness that Papa might have expected her to deliver. Instead, she asked her sister whether she'd taken leave of her senses, just standing there, picking off bits of hedge when they should be running for home as fast as their satin slippers and narrow skirts would permit.

"No need for that." Lucy proffered a half-dozen black thorns on the palm of a slightly pricked white kid glove. "Here. Pin me."

"You're funning, aren't you?" Camilla's voice held more hope than it did conviction. Even Papa had been known to say that Lucy had a touch of the hoyden in her makeup. "Lucy, you can't be serious. You can't arrive in our aunt's withdrawing room in a gown held together with black thorns!"

"Why ever not? It's better than having the torn part flapping behind me like a banner and most likely ripping worse. Besides, I can cover it up with Mama's shawl." She demonstrated by shifting the triangle of Norwich silk she wore round her shoulders to the crooks of her elbows, allowing it to dip down far enough to hide the offending tear.

"T-that looks ridiculous." In her nervousness Camilla was reduced to giggles. "N-no one wears a shawl across her bottom."

"Gypsies do. Oh well, I collect you have a point." Lucy sighed and reshouldered the borrowed garment. "But come on, pin me. Thorn me? Then walk close behind me when we get there. After that I'll be sitting on the tear all evening anyhow, and unless one of the blasted things sticks me and I shriek, no one need ever know."

The sisters, only fifteen months apart in age, had never appeared closer than when they entered the spacious withdrawing room of Tilney Hall (which tried to ape the Prince Regent's Oriental taste with a profusion of beechwood furniture posing as bamboo) under the censorious eye of the Dowager Lady Tilney. To her nieces' relief, her ladyship did not see fit to terminate the conversation she was engaged in with several other mothers of marriageable daughters whom she'd included in the company. It was far too satisfying to find her opinion shared that Mr. Carnaby More, besides being a tulip of fashion and handsome beyond the raptures of report, was also the soul of amiability and not above his company in the least. And it was most edifying to learn that his friend, Mr. Drury, who'd come down from London with him, was of no consequence whatsoever and that it would be a waste of time for any of the young ladies present to try to fix his interest. She did, however, direct a speaking glance in her nieces' direction as the two Misses Haydon scurried, in tandem, toward the harp and pianoforte, banked so as to be almost hidden by tall baskets of cut blossoms in the corner of the room.

If any among the company were aware of Lady Tilney's stratagem to keep her nieces tucked out of sight, they would have been hard put to blame her. It was understandable that her ladyship had grown desperate since her daughter's engagement had been broken off in such a shocking manner. And it was generally acknowledged that the Haydon girls, in spite of their straitened circumstance, were formidable rivals for their cousin, especially Camilla, whose large blue eyes, flaxen hair, dainty features, and flawless complexion had inspired more secret sonnets from fledgling Byrons and more envy in the breasts of

5

her female contemporaries than any other young lady in the whole of Sussex.

True, while there was a striking resemblance between the vicar's fourth and fifth child, Lucinda did not quite meet her sister's diamond-of-the-first-water standard. Her hair was darker by at least a shade. Her eyes, more gray than blue, not only defied being described as "limpid pools," but generally seemed to see too much by half. Even so, it was generally conceded that Lucy Haydon could be just enough out of the ordinary to attract a certain type of gentleman whose tastes might be the least bit eccentric. Their aunt was merely looking out for the best interests of her own daughter by trying to keep the sisters as inconspicuous as possible. A lesser personage would have seen to it that they remained in the obscurity of the vicarage. But perhaps their cousin Nigel, Lord Tilney, would not have countenanced that kind of slight. No, it was far better just to distance the vicar's daughters from the guest of honor, for it was a documented fact that Mr. Carnaby More hadn't the slightest need to dangle after an heiress unless he simply chose to and might be susceptible to their charms.

Mr. More was, in fact, a nabob, the owner of one of the most prosperous estates in Sussex. That he had not so much as visited that estate since inheriting it from an uncle some five years before had been a source of considerable vexation to his neighbors. Now that he'd finally seen fit to leave his London haunts to inspect his property, it was hoped he might be persuaded to settle on it. Lady Tilney had been the first to cast out a lure toward that result. Other hostesses planned to follow her example.

While her fingers moved skillfully upon the ivory keys of the pianoforte, Lucy peered at Mr. More through the foliage as he and the other gentlemen, their port consumed, entered the withdrawing room to join the ladies. She soon concluded that all the attention being lavished upon him would prove a waste of time. Though Mr. More was apparently exuding all the considerable charm that early reports had credited him with, he appeared to have far too much town bronze to be at home for long in a bucolic setting. Lucy was not familiar with the revered name of Weston, but she recognized immediately that no provincial

6

tailor had cut the perfection of his blue, long-tailed coat. Nor had she ever seen so intricate a cravat as the one now being covertly studied by several rural young men with secret longings to become pinks of the ton.

As the gentlemen began to distribute themselves around the room, Lucy reached out a foot and shifted a floral basket to gain a better view. She suppressed a grin at the deft way in which her aunt intercepted her guest of honor, leaving his friend as second prize for Mrs. Elliot and her daughter, who had placed themselves strategically near the door hoping to establish a claim to Mr. More's attention. Lady Tilney's smile of triumph at these disappointed rivals caused Lucy to giggle and repeat a measure she'd just played, forcing poor Camilla on the opposite side of an enormous arrangement of hollyhock to clap both hands upon her harp strings till she could find her place again.

After this mishap, Lucy dutifully concentrated upon her music for some thirty seconds. Then her attention wandered back to observe the scene. Several of the more determined females had drifted over to join their hostess and the honored guest where they were admiring the Reynolds portrait of the late Lord Tilney above the fireplace. Lady Tilney's efforts to push Ada into the conversation were soon thwarted by a determined miss who proceeded to ply her fan in time to some animated anecdote right under Mr. More's aristocratic nose. Lady Tilney gave her daughter speaking looks. But her message seemed doomed to remain undecoded.

Now if Mr. More were only a horse, Lucy thought irreverently, Aunt Tilney might get more cooperation. These equine creatures were of far more interest to her tall and gangly cousin than any number of eligible young Bond Street beaux. It was a pity, she mused, that her aunt had not given a hunt instead of an evening party so that Mr. More could have observed Ada at her best. All her awkwardness miraculously evaporated in the vicinity of the stables. Lucy, an able horsewoman in her own right, had been known to envy her cousin's ability to ride neck or nothing over any obstacle in her path. And certainly a riding habit was more becoming to her mannish angularity than the yellow lace over a white satin slip ornamented with satin

7

cockleshells and full-blown roses her mama had chosen to impress Mr. More. And while her heavy emerald necklace did shout "heiress," it did little to enhance either the wearer or her costume.

"You look quite charming this evening, cousin." A voice at Lucy's elbow interrupted this reverie. "Aren't you wearing a new gown?"

"Oh for heaven's sake, Nigel. You must have seen this frock at least a half-dozen times. First on Eleanor and now on me." But she smiled affectionately, realizing that even the most banal social conversation came hard to Nigel and that it was the obscurity of their location quite as much as the familiarity of their company that had caused him to seek his cousins out. He leaned upon the pianoforte as Lucy launched into another tune and Camilla, after a few seconds' lag for the purpose of identification, was able to join in.

Lucy was seldom in her cousin's company without marveling at the caprices of heredity. With his retiring nature and love of scholarly pursuits, Nigel should have been Papa's son and not his nephew. Her own two brothers, on the other hand, had resisted all attempts to point them toward the church and had opted instead for a life of adventure in the navy at the earliest opportunity afforded them. Also, it seemed further poor management on nature's part that Nigel had been endowed with the family good looks while his sister had the attributes that should have been part and parcel with inheriting the title and estate.

"It's odd," Nigel was saying, "but I don't remember that gown at all." He frowned, seriously considering the problem as if it were some genealogical muddle found in his research. "That would not be so strange if I had only seen it on Eleanor. For you and your oldest sister are quite different, and don't you agree that garments look very different on different people? All those frills and flounces Ada's wearing, for example, quite fail to do whatever they're intended to do on her but might be just the thing for your sister Camilla. Oh I did not mean—" He colored as Lucy laughed at his confusion. "I did not mean that your gown would have looked odd on Cousin Eleanor—who's quite attractive in her way though not a bit like you and Camilla in appearance. Anyhow," he finished hopelessly, "I'm sure to know that gown the next time you wear it."

"Actually, Nigel, recognizing gowns from previous wearings is definitely not a social asset. And if I've led you to believe so, then I've a lot to answer for and do apologize. Anyhow, as far as this one goes, the occasion won't arise. It's done for. I ripped it on the way over here and am now sitting on the tear."

"You're roasting me."

"Indeed I'm not." She winced as she shifted her position and felt a thorn prick. "In fact, I may have to rely on you to create a diversion, such as setting the draperies afire, so that I can make my exit without disgracing us all. No, no." She hastened to wipe the look of anxiety from his face. "I really am roasting you this time. I got in here unobserved and I can get out just as well. All eyes are glued on the magnificent Mr. More and aren't likely to waste time on Eleanor's old gown."

Then, as if to belie her words, she glanced across the room to see her aunt's eyes fastened upon the two of them. Their message was quite clear. Lady Tilney had never bothered to disguise the fact that she was anxious to discourage any intimacy between her son and his attractive cousins. The shy viscount's apparent ease with Lucy had certainly not escaped his mother's attention. She was determined that no tendre should develop there. Lucy found her attitude more amusing than distressing. She had no aspirations to become Lady Tilney.

"I think your mama expects you to do your hostly duties, Nigel. Mr. More's friend seems to be neglected." She nodded toward Mr. Drury, who stood apart from the company, balancing a teacup, looking bored and watching his friend holding court. "Perhaps you'd best go talk to him."

Nigel looked alarmed. "Must I? Yes, I suppose so." He sighed. "But heaven knows how we shall manage. Miss Meredith only extracted monosyllables from him at dinner and you know what a chatterbox she is."

Lucy was glad to note, however, that her cousin's pessimism proved unfounded once he'd joined his laconic guest. They were soon conversing fairly easily, by Nigel's standards at any rate, which was to say that the newcomer carried the lion's share of the social burden.

As she automatically slipped into another tune, leaving the faltering harp to follow as best it could, Lucy watched the two men with interest. Compared with his friend, Mr. Drury had been a definite disappointment, indifferently dressed and only moderately good-looking. But away from the sun of Mr. More's Adonis visage and charming manner, he didn't seem all that bad, she concluded fairly. Certainly his physique passed muster. He was above the average height, trim, and muscular. His dark hair was neatly cut above his collar but its careless arrangement followed no particular style that she could recognize. Nature had not seen fit to curl it and he certainly had not tried. His face was strong but rather craggy, with prominent cheekbones and a slightly hawkish nose. His eyes might be rather fine at a closer range, she'd concluded, when he must have felt her scrutiny and turned them her way. She quickly averted her gaze and returned her attention to the group of ladies clustered around Mr. More.

Lucy was taking considerable amusement from all the vying for the beau's attention and chuckling at her aunt's superior skill in thrusting Ada forward, when all of a sudden she was struck by a sobering thought. It was the height of hypocrisy to ridicule this scene. The truth was, this business of matchmaking was deadly serious, and the more conscientious the mama, the more skilled she became.

Lucy peered thoughtfully through the hollyhocks. Camilla was plucking her harp with her usual skill, the action second nature, while like Lucy she was busy observing the group gathered round Mr. More. Camilla was obviously enjoying her role of spectator. Lucy knew that her sister was storing away every detail of the evening to be discussed over their needlework. And there'd not be the least bit of envy in her recollection or any resentment of her cloistered position behind this indoor garden, whereas nature had fashioned her to be the belle of every ball. The situation suddenly struck Lucy as intolerable. What, she asked herself, would Mama do?

And to her astonishment, the answer was obvious. Mama would play the game with the other matrons. Oh, with a great deal more subtlety certainly than Lady Tilney, but she would play it all the same. And for the first time it occurred to her daughter that Mrs. Haydon was a very worldly woman. For hadn't she been the moving force behind Eleanor's marriage to the Reverend Mr. Landseer? Admittedly, a curate was far less a prize than the wealthy Mr. More. But then Eleanor was not possessed of Camilla's beauty. Who was to say that this London nabob was above her younger sister's touch? Besides, that was not the point. The point was, so Lucy now concluded, that her mother would somehow manage to bring her sister to the gentleman's attention. What came of the introduction would be squarely up to fate.

"Camilla!" she hissed. Her sister wrenched her attention away from Mr. More. "Sing!"

"Oh no, I couldn't." Camilla shrank back farther among the flowers.

"Of course you can. The party's dragging. These guests need to be entertained."

Camilla looked doubtfully about the drawing room, where most of the thirty or so people were engaged in animated conversation accompanied by the clink of cups. "I don't really think—" she had begun when Lucy interrupted.

"Our aunt will expect it." She squelched the vision of her reverend father that floated before her eyes at that whisker. Their aunt had most specifically requested background music only, from harp and pianoforte. Lucy substituted her mother's image for her father's. She had now convinced herself that Mrs. Haydon would understand the necessity for the little lie. "Now, Camilla!" she commanded as they concluded the duet they'd been engaged on.

Camilla was accustomed to being bear-led by her older sister. Though obviously all aquake, she still rose obediently and approached the pianoforte. "W-what shall I sing?"

" 'Greensleeves' " was the prompt reply. Best not try to be too showy, Lucy had decided. The plaintive ballad fit Camilla's voice, which was sweet and true, but lacked the dramatic flair to do real justice to the operatic selections well within her technical capabilities. "Don't stand here." Camilla had taken up a position behind Lucy's chair. "They'll never hear you. Go over there." She frowned her timid sister to a spot well cleared of the foliage and quickly began to play an introduction.

Oh blast, this isn't going to work, she thought despairingly. For as her sister began to sing, the conversational noises increased. Camilla's volume was negligible at the best of times. Now, intimidated by the company and the chatter, she could barely be heard a yard away.

Well, I'd best get their attention, Lucy thought. Her hands came crashing down upon the keys in a chord that stopped Camilla in midnote and caused all heads to turn in their direction. Thereupon Lucy rose to her feet and, mindful of her ripped dress, carefully stepped around the flower baskets. "Ladies and gentlemen," she announced in a carrying voice, "Miss Camilla Haydon will now favor you with a solo. Miss Haydon will sing 'Greensleeves.' "

Back once more at the pianoforte, she tried unsuccessfully to wipe her mind free of a welter of disturbing impressions while she played the musical introduction once again. Her outlandish behavior had caused the guests to look astonished, her sister to appear ready to sink, her aunt to be on the verge of some kind of fit. Mr. More had appeared politely interested. His friend, on the other hand, had looked amused.

Chapter Two

HER SCHEME WAS WORKING BETTER THAN SHE COULD HAVE imagined. The assembly was all rapt attention. And after a rather faltering beginning, Camilla had lost herself in the beauty of the melody and lyric, and her performance was now hauntingly lovely, freed of all self-consciousness.

Mr. More, especially, seemed entranced, shushing Miss Meredith rather rudely when she whispered something in her ear. He might have been Odysseus straining to hear the Siren's song. Mama, Lucy felt, would have been proud of her. It was no small achievement to have made her retiring sister the center of everyone's attention. Well, almost everyone. Her aunt Tilney was ignoring Camilla and glaring daggers straight at her. And Lucy had fixed Mr. Drury's interest as well. He was still studying her with the same detached amusement, as if he'd seen through her stratagem and was ready to offer congratulations on a well-executed campaign. Lucy was beginning to think him decidedly odious, too knowing, it would appear, by half. Well, her aunt's displeasure and his ridicule were a small price to pay for Camilla's success, she thought with satisfaction as the song concluded to enthusiastic applause. Then she could hardly contain her glee as Mr. More detached himself from the group around him and moved purposefully their way.

Camilla blushed in attractive confusion as he complimented her on the loveliness of her song while all the time his eyes implied that the song was not half as lovely as the singer. "Could I join you in a duet?" he asked her.

The other guests had followed Mr. More like a lodestar and now gathered around the pianoforte, transferring flower baskets hither and yon with no regard for the aesthetics of their arrangement, while the singers and their accompanist conferred. After several suggestions and rejections by first one musician and then the other, it was at last discovered that they could all three deal with "Flow Gently, Sweet Afton" and Lucy struck an introductory chord.

Mr. More, Lucy soon concluded, was really far too good to be true. Besides his looks and fortune, he was possessed of a fine tenor voice that blended with Camilla's sweet soprano in a manner that gave rise to speculation concerning a permanent duet arrangement. Lucy was not the only one so affected. The notion that the handsome couple with the harmonizing voices were obviously meant for each other was reflected in the disgruntled looks of more than one mama and marriageable daughter in the company. Lady Tilney appeared ready to blow the candles out and declare the party at an end.

The applause, except from those few with noses out of joint, was spontaneous and enthusiastic when the duet concluded. And then, rather like Napoleon's escape from Elba two years before, Lady Tilney made one last desperate attempt to stave off the inevitable. "What a glorious voice you have, Mr. More. We'd no notion of your talent. Perhaps now you will give us the full benefit of it and sing a solo. I'm sure my niece would like to rest her voice awhile and have some tea." She frowned pointedly at Camilla, who murmured, "Oh yes, thank you," and edged away from the guest of honor's side.

Lucy was not to be so easily outflanked. "Could you take my place, Camilla dear? You are the better accompanist and a voice like Mr. More's deserves the best."

"Nonsense!" Lady Tilney spoke sharply. "You are the expert on that instrument, Lucinda. Why, she even instructs the neighborhood children, Mr. More."

"Oh but I'm sure the other Miss—Haydon, is it?—will do nicely." His smile tugged Camilla toward the pianoforte, and before Lady Tilney could regroup her forces, Lucy rose and, carefully averting her back from the company, sidled away.

Accompanied by the strains of

> Oh in the days near Mortmas time,
> When the green leaves were fallin',
> Young Sir John Graeme in the west country
> Fell in love with Barbara Allan . . .

she eased her way, crablike, out of the withdrawing room, then dashed down the deserted hall. She poked her head cautiously into the library and sighed with relief to find it empty. After a quick scan of the shelves that ranged along three sides of the paneled room, she pulled out a volume and plunked down in a large wing chair that faced the empty fireplace. "Ouch!" A thorn made its presence known. Lucy tucked her legs beneath her to ease the contact, pulled the candelabra on the tripod stand beside her a little closer, and was soon engrossed in *The Mysteries of Udolpho*.

Time lost all meaning. But it was almost two chapters later when Lucy was wrenched from the story by the sound of someone entering the room. A peek around the leather wing disclosed Mr. Drury, his back toward her as he stood in the open garden doorway lighting his cigar, prepared, evidently, to blow his cloud in the out of doors rather than contaminate his host's library. She decided against making her presence known and immersed herself once more in her heroine's perils.

"Well, there you are."

Lucy jumped and almost answered before she realized the words weren't meant for her.

"I've been looking everywhere for you. You should know you've greatly displeased your hostess by disappearing this way."

"Why?" Mr. Drury's bored voice answered Mr. More's. "God knows I've heard you sing often enough to be excused from that particular treat."

"You've no appreciation of good music at all, have you, Jerrold? Well your Philistine attitude is no longer the point. The concert's over. Lady Tilney's organizing dancing. And you're needed."

Mr. Drury groaned. "That's all that's lacking—watching those pathetic females trampling over one another for the honor of standing up with you. My God, they're desperate. It's frightening to observe. Aren't there any eligible men at all in Sussex? It's no wonder you're so insufferable, Carnaby. I've never known anyone to be so toad-eaten. Or seen so many lures cast toward one poor fish."

"I do believe you're jealous."

"Jealous? Me? I assure you I've no desire to have a bunch of rustics fawn over me."

"And I'd say you've managed to make that fairly evident. Might I remind you that you were the one who insisted that we come?"

"True. But might I remind *you* that the person I had hoped to see isn't among the company. We could have taken our leave ages ago."

"Not I," his friend replied. "I'm having a perfectly marvelous time. By Jove, it was fate! Fate in your ill-favored, top-lofty guise that brought me here. By heaven, Jerrie, I've just met an angel."

Lucy heard a heavy, speaking sigh. "You, my friend, have been led sadly astray by the fact the lady you no doubt refer to plays the harp."

"The harp has nothing at all to say in the matter. Surely even you must admit she's the most exquisite creature alive. And so unspoiled. And shy. When did you last see such blushes?"

"Vicars' daughters are supposed to blush. It's part of their training. Really, Carnaby, don't expect me to join in your transports. Your propensity for falling in love with every moon change has become a trifle boring."

"Oh, but this is different."

"Isn't it always?"

"No! I tell you, I've never met anyone like Miss Haydon. She's a breath of fresh air after all those spoiled sophisticates in London. Why, she doesn't seem to have the slightest notion of how exquisite a creature she is. You certainly can't accuse *her* of casting out lures for me. She wouldn't have the slightest notion how to go about it."

"She doesn't need to know," was the dry rejoinder. "Her sister saw to that part."

Lucy stifled an indignant gasp. She'd been most uncomfortable up to now with her eavesdropping, just waiting for an opportune moment to make her presence known. Now she scotched her scruples and pricked up her ears.

"Her sister? I haven't the least idea of what you're talking about. Miss Lucinda Haydon's cast no lures at me, though I must say I wouldn't have minded if she had done. By Jove, I'm curious to meet the vicar, I must say. For when it comes to producing daughters, he appears to be in a class all by himself. True, the older one's no nonpareil like my Camilla, but she is quite fetching. Oh, I say, Drury, you might do worse than make her one of your flirts while we're down here. She is a taking little thing, don't you think so?"

"No."

That flat monosyllable did nothing to mollify the dislike of Mr. Drury that Lucy was forming. Nor did his next speech.

"By the by, Carnaby, let me give you a wasted word of warning. The Haydon sisters are no doubt desperate to marry fortunes. For I understand they're poor as their own church mice. The vicar's the late Lord Tilney's younger brother, another classic case of everything to the firstborn while the second son winds up with nothing but a rather impoverished living.

The young ladies are reduced to giving lessons to eke out their meager income, I understand."

"And so? Since I've no need to dangle after a fortune, you really are wasting your breath, old man. But I still don't understand why you've taken so against Miss Lucinda Haydon or why you should imply she'd set her cap for me. Why, I hadn't even noticed her until she played for the goddess and myself to sing."

"Of course not. That was not the design. It was her sister you were supposed to notice. And she saw to that like an old campaigner. My God, the girl can't be a year over eighteen"—here Lucy barely restrained a sniff—"and she made all the scheming mamas appear amateurs. She especially undid all of Lady Tilney's stratagems."

"Really, Jerrold, your attitude does grow tiresome. You're too cynical by half, seeing plots everywhere. Why can you never accept people at face value?"

"Because they're too seldom what they seem. Take you, for instance. Fresh-faced. Boyish. Enthusiastic. None of these poor deluded people that seem so eager to have you settle among them has the slightest notion that you're as jaded as Lord Byron's corsair."

"That's not true," the other said indignantly.

"Well, a slight exaggeration, I'll admit," his friend conceded. "Jaded may be coming it too strong. Fickle, then."

"Only because I've never met the right girl." There was a long, dramatic pause. "Till now."

Then after another extended silence, Carnaby More laughed wryly. "No need looking at me like that, Jerry. This really is different. You'll see. But come along. We mustn't keep our hostess waiting. The sets are forming. By the by, you haven't by chance seen the other Miss Haydon, have you?"

"No. Why?"

"She seems to have disappeared, too."

"Well, does it matter? Isn't one vicar's daughter enough for you?"

"No, actually. I need her to play the pianoforte so that I can stand up with her sister. Lady Tilney insists that we have dancing. So it's fallen to Miss Camilla's lot to play."

"High marks then to Lady Tilney. Run on and take your medicine and stand up with her ladyship's daughter like a man."

"I don't go back alone. These people are my neighbors. I'll not let your ragtailed manners put me to the blush."

"Must I? Oh very well. But a brief reprieve, all right? I tell you what. We'll strike a bargain. Allow me one more cigar and then I'll go in search of the missing Miss Haydon and point her toward the pianoforte so you can dance with your goddess. A bargain?"

"Done." There was the sound of shoulder clapping, footsteps, and the library door opened and then closed again.

Lucy felt turned to stone, too angry to permit herself to ease her cramped position even slightly lest the temptation to spring up and start hurling things toward the insulting Mr. Drury prove too strong.

She did, however, cower down in the wing chair a bit more as the sound of footsteps came her way. They stopped in the nick of time, however, and from the rapid succession of puffs that followed, Lucy concluded he must be lighting his cigar from the candles on the library table a few feet behind her. A cloud of smoke drifted her way to confirm this, and soon a stifling aromatic haze was settling all around her. Despite all effort she could only hold her breath so long. Her gloved hand clapped across her mouth was quite inadequate to muffle her fit of coughing.

"Ah. The elusive Miss Haydon, I presume."

Chapter Three

LUCY LOOKED UP THROUGH WATERING EYES TO SEE MR. Drury looming over her. He'd removed the offending cigar from his mouth but made no move to extinguish it.

18

"Would you throw that foul thing away?" she managed between spasms.

"Must I? Well, yes, I suppose so." He sighed, walking over to the fireplace and stubbing it out. "Though it's rather undiscriminating of you to call it foul. The tobacco's a special Turkish mixture. Quite top of the trees. The things cost me an arm and a leg, actually." He'd resumed his position and was again looking down at her, his expression thoughtful. "But then I expect it's not just my tobacco you've taken against, but me. Your own fault, you know, Miss Haydon. Eavesdroppers seldom hear good of themselves, as the saying goes. You might have coughed earlier, you know," he added reasonably.

"I was not eavesdropping," she retorted with considerable heat, then forced herself to be more calm. How dare he put her on the defensive when he was the offender? "It must be obvious even to you that I was in the library first. And despite the scarcity of eligible men in the neighborhood, I was *not* so desperate as to desire your company above my book."

"Touché."

She was indeed rather proud of hurling his own words back in his teeth and warmed up to deliver a more quelling setdown. "I had assumed you'd smoke your filthy weed and soon be gone and that there was no civil necessity on my part to make my presence known. But then when your friend joined you, I must admit I was too fascinated by hearing my own and my neighbors' characters ripped to shreds to dream of interrupting. Why, after all, should I do the civil in the teeth of slander?"

"Why indeed?" Mr. Drury appeared more amused than mortified, Lucy noted with a new annoyance.

"The hypocritical would, I collect, consider it a requirement of good manners to pretend to have been so engrossed in their reading as not to have heard a word of what was said."

"Really? Hardly convincing, I should think." He reached over and took the book from her lap to study its title. "Hmmm. *The Mysteries of Udolpho*. Haven't read it myself but I understand it's a real hair-raiser. A person just might possibly get by with such a pretense as that."

"I don't intend to try."

"Something warned me that you would not."

"Rather than stand on ceremony, I think it much more beneficial to set you straight on a few points."

"Plan to ring a peal over me, do you?"

"Not at all. But since you are a stranger in these parts, I think someone needs to point out the difference between London and Sussex manners. For example, the conduct toward Mr. More that you called 'toad-eating,' we would describe as merely doing the civil."

"Oh well then, I stand corrected."

Lucy rather thought his expression belied his words.

"And if this 'civility' appeared perhaps a bit excessive—even by 'rustic' standards—I assure you there was a good reason for that too."

"Oh, I'm convinced of that. As I recall, I implied as much."

"You gave the matter the wrong interpretation entirely. You seemed to think Mr. More's bachelorhood was his greatest asset."

"Well yes. Along with his fortune, of course."

"Well, I can assure you that Mr. More would have been treated just as cordially if he'd possessed a wife and a brood of children."

"A brood? Carnaby? That notion rather staggers the imagination, but if you say so. Fond of children in Sussex, are you?"

Lucy feared that perhaps she was coming it a bit strong and modified her position slightly. "Oh, I will admit that a few here might first consider Mr. More in the light of his matrimonial eligibility, but the foremost consideration with most is that he cease being an absentee landlord and live on his estate. You've no idea how unsettling it is to have so fine a property neglected."

"I must confess I've given the matter little thought. But then I haven't really noticed the neglect that you must have seen. I'd understood that Mr. More's bailiff is first-rate."

"Oh, Mr. Webster does very well, I suppose, as bailiffs go. But it's not the same thing at all as having the owner in residence. Mr. More's absence shows a kind of contempt for the neighborhood, don't you see?"

"No I don't." Mr. Drury looked longingly at the fireplace, no doubt regretting the good manners that had parted him from his cigar. "The only people Carnaby might possibly show contempt for are the people who welsh on their gaming debts or dress improperly for Almack's. As you must have heard him say, he finds the company here charming. And"—Mr. Drury seemed to put unnecessary emphasis on his next words—"he will continue to do so for a little while. But I think you should know this about Carnaby before you set your hopes too high—about his settling here permanently, I mean of course—while he may enjoy the novelty of rusticating for a bit, the metropolis is his natural habitat. You can keep a fish out of water longer than you'll keep Carnaby More away from White's and Watier's. No, he won't become a country squire. To speak even more plainly, I don't think the beauty has been born who could bring about that conversion."

"And to answer back just as plainly, where you got the maggoty notion, Mr. Drury, that I was throwing my sister at your friend's head I can't imagine. Any interest in that direction is of his own making."

"You deny then that you were at some pains to bring her to his notice?"

"I most certainly do." Her heightened color robbed this assertion of some of its conviction. "It was my aunt who arranged that we perform."

"And then arranged the flower baskets to hide you." He grinned. "I noticed how extraordinarily pleased she was when you thrust your sister center stage."

"You seem to make a habit of giving odd interpretations to the most ordinary behavior." Lucy spoke witheringly. "Believe me. There is no need for me to resort to stratagems for my sister's benefit. Camilla does not lack for beaux." She started to rise to emphasize her words, felt a thorn prick, and thought better of it. "True, they may not be able to match your friend's annual income, but that does not signify. Our church mice, sir, manage a great deal better than you think."

"Oh God. I did say that, didn't I?"

"You did. I'll have you know, sir, that Camilla and I are not 'reduced to giving lessons.' I do have one pupil who my mother felt should have music lessons, more because he needed a diversion, I might add, than to 'eke out our meager income.' And

21

just to set the record straighter still, I am nearly twenty years old, not 'barely eighteen.' "

"So ancient?" he murmured. "I would not have thought so."

"Though you'll still find me young for a 'scheming mama,' I've no doubt."

"Precocious, in fact. What you'll become in twenty-odd more years with a daughter of your own on the marriage mart staggers the imagination."

"Since I've no plans for marriage, the occasion will hardly—"

"Lucy Haydon! Whatever is the meaning of this?"

The Honorable Ada Tilney's scandalized voice from the doorway sent her cousin leaping to her feet before she thought. Since this exercise had caused her back to be turned toward Mr. Drury, it was fortunate that his eyes were also fixed upon the newcomer. Recalled to her predicament, Lucy quickly backed up a bit to stand quite next to him, a maneuver that caused him to look startled and Ada to appear even more shocked.

"Really, Lucy, you can't have thought," Miss Tilney chided, striding into the room at the peril of ripping the seams of her narrow skirt. Four years older than Lucinda, with all the authority of the manor house bred into her, she, like her mother, was accustomed to telling the vicarage girls what they should or should not do. Unlike her ladyship, however, it had never occurred to her to be jealous of her cousins. Now she shook her head at Lucy in the same way she might correct a favored stable lad who had failed to rub down her horse properly. "Don't look right, you know, you and Mr. Drury disappearing together this way. Sets tongues to wagging. Bound to. Especially with no one really knowing what Mr. Drury's like." That gentleman choked suddenly but recovered rather quickly. "Mama's already noticed that the two of you are missing. Other people are bound to remark upon it. Thought I'd better come and find you before someone else begins to snoop."

"Mr. Drury and I did not disappear together," Lucy sputtered. "The idea's ludicrous."

"You're both here, ain't you?" Ada looked puzzled at having to state the obvious.

"Yes, of course we are. But that's hardly the same thing as

disappearing together. I came here to read. He came here to smoke. Separately. It's not the same thing at all."

"Maybe not. But it don't signify since folk will think what they please anyhow. But come back with me now, Lucy. You'll be needed for the set that's about to be formed. Mrs. Farnsworth's dropped out. Winded, don't you know. Must weigh twelve stone."

"Well then, Miss Haydon, may I have the pleasure of standing up with you?"

"No."

Though Lucy herself felt the monosyllable quite adequate, Ada's shocked expression forced her to add, "I am much obliged to you, of course, but I'm not dancing this evening. I'm sure my cousin will be glad to take my place."

"No, I won't." It would have surprised Miss Tilney to learn that she sounded no more gracious than her cousin. "Promised the squire. Tell you what though, Lucy. You take Camilla's place at the pianoforte, then she can stand up with Mr. Drury. That will fix everything right and tight."

"Very well then." Lucy, however, made no move to go.

"Well, come along." Ada spoke impatiently. "They'll be ready to begin."

"You two go ahead. I won't be a minute." She forestalled her cousin's protest by pointing to her novel. "There's sure to be a ghost walking soon. I'll be along as soon as I discover just what happens."

"Nonsense. You can take the book home with you. Come now." Ada put an arm around her cousin's shoulders and propelled her toward the door. Behind them there was a sharp intake of breath.

Ada glanced around and followed the direction of Drury's eyes. "Good God, Lucy! What on earth has happened to your gown?"

"Oh for heaven's sake!" Lucy snapped. "Isn't it obvious?"

"Well, it looks," the literal-minded Ada answered, "like it's pinned together with a bunch of thorns. Oddest thing I ever saw. Have you run out of needle and thread at the vicarage?"

Though she studiously avoided looking at him, Lucy was all

too conscious of the fact that Mr. Drury was having to struggle to maintain composure. "Of course we have needles and thread at the vicarage. I ripped it on the way up here. There wasn't time to go back and change."

"Why didn't you borrow something of mine then?"

Since her cousin was some four inches taller than herself, Lucy didn't bother to justify not raiding the other's wardrobe. "Nobody's noticed it up till now," she muttered.

"But hasn't it been painful? Having to sit on all those stickers, I mean to say?"

"And to think I believed that I was the only thorn in your flesh," Mr. Drury remarked sotto voce. Then, as she glared up at him, he added ingenuously, "At least I'm relieved to know the real reason you refused to stand up with me. For a moment there I feared it might have been something that I'd said." An odious grin made Lucy long to throttle him.

"Well, you can't keep skulking here," Ada said practically. "Mama's bound to flush you out. Here's what we'll do. You go first and Mr. Drury and I will walk close behind you. That way no one will notice."

"No one will notice Mr. Drury walking close behind me?"

"Hmmm. Well, yes. See what you mean. No use giving the gossipmongers any more to work on. Take no notice, Mr. Drury." Ada turned toward him graciously. "Strangers in the country are alway notorious."

"So I've observed," he replied solemnly. "How would this be? Why don't I go on ahead and inform the other Miss Haydon that she's soon to be replaced at the pianoforte. And then perhaps you can contrive to block Miss Lucy's—err—posterior from view. Pity we don't have Mrs. Farnsworth. Oh really, Miss Haydon"—he reacted to a venomous look—"I did not mean to imply—surely anyone as slender as you need not be so sensitive." His grin grew wider.

Somehow she managed to nod coolly to his bow with all the dignity her thorny condition would allow her. As he went striding from the room, she vowed to herself that she'd have no more to do with the insufferable Mr. Jerrold Drury.

Still, it was not easy to avoid stealing glances at him throughout the remainder of the evening while she accompanied the country dances. And she took some satisfaction in noting that he stood up for every dance and was at some pains to entertain his partners. Her lecture on civility had not been entirely wasted, it would seem.

Nor was it easy to forget his mocking face once she and Camilla had arrived back home. Not only was that image prominent in the memory of her own humiliating evening, it intruded as well upon her sister's social triumph.

Now that the other three Haydon children had left the nest, Lucy and Camilla had acquired the luxury of a room apiece. But when her sister suggested that they spend what was left of the night together, Lucy hadn't the heart to refuse. After exchanging their party frocks for nightgowns and caps, they climbed into Lucy's high four-poster bed, blew out the candle, and snuggled together as they had done when they were little girls.

As a rule it was Lucy who talked while Camilla listened, but now the positions were reversed. And thanks to Mr. Drury, Lucy grew more and more uneasy at her usually reserved sister's transports over Mr. Carnaby More's countless perfections. Could anyone match that gentleman's looks, his voice, his amiability? And if Lucy's own enthusiasm seemed tempered, her sister was too far gone to notice it.

Lucy, though, was angry with herself for her reservations. Why should she allow Mr. Drury's opinions to bother her? He was obviously no judge of character. What did it signify if Mr. More had been in love before? Had she not heard from that gentleman's own lips that this time it was different? She must not allow Mr. Drury's dog-in-the-manger attitude to spoil her pleasure in her sister's triumph. And he could poke fun at her maneuvers all he wished to. She would not be put to the blush for bringing her sister and Mr. More together. Her instincts had told her those two would deal famously together, and the evening had certainly proven her right. She'd done no more than their mother would have. Only Mama would have been a lot less obvious. Lucy's face burned at the memory of her crashing introduction to Camilla's solo performance. Well, the end had justified the means at any rate.

With a supreme effort, she pushed Mr. Drury and his opinions from her mind and chimed in to help her sister recreate every moment of the most glorious evening of Camilla's life.

Dawn was breaking when Camilla at last went smilingly to sleep. Lucy had yawned prodigiously, turned over twice, and was herself finally drifting off when she was suddenly jerked awake by a buried thought.

Who on earth was absent from the party that the odious Mr. Drury had hoped to meet?

Chapter Four

"Do you know, I believe Mr. Drury is quite taken with you."

"Fiddlesticks!" Lucy jabbed the needle viciously into the shirt she was hemming.

She and Camilla were seated by the small parlor window to catch what light there was on the dreary, overcast day that had followed Lady Tilney's party. Camilla's mood, however, had not been dampened by nature's glumness. Indeed, Lucy, suffering from the headache, had concluded that her sister was, in fact, turning into a confirmed rattle. She did wish Camilla would find another topic of conversation.

"I didn't refine upon it at the time," Camilla continued thoughtfully as she made her neat, small stitches, "but when Mr. Drury stood up with me for the boulanger, most of his conversation had to do with you."

"It did?" In spite of herself, Lucy's curiosity was aroused.

"Of course I could be making too much of it. I felt quite tongue-tied with him, you see, and he had to talk of *something*. I suppose you were the only topic he could think of that we held in common."

Why Lucy should have been piqued by this naive observation passed her understanding. She blamed the headache for making her waspish. "Well, whatever he said must not have made much of an impression since you've repeated every word Mr. More saw fit to utter at least a dozen times and this is the first I've heard that Mr. Drury spoke at all."

"It simply slipped my mind. But now I recall he did mention that you and he had a most comfortable coze together in the library."

"Humph!"

Camilla glanced up, startled. The ejaculation had actually come from her sister. For a moment she'd thought that Lady Tilney had entered the room.

The sisters sewed in silence for a bit. Then Lucy's curiosity got the better of her. "Tell me. Did you find out anything about him?"

"About whom?"

"Mr. Drury, of course. We were just speaking of him."

"No, not really, except that he and Mr. More have been friends forever." This fact seemed recommendation enough as far as Camilla was concerned.

"He didn't say, then, where he comes from or what he does?"

"Well, he's from London, of course. We knew that already. And I suppose he does whatever gentlemen do in London. Visit the clubs. Ride in the park." Camilla seemed rather vague about the pursuits of the Smart Set. "Cousin Ada thinks he's no one of any consequence, that he's simply attached himself to Mr. More. It's quite common, she says, for rich gentlemen to attract sycophants. But I suspect that Ada has grown cynical of late, don't you? For I must say that Mr. Drury did not strike me as that sort at all."

"How could you possibly tell if he's a sycophant or not? I'm amazed you even know the term, and you've certainly never met one." Despite this defense of Ada's viewpoint, Lucy felt quite disappointed in Mr. Drury.

"Well, even if he is a toad-eater, I thought he was nice," Camilla said. "He certainly went out of his way to take an interest in our family. He even asked about Eleanor, for instance."

"Whatever for?"

"How should I know? Just doing the polite, I suppose. But I do recall that he said our cousin had mentioned Eleanor's uncommon taste in clothes."

Lucy's needle jabbed the material viciously. She considered taking out the resulting stitch and then decided not to, though if Mama ever saw it, goodness knows what she might say.

"That struck me as rather odd," Camilla mused, "though of course I never said so."

"Mr. Drury is a very odd gentleman."

"I wasn't referring to Mr. Drury. I meant it was odd of Ada, who never notices what anyone has on, to mention Eleanor's taste. Eleanor, of all people, who hasn't any that I ever noticed." She frowned, trying to recall the details of a very dull exchange that had soon been overlaid with the memory of Mr. More's sparkling conversation. "Then, after we'd discussed Eleanor, Mr. Drury went on to remark on your skill at the pianoforte. And he seemed most interested in the fact that you give music lessons."

"Indeed?"

"Oh yes. He inquired who your pupil was, and after that asked how often you instructed him."

"He certainly was at a loss for topics to discuss."

"Well, yes, I suppose so. I haven't your address, you know, and gentlemen, I suspect, do find me rather difficult to talk to, though nothing could have been farther from the case than Mr. More. He put me at ease immediately. Can you believe it, Lucy, I found myself chattering like a magpie."

Lucy certainly could believe it, but stopped herself just in time from saying so. She was grateful for the diversion the sound of carriage wheels afforded and jumped up to peer out the window. "Speak of the devil!" she exclaimed.

"Lucy!" Camilla was scandalized. "The things you say. What if Papa were to hear?" She came to stand behind her sister and watch the curricle approach along the lane that lay just beyond their hedge. "Oh my heavens! It's Mr. More and Mr. Drury."

"So I just said."

"They're on their way to the hall, I suspect."

"Undoubtedly. Oh no!" The smart team of matched grays was slowing down. "They're coming here."

The sisters looked at one another in confusion. "Am I all right?" Camilla's cheeks had turned as pink as the muslin gown she wore.

"Of course." Lucy sighed. "Whenever weren't you?" She looked ruefully down at the ancient gray morning dress she was wearing. Well, at least it was intact. That was something.

They stood transfixed a moment longer while the two gentlemen, Mr. More dapper in a cherry-colored riding coat, Mr. Drury more subdued in an earthy brown, jumped down from the smart equipage and approached their gate. The spell broke with the unfastening of its latch, and the two young ladies sprang into action, cramming the shirts into the recesses of their worktable and snatching up their tambouring, only, in Lucy's case, to immediately throw it down and rush off to the kitchen to alert Emma, their cook and housemaid, that distinguished guests were arriving at the door.

"Fetch Papa before you go answer it," she hissed, while Emma finished the pot she was scrubbing and wiped her hands with maddening deliberation. "Then show the gentlemen into the parlor."

"Where else would I show them, miss? Back here?" Emma had been with the family since the eldest lad was in leading strings and stood on no ceremony with any of its members, with the exception of the Reverend Mr. Haydon.

Lucy paid no heed to the sarcastic mutterings. She was speeding back to her chair in the parlor, where she took up her tambouring hoop and fanned herself with the picture in silks that she was working. She then began to ply her needle as though embroidering was the most absorbing activity in the world.

It was obvious that the Reverend Mr. Haydon, interrupted during the composition of next Sunday's sermon, hadn't the vaguest notion of the identity of the two gentlemen he was ushering into the parlor. He looked greatly relieved to find Lucy and Camilla there. "Allow me to present my daughters—" he'd begun when Lucy, trying not to sound exasperated, interrupted.

"The gentlemen have already met us, Papa." As a rule she

was less bothered by her father's absentmindedness than proud of his distinguished appearance. Indeed, next to Camilla, he was still, at fifty-five, the family's handsomest specimen and had been, so it was reported, an Adonis in his youth. But then as a rule her socially adept Mama was present to counterbalance her husband's vagueness. Now it fell to Lucy's lot to step into the breach. "We were presented to Mr. More and Mr. Drury at our aunt's evening party. Just last night. Remember, Papa? You were not able to attend."

The clergyman's face cleared. "Of course. How stupid of me. Dighton House. You've taken up residence at Dighton House, Mr. More, I understand."

But even with the mystery of the guests' identity now cleared up, the conversation proved heavy going. Mr. More and Camilla seemed content to gaze covertly at one another and smile fatuously when their eyes did meet, while Mr. Drury proved rather less than expansive on the topic of the weather that Lucy, in desperation, broached. He appeared entirely engrossed in observing his friend's smitten aspect and remained oblivious to his hostess's floundering attempts at social discourse. The Reverend Mr. Haydon, whose mind also seemed to have wandered off on some scholarly tangent of its own, finally became aware of the unnatural silence that had descended on the parlor and came back to the present to find his older daughter looking at him in desperation.

"Well, well, well, then." He rubbed his hands and spoke heartily. "You young gentlemen are most eager to see the church, of course. St. Botolph's has several interesting features, you know. I regret that my duties make it impossible for me to show it to you myself. But my daughters can serve as guides. And you'll most likely find my nephew there. Unless he caroused too much last evening and is still abed." He paused to allow them to chuckle at his little joke. But since no one but Lucy, who smiled wanly, realized he'd made one, Mr. Haydon was forced to carry on.

"Actually, my nephew, Lord Tilney, is the leading authority on St. Botolph's. He's working on the parish history and quite casts his vicar in the shade. You can rely upon him to answer any questions you may have. That is to say, you may rely upon him if he is there. In any case my daughters will be happy to show you around." He smiled and rose dismissively.

Since neither of the two gentlemen seemed inclined to pass up the church treat, Lucy led the way across the damp grass of the vicarage lawn and toward a gap in the hedge that separated it from St. Botolph's. As she brushed through the shrubbery, she heard an exaggerated sigh of relief behind her. "My felicitations, Miss Haydon. Your gown is still all in a piece. But I don't wonder that your habit of avoiding gates plays havoc with your wardrobe."

Lucy shot a quelling glance back over her shoulder, then threaded her way among the gravestones to the front entrance of the church. She stood impatiently upon the marble steps while Camilla and Mr. More, deep in conversation, dawdled along, oblivious that anyone was waiting for them. Mr. Drury stood silently at her side staring at the swollen clouds that looked ready to spill over at any minute rather as if he were testing her earlier hypothesis that it must surely rain. Well, she was certainly not going to strain for conversation now. She felt no compulsion, away from Papa, to continue doing the polite. Mr. Drury had obviously only come calling for his friend's sake.

Much to Lucy's relief, Nigel was inside and declared himself delighted to show the strangers around the church. Lucy's family, she sometimes thought, was equally divided between the reticent and the overbearing. But while Nigel clearly belonged to the former group, he was able to lose all self-consciousness when he mounted his favorite hobbyhorse.

The foursome trailed along after him while he enthusiastically pointed out the medieval carvings, the screens, the glass and paintings that had miraculously survived the horrors of the Reformation. Much to Lucy's surprise, Mr. Drury seemed to pick up on her cousin's enthusiasm. He asked several intelligent questions that smacked of genuine interest. This interest served to divert Nigel's attention, in part at least, away from Camilla and Mr. More, who seemed oblivious to anything beyond themselves. But from time to time Nigel did gaze with some bemusement at his younger cousin. Camilla was the one who usually shared his interest and often aided him in his scholarly pursuits. Now she hardly seemed aware of where she was. But the puzzle of his cousin's odd behavior was soon obscured by the chance to discuss the splendors of the church with the obviously intelligent, surprisingly well-informed Mr. Drury.

They had entered an open chapel in the south transept and Mr. Drury's attention had been claimed by the splendid brass effigy of a knight in armor that lay atop a Purbeck marble tomb chest. It was, undoubtedly, an arresting bit of sculpture. Though intimate with its every detail, Lucy had never been able to sufficiently appreciate its aesthetic qualities from the necessity of having to polish it with disgusting frequency. Mr. Drury suffered no such deficiency.

"Oh, this is splendid," he breathed, as his fingers lightly traced the veins in the brass hands that were brought together in a prayerful attitude and Lucy flinched at the possibility of smudges. "An ancestor of yours, Lord Tilney?" He looked vainly at the tomb for an identifying plaque.

"Well—err—no. That is to say, not precisely." His lordship smiled while at the same time he looked rather embarrassed, an accurate indication of his ambivalent attitude toward this, the most arresting feature of the church. It tickled his fancy, while at the same time it offended his fastidious soul.

"There's certainly a family resemblance," Mr. Drury, studying the cleft chin and classic features, observed. "An early Sir Nigel. I would have wagered on it."

"I'm sure that was done deliberately." Lord Tilney's smile got the better of him and widened. "You see, when one of my ancestors had the place restored in the seventeenth century, he felt that it reflected poorly upon St. Botolph's that we had no resident crusader, as it were. Any other old church usually boasts several. So my ancestor hired an artisan to make one. He did not, however, go quite so far as to give the fellow an identity. I'm sure he viewed it merely as another work of art. To the glory of God, of course," he added piously. "But some local wag of the time christened our bogus crusader 'Sir Sham,' and I fear the name has stuck."

Even Mr. More had wrenched his attention away from Camilla's cornflower blue eyes to listen, and now both gentlemen laughed heartily. "And there's no one at all in this magnificent tomb then?" he asked.

"Well, yes, actually there is. Or at least tradition has it that the artist himself is buried there. He chose anonymity, so it is said, rather than detract from his masterpiece."

The group moved out of the little chapel. As always, Lord Tilney had saved his crusader for the last. The tour concluded, and for the first time since the unexpected arrival of the London gentlemen at the vicarage gate, Lucy recalled her afternoon's obligations.

"Oh my goodness! Louis's lesson! I completely forgot. Do please excuse me."

"Lucy is supposed to tutor Master Louis Aldington on the pi-anoforte this afternoon," Camilla explained as her sister hurried from the church with the others following.

"Slow down, Miss Haydon," Mr. Drury called after her. "I'll drive you there."

"That's not necessary. Louis won't mind that I'm a trifle late. And it's quite the opposite direction from Dighton House."

"So much the better." He'd caught up with her as she hurried through the graveyard. "Carnaby has been urging me to try out his new equipage. Wants my opinion of his pair."

Lucy was of two minds. She had no desire to be forced into the intimacy of a two-mile ride with Mr. Drury. Still, the yellow curricle with its shiny black leather seats was certainly a temptation.

"Very well then. I'll just get my music and be right back."

"It's nice to know that you can be corrupted." Mr. Drury, who had observed her struggle, grinned a very knowing grin.

Chapter
Five

CAMILLA AND MR. MORE WERE STANDING BY THE CUR-ricle when Lucy emerged. Camilla's eyes were wide with the splendor of the sporty vehicle and its perfectly matched grays.

"Try not to be too cow-handed, Jerry," Mr. More remarked as his friend handed Lucy up.

"What you mean is, try not to spoil your team too much," the other answered with a similar straight face. "The shock of having a competent whip in charge may quite overset them." To emphasize his words, he shot the leather out over the backs of his friend's cattle in an earsplitting crack that sprang them instantly. Lucy regretted that her hands were too full to anchor herself properly and feared she might go flying off the leather seat.

He slowed down as soon as they were out of sight and laughed at her heartfelt sigh of relief. "You did say you were late, Miss Haydon."

"Yes, but I wish to arrive at Lockhart Place, not land in the ditch."

"No danger of that. I only slowed down for fear that thing might take off with you over the treetops." He nodded at the object which, along with some rolled up music, she was clutching in her hand. "Odd sort of music sheets, Miss Haydon."

"It's a kite, of course," she said defensively. "I promised Louis that we'd fly it if he'd learn his piece."

He kept staring at the pale blue silk creation, then took it from her and examined it dubiously. "Do you think he's likely to have done so? Frankly, Miss Haydon, on further consideration, my concern for our speed was ill-judged. I don't think this thing will fly."

"Why ever not? My brothers used to make them all the time and they flew splendidly."

"Like this, were they? Well, we'll see." He handed the kite back with a dampening shrug and turned his full attention upon the horses.

After a long drawn-out silence during which they'd sped up and slowed back down with a frequency that had her giddy, she remarked civilly, "They're a beautiful pair."

"They're slugs. Carnaby's done it again. He's notorious for his wretched horses."

Sour grapes if I ever heard it. Kites. Horses. Mr. Drury con-

34

siders himself an expert in every field. Lucy kept the comment to herself, however, while vowing she would make no more polite attempts at conversation.

But Mr. Drury seemed to recall some obligation on his part to do so. "I must have met the Lockharts last night, Miss Haydon, but I fear I haven't been able to sort out your neighbors. Which were they?"

"They were not there."

"Really? Unsociable, are they? I mean to say their absence does seem rather odd, what with the Lockhart estate and Lord Tilney's marching together."

"Not at all," she replied stiffly. Mr. Drury evidently had a nose for scandal. Or more likely, someone had already told him that her cousin Ada and William Lockhart had had an understanding till William made a trip to London and returned home with a bride. The sudden marriage had rocked the neighborhood and had, of course, severed relationships between the Lockharts and the hall. But if Mr. Drury thought she was going to be so rag-mannered as to chew over this juicy bit of gossip with him, he much mistook the matter. "Mrs. Lockhart is away. In Brighton, I believe."

"Oh really? The matrons of your community seem quite travel-prone. Your mother is also away, I believe, Miss Haydon."

"My mother is attending my sister's lying-in." That piece of indelicacy should shut him up.

"That would be Eleanor, I collect. The sister whose evening frock you finished off." He grinned at her and the thought crossed her mind that if the motivations for his smiles weren't always so odious, they would really make him appear almost attractive. Rather than reply to his latest attempt to provoke her, Lucy pointed out the entrance to the Lockhart estate that lay just ahead.

The gatehouse was uninhabited, its windows festooned with spiderwebs. Several of the panes were either cracked or missing. Mr. Drury got down to open the gate himself. The deep arced grooves in the dirt driveway gave ample warning that it would sag upon its hinges.

The winding carriage drive was rutted, the grounds wildly overgrown. The house, when it came into view as they rounded a bend, showed the same neglect, its once-handsome Caroline facade marred by crumbling chimneys and windows as neglected as the gatehouse. "I thought Lockhart was supposed to be a nabob," Drury remarked.

"Really? Wherever did you get that notion? The Lockharts are an old, established family here, but they haven't been wealthy for generations." She could have added that a propensity for gambling among the heirs had caused the once-vast estate to dwindle down to nearly nothing, with the Tilney family the leading beneficiary of their necessity. But she refused to feed Mr. Drury's curiosity. Really, the man hadn't the least notion concerning proper topics of conversation.

He came around to help her down and forestalled her thanks. "You can't get rid of me quite so easily, Miss Haydon. I'm coming in to wait for you."

He dismissed all of Lucy's protests. Mr. More would be in no hurry for his equipage; her sister would keep him entertained, he was sure. Well, if Miss Camilla Haydon's duties prevented that, then Carnaby could walk home. The exercise would do him good. No, he did not mind at all waiting through the lesson. It would give him time to make some adjustments in the kite. Then perhaps young Master—Louis, was it?—just might be able to get the thing aloft. Mr. Drury gave the brass knocker several resounding whacks, taking apparent satisfaction in the fact that it at least seemed in good repair. "Good afternoon, Bert," Lucy greeted the strapping young butler-cum-groom-cum-gardener who had answered the door and was looking curiously at Mr. Drury. "Is Master Louis in?"

Bert's curiosity turned to astonishment when, after ushering the arrivals into the hall, he was dispatched by the strange gentleman to round up some cloth and scissors.

"You can wait right there." Lucy indicated a rather uncomfortable-looking bench, the only remaining piece of furniture in the expansive, marble-floored hall. The walls, too, appeared to have been stripped. Several lighter-colored rectangles on the dark paneling testified to long-gone paintings and tapestries.

Mr. Drury ignored Lucy's suggestion and followed her into a long withdrawing room that, like some ancient crones, still managed in its ruin to retain a vestige of long-lost beauty. The colors of the well-worn carpet had mellowed with the years to become a lovely muted crimson-gold ensemble. The gilt of the furniture still managed to appear opulent, even though the once-rich brocade upholstery was worn and frayed. The gold damask curtains had been carefully arranged so that most of the splits in the material were hidden in the folds. But the object that gave the room an undeniable elegance in spite of its drawbacks was a ceiling-to-mantel portrait that hung above the fireplace. Mr. Drury's eyes went to it immediately, Lucy saw, even before they traveled to the corner of the room where a small boy, almost hidden by the grand pianoforte, was laboring with the keys. He looked up anxiously at their approach. "Oh, Miss Haydon, did you bring—" He broke off in some confusion at the unexpected appearance of Mr. Drury, then brightened at the sight of the blue silk object in the strange gentleman's hand. "Oh, is that my kite, sir?"

"Well, that issue is still in doubt. But, yes, Miss Haydon intends it for a kite." His smile was warm and friendly, a sort of man-to-man salute, patronizing a female's well-intentioned bungling.

"This is Mr. Drury, Louis." For the child's sake, Lucy managed to sound only slightly waspish. "He's visiting Dighton House and I have his own word for it that he's an expert in all sorts of matters—horse flesh, kites, almost anything you might think of seems to fall within the province of his genius."

"Miss Haydon exaggerates, Louis," Mr. Drury said as the child rose politely from his stool. The seven-year-old was tall for his age and thin, with large gray eyes in a solemn, oval face. The boy studied the man with frank curiosity as Mr. Drury continued, "I do know quite a lot about horses and a bit about kites, but nothing whatsoever about music. Can you play that thing?"

"Not very well," Louis admitted, but added quickly, "I have learned my piece, though, Miss Haydon, so please can we fly the kite?"

The servant reappeared just then with the scissors and material he'd been sent for placed upon a large and tarnished tray. He deposited it upon a sofa table and then left, looking curiously back over his shoulder as he did so.

"That was our bargain," Lucy said. "But first let me hear how you've got on. While Louis plays for me, Mr. Drury, you can take the kite to the library across the hall and do whatever unnecessary thing you plan to do with it."

Mr. Drury ignored her instructions and sat down on the sofa a few feet away, where he began to cut the cloth into strips.

"Really!" she exploded in exasperation. "You can't expect us to have a lesson with you in here."

"Why ever not? I'll not say a word. You don't mind, do you, Louis?"

"Oh no, sir." The lad seemed fascinated, in fact, by this newcomer. His face had taken on an unaccustomed animation as he watched Mr. Drury cut the cloth with all the precision of a fashionable tailor. "Oh I say. Are you going to make it a tail?"

"Exactly." The other sounded approving of such insight.

"Play, Louis."

Lucy resigned herself to the audience and gritted her teeth as Louis labored his way through the simple tune she'd set for him to memorize. Though the errors were frequent, Lucy could not in all fairness blame them on Mr. Drury's presence. Louis was simply not musical. But when she had pointed this fact out to her mother and gone on to say that she considered the lessons a waste of her time and his stepfather's money, Mrs. Haydon had been adamant that she should continue them. "It's the attention Louis needs, not the training. He's a lonely child. You'll be good for him." It had been Lucy's own idea to bring the kite.

As Louis backed up to repeat a troublesome three measures for the third or the fourth time, Lucy noted with pleasure that even the unmusical Mr. Drury was beginning to wince. Serves him right for intruding this way, she thought, wondering once again what had possessed him to do so. He couldn't be so bored as all that, not possibly. Oh, of course, she decided as she played the correct version of the piece for Louis, how dense of me. Mr. More has put him up to this so he could be alone with Camilla. "All right now, Louis. Let's see if you can make it all the way through this time without stopping."

He did just that. With tongue placed between his teeth in awesome concentration and with small fingers pounding, he went from first to last while Lucy battled her own musicianship every inch of the way in order to overlook the notes he missed and allow him to conclude his performance. Her mother was right. Louis needed to run and play outside more than he needed to achieve some dubious mechanical perfection.

The child's face glowed when she pronounced the lesson concluded, then fell as his stepfather came into the room at just that instant.

William's changed, was Lucy's first thought. He was but a few years older than she, a close friend of John and Paul. They'd all played together as children and he'd fallen into the role of third big brother. She'd seen very little of him since he'd left her cousin at the altar, figuratively at least, and had brought his beautiful bride and her son to Lockhart Place.

It was not only that William looked considerably older than she'd expected; his dress also bespoke a carelessness that seemed quite foreign to his past. Of course his wife's away, she thought. She excused his none-too-clean linen and the crudely folded cravat he wore.

It was not quite so easy to dismiss the signs of dissipation beginning to mar the handsome face with a telltale puffiness around his bloodshot eyes. He was losing his athletic trim, she noticed. Ada would have kept him in the saddle too much for that.

"How are you, Lucy, and how was the lesson?"

It was sad that William seemed to feel awkward in her presence now, but natural enough, she thought. She also sounded a bit stilted as she replied, "Quite well. In both instances, I mean. Allow me to present Mr. Drury, William. As you've no doubt heard, he's staying at Dighton House with Mr. More."

"Ah yes. Your servant, sir." Mr. Lockhart bowed toward the visitor. Lucy's introduction had failed to explain why the gentleman happened to be an audience to his stepson's music lesson. He looked curiously at the kite Mr. Drury had laid aside when he'd risen to his feet. Too well bred to comment on such peculiar circumstances, he settled for a forced heartiness. "Glad to hear that More's in residence. An estate needs to have the master spend time there." It possibly occurred to him that the statement could seem odd, coming as it did from the resident owner of a far from model estate. At any rate he allowed no time for comment but hurried on to say, "I hope you're enjoying your stay, sir."

William Lockhart soon grew expansive in his role as host, a rare enough position for him since he'd jilted Ada Tilney. Nothing would do but that Mr. Drury must sample his brandy while Lucy and Louis partook of lemonade.

Louis's face had been shuttered tight since his stepfather's entrance. Lucy felt, rather than saw, his impatience.

"Louis and I will go fly our kite and leave you gentlemen to your brandy," she said, but Mr. Drury would have none of it. "I still need to lash the bow and spine sticks properly. We'll go in just a moment."

Then, while Lucy and Louis champed at their bits, he abandoned his quite unnecessary alterations in her kite engineering to go stand with legs wide apart and hands clasped behind him before the fireplace to gaze up admiringly at the portrait.

William Lockhart, who had called his guest's attention to the work of art, stood beside him. "Lovely, isn't it?"

"Magnificent. Thomas Phillips, I collect?"

"Yes. Cost me a fortune of course. But no one else could have done her justice."

"This is Mrs. Lockhart, I presume."

"Yes." Mr. Lockhart answered with simple pride. His heart was in his eyes.

Lucy, who had only caught occasional glimpses of Mrs. Lockhart, studied the painting now with more interest than she'd accorded it before. Perhaps it was the sight of two males transfixed that demanded a closer scrutiny.

Golden ringlets framed the oval face. The flawless skin glowed against a pale blue background of sky. The eyes were an almost emerald green, an artistic exaggeration, surely. Until this moment, Lucy had thought the pose a trifle silly. The lady stood, body in profile, head turned toward the viewers as though gazing just beyond them, while, for all the world like someone's footman, she held aloft a silver tray of fruit. Now, as Lucy looked back and forth from the gentlemen to the painting, she began to wonder if the subject was actually offering far more than met the eye. Poor Ada. She was surprised by this seemingly inconsequential thought.

The servant Bert reappeared with their refreshment and the spell was broken. Mr. Drury accorded his host's brandy almost the same appreciation he'd shown Mrs. Lockhart's portrait. Instead of applauding this improved sociability, Lucy found it irritating. I'll bet a monkey he's cultivating William simply because everyone else in the neighborhood shuns him nowadays. Well, if Mr. Drury thought to teach her a lesson in Christian charity, he wasted his time. Papa's daughter was not in the habit of casting stones.

Mr. Drury was meanwhile inspecting his glass with satisfaction as he swirled the liquid round and round. "You people do yourselves well here in Sussex. Don't think I've ever tasted as fine a cognac."

"I'm sure you haven't. Ain't generally available, you know." William Lockhart gave his visitor a knowing wink.

The other grinned. "Oh, I see. I've heard tales, of course, of Sussex smuggling, but always thought the stories were greatly exaggerated."

"A lot of Banbury tales for the most part, I assure you. But then 'smuggling' is not a popular word in these parts. 'Free trade' is what folk here are apt to call it."

The guest sipped contentedly. "I must say it's not hard to appreciate the local attitude. And the government's tax law seems fashioned to encourage this 'free trade,' as you call it."

Lucy, whose lemonade evidently fell far below the quality of the drink in question (indeed she wondered if it had ever seen a lemon) had had enough of both her weak beverage and the company. She rose. "If you gentlemen will excuse us," she said firmly, "I did promise Louis that we'd try out the kite *this* afternoon. Please don't disturb yourself, Mr. Drury." She tried to forestall that gentleman as he too stood up. "Finish your refreshment. Louis and I can manage quite well on our own."

"She can, you know." William Lockhart had grown expansive under the influence of his brandy. "Used to trail after her brothers and me all the time. Tried to do everything that we did. Succeeded in most."

"I'm sure she did," Mr. Drury said.

Perhaps it was all that flagrant femininity in the painting that made Lucy conclude she'd just been insulted. The fact that

41

Louis's expressionless face brightened as Mr. Drury tossed off his brandy and picked up the kite only added to her disgust. She longed to shake the little traitor.

But outside in the meadow, she was forced, against her will, to stifle her resentment of Mr. Drury's intrusion. She never would have thought he'd bother with a seven-year-old at all, much less be at such pains to teach the child the art of getting the kite into the air and keeping it aloft. Nor could she fault his technique with Louis. He never talked down and his patience seemed inexhaustible. If she felt the least bit annoyed that she'd been shunted aside in a project that had been of her own devising or the slightest bit of irritation when Mr. Drury's alteration to her creation made him appear a veritable Leonardo after she'd done all the real work, it was a small price to pay for the pleasure of seeing Louis running pell-mell down the field with the kite jerking and swirling in crazy loops behind him and hearing his shout of triumph as the blue diamond of silk rose in the air. It was the first time ever that she'd seen him acting like a child.

That was why it seemed so tragic that when Louis was running with the kite, a miniature of itself now, sailing high above him, his toe encountered a boulder and he stumbled, letting go the string.

Louis scrambled to his feet, looking stunned, as the kite, freed of its earthly moorings, soared even higher, a rapidly disappearing speck. The child burst into tears as Lucy jumped up from the grassy mound where she'd been sitting and sped toward him. It seemed perfectly natural to kneel down and clasp her small pianoforte pupil in her arms as he sobbed his heart out against her shoulder. "There, there, Louis, never mind," she crooned. "We had to stop for today anyhow. And I'll make you another kite. I promise."

"Y-you will? You won't forget?" The tearstained face gazed up anxiously, but the sobs abated.

"I'll make it this time." Mr. Drury appeared to be speaking man to man once more, making Lucy long to kick him. But since his matter-of-fact approach was having such a restorative effect on Louis, the notion seemed unworthy.

"Oh, would you really, sir?" There was no doubt that this

offer rated much higher than Lucy's. The child's eyes were shining.

"You have my word on it. Practice hard and Miss Haydon and I will be here next week. With a bigger and better kite."

There was no way Lucy could express her opinion of this high-handed intrusion into her music lesson without causing Louis further upset. She contented herself with retorting, while dampening down her annoyance the best she could, "You certainly may make him a bigger kite, Mr. Drury. But I defy you to design one more air-worthy than mine." She gestured dramatically toward the sky where her creation had all but vanished.

"It will be my challenge, Miss Haydon." He grinned his odious grin.

Chapter Six

*T*HE NEIGHBORHOOD HAD RARELY BEEN SO BLESSED. FOR now that the scandal of William Lockhart's sudden marriage had just begun to pall, the word was spreading that the bright yellow curricle was tethered at the vicarage gate far more often than was really proper. And even though it was acknowledged over the teacups that had Mrs. Haydon been at home her daughters would not have been allowed to be nearly so much in the newcomers' company (the vicar, of course, never saw anything beyond his nose), still most, except for a few spiteful mamas with marriageable daughters of their own, felt it would be a very good thing if Mr. More should marry "sweet Camilla" and settle down amongst them. As for the friend who was dangling after Lucy Haydon, well that was another matter altogether. For who knew anything of him? Even the most skillful digging had failed to unearth anything more concrete than that he and Mr. More had been at school together. Who could say what his intentions were?

Lucy was as puzzled as anyone. Oh, it was easy enough to account for Mr. Drury's visits to the vicarage as a sort of chaperonage of Mr. More, who appeared to grow more and more enamored of Camilla each time they met. But it was not so easy to dismiss the fact that she was the only female with whom he'd stood up twice at the Langleys' ball. (To dance with one partner more than that would be a solecism beyond even the pale of Mr. Drury.) Or that she was always running into him "by chance" as she took over her mother's charitable rounds, carrying calf's-foot jelly to parish invalids and distributing used clothing to the needy. When she had commented rather dryly on his unexpected propensity for good works, he'd shrugged and pointed out that he'd little else to do.

Which as far as she was concerned explained everything. Lucy made this point to Camilla when the two resumed the shirt hemming they'd abandoned the week before. Her sister was insisting that Mr. Drury had developed a tendre for her.

"Fustian!" she exclaimed emphatically, then went on to repeat his very words.

"Why there are all sorts of other ways he could amuse himself." For once Camilla refused to allow Lucy the last word. "There certainly is no shortage of young ladies in the neighborhood. Charlotte Langley, for instance, quite threw herself at Mr. Drury's head at her own ball. Surely you noticed. She wound up looking daggers at you."

"Yes, but Charlotte doesn't have a sister whom his friend's pursuing. If she had, I'm sure the case would be quite different. I'm simply more convenient for both gentlemen."

Camilla sighed over her sewing. "Really, Lucy, I don't know why you keep arguing when it's perfectly obvious to everyone else that you've made a conquest. I think yours is a classic case of 'the lady doth protest too much.' For the life of me, I don't see why you do it."

Her sister thought a moment while she frowned. "I don't know either," she finally said slowly, "for there's no denying his attentiveness. In fact, I think he's deliberately gone to a great

44

deal of trouble to give the impression that he's smitten. But somehow it just does not ring true."

"That's nonsense. How can you even think it?"

Her sister colored a bit. "It's just that—Camilla, do you remember George MacDonald?"

The ensign had been a close friend of their brothers and had spent several weeks at the vicarage two years before when their frigate was in port.

"Of course I remember him. But what does George MacDonald have to say to anything?"

"It's just that—well—he really did have a tendre for me. In fact he wished to speak to Papa, but I discouraged it."

Camilla put down her sewing to stare at Lucy in astonishment. "George MacDonald wished to marry you? Why did you never tell me?"

"I don't know. I suppose I didn't want to be teased about it. Also I hated to hurt him. And simply wished to forget the incident, I suppose. The only reason I bring it up now is to prove I really do know what I'm speaking of. I know what it's like to have a gentleman in love with me and Mr. Drury isn't."

In spite of herself, Camilla seemed impressed. Still she was unwilling to give up without a struggle. "Mr. Drury is quite a bit older than George was," she offered. "And much more worldly, don't you agree? I'm sure he's not the type to wear his heart upon his sleeve."

"Well, I'll grant you that much. In fact I'm not sure that he even has one. But I am quite sure he's simply using me. Oh, I don't mind that so much," she responded to her sister's scandalized expression. "What really annoys me is that I haven't the slightest notion why."

Lucy was determined to probe that gentleman's motives that very afternoon as they rode toward Lockhart Place. He had called for her in Mr. More's smart curricle. Though she had immediately noticed the kite tied behind the leather seat, she pointedly declined to remark upon it but privately felt it not one whit superior, except in size, to the one that she had made. Her expression just possibly betrayed her, for Mr. Drury chuckled for no apparent reason as he whipped up his team.

They drove in silence while Lucy tried to think of a subtle

way to explore what she had now convinced herself was an actual mystery. She soon despaired of subtlety and instead said bluntly, "I must say it amazes me, Mr. Drury, that you should put yourself out to this extent to entertain a seven-year-old boy."

"Oh? Why should it?"

"I don't know. I suppose it's just that you don't seem the type who'd take pleasure in the company of children."

He gave her a long, sideways look. "Perhaps it's not the child's company I take pleasure in, Miss Haydon."

"If that speech was supposed to throw me into confusion, all I can say is, it misses the mark."

"It does? Well, that is a leveler. I thought it rather effective, myself." He heaved an exaggerated sigh. "Do you know what I find particularly lowering?"

"No, but I suppose you'll tell me."

"It's expecially humbling"—he ignored her snide remark— "that I've kept company with Carnaby all these years without cultivating any of his ability to charm. What is it he has that I lack, Miss Haydon?"

"Sincerity perhaps?"

"Sincerity?" He seemed to be taking the flippant remark quite seriously. "I shouldn't think so. As I said, Carnaby does have charm by the bucketful. And no one can touch him when it comes to amiability or generosity. But sincerity? No, I'd not list that among his finer traits. Still though, to be fair, Carnaby *thinks* he's sincere, so perhaps it amounts to the same thing."

"Are you always so hard on your friends, Mr. Drury?"

"Inevitably." He had slowed the grays down to a plodding pace, possibly to take advantage of the sun, which was making its first appearance for several days or, more probably, to prolong the conversation. "I do air my opinions to my friends' faces as well as behind their backs, let me assure you."

"Then I find it a wonder that you have any. Does Mr. More, for instance, know your opinion of his cattle?"

"He does—and lets me drive them anyhow. I told you that Carnaby is the soul of generosity."

"I must admit then I'm at a loss to understand either of you."

"We really aren't that puzzling. Do you stand on ceremony

with your sister, for instance, Miss Haydon? Of course not. Carnaby and I have known each other too long and too well to deal in Spanish coin. And I doubt that either of us spends much time trying to puzzle out why we do what we do. Or whether we'd recognize our real motives if we did so. If you were right, just now, that I really am not the type to want to fly a kite on a perfect summer's afternoon with a delightful little boy—or in the company of the prettiest young lady in Sussex—second prettiest then?" he amended in reaction to her disgusted look. "Oh well then, how about the most *fascinating* lady in Sussex? That won't do either? Oh lord, Carnaby, where are you when I need you most?"

In spite of herself Lucy had to laugh. "I thought you just said that you didn't deal in Spanish coin."

"I don't. It's just that I always seem to lack conviction. A pity, but never mind. As I was saying, if I'm not doing this kite flying business for Master Louis Lockhart—"

"Aldington."

"Beg pardon?"

"Louis Aldington. He's William's stepson."

"Oh yes. I had forgotten. But the goddess in the portrait is his real mother, right? Well, as I was saying, again, if I'm not eager to play with Master *Aldington* or to spend the afternoon with you, neither of which perfectly good explanations of my presence you seem willing to allow, that only leaves one thing." He paused dramatically.

"Am I supposed to say, 'And what can that possibly be?' "

"Certainly. With bated breath."

"Well then. And what can that possibly be?"

"Mr. Lockhart's brandy! I can only be going to all this trouble hoping for another sample. It was without a doubt the finest I've ever tasted. Where do you suppose it came from, Calais?"

"I wouldn't know. It's not one of Papa's vices."

"A pity. But one of the crosses a man of the cloth has to bear, I collect. Anyhow, I've been making inquiries, and from what I've been led to understand the vicarage must be the only place around whose cellar isn't stocked by the free trade." He gave her a searching look. "Come now, Miss Haydon, you don't appear especially shocked. And I find that rather shocking in a clergyman's daughter, I must say."

"Do you? I've never really thought about it, I suppose. Smuggling's a thing I've always been aware of, more or less. At least John and Paul used to say they really should take it up rather than join the navy, that there was more adventure to be had right here at home. They were only funning, you understand."

"Naturally. But their point was well taken. At least, according to Carnaby's head groom, whom I suspect of having firsthand knowledge, by the by, most of the folk around here are involved one way or another. And you think Londoners are dissolute. Tsk, tsk, Miss Haydon." He pulled his team to a halt and climbed down to open the Lockhart gate.

"Well, I don't really see what's so terrible about smuggling." Lucy renewed the topic as they continued along the rutted drive. "Folk around here have always traded back and forth across the channel. It's their way of life. They depend upon it."

"It's too bad the government doesn't share your tolerance, Miss Haydon. But London does seem to take a dimmer view of all that lost revenue. And it's my understanding that now the war's over, they plan to make a big push to stamp out the trade."

"You certainly seem quite well informed." She looked at him suspiciously; a new idea was slowly beginning to take form. "Why all the interest?"

He shrugged. "No reason particularly. We must talk of something, must we not? And you weren't impressed by my attempts to charm you."

Lucy found this explanation a trifle lame but for once kept her opinion to herself. She had a more pressing problem to deal with. She was determined that this time Drury should not be present while she gave Louis his music lesson. "It's useless to expect a child to concentrate with you watching him," she said firmly as he helped her down from the curricle. "Please leave us alone."

"I would say it's useless to try to teach Louis to play at all. What's the musical equivalent of 'cow-handed'?"

"Never mind about his aptitude. I'm being paid to try. Besides, even if he's not especially talented, his efforts should produce some musical appreciation."

"You think so?" Drury looked doubtful. "I should rather think he'd be put off it for life."

If he'd hoped for Mr. Lockhart's company to help him pass the time, Mr. Drury was doomed to disappointment. The servant answered his inquiry by saying his master was away.

"Oh well then, I'll just wait, all alone, in the library. I'll pass the time somehow. Warm though, isn't it?"

Lucy smiled broadly as his expectant look brought no answering offer of refreshment from Bert.

"Do find something to read, Mr. Drury. And don't disturb us until two o'clock. I insist upon being allowed to give Louis his entire lesson." Rather to her surprise, he obeyed this directive.

It was Drury's idea that this time they should fly the kite down by the seashore. Only St. Botolph's, as befit its calling, was placed higher on the down than Lockhart Place. Louis led the way for the quarter mile that brought them to the edge of a rather daunting cliff. The path leading down from this precipice was quite worn with travel, though, and so well angled and so abundantly furnished with rocks and shrubs for hand and foot holds as to make their descent hardly hazardous at all.

The tide was out. They clambered over the bank of shingles that the waves had flung up on the high shore and then descended onto a wide stretch of sand. "You'd best take your shoes off, Louis," Lucy observed, thinking the lad was bound to ruin them.

"Why don't we do the same?" Mr. Drury was suiting the action to the word, tugging at his gleaming Hessians. He laughed at her scandalized expression. "Don't believe in untying your garters in public, or however the saying goes, Miss Haydon? Well, Louis and I will turn our backs like the gentlemen we are, and there doesn't seem to be anyone else around for miles."

It was glorious to be a child again and run barefoot behind Louis as he raced down the sand with his kite bobbing behind him. Lucy splashed daringly in the edges of the foam, snatching the ruffle of her skirt out of danger as a sudden wave threatened to drench it and sticking her tongue out at Mr. Drury, his pantaloons soaked to the knees now, who laughed over his shoulder at her.

The day was gloriously bright, with only a few wisps of clouds to vie for contrast with the vivid red of the kite against the clear blue sky. The sea breeze tugged at Lucy's chip straw bonnet, trying to rip it from her head and send it soaring into the heavens with the kite. She wished she might discard it like her shoes. But the thought of what Mama would say if she came home to find her daughter burned to a mahogany was too intimidating.

"Oh I say, this is famous!" Louis crowed. "Better than the meadow, don't you think?" He let out a bit more of the string wound round a heavy stick that he gripped tightly to prevent a repetition of last week's mishap.

"It's the best possible place for kite flying," his mentor called back, as if to reinforce his superiority to Lucy in every aspect of that art. She refused, however, to rise to the bait; like Louis she was finding the outing famous. She paused to admire the vista of sun-sparkling sea with headland after headland jutting out into it, then hurried on to catch up with her male companions as the wind tugged Louis farther down the shoreline.

They rounded a point of unusually high land and came upon a creek spilling out into the ocean. A yawl lay there at anchor.

"We used to come here when we were children!" Lucy exclaimed. "I'd almost forgotten. William had a skiff then. Is this his, Louis? Well then, he's certainly come up in the world since those days. Have you been out in her?"

She instantly regretted the question as Louis shook his head. "It's not a pleasure boat," he explained reasonably enough, but his face betrayed his disappointment. "My steppapa uses it for fishing."

Mr. Drury was looking at the vessel through narrowed eyes. "Should hold quite a haul, I'd say. Looks speedy, too."

"Oh, really!" Recalling their earlier conversation, Lucy gave him a withering look. "You can't actually be thinking—I mean to say, you mustn't go looking under every bush here in Sussex for—" She bit off the word 'smugglers' for Louis's sake.

"Don't you mean in every cove? Well, perhaps you're right. Possibly I have let myself get carried away by the local lore."

They started back the way they'd come with Louis once more leading the way. Mr. Drury paused and pointed out over the water. Shading her eyes with her hand, Lucy squinted in that direction. A cutter was plowing its way through the sea, following the shoreline.

"Part of the new naval blockade," he explained.

It occurred to her to wonder how he happened to be so well informed.

"Mr. Drury and I have to go now," Lucy informed her charge when they'd arrived back at the cliff path. The way Louis's face fell was harder to deal with than any spoken protest. "We're supposed to meet my sister and Mr. More," she explained, "and we're already late for that appointment. But we'll do this again," she promised, with a twinge of guilt that any interest Louis might have shown in music was surely now subverted.

Again, Drury trailed along unnecessarily as Lucy went back into the house to collect the music that she'd left there and to give Louis some final instructions concerning next week's lesson. Her back happened to be toward the withdrawing-room door when it opened.

"Mama, you're home!"

Even over Louis's exclamation, Lucy heard a quick intake of breath, and when she glanced up at Mr. Drury, he appeared to be struggling with some powerful emotion. But so quickly did he wipe his face clean of all expression that it gave no opportunity to read whatever had been written there.

Lucy was convinced of one thing, however. All of Mr. Drury's attention to herself—and through her, to Louis—was simply a prelude, a means to this predestined end. She was sure that he had carefully orchestrated events to lead him to this moment and this meeting, which was now, inevitably, taking place.

SOPHIA LOCKHART GAVE LUCY A COOL NOD, BENT HER cheek for Louis's kiss, but never took her eyes off Jerrold Drury. Lucy watched her slow, intimate smile with fascination and waited for some word that would prove the two were old acquaintances.

"You must be the owner of the magnificent rig I saw our Bert bringing up from the stables, sir. Louis, pray present me to your friend."

"This is Mr. Drury, Mama."

"Your servant, ma'am." He bowed above her hand, taking much too long about it, Lucy thought, while experiencing a stab of jealousy that both surprised and annoyed her. "I'm afraid I can't take credit for the curricle, though," he went on to say when he'd finally released the hand. "It belongs to a friend of mine."

Her eyes forgave him. "But I'm sure you must look quite dashing driving it."

She and Louis might just as well not be in the room for all the attention those two paid them, Lucy thought. They were too busy assessing one another, too pleased with what they saw.

She's older than the painting, Lucy decided. This was the only silent setdown she could come up with. She had taken it for granted that the artist, following a time-honored tradition, had flattered Mrs. Lockhart; while the lowering truth was, he had not begun to do his subject proper justice. The canvas was but a pale copy of the lady's magnetism.

Louis, too, seemed bothered by all the currents swirling around him. "Mr. Drury made me a kite, Mama," he offered suddenly. Lucy wondered if he, too, was not sensing the defection of his new friend.

"And you've been flying it? How extremely kind of you, Mr. Drury, to take so much interest in my child."

The gentleman shrugged modestly, for all the world as if it had been his own idea entirely. Lucy was disgusted to see how easily this aloof sophisticate was succumbing to the siren's spell.

It was interesting to note, however, that although Mrs. Lockhart asked most of the usual questions put to someone newly met, Mr. Drury was no more forthcoming with the beauty than he'd been with anybody else. Indeed, judging from his answers to her queries, his friendship with Mr. More appeared to be his entire claim to fame.

I'll wager he's a Cit. Miss Haydon, who boasted a viscount on one side of her lineage and a duke—though somewhat distantly removed—upon the other, took a snobbish satisfaction in so disposing of the fickle Mr. Drury. She could not fail to note that her nose was becoming alarmingly out of joint. She was therefore most relieved when the entrance of her sister and Mr. More broke up the tiresome tête-à-tête.

"I say, Drury, what kept you? We waited and waited, then decided to come along and see if you'd put my curricle in the ditch. Now here you are, dawdling—" Mr. More was in full spate as he strode into the room, but he shut off in midtirade at the sight of the lady standing next to his friend. And though in actuality his jaw did not then drop, his rather stunned expression managed to convey something of the kind.

It's like sitting in at a rehearsal of a play, Lucy thought, and being forced to watch the second run-through of a scene. Only this time the performance was much heightened. Mr. Drury might have been a mere understudy to the star.

Mrs. Lockhart was charmed to make Mr. More's acquaintance. There was certainly nothing original about that. Nor about the fact that she and Mr. Lockhart had been longing for the owner of Dighton House to take up residence there. That sentiment had been flung at Carnaby More's head since his arrival in the parish. But this time the phrases were said with a difference that seemed to put that gentleman in a daze. Lucy, who, the second time around, was studying the bewitching Mrs. Lockhart's technique with a greater degree of detachment than she'd shown before, observed that once again the object of the beauty's interest might have been alone with her on a desert isle, so effectively did she shut out all the others in the room.

Lucy stole a slightly malicious glance at Mr. Drury to see how he was taking this exclusion after his own brief moment in the sun. If he was consumed with jealousy, he failed to show it. Indeed, he seemed to be observing his friend's captivity with a fascinated interest that outdid her own. She felt an un-Christian surge of disappointment that he was not getting the comeuppance he deserved.

Mrs. Lockhart insisted that they must have some tea, which Louis might have with them "since he and Miss Haydon and Mr. Drury are such particular friends." And when Camilla timidly reminded Mr. More that if they did so, it would be too late to go to Rye as they had planned, "We've worlds of time," that gentleman had replied. "Besides, we mustn't disappoint Louis." Then, too, he and Mrs. Lockhart had just discovered that they had some fascinating friends in common. Furthermore, she was just back from Brighton and he longed to hear her views of Prinny's pavilion.

As they dutifully drank their tea, which surely must have been turning to dust in Camilla's mouth, Lucy did wish that her sister had some of Mr. Drury's skill at masking all emotion. Perhaps she'd been reading too much of Mrs. Radcliffe. "Stricken" was the only word she could think of to describe the impression Camilla conveyed. She longed to shake her sister, even while commiserating with her, as they listened to the other woman's recital of the latest on-dits concerning the Prince Regent's architectural excesses, punctuated by her delightful, infectious laugh.

Lucy felt Mr. Drury's gaze and for an instant thought she detected an I-told-you-so expression in it before he looked away. Well, he didn't have to underscore the fact that, for the moment anyhow, Camilla had simply ceased to exist as far as Mr. More was concerned.

It wasn't that Mrs. Lockhart was any lovelier than Camilla, Lucy loyally concluded as she sipped the tiresome tea. But it was rather like comparing lily of the valley to an exotic orchid. On some abstract aesthetic plane the small white flowers might even be superior. But who would ever notice?

When Lucy finally roused herself to say, "We really should be going," it was more to release Camilla from her misery than from any desire to go on to Rye. As far as she was concerned, Rye could go to perdition and take Mr. More—and Mr. Drury—with it. It was the sanctuary of the vicarage that she longed for, with a few of Papa's platitudes thrown in. But no, they mustn't leave, Mrs. Lockhart insisted, before Louis played for them. "We shall all reap the fruits of Miss Lucinda Haydon's labors."

Lucy longed to protest as Louis turned quite pale. But since the child's mother had placed her teaching skill squarely on the line, she knew that her motives might be suspect. All she could do was to give the child a smile of encouragement as he rose obediently and marched woodenly toward the pianoforte.

At his very best Louis was an inept performer, but with five pairs of adult eyes upon him, the result was painful. When the piece, after several false starts and multitudinous repetitions to rectify missed notes, finally stumbled to its conclusion, his mother heaved a sigh of relief for all of them.

"Oh well, Louis"—she laughed off his poor performance—"the fault is mine. And to think I've always despised the type of mama who insists upon exhibiting her offspring to everyone's discomfort. Never you mind, Miss Haydon"—Lucy found herself dazzled by a forgiving smile—"I'm sure you've done your best. Louis, I fear, takes after his father's family. The Aldingtons are not musical in the least. Still, there is a great deal of discipline to be gained from a pursuit of the pianoforte, I collect."

"A pity," Mr. Drury offered, "that you did not ask Louis to demonstrate his ability to fly a kite. I can assure you that in that particular undertaking he's a nonpareil."

Louis's smile was a mixture of pride and gratitude.

This time Lucy was firm in insisting that they must go. "Papa will be wondering where we are, Camilla." The sisters rose to their feet as Lucy looked pointedly at their laggard escorts. The gentlemen stood, reluctantly.

"Oh dear." Mrs. Lockhart's voice was distressed as she looked at the ormolu clock that stood on the mantel. "I've spoiled your outing. You must forgive me. We have so few visitors that I fear I've selfishly reveled in your company and had quite forgotten that you had your own plans for the afternoon. The truth is"—she rushed on with an embarrassed candor that Lucy found suspect—"I had hoped to detain you until my husband came home. Poor William, you see, has had to pay rather dearly for his rashness in marrying me. You see"—she turned her attention back exclusively to Mr. More—"my husband had an understanding with one of the local ladies—in her mind, at least"—Mr. Drury glanced at Lucy as she bristled—"when he met and married me. And I'm sure the Miss Haydons will not mind my saying so, the people here are clannish to a fault and not quick to forgive any slight, true or imagined, to one of their own. So we've received no invitations—which bothers me not in the least, as you can well imagine." She spoke to Mr. More as one sophisticate to another. "But it has distressed poor William a great deal. And I was hoping he would find me receiving callers. That was why I was so thoughtless as to ruin your outing. Do, pray, forgive me. No, better still!" She clapped her hands delightedly as a thought seemed to occur spontaneously. "Allow me to make it up to you. Allow William and me to show you Seacliffe. Oh please, Mr. More, don't tell me you have already seen it. I won't be able to stand the disappointment."

"Seen it? I have not even heard of it. What is Seacliffe?"

"You don't know? Well then, that settles it. We really must all go there. Seacliffe, I'll have you know, sir, is our local rival to Ramsgate. Mr. Hawkins, its chief developer, assures me that it's destined to put even Brighton in the shade. Really, you must see it. Will a week from today suit? I'm sure one lesson more or less will make little difference to Louis here. He'd much rather go to Seacliffe, wouldn't you, dear? Well then, shall we consider it settled? We can go in our carriage. William will be in raptures when I tell him."

Mr. More, however, declared himself unwilling to wait an entire week to make that gentleman's acquaintance. He seemed to have taken the uncivil attitude of the neighborhood very much to heart. "Actually there's really no need to drive both our rigs to the vicarage. You won't mind going home with Jerry and your sister, will you, Miss Haydon?" For the first time since they'd arrived at Lockhart Place, he appeared conscious of Camilla's presence.

"No, of course not." Lucy was proud of her sister's dignity. Camilla even managed a small smile.

And once the threesome was on its way, with Camilla squeezed in between Mr. Drury and her sister, she was the one who kept the conversation alive when the other two would gladly have settled for silence. She began by commenting brightly upon this or that aspect of the scenery, then moved on to dwell enthusiastically upon their upcoming trip to Seacliffe, bringing up several other treats there that Mrs. Lockhart had failed to mention. "It really is thoughtful of Mrs. Lockhart to plan this outing for William's sake. I'd no idea we'd caused him such unhappiness. I'm sure that Mrs. Lockhart is wrong, though, when she says it was intentional. People merely wished to allow the honeymooners time to themselves, don't you think so, Lucy?" The question must have been rhetorical for she gave her sister no opportunity to reply before adding, "I shall tell Papa of his unhappiness, nonetheless, for it makes no difference whether the cause is real or imagined, does it? The misery would be the same. I will tell Papa to call upon William right away."

"Oh for heaven's sake, Camilla, don't be goosish! I don't know which idea is more preposterous, William Lockhart's martyrdom or the notion that if he does care a fig what anyone else thinks about the way he treated Ada, a visit from Papa would set it to rights. Why Papa and William could never think of two words to say to one another when the boys were still at home and William was in and out of the vicarage all the time."

She was immediately sorry for her outburst. Even Mr. Drury came out of his abstraction long enough to give her a censorious look as Camilla's eyes filled with tears.

And that night Lucy paid dearly for her thoughtlessness. The fact that she had been guilty of adding to her sister's misery was the last straw. She tossed and turned in bed while she rehashed every moment of their disastrous visit with Mrs. Lockhart. Surely Mr. More's incivility toward Camilla was only temporary. It would be the rare man indeed who would not succumb to Sophia Lockhart's spell. But once removed from the dazzle of her presence, he was bound to come back to his senses and appreciate Camilla's superior worth.

This conclusion would have been quite reassuring and Lucy would have thereupon gone to sleep had she not kept recalling the conversation she'd been so unfortunate as to overhear at Lady Tilney's evening party. How often, according to Mr. Drury, did Mr. More fall in love? Every moon change, was it? Oh blast Mr. Drury for a know-it-all! Lucy gave her pillow a punishing thump. But there was no need thinking she'd go to sleep now.

She gave up trying and got out of bed. Disregarding the chill of the floor upon her bare feet, Lucy walked across the room to look out the window, hoping perhaps to find a star to wish on. But as if to match her mood, the sky was an uncompromising black. She leaned out the window, drawing in deep, calming breaths of the heavy air.

Then, glancing up, she saw the signal light.

Chapter Eight

A T FIRST LUCY THOUGHT IT A FLASH OF LIGHTNING, glimpsed out of the corner of her eye, too far away for the noise of thunder.

But in a bit it was repeated, followed by two more flashes in quick succession. She leaned still farther out the window and peered in the direction it had come from.

Never had she seen a night so dark. It was impossible to discern even an outline of anything outside or to recall the scene's homely familiarity, so eerie did the out-of-doors now seem. Heaven alone knew what might walk abroad on such a night as this. For the first time in her life the thought of the graveyard that lay so near caused Lucy's scalp to prickle.

Nonsense! What would Papa say to such heathen superstition? And even if one did believe in the dead clambering out of their graves at night to take up haunting, who'd ever heard of ghosts behaving in this manner?

See! There it was again. Three rapid flashes. And high. Too elevated entirely for the graveyard inhabitants, one would think. (But what, in heaven's name, were fairy lights?) She had her bearings now. The light must be coming from the church tower. And if its origin was supernatural, well then, she was a Frenchman.

Her first impulse was to wake her father and inform him of the mysterious lights. On second thought it seemed better not to. Papa, she was sure, would simply march straight into the church, wearing the breastplate of righteousness, and demand of the person or persons unknown just what they were up to. No, Papa was really much better in spiritual matters.

Reason told her that whoever was sending out signals in the dead of night was up to no good. Circumspection seemed definitely in order. Best to know first what was going on; then one could decide just what to do about it. She'd watch awhile.

This, Lucy soon realized, was an exercise in futility. Her present situation offered an uninterrupted view of the church tower and nothing else. Even if the night were not as dark as a bunch of black cats in a witch's caldron, her view of the church entrance would still be obstructed by all the foliage that lay between. Whoever was up there in the steeple must eventually come down. (She stifled the thought that he—or they—might already be down and prowling about.) And when that descent occurred, she needed to be close enough to see who it was.

Acting on the thought before an attack of prudence could set in, Lucy turned back into her room for her dressing gown and slippers. Her nightcap, somehow, seemed inappropriate for a nocturnal expedition. She took it off, eased quietly out her bedchamber door, and tiptoed down the stairs.

As a child, Lucy had often exited the house by way of a ground-floor window since her parents' room commanded a good view of the front door and Emma's bedchamber overlooked the back. It was not a route, however, she had taken lately. So when she gathered up her skirts and climbed over the sill, her instincts were operating from a ten-year-old's perspective. The drop should have been farther. The ground came up too suddenly and rattled her teeth.

She fought her way through the boxwoods that surely had doubled their branches during the night, then paused a moment to get her bearings. This is ridiculous, she chided herself. I could walk to the church blindfolded. No need to see now. She fought off the delayed fit of prudence that was telling her to climb back in the window and pull the covers over her head, and began walking, so she hoped, in the direction of the church.

From the perspective of her chamber, the darkness had been an obscuring screen. Out here it was a palpable thing. She could feel it settling over her like a—shroud? She shivered, then clenched her teeth to stop their rattling. She blamed both conditions on the midnight chill.

"Blanket." There, that was a much better figure of speech. And certainly as apt a one as "shroud." Or "cloak"? That was even better. The cloak of darkness. Now there was comfort for you. For if she couldn't see her hand before her face, at least she knew the darkness worked both ways and she'd not be seen herself. Lucy barely repressed a shriek as she blundered into the hedge.

It took a few moments of groping up and down its length before she found the opening and squeezed through. Then once inside the churchyard her night vision began to improve slightly, not an entirely unmixed blessing, for now the gravestones seemed to be springing up all around her like dragons' teeth, dimly perceived and ominous in the nether gloom.

Get hold of yourself, Lucinda! Her inner voice scotched a sudden impulse to bolt and run. You've played among these tombstones since you were in leading strings. They're like old friends. "Saints laid to rest," Papa calls them. But then the lowering thought intruded that amongst so many they couldn't all have been that saintly. Some tormented ones might not be at rest at all and might choose this very moment to walk abroad.

Fustian! The inner voice dripped scorn. You don't really believe that nonsense. Get along with you.

She weaved her way purposefully through the gravestones, bound for a concealing bush she knew of in good position for

60

observing the church door. One of the larger gravestones gave her her bearings. The bush lay just a few yards beyond. She'd been moving noiselessly up to now, but close to the church her breathing became a blacksmith's bellows, her heartbeat the hammer on the anvil. She stopped a moment to gain control and to stare up in the general direction of the steeple. No telltale light. The signaler was still up there waiting for—whatever. Or else gone by now. Or out here prowling. The bush suddenly became a sanctuary, a goal to be reached as quickly as possible. Lucy hiked her skirts and bolted, holding her breath, running on tiptoe. Then, just as she came abreast the monument to Josiah Crowell ("departed this life, March 25, 1684"), a shadow materialized.

You're simply seeing things. It's the natural outcome of your panic. Lucy's inner voice made a last-ditch effort.

But there was nothing imaginary about the fingers that reached out and grabbed her or the muscular body that held her tight, arms pinioned. And the rough hand clapped across her mouth just in time to cut off a rising scream was a much more effective silencer than her inner voice. At this point, certainly, one of Mrs. Radcliffe's heroines would have swooned. But Lucy was granted no such deliverance. Lacking it, she bit her captor's hand.

"Damnation! Be still, will you!"

Since he'd been the only one to speak, Lucy seethed at the injustice of the order till it occurred that he might possibly be referring to the struggle she was putting up. She decided to oblige and ceased her kicking.

"It's me, you addle-pated vixen!"

He hadn't needed to hiss this piece of information into her ear. She'd just figured that out for herself. For once the quite novel sensation she was experiencing had battered down her wall of terror, there'd been a familiarity about the male body she was pressed against that defied all reason since his and hers had certainly never been in such close proximity before. Standing up with him twice at the Langley ball was not to be compared to their present position as they stood together like two pages in a book. So why she so instantly recognized her captor was a puzzle that for a moment obscured all the much more important considerations.

Mr. Drury brought her back to reality with a low growl. "If I let you go, you aren't going to shriek or faint or do anything else silly, are you?" She shook her head violently and he released her. "Now what the hell are you doing out here?"

"I'm going to that bush," she whispered back.

He must have found that explanation lacking, for he took her hand and jerked her behind the monument that previously had concealed him and pulled her down beside him on its base. "Tell me what you're up to, Miss Haydon. But for God's sake keep your voice down," he added as she started to comply.

"I saw you signaling from the church tower," she whispered, "and came out to investigate. Now you explain yourself, Mr. Drury."

"*I* wasn't signaling. Like you, I saw the lights and wondered what was going on."

"You could not possibly have done so. The church tower's not *that* tall. There's no way you could see it from Dighton House."

"As a matter of fact, I didn't. I saw it from the beach."

"And just what were you doing on the beach?"

"Walking," was the succinct if not quite satisfactory reply. "But never mind about me now. Whoever was flashing that light is most likely still up there. That is to say if he hasn't had heart failure at the sight of you."

"Don't be ridiculous. He couldn't possibly have seen me. It's too dark out here. I can't even see you properly."

"My dear Miss Haydon, promise me you'll never take up a life of crime. Obviously you're not cut out for it. If you hope to remain unobserved, don't go abroad at night dressed in white." He chuckled softly. "I must say you did give me quite a turn when you materialized among the gravestones. I'm trusting that our friend up there believes you were a dread specter of some sort."

"I didn't have time to think," she said defensively. "After all, I'm not in the habit of—" She broke off suddenly as the thought struck her that there'd been something rather odd about the feel of him. She reached out and ran her hand over some coarse material that was definitely not gentlemen's superfine. "You're wearing a smock!" Her voice was incredulous. "Pretty odd clothing for an innocent stroll along the beach, I'd say." She peered quite close. "Is your face blackened?"

"Don't be absurd." For a denial it lacked conviction. "Really, I think we've discussed our sartorial peculiarities quite enough. Go home, Miss Haydon."

"I'll do nothing of the sort."

"Use your head, woman. Those signals had a target."

"Well, you should know." She could have bitten off her tongue. If he'd been summoned for some unsavory purpose, it really would have been wiser not to let him know that she suspected.

"Miss Haydon." She didn't need to read an expression to know his patience was sorely tried. "Believe me when I say that I am neither the signaler nor the signalee. Believe me when I say that whoever is involved in either of those occupations is up to little good."

"I know that. Why do you think I'm here? Papa will have to be told who's misusing the church. And why. What do you think they're up to?"

The intimacy involved in breathing a conversation into one another's ears was having an odd effect upon Lucy's equilibrium. Mr. Drury, she noticed, was slow in answering this time, and when he did so his whisper was rather strained.

"The possibilities are endless. Could be just some lads out for a lark. My best guess, though, is that it's smugglers."

"Smugglers! Here?"

"For God's sake, keep your voice down."

"But that's daft. We're too far from the sea. What can smuggling have to do with St. Botolph's?"

"That's what I plan to find out if possible. Now please be a good girl, Lucy, and go home before your father misses you and raises the hue and—"

It was her turn to clap a hand over a mouth. "Listen!" she hissed. At first she thought she'd been imagining things. Then she felt Drury relax from the strain of listening, only to stiffen once again as the sound grew unmistakable.

"Sit still," he breathed. "It's too late now to run for home."

As though she would. What did he take her for?

"And for God's sake remember how visible you are. Don't move. With luck, if anyone sees you, they'll think you're another tombstone."

She clapped her hand over his mouth again. Really, he was prosier than Papa.

The horses' hooves were evidently muffled, for they made little sound as they turned off the main road. Drury shifted his position silently to peer around the gravestone. Despite his earlier warning, Lucy used his body as a shield and peeked across his shoulder.

She could barely make out two horses, heavily laden, their outlines so grotesque with packing cases that they might have been mistaken for mythological beasts instead of English cattle. The men were more difficult to see. They certainly were not wearing white. Squinting through the gloom, Lucy decided there were three of them—no, possibly four. Before she could pin down the exact number, they had passed on out of sight.

For the next few minutes, Lucy and Drury strained their ears toward the sounds of St. Botolph's heavy carved doors opening, followed by strained grunts, a horse's stamp, the thud of something dropped, a muffled oath. Lucy deeply regretted never having reached the bush that commanded so excellent a view of the church entrance.

Drury must have been thinking along much the same lines for he whispered, "I'm going to try and get a better look. You stay here. And don't move, unless you want your throat cut."

How long Lucy sat pressed up against the smooth white marble was impossible to calculate. She only knew that the cold had gradually seeped into her body till she felt like a part of the stone itself. She thought longingly of the heavy—and dark—cloak hanging in her wardrobe. It topped the mental list she began making of all the things she'd bring along the next time she set forth to investigate any midnight mysteries. It was followed by a weapon, a means of light, something to eat, perhaps? Forming the list kept her mind off her discomfort for quite a while, but where was Drury? Strolling on back to Dighton House most likely, leaving her here to freeze to death like some poor dumb hunting dog immobilized by the command to stay.

She'd been staring toward the row of stained glass windows on her side of the church since he'd left her and had glimpsed only an occasional faint gleam of light. Whoever had gone in there was doing whatever he was doing in near darkness. Stealing the plate perhaps. It wouldn't take good visibility to find the altar. Lucy quickly squelched any relief at being liberated from polishing all the brass and silver the church contained, quite shocked at her momentary reaction to such sacrilege. She did, however, allow herself to be relieved that the intruders were more likely thieves than smugglers. Undoubtedly they were part of the gypsy bands that wandered the back roads from time to time, pilfering as they went. She found this far more palatable than the notion that her Sussex neighbors were using the church for nefarious purposes. If only she were sure.

The only thing she was certain of was that it was ridiculous to stay there till she atrophied just because Mr. Drury had told her to. For all she knew he might be hand in glove with the intruders. He could have flashed the steeple light, then simply sat down in the graveyard to await their coming. Of course, this view of things rather played havoc with her gypsy theory. Try as she might, it was hard to cast the sophisticated Drury in that role. Of course he did have the misplaced arrogance of a gypsy king. Oh come now. That notion really was preposterous.

But the more she thought about it, the more she became convinced that there was some kind of collusion between Drury and the night prowlers and that he'd cleverly hoodwinked her into immobility. Why, she even doubted that she was all that visible. It was one more effort on his part, most likely, to keep her from discovering what was going on.

Lucy rose to her feet cautiously. They responded with the pricking of a thousand needles. She flexed her toes inside her soft leather slippers, trying to coax the circulation back. When they were once again in working order, she scampered toward the bush.

Her elation at reaching it undetected was soon dampened by the realization that she was the only person cowering there behind it. She'd hoped, in spite of all her earlier conclusions, to find Drury there. If he were a mere observer like herself, this is certainly where he would have gone. Ergo, he must be a participant in whatever unsavory business was going on. The need to know what part Drury was playing, far more than her original goal of spying on the strange intruders, propelled Lucy toward the door.

It was locked. This destroyed her last hope, that Drury had simply crept into the church to identify the thieves—or smugglers. He'd hardly have cut off his own retreat if he were innocent. She tried the door more forcefully in case it was merely stuck from dampness, which had been known to happen from time to time. The knob jiggled in her hand. And it took a moment for the fact to register that she was not the cause. The key was being turned on the inside.

Lucy ran. Ran with all her might at the sound of the door's opening. But as she sped around the corner of the church, a hissed "What's that!" warned her that possibly she'd been spotted. The sound of running feet on the marble steps confirmed it.

In a blind panic she bolted toward the vicarage, weaving in and out among the gravestones. The noise of pursuit slacked suddenly, then stopped altogether. "Oh my God, it's a ghost!" a quavering voice exclaimed while another gasped "Lor' save us!"

Since the vicarage seemed a less likely specter's destination than where she was, Lucy forced herself to halt there in the graveyard. She turned slowly back to face the way she'd come and made out the outline of two forms by the corner of the church and heard a muttered argument. The disputants appeared to be of separate minds about pursuit. In an effort to influence their decision, Lucy slowly flapped the skirts of her white dressing gown and moaned a long, low quavering moan whose macabre quality owed as much to fear as to innate dramatic talent. Did she just imagine that one of the figures crossed himself? Impossible to tell at this range. But certainly they'd begun to inch away.

Hoping to clinch the matter, Lucy raised her arms on high and moaned again, a sound that improved with practice both in eeriness and in volume. To heighten her performance, she began to sway from side to side; then in a burst of inspiration she sank slowly behind the gravestone where she was standing; creating, she fervently hoped, the impression she was reentering her grave.

It worked. There was a sudden sound of running, followed almost immediately by the gallop of horses' hooves. Lucy leaned back against the marble and broke out in a cold sweat.

"A most effective performance, Miss Haydon."

"Eeeeek!" The apparition leaped upward from its grave. "You scared me senseless," she accused when she'd finally recovered.

"No more than you deserved." Drury was convulsed with not-quite-silent laughter. "Those villains are still running, I'll bet a monkey. Hey, hold on now. You're shaking like a leaf, girl." He'd quickly sobered. "Cold or scared?"

The remedy for either condition, evidently, was to enfold her in his arms. He held her close, which did little to stop the trembling but in point of fact increased it. He possibly hoped for a better solution to the problem as he bent down and kissed her.

Of all the sensations she'd thus far experienced throughout the long, eventful night—up to and including being hounded by cutthroats through a graveyard—this meeting of male and female lips was by far the most devastating. And the more it was prolonged, the more convinced Lucy became that the result of this strange new sensation would be to leave her weightless, disembodied, floating forever like the wraith she'd pretended to be, here among the gravestones.

He finally released her, reluctantly it seemed, but then reached out to steady her once more. At least that was probably his intention. Lucy, though, had different ideas upon the subject. She had just concluded that if she ever hoped to regain her equilibrium, they needed to be separated entirely. To test this theory, she removed the hand that was clasping her by the shoulder.

"Go home, Lucy," Drury said. His voice sounded a great deal huskier than usual. "Go home and lock your doors, and if you ever see lights in the church steeple again, crawl back into bed and go to sleep. Of all the daft, chuckle-headed things to do—

67

coming out here, and in your nightclothes at that. My God, girl, have you no sense in that lovely head at all? Don't you realize—"

"Don't lecture me!" She broke into his tirade. "For I'll not listen." She turned away and started toward home, not because he'd said to, but because she wished it. Then, when she'd reached Josiah Crowell's last resting place, she paused just long enough to deliver a Parthian shot.

"It seems to me, Mr. Jerrold Drury, that I'm not the one that needs the sort of tongue lashing you've just delivered. For it seems to me, sir, that you yourself have a great, great many things to answer for this night."

Chapter Nine

*L*UCY HAD NOT EXPECTED TO SLEEP A WINK. BUT IN POINT of fact she did not open her eyes till ten and then lay in bed several minutes longer, recalling, in selective snatches, the strange dream she'd had. When it finally penetrated her consciousness that it had been no dream (the realization coming rather providentially just before she'd be forced to relive the evening's shattering conclusion), she came tumbling out of bed.

This time, after tea and toast, she left the vicarage properly—through the door. And she went the long way around by the walkway instead of taking the shortcut through the graveyard. But after all this propriety, when she stepped inside the church, it was all that she could manage not to curse, a bad enough impulse at any time, unthinkable in the sanctuary.

Mr. Drury rose from the back pew where he'd been sitting with his eyes closed. "What kept you?" he asked.

"Didn't you go home at all?" she answered crossly, though

obviously he had, for whatever rustic sort of garb he'd worn the night before had been traded off for buckskin breeches with top boots and a dark green riding coat.

"You look different, too." He'd not missed her scrutiny. "Not nearly so sepulchral. Yours or Eleanor's?" He nodded at the pale blue jaconet muslin morning dress she wore. "Sorry. The question was rag-mannered. It's most becoming."

"What are you doing here?" She cut through all the small talk.

"The same as you. I wanted to look around. But since I knew you'd be coming, I decided just to wait. Thought you'd know of nooks and crannies I might miss. Still, had I known you were such a slugabed—" He pulled out his watch and consulted it. "I've been here for the better part of an hour."

"Spending a bit of time in church won't do you any harm. I doubt it's a thing you do all that often."

"Got up on the wrong side of the bed, did you? What an unkind cut, Miss Haydon. Still, the point is well taken, I collect. For I must say this is an excellent spot for meditation. Though I'm not certain all my thoughts would meet with the Reverend Mr. Haydon's approval." He gazed up at the pulpit.

Lucy's face grew hot as she recalled one likely direction of his thoughts. But once again she was spared any serious consideration of her shocking behavior as her own gaze drifted off the pulpit and focused on the altar. The sight of it erased all else from her mind.

"Why, there's nothing missing!" she exclaimed.

"I beg your pardon?"

"It's all there—the gold cross—and the candlesticks—the chalice. Nothing's missing."

"Did you think there would be?"

"Of course. The horses were still loaded when I tried the church door."

"They couldn't have been. You must be mistaken."

"I am not. I not only saw—well, more or less—that they still carried their packs, I reached out to touch the cases to make sure as I went by. That's why I was so certain that the men were thieves, not smugglers. I thought they must be making one last stop for the church valuables."

"It makes no sense. Granted, I could see very little either, but I could have sworn they were unloading something that they took inside. I suppose it could have been the other way around."

Lucy gave him a hard look. "And just where were you, Mr. Drury, all that time? Strange that I didn't stumble over you anywhere. I couldn't help but wonder," she said with deliberation, "if you'd joined up with some friends of yours."

"So that's what you've been thinking." He looked less insulted than amused as he perched upon the pew in front of him and studied her while she glared accusingly from the aisle. "And just how did you arrive at that maggoty notion?"

"Well, I don't really know all that much about you, do I?"

"Perhaps that's because there's not really all that much to know."

"And I've only your word for it that you saw the signals from the beach. For all I know, you could have just come down from the church tower when we—uh—met in the graveyard."

"You mean when I grabbed you in the graveyard, don't you? It's a bit late to put a period to your plain speaking, don't you agree? Would you like to know what I think, Lucy? No? Well, I'll tell you anyhow. I think it was my ungentlemanly behavior last night that's made you decide I'm a villain. But just because a man loses his head and steals a kiss doesn't necessarily mean that he's in collusion with a band of smugglers."

"If that's what they were."

"Well, I don't think they came in here to pray, do you? I still believe they must have hidden something somewhere, and all this talk won't help us find it." He slid off the pew back. "Let's go have a look around."

Their search was exhaustive and exhausting. Mr. Drury even insisted that they explore the subterranean passage between the sacristy and the vestry twice. Festooned with cobwebs and reeking with the mildew of neglect, the passageway did seem the ideal hiding place. But though the corridor was piled with worn-out prayer books, priedieux vainly waiting for repair, tattered altar cloths, bits of candles, and topping the debris, a lady's garter that Mr. Drury picked up and gazed at thoughtfully, they found nothing whatsoever to account for the previous night's invasion. The lowering truth was that in the whole of St. Botolph's from its steeple cross to its firm foundation, they had been unable to discover that anything had been added or subtracted at all.

"Of course there is one place that we haven't looked." They'd returned, dusty and weary, to sit in the back pew that Mr. Drury seemed now to think he'd rented, and he was breaking a rather lengthy silence.

"Surely you don't think! Why, that's ridiculous."

"It's a day for ridiculous notions, Miss Haydon. I don't see why I should be any less suspicious of Lord Tilney than you are of me. Scratch a Sussex man and if you don't actually find a free-trader, you'll find a sympathizer. Or so I'm told. Why shouldn't he be in cahoots with those shady characters we saw last night? The cellars at the hall may need replenishing."

"Well even if he were—oh, you really are absurd, you know—Nigel would never desecrate St. Botolph's. It's his passion."

"Just the same, it doesn't make sense to have prowled all over this place"—he flicked the remnants of a cobweb off his sleeve to emphasize the point—"and then declare one area to be off limits."

"Very well then." She rose. "If nothing else will satisfy you. But even though he's far too nice ever to show it, I happen to know that Nigel hates to be interrupted in his work. Besides, unless those men last night were smuggling documents of some kind—and the war *is* over, you may recall—there's no place in there to hide anything. But I can't expect you to take my word for that."

"As an accused smuggler myself, Miss Haydon, I'm feeling less than charitable. Lead on."

Lucy tapped at the door of the vestry and then opened it. "Oh there you are, Camilla," she said brightly, as though furnishing an excuse for their intrusion. Her sister and Nigel were seated at opposite ends of a library table piled high with parish records. The viscount looked up, still keeping his place with an index finger, then rose politely to extend a rather abstracted greeting. Camilla's face lighted when she saw Mr. Drury, then changed to disappointment as she realized he'd come from Dighton House alone.

"Did you want me?" she asked her sister in a voice that attempted to sound cheerful but failed.

"Oh no, not really. Please go on with what you were doing, Nigel. Don't let us interrupt you. It's just that Papa was wondering where you were, Camilla," Lucy improvised as Drury's eyes scanned the room.

"That's peculiar. Papa knows I'm helping Nigel with his research."

"Oh well," Lucy's laugh was rather forced, "you know how absentminded Papa can be at times." She glanced again at Mr. Drury and found him staring pointedly at a large wooden cabinet. Repressing a sigh, she walked over and opened it to disclose nothing but stacks and stacks of registries as Camilla asked, "Does Papa need me?"

"No, no. He was just wondering, that's all. How is the history coming, Nigel?"

"Eh?" Nigel was frowning down at the record book again. "Oh very well. Very well indeed. Thanks largely to your sister's excellent assistance." He glanced up, though, when Drury walked over to the cupboard to peer over Lucy's shoulder. "Were you looking for something?" he inquired politely.

"Er, yes, more or less," Lucy answered. "I've mislaid a handkerchief somewhere. It just occurred to me it might have been in here."

Camilla was looking at her sister rather oddly, but Nigel appeared to find nothing out of the ordinary in that preposterous statement. He turned his abstracted gaze upon the cupboard. "I think I would have seen it in there, Lucy." He stooped to look underneath the table and then gazed rather helplessly around the room. "I don't recall having seen—how long ago did you lose it, you say?"

"Oh never mind." Lucy closed the cupboard door. "It's not important. Forgive us for interrupting you. It's just that Mr. Drury wished to see the church again, and while we were here, I thought I'd check on Camilla's whereabouts. And look for my handkerchief. Two birds with one stone, you might say." She avoided her sister's puzzled gaze.

Lord Tilney had brightened at the news of Mr. Drury's enthusiasm. "St. Botolph's is well worth a second look, is it not?

72

Could I be of any assistance in pointing out some of its more unusual features?"

"Oh no. No, thank you very much. I wouldn't dream of disturbing you any further. Miss Haydon is a very competent guide."

"Your friend Mr. More did not come this time?" Nigel inquired.

"No, I'm afraid not. It's not from lack of interest in St. Botolph's," he hastened to add, "but he's closeted with his bailiff, actually."

After a few more apologies for their intrusion, Lucy and Mr. Drury left the researchers to their work and walked out of the church in silence. But once outside, "Well, why don't you go ahead and say it?" she asked peevishly.

"Say what?"

"I told you so."

"But that should be your line. You're the one who insisted there'd be nothing to find in Lord Tilney's workplace. And you were right. We're miserable failures as spies, Miss Haydon. We still don't know who was in the church last night or why."

"I didn't mean that and you know it."

He sighed deeply. "I know nothing of the kind. If you think I've any competence at all in following your shifts in conversation, not even to mention in reading your mind, you much mistake the matter." He led her over to a marble bench beneath a large willow among the gravestones. As they sat down, Lucy gazed around her—at the peaceful graveyard—the church—the vicarage. "It doesn't seem like the same place at all, does it?"

"As last night? No, you're right there. This morning it's a painting by Constable. Last night it was pure gothic. Well, not entirely." He gazed significantly at the gravestone where he'd kissed her. "But let's not wander from the point. I think you were just about to ring some sort of a peal over me, Lucy."

"Miss Haydon. Last night's lapse of conduct does not give you the right to make free with my name, sir."

"It doesn't? Oh well, then. Just why, *Miss Haydon,* was I supposed to say 'I told you so'? A phrase I abhor, by the by."

"Nevertheless you are dying to say it about my sister and Mr.

More. You knew all along that Camilla was just one of his flirts, no more. But I took his word for it that his feeling for her was different."

"And now you've changed your mind? Aren't you—and your sister—placing too great a significance on the fact that Carnaby's not with me this morning? I couldn't help noticing that she seemed upset. But you of all people should know that I took pains to come alone."

"And you of all people should know that it's not his absence this morning but his conduct yesterday I refer to."

"Oh yes, that. It was inexcusable of Carnaby not to escort your sister home. But then I'm afraid he's inclined to be thoughtless."

"For someone so given to plain speaking, Mr. Drury, you are certainly shying away from the main issue. It could not have escaped your notice that Mr. Carnaby More was quite swept off his feet by Mrs. Lockhart. Camilla might never have existed for all the attention that he paid her."

"Well, yes," the other admitted, "but don't be too hard on him. The lady does have that effect."

"You'd met her before, hadn't you?" she blurted.

He looked startled. "Why no. I'd never set eyes on her till yesterday. What gave you that notion?"

"I don't know really. You just looked as if you knew her, I suppose."

"I did? Well it must have been the portrait then. Which, amazingly enough, doesn't really do her justice, or don't you agree?"

"Oh, I agree all right." Something in her tone caused him to chuckle. "You think I'm jealous, don't you?" Her hackles rose.

"Let's just say I'd be surprised if Mrs. Lockhart doesn't have that effect upon most females."

"Upon those who have husbands or sweethearts who come into her range, certainly. I, for one, would hate to be among their number. She seems to bowl men over like tenpins."

"Come now. Just because she bowled down poor, susceptible Carnaby? That's no true test."

"And you."

"Me? I emphatically deny it."

"You needn't. You practically groveled at the lady's feet till Mr. More arrived and she abandoned you for bigger game."

"You mistake the matter, I assure you. I hesitate to say so, but possibly you *were* jealous."

"Me? Never! Well," she amended, "a little perhaps, for Camilla's sake. For lovely as she is—and Camilla is beautiful, even if I shouldn't say so—"

"Oh I quite agree," he said hastily since she'd paused expectantly.

"But even though she's far nicer looking than our cousin, there's no reason to expect that Camilla will have any better chance against Mrs. Lockhart than poor Ada had."

If Lucy had hoped for any argument here, she was disappointed. Mr. Drury leaned back against the willow, crossed an ankle above a knee, and waited for her to continue. She did so, thoughtfully. "You know, I've only just come to realize that I don't understand men at all."

"You amaze me!"

"Don't make fun. I'm serious. Growing up in a house with two brothers—and Papa, of course—I thought I had a considerable understanding of the other sex. And in most things I do find males quite predictable. But I'm learning there's no need to expect any rhyme or reason from them when it comes to matters of the heart."

"Oh, I daresay you're right about us there. Only females remain logical in that area, with a weather eye out for the better chance."

Lucy was too busy pursuing this train of thought to pick up on his bitterness. "Take my cousin Ada and William Lockhart, for example. I would have said that they were perfect for one another." Drury looked a bit skeptical. "No, I mean it. Oh I know Ada's no beauty, while William's quite good-looking, or used to be at any rate. But they have practically everything else in common—their background, their love of horses, hunting, racing. All types of sporting things. And they had always dealt famously together. They were so—so"—she groped for the proper word—"comfortable."

"That's a damning thing to say."

"Why should it be? I certainly don't think William's as

75

happy now as he would have been with Ada, no matter how completely he was swept off his feet. Indeed, I might go so far as to say he looks downright wretched. And I don't for a minute believe all that fustian Mrs. Lockhart talked about their being sent to Coventry by the neighborhood. Even if it's so, I don't think that would bother William a fig if theirs were a happy marriage—and he could hunt and fish and attend an occasional mill."

"Your recipe for domestic bliss, Miss Haydon?" He laughed.

"In William's case at least. I can't help thinking he'd been better off not to have fallen in love."

"It can be a most uncomfortable business. Or so I'm told," he added hastily as she turned to look at him.

Once again it occurred to Lucy that she knew next to nothing about this man. And as she had just observed, it was folly to take anything about the other sex for granted. "Are you by chance married, Mr. Drury?"

"Good God, no!" he exploded. "What next, Miss Haydon? First a smuggler. Or was it a thief? Now this. No, though I hate to disappoint you, I've left no bedlamite wife chained in my attic."

"No need to fly off into the boughs. I thought the question reasonable enough. Haven't we just been talking about the inconstancy of men?"

"You tend to go more than a bit overboard with your generalizations, Miss Haydon. I'll grant you Lockhart's inconstancy, certainly. And Carnaby's, though I still say it's early days yet to judge the nature of his feelings for your sister. But just why these two instances should turn me into a Bluebeard—"

"No one but you mentioned Bluebeard. Or wives in attics. I just wondered if you were married, that was all. Most men your age are, you know."

"Let's just say that one of the things that Carnaby, who is quite as ancient as I am, by the by—more so, in fact, since he'll be thirty a whole month before me—anyhow, one of the things we've always had in common is that being leg-shackled holds little appeal for either of us. Of course if your theories about male inconstancy are right, we're both bound to change our minds."

"Except that Mrs. Lockhart's already married."

"But then Mrs. Lockhart's not the only fish in the sea, you know."

"True," Lucy replied thoughtfully. "But she does seem to have the power to dissuade most anglers from casting out lures for any other."

"Well, I won't deny that," Drury answered.

Somehow Lucy wished that he had tried.

Chapter Ten

THE FIVE DAYS LEADING UP TO THE EXCURSION TO SEAcliffe dragged on interminably. It seemed to Lucy that for the most part the time was spent looking and listening for one particular visitor while pretending not to.

Camilla made all sorts of excuses that kept her constantly in the house to the exclusion of her other duties. On the surface Nigel was all polite understanding when she sent word that she'd be unable to assist him for a while, but it was Lucy's opinion, which she freely shared with her sister, that their cousin had been a little hurt.

"Nigel can get along without me for a few days," Camilla had replied defensively. "Whereas you know that Emma cannot possibly deal with the green gooseberry wine by herself. Mama always helps her and would expect one of us to take her place."

Since Lucy had no desire to volunteer for that duty herself, she dropped the subject. But she knew that gooseberry wine had nothing to say in the matter. Camilla was waiting for Mr. More to call.

But the yellow curricle that had given rise to so much gossip because of its frequent stops at the vicarage gate was now conspicuous by its absence. And that circumstance was beginning to get on Lucy's nerves.

Perhaps it was only her fancy that Camilla turned pale every time they heard carriage wheels outside. But the notion was enough to send her constantly to the window to casually identify the nature of each vehicle that approached, for all the world as if she were the proprietor of a posting house announcing the Brighton stage.

Then when Lucy woke up to the fact that she herself had been watching for Mr. Drury, she decided that things had gone too far. The realization that she was actually longing for the sight of the top-lofty Londoner shocked her into action. "Put on your bonnet, Camilla; we're going out."

And over her sister's protest, she insisted that both of them should make the two-mile tramp required to take a pail of soup to a parish invalid. "We've neglected Mrs. Choate shamefully. What would Mama say?"

"That it doesn't take two people to carry one pail of soup." Camilla answered with a touch of healthy asperity that Lucy found encouraging.

But except for nourishing Mrs. Choate, the expedition proved a disaster. For as the sisters were walking back up the lane from the elderly widow's house, they spied the yellow curricle on the highroad. Mrs. Lockhart and Mr. More were so engrossed in conversation that they did not notice the Misses Haydon, not even when Camilla dropped the empty soup pail. Louis, however, having nothing else to do but look around, spied them and waved.

Later, back in the vicarage, while drinking cups of tea, Camilla brought up the subject they'd so far been avoiding. "I won't go tomorrow," she said.

"Indeed you will!"

"I can't possibly do so. You musn't try to force me. It's obvious that Mr. More wants nothing further to do with me. Oh Lucy, how could I have been such a fool as to mistake all his attention?" She burst into tears.

"It's Mr. More who's the fool. But never mind all that. The important thing is not to advertise to him or to the world that you care about it in the least. Oh, I know that Papa says pride is a deadly sin, but I don't think he means the kind of pride that forces you to hold your head up high as if you didn't care a fig that Mr. More's making a perfect cake of himself over a married female. Besides," she added practically, "we don't actually know that his affections have altered. The fact that we saw them together today means little. It was likely all Mrs. Lockhart's doing. She's certainly one for arranging things that no one else wants to do. Like a trip to Seacliffe, for instance."

Camilla refused to be cheered up. "Maybe so. But you can't possibly hold Mrs. Lockhart responsible for the fact that Mr. More has neglected us entirely for this past week, now can you? That has to be his own doing, entirely."

Even if Lucy could have thought of a rebuttal to this piece of logic, it possibly would have been kinder in the long run not to use it. "Well, you may be right, Camilla. But I still insist that you should do your best to appear indifferent."

"But if I furnish a good excuse as to why it's impossible for me to go to Seacliffe—"

"Oh, surely not the green gooseberry wine again!"

Camilla managed to smile. "Very well then. If you really think I must, I'll go."

Lucy was to regret all her sage advice and to wish she'd sent a note herself to Lockhart Place saying they'd both just contracted leprosy. Indeed, there were times during that long and trying expedition to the watering place when the vicar's daughters might actually have been victims of that dread disease, so completely were they made to feel that they were outcasts.

No one, for instance, seemed inclined to offer any explanation when the carriage was a good thirty minutes late arriving at their gate, though Lucy was convinced that it was entirely Mrs. Lockhart's doing, for it must have taken an incredible amount of time, involving recourse to a variety of cosmetics, to achieve such perfection. Their hostess was looking especially ravishing in a gray bombazine carriage dress trimmed with black gauze, a perfect background for her vibrant coloring. Confronted with such Parisian smartness, Lucy was reminded of Mr. Drury's earlier references to "church mice." Certainly she and Camilla looked quite dowdy by comparison.

"Why, where's William?" she asked when she and Camilla

had settled in to ride backward on either side of Mr. Drury, Mrs. Lockhart having excused her lack of courtesy to her guests on the grounds that such locomotion always gave her the headache. The worst part of the arrangement was that Camilla was forced to sit opposite Mr. More, and during the entire twenty-mile journey hardly seemed to know quite where to look.

"William asked me to convey his deepest regrets, Miss Haydon. The press of business keeps him at home. Really, as I'm wont to tell him, he's far too conscientious a landlord. His tenants take shameless advantage of his time."

Well, if that was so, Lucy had never heard of it. Any more than William had heard of this trip, she'd bet a monkey. But then the vicar's daughter upbraided herself for her lack of Christian charity. Her prejudice against Mrs. Lockhart was getting out of hand. William had probably merely thought the outing a dead bore and, not having the face-saving motivation of Camilla and herself, had simply gone fishing instead.

As a penance, Lucy exerted herself to make the best of a bad situation. She began by attempting to exchange pleasantries with Louis. But after a shy smile of greeting, the child seemed too self-conscious among so many adults to do more than answer her in monosyllables. Mr. Drury proved even less communicative. Her duty done, Lucy abandoned all attempts at sociability. The burden of conversation was left to Mrs. Lockhart and Mr. More, who, apparently unaware of the blue devils afflicting their fellow passengers, effervesced and sparkled, though entirely between themselves.

When the party reached its destination, Lucy's spirits rose, as did Louis's. But the fact of a rare, cloudless day with sunlight dancing on the water and reflecting off the white, dazzling sand, or the sight of so many of their fellow creatures, of every size, class, age, and description frolicking, strolling, picnicking, fishing, boating, seemed to have little effect upon Camilla's dejection or Drury's taciturn preoccupation. As for Mrs. Lockhart and Mr. More, they might have been in Timbuktu, so oblivious were they of anything and everyone except each other.

"Well now, what shall we do first?" Drury broke his vow of silence as they climbed out of the coach. He looked pointedly at

Sophia Lockhart as though to remind her of an obligation to all her guests.

She replied by suggesting that they first stroll along a row of shops and houses situated on a small rise and separated from the beach by a wrought-iron fence. She and Mr. More led the way, her gray silk parasol effectively framing their intimacy. Mr. Drury offered his arm to Camilla, who took it with a shy smile of gratitude. Lucy was glad to bring up the rear with Louis. "Don't worry, we'll have plenty of time by the sea later," she whispered as the child reluctantly turned away from all the glories there.

Seacliffe, like several other small communities along the coast, spurred on by the success of Ramsgate, Brighton, Worthing, and the like, had decided to take advantage of its location and the current boom in the seaside-holiday industry and convert itself into a fashionable resort. And while it still fell far short of those well-established watering places, there was ample evidence that Seacliffe was well launched.

Most of the houses that they passed were newly painted, with fresh white curtains blowing in the breeze. Several signs boasted LODGINGS TO LET. And in addition to the usual collection of necessary shops, there was a circulating library and a brand-new hotel complete with assembly rooms, where fortnightly assemblies were held throughout the season. And of course Seacliffe could not fail to provide a tea room. Mrs. Lockhart was all for patronizing it immediately.

"Could we not do so later?" Lucy objected, seeing the anxious look on Louis's face. "The tide will be turning before long, I expect. We should do our bathing right away."

"Surely you do not intend to bathe, Miss Haydon." From the altitude of Mrs. Lockhart's eyebrows, Lucy might have just proposed to tie her garters in public.

"Why of course. I had supposed that was the chief reason one came to Seacliffe."

"Some undoubtedly find it amusing." Mrs. Lockhart wrinkled her fetching nose. "Though for the life of me I can't think why. It looks exhausting. Not to mention hazardous."

"Actually, it's said to be quite healthful." Camilla addressed her hostess for the first time since her initial murmured greeting. "Dr. Lawson recommends it very highly. Providing one does not overdo, of course."

"Oh Mama, could we?" Louis pleaded.

"Certainly not."

"I'll take you, Louis." Mr. Drury's peremptory tone drew a scowl from Mr. More.

Mrs. Lockhart merely shrugged charmingly. "I can see that if I object further, my son will never, never forgive me. Really, it's most kind of you, Mr. Drury, to indulge the lad." Her lovely smile seemed to lighten Drury's mood. His "My pleasure, I assure you," sounded most civil.

Mrs. Lockhart and Mr. More decided to stroll along the cliff path while the others bathed. The party set a time to meet back at the tea room.

"Oh Lucy, couldn't I just watch?" Camilla whispered a bit later as their foursome crossed over a strip of shingle and reached the wide stretch of sand that the waves were decorating with a border of lacy foam. "Mrs. Lockhart's right, you know. It does look dangerous."

"Fustian. What could possibly happen? Each machine has a dipper. Besides, we did bring our bathing costumes all this way. I for one intend to use mine. Of course if you had rather rejoin Mrs. Lockhart and Mr. More—" This suggestion had the effect Lucy intended. Camilla would brave the perils of sea bathing after all.

Seacliffe boasted six bathing machines, one of which was standing idle on the shore when their group arrived. "You take it, Mr. Drury," Lucy said graciously. "Camilla and I won't mind the wait at all. Louis should have the first turn."

Louis beamed his gratitude, but Drury shook his head. "No, thank you, Miss Haydon; I wouldn't dream of engaging the last machine. It's yours. Louis and I will fend for ourselves."

The lad looked crestfallen. But he followed Drury without a protest down the beach toward a man wearing a blue short coat, pantaloons, and a jockey hat, who had a rusty teakettle heating on coals nested in a sand pit. Lucy watched Drury pause and bend down to whisper something in the child's ear. When they returned with the owner of the bathing machine in tow, Louis's eyes were sparkling.

Mr. Drury paid the man their fee—one and sixpence each for ladies—bade them enjoy themselves, and went striding off with Louis positively skipping beside him. What can they be up to? Lucy wondered, but soon forgot them entirely, so engrossed did she become in her own adventure.

While Mr. Hawkins hitched the horse to his machine—a wooden shedlike structure on four wheels with a green hood of canvas over its entrance—an enormous broad-shouldered female wearing a loose long-sleeved garment of the same shade of green, with a scarf over her hair topped by a man's felt hat, emerged from the caravan and announced that she was their dipper, Mrs. Hawkins.

The sisters stepped inside, where Mrs. Hawkins helped them with their flannel bathing gowns and caps. Then, when they were ready, she called out to her husband, who urged on his ancient horse with deafening shouts punctuated by a great deal of whip cracking while it backed the creaking, groaning bathing machine into the sea.

Mrs. Hawkins let down the hood in the front of their caravan and hooked a ladder into position. She then turned expectantly toward the two young ladies. Camilla stared down at the waves lapping below them in a steady rhythm and clutched her sister's arm. "I can't possibly go in." She shuddered.

"I'll go first," Lucy announced bravely, and earned an approving nod from Mrs. Hawkins, who took her firmly by the arm.

With the sun beating down upon its roof, the machine had been like an oven. At each rung of the ladder Lucy gasped as her bare feet—her legs—her waist encountered the chilly water. She clenched her teeth in earnest as her feet touched bottom and the sea surged terrifyingly around her. Mrs. Hawkins pushed the canvas hood back up.

But soon the rhythmic splash of the waves against her body seemed exhilarating and Lucy began to jump and splash against them while the dipper retained a firm grasp upon her arm.

"Oh, this is famous!" Lucy gazed with fascinated eyes at the ocean vista. A tall mast, reduced to toothpick size, was disappearing over the distant horizon. Nearer shore were several smaller boats, on hire to the holidayers who sailed them. The other bathing machines were still in the water, with squealing patrons bobbing up and down propelled less by the surf than by their dippers. And well down the shoreline, away from the crowded beach, she spied some intrepid swimmers splashing on their own.

"Oh, do come in, Camilla. You'll like it above all things."

"You just hang on to the canvas, miss, whilst I help her." Mrs. Hawkins released Lucy's arm and began guiding her quaking sister down the ladder rungs.

"You'll soon get used to it," Lucy said encouragingly. "It just takes a moment."

"Do you think so?" Camilla's teeth were chattering. She shrieked as she was struck on the bosom by a swelling wave.

"You keep right on hanging there a bit, miss," Mrs. Hawkins said over her shoulder to Lucy, who was still anchored to the canvas, "whilst I give your sister me full attention. Soon as she's used to it, I'll dip you both, no trouble."

But with the dipper's back turned, Lucy gradually grew brave. She let go the canvas and greeted each wave like a new friend, stepping forward eagerly to meet it. She soon learned to time her jump with an exact rhythm as the wave threatened to engulf her. It was rather like waltzing, she decided, only much more fun.

A sailboat with three young men on board waving saucily came within a hundred yards of their machine. Lucy waved back. What would Papa say?

The free-spirited swimmers, well out beyond the surf, drew parallel. A man and a child, so it appeared. Like the sailors, they seemed especially interested in the Hawkins's machine. Lucy looked more closely. It was Mr. Drury way out there, with Louis on his back.

She shaded her eyes with her hand to peer against the glare. Drury was swimming with strong, sure strokes, quite unhampered by the child's arms clasped round his neck. Their freedom made a mockery of the bit of untethered romping she'd indulged in. They might be two dolphins out there in the deep, moving so effortlessly with the sunlight sparkling on their—skin!

Her eyes surely had deceived her. Lucy rubbed them and

84

looked again. There was no mistaking the fact that Louis was entirely nude. As for Mr. Drury—oh, surely not—but then she saw the flash of white limb as he gave a powerful kick, and the gleam of his buttock as, porpoiselike, he dove underneath the water then bobbed back up with Louis sputtering and laughing on his back.

Drury raised a bare arm in a salute just as an extra-large wave caught Lucy completely unawares and knocked her off her feet. She was sent head over heels, swirling, tumbling underneath the waves, and was dragged mercilessly out to sea.

She had just presence of mind enough to keep her mouth and eyes tight shut as she struggled to regain her footing. But when she was immediately dragged under once again, drowning became inevitable. She waited for her life to flash before her eyes but could only see her father's reproachful face. Then at the precise moment when she knew she could no longer hold her breath, she was dragged up and out of her briny grave and held suspended, head and shoulders above the water, coughing and gasping great gulps of air through the streaming hair and seaweed on her face. But the hold upon her waist seemed insecure. She snatched at her rescuer with both hands and plastered herself against him.

"For God's sake, girl, you're clawing Louis! Hang on, lad. Lucy, you're all right. You're safe, I tell you." She increased her stranglehold.

"Lucy! I've got you. Don't unseat poor Louis. It's all right, girl. Let go and stand up on your own. It's not over your head here."

His appeal to reasonableness finally penetrated Lucy's consciousness, stilled her panic, made her realize at last that she was not about to drown. But along with that realization came a new awareness. She was clinging like a limpet to a naked man.

Her moment of stunned silence was followed by a quick intake of breath.

"Would you prefer death?" Mr. Drury asked.

Chapter
Eleven

"OH LUCY, YOUR HAIR!" CAMILLA WAILED AS THEY stood on foot warmers within the bathing machine vigorously toweling themselves. Lucy's immersion had put an abrupt period to their bathing—not that it mattered, since fifteen minutes, twenty at the outside, was considered as much stimulation as a female should endure. The more immediate problem, as Camilla indicated, was Lucy's hair, which was streaming with salt water.

Mrs. Hawkins found the incident an especial source of grievance. "Folk are bound to have noticed what happened to you. And I always tell me ladies they've naught to fear with Mrs. Hawkins for a dipper."

"Oh, it was my own fault entirely."

"Yes, but who's to know that?"

Lucy clapped her chip straw bonnet on top of her sea-soaked hair. It hid the mess, except for the tendrils that continued to drip around her neck and face and ears.

The rest of their party had been waiting for some time in front of the tea room when the two young ladies arrived. No wonder Louis and Mr. Drury got here first, Lucy thought. They didn't have to change or to carry wet bathing costumes to the carriage. She studiously avoided looking at her rescuers as they joined the others.

"I hope you've enjoyed your bathe as much as Louis has," Mrs. Lockhart said politely. She had exchanged her carriage bonnet for a fetching new headgear that consisted of a laced cap with a detachable green silk eyeshade worn underneath a modish creation of Dunstable straw. She noticed Camilla's stare. "Do you like it? Mr. More insisted I must have it. The shopkeeper says they're all the rage in Ramsgate. They're especially designed to protect the hair and eyes from the sun and wind."

"How convenient," Lucy murmured, while wondering if such utility would have mattered if the bonnet had not also framed the wearer's face so becomingly.

"Perhaps you, too, would like one, Miss Haydon?" Mr. Drury's face was perfectly straight as he offered to go make the purchase, but his eyes twinkled outrageously as the others made a point of not looking at Lucy's hair.

"No, thank you." Her voice was quite as stiff as her salt-encrusted locks, now rapidly drying in the sun.

Nor did he cease his innuendos once they were seated at a table inside the tea shop. "The bill of fare strongly recommends drinking sea water, I see. It claims this cures all sorts of specific ailments in addition to being a marvelous tonic for the system. Miss Lucy Haydon, I understand, has drunk hers already. And I must say I do detect a new glow of health. Would anyone else care to try? No? Well it does, I admit, sound a bit revolting. We'll settle for your tea then." He smiled at the young girl taking their order. Lucy could only regret that she had not succeeded earlier in choking him.

Conversation grew strained once more. But when the tea arrived, it gave rise to a discussion of its remarkable lack of brackishness, considering the fact that it was made from seaside water. Lucy was too busy devouring cakes to give an opinion. Sea bathing certainly stimulated the appetite. She caught Mr. Drury's amused stare and with an effort slowed down her consumption.

"Oh Miss Haydon." Mrs. Lockhart broke another awkward silence, then threw up her hands as both sisters turned her way. "Really, this is too confusing. May we not stand on points and use our first names? You are Camilla and Lucy from now on and you must address me as Sophia.

"Now, Lucy." She smiled at having this time made the object of her communication clear. "It had slipped my mind to tell you earlier that William and I have decided to discontinue Louis's music lessons."

"You have!" Louis blurted through a mouth full of seed cake.

"Yes, dear. I knew you'd be pleased by that decision."

Louis, in point of fact, did not look pleased. He looked distressed. Lucy had no illusions, though. It was not the lessons he would miss, but the kite flying.

"I'm sorry to hear it," she said. "I felt he was beginning to make some progress."

"Did you indeed? Believe me, it is no reflection upon you when I say that William and I have failed to discover any. Alas, I fear that Louis is hopelessly unmusical." She smiled at the boy teasingly. He ducked his head and colored.

"I understand," Mr. Drury said, "that you yourself are quite talented musically, Mrs.—err, that is to say, Sophia."

"Only indifferently so, I fear."

"Come now. Aren't you simply being modest? You sang at Covent Garden, did you not?"

Suddenly the click of teacups and the chatter of conversation at the tables all around them seemed to increase in volume, so still had their own group become after Mr. Drury burst his bombshell. Lucy, who was looking straight at Sophia, saw her turn a trifle pale, but in no other way did she betray her true reaction to the question. Her beautiful guileless eyes looked thoughtfully at Drury. "What an odd thing to say. Wherever did you get such a notion?"

He shrugged. "Really I can't recall now just where I heard it."

"Then by God, Drury, I think you'd be well advised not to repeat such malicious slander!" Lucy would not have believed the amiable Mr. More capable of such fury.

"Pistols at ten paces, Carnaby?" His friend raised an eyebrow. "I had thought to compliment, not slander."

"The devil you did!"

"Oh really, Carnaby, do calm down. I'm sure Mr. Drury did not intend to insult me—though I doubt my dear departed papa would have shared my broadmindedness. It would have upset Sir Windom dreadfully, I fear, to have his daughter's name linked with the stage."

To Lucy's horror, Sophia's eyes now brimmed with tears. She gave Mr. Drury a speaking look. She might not like the lady above half, but that had been a shabby thing to say. "Is anyone else interested in visiting the curio shop?" was the first thing that popped out of her mouth to ease the tension.

"Why don't we go there right after tea?" Sophia managed a bright smile that even included Drury.

Later on, as the party wandered among the collection of seaside souvenirs that could be purchased in the circulating library, Mr. Drury stood alone, gazing with apparent disbelief at a framed bouquet of so-called flowers made entirely out of seaweed. Lucy, who had been seriously considering purchasing the same picture before she'd seen Drury's scornful appraisal, had just gone over to examine a counter filled with shell boats, shell pictures, shell frames, shell boxes, shell broaches. It seemed that anything that could possibly be done with a seashell was on display here. She began to rummage through the lot, vowing that her selection would not be subjected to any critical scrutiny, as Carnaby More left Sophia Lockhart's side and approached Drury.

Her new position did not put Lucy out of earshot. She was soon confirmed in her earlier impression that the two boyhood friends had had a serious falling out and were likely to reach the daggers-drawn stage at any moment.

"How dare you throw Sophia's past in her teeth that way. You humiliated her before the Haydons. That was despicable."

"Perhaps." Drury spoke so softly that Lucy had to strain her ears to hear. "But never mind. The Haydons are not gossip-mongers. I said what I did mainly as a reminder to you, as well as to get the lady's reaction—which you must admit was rather interesting."

"Of course she denied it! Would you have expected her to do otherwise? You of all people have no right to condemn her for it. You're more devious than she has ever been. By God, before you start rattling other people's skeletons, you should stop to remember that your own closet isn't exactly open to inspection."

"Are you blackmailing me, Carnaby?" His eyes had narrowed.

"No, dammit, but you push me hard."

"Maybe that's because you've forgotten what this is all about."

"Oh I haven't forgotten anything. But you can be wrong, you

know. There's always another side. Maybe *you* need to be reminded of that."

"Very well then, the point's well taken. There's one thing I am sure of, though. We've been friends too long to fall out over this. There's been enough harm done without us adding to it."

At that moment Louis came rushing up to show Drury his purchase, a toy sailboat painted a bright red. And Lucy quickly went to pay for the shell box she'd selected and have it wrapped before anyone else would have a chance to diminish its charm for her.

Louis was their salvation during the carriage ride home. Oblivious to any tensions the adults might be feeling, he lost his shyness in the pleasure of recalling every moment of his visit to the seaside. Camilla, anxious that it be known that she was not in the least upset over Mr. More's transfer of affections, chattered almost as much as he did. And Lucy, wishing to give her sister moral support, joined in, so one way or another they managed to pass the time. Even so, the twenty miles seemed to drag out to fifty, and when they were finally deposited at the vicarage gate and Lucy watched the Lockharts' ancient carriage pull away, she told herself that if she never saw any of the three Londoners again, it would still be far too soon.

A letter from their mother was waiting for them, written in Mrs. Haydon's small, neat script, crossed thriftily. Eleanor had had her baby, a boy, called Edward after its grandfather.

"Oh, Papa must be pleased!" Camilla clapped her hands and forgot her misery when Lucy read that part.

But the letter then went on to say that Eleanor had had a difficult lying-in and Mrs. Haydon planned to stay a little longer to care for the Landseer family. It was a comfort to know, she concluded, that she could rely upon Lucinda and Camilla to do everything that was proper in her absence.

Later that night, as she lay in bed unable to sleep, Lucy kept wondering what her mother would think when she did come home. Would she find them changed past all recognition? It seemed to Lucy that she and Camilla were two entirely different persons now. But then Papa had not noticed any change. Of course that proved very little. They could each have grown a second head, she giggled in the darkness, and Papa would never notice it at all.

But could one have loved and lost as Camilla had done and still not show it? And would Mama know at a single glance that she'd been kissed in the graveyard and rescued from drowning by a naked man?

She put her head underneath the pillow, hoping to smother further thought. But the image of Ensign MacDonald came floating before her eyes. She did wish that she'd been kinder. If only she had had the understanding then that she had now. Did he still think of her? she wondered. Probably. For during all those months at sea, he'd little else to do.

She sighed a muffled sigh for all their muddled lives. For Ada who had loved William who loved Sophia who appeared to be in love with Mr. More whom Camilla loved. And for Ensign MacDonald who had loved her who loved—certainly not! She jerked wide awake. It was unthinkable!

Even so, she tried to work Jerrold Drury somewhere into the pattern of unrequited love that she'd been weaving. He surely must have suffered some kind of disappointment in his nearly thirty years. What was it that Carnaby More had hinted about Drury's deceitfulness and about his past? There was a skeleton in his closet, his friend had said. A female skeleton, she had no doubt. And on that lowering thought, Lucy finally drifted off to sleep.

Chapter
Twelve

THE FOLLOWING WEEK LUCY, RETURNING FROM A BERRY-picking expedition Emma had sent her on, saw Nigel sitting forlornly on one of the stone benches in the graveyard. She went over and sat down beside him, placing the brimming bucket in between.

"Why on earth aren't you working? It's unlike you, Nigel, to come up for air from your dusty tomes."

He smiled. "I know. But somehow I couldn't force myself to work on the history this morning. The pull of the out-of-doors grew too strong."

Since the low-lying clouds looked as though they might open up and pour at any moment, Lucy found this a rather odd excuse but didn't comment.

"Oh, I say, Lucy." Nigel helped himself to a handful of berries as he peered down. "Did you know you've torn your dress?" There was a V-shaped rip in front just above the hem-line ruffle.

"Caught it on a briar, but no matter. It's the same one I ripped on the thorn hedge on the way to your evening party. Even Camilla couldn't mend that tear so it wouldn't show. Now the gown's only fit for berry picking." She absently popped a blackberry in her mouth with blue-stained fingers.

"Uh—speaking of Camilla." Nigel quite failed in an effort to sound casual. "Do you know where she is this morning?"

"Why, I thought she'd gone back to helping you."

"No. I haven't seen her for several days. She'd always been so kind about assisting me that I've taken advantage of her good nature. It's dull, tedious work for a young girl."

"Oh no," Lucy protested, but then amended. "Well, I shouldn't like it, I'll admit, but Camilla really does. Of all us children, she's the most like Papa in that respect. Which, by the by, is probably where she is right now. Looking up obscure bits of information for Papa's sermon."

"No doubt you've received a card of invitation to the ball that More fellow is giving."

Lucy was accustomed to her cousin's abrupt conversational switches and could usually leap about after him with ease. This took a moment. "Mr. More's giving a ball? Why no, we've had no invitation. Not to my knowledge at any rate."

"Mine—ours, I should say—came just this morning. Yours is probably waiting for you. You and Camilla will be asked, of course."

"Well, I suppose so." The prospect did not send her into raptures. She dipped her hand into the berry bucket.

"Mama says that she and Mr. More have formed a tendre for one another."

For a brief moment Lucy was quite stunned by this revelation. "Oh you mean *Camilla* and Mr. More."

"Naturally." He looked puzzled. "Didn't I just say so? Mama says it was evident at our party that he was dangling after her. Stood up with her twice, Mama said."

"Well, yes he did. But just when did my aunt tell you all this, Nigel?"

"Oh, quite some time ago. I really can't recall exactly when." He helped himself to berries once again.

"I'm afraid it's no longer true. Mr. More was very attentive for a while. He quite turned Camilla's head, if the truth be known. But he has dropped her since. Which, so I've been told, is not unusual behavior on his part. Please don't mention this to my aunt, Nigel, but that's probably why you haven't seen Camilla lately. She has been quite blue-deviled over the business and keeps moping around the house."

Two bright spots burned in Nigel's cheeks, which for all Lucy knew might actually indicate anger. Since she'd never observed her cousin in such a state, she was unable to decide.

"That sort of conduct may do very well in London, where, I'm told, idle flirtation is à la mode. But it is not appropriate here in Sussex. I believe I should have a word with Mr. More. You may think I'm usurping your father's prerogative, but frankly I doubt Uncle Edward would be any good at that sort of thing."

Lucy had been thinking that Nigel himself would be the least likely person to ring a peal over a wrongdoer and was amazed that he saw himself otherwise. But then, she was beginning to think she didn't really know anyone all that well.

"Your father probably isn't even aware of the situation," he continued. "Besides, I am the head of the family as a whole."

"That's true, but you mustn't speak to Mr. More, Nigel. Camilla would die."

"She would?" He looked bemused. "But I merely wish to set things right for her."

"I know you do. And it's perfectly splendid of you," Lucy

said sincerely, astounded that someone of Nigel's nature would willingly take on such an unpleasant task. "But you can't just command Mr. More to reciprocate Camilla's feelings. It doesn't appear to work that way. And in this case, it's much too late. He seems to have fallen in love with Sophia Lockhart."

"William's wife?" He peered at her closely. "Lucy, are you funning?"

"Certainly not. I wouldn't joke about such matters. This is Mr. More's way, or so I've heard. He falls in and out of love with amazing regularity."

"Mrs. Lockhart is a married woman."

"I'm well aware of that."

"William's folly seems to have caught up with him." Nigel did not appear to gain any satisfaction from that particular bit of poetic justice. "Well, one thing's certain, at any rate." He sighed. "Mr. More is clearly not worthy of Camilla. I won't speak to him after all."

He rose abruptly. "Now if you'll excuse me, Lucy, I must get back to my history. I'm glad we had our little talk. It's been most illuminating."

It wasn't until she'd carried the bucket home and set it on the kitchen table that Lucy noticed there weren't enough black-berries left in it for Emma's syllabub.

As Nigel had predicted, a card of invitation to a ball at Dighton House was waiting. "I'm not going," Camilla announced stubbornly.

"But won't it look odd?" her sister countered.

"Then let it. Why not give the gossips something else to feed on? I'd find that preferable to being forced to spend an evening in the same company with Mr. More and Mrs. Lockhart—I will not call her Sophia. My attitude has nothing whatsoever to do with Mr. Drury's insinuation that she was on the stage, which I did not believe for even a moment." Camilla paused to look inquiringly at Lucy.

"No more did I. Any more than I believed that her father was Sir—whoever she said."

"Whether Mrs. Lockhart was on the stage or not has nothing to say in the matter. I will not be on a first-name basis with her." Camilla looked as mulish as Lucy had ever seen her. "You may call her Sophia if you wish, Lucy, but I shan't. Nor shall I attend the ball. I allowed you to talk me into going to Seacliffe when I did not wish to and it was horrible. This time I shall do as I please."

In the end, it was Nigel who persuaded her to go. Lucy had no idea just how he accomplished it, but she was beginning to discover qualities in Nigel she had not dreamed of. It was arranged that the sisters should go with the Tilney family in their crested carriage, an arrangement that would not please Lady Tilney, she'd bet a monkey.

Although in general Lucy was not looking forward to the evening any more than Camilla was, she was curious to see Dighton House, which was said to be the most elegant in the area, making even Tilney Hall pale by comparison. Then, too, she was curious to see whether Mr. Drury would be there. She had neither seen nor heard of that gentleman for days and wondered whether, in light of his rift with Mr. More, he had not gone back to London.

The house surpassed her expectations, the exterior an anglicized Baroque, the interior resplendent with a marble hall, riotous plasterwork, and furnishings that reflected both wealth and taste. Lucy could not but feel a pang that her younger sister would never be mistress here. Papa would be horrified by such worldliness.

She quickly shifted her thoughts to Mr. Drury, for once a lesser evil, and scanned the ballroom for him as she inched forward in the line formed to greet their host, who was receiving guests with all his usual charm.

Drury was there, standing with a group of men deep in conversation. As his eyes turned toward her, Lucy quickly looked away.

For Camilla's sake she dreaded this formal meeting with their host under the eyes of their curious neighbors. Ahead of them, their aunt was playing Lady of the Manor to the hilt, extending a gloved hand with condescension. Lady Tilney had not forgiven Mr. More for his lack of interest in her daughter and seemed bent upon making it quite plain that, despite his wealth, the Tilneys were the crème de la crème of this society.

Ada herself was cordial, Nigel even more reserved than

usual. Lucy braced herself for Camilla's turn, saw Mr. More take her hand and begin some word of greeting. It died suddenly on his lips as he ceased to be aware of Camilla's presence and passed her along as if he were in a trance. As Lucy murmured her own greeting, she followed his gaze over her shoulder and was not in the least surprised to see Mr. and Mrs. William Lockhart joining the line.

Lucy thought she had grown accustomed by this time to Sophia's loveliness. But tonight the nonpareil had outdone herself. She was wearing a ball gown composed of a slip of sapphire satin, topped with a white lace robe edged in pearls. The bust was cut daringly low, but some of the attention was drawn away from the décolletage by a sapphire necklace that almost rivaled the brilliance of the beauty's eyes.

"I wonder where the jewels came from." Ada, at Lucy's elbow, sounded merely curious and not cattish. "William's mother never had any sapphires that I heard of."

"If she had, they would have been pawned years ago," her mother said with a sniff as their party moved across the ballroom toward a row of unoccupied gilt chairs.

The orchestra, consisting of a pianoforte, two violins, a violoncello, and a harp, struck up a melody and the first set began to form. Lucy held her breath and Camilla turned a trifle pale as Mr. More left his post and came across the ballroom toward their group. But it was Lady Tilney's hand he claimed. As she was led out onto the floor, her ladyship's hauteur seemed to be vanishing rapidly at this public acknowledgment of her consequence.

William Lockhart was leading his wife into the set. Nigel asked Camilla to partner him and took her away. Ada's hand was claimed by the village doctor. Lucy sat very much alone. She risked a peep over her fan in Mr. Drury's direction. That gentleman was still engaged in the same fascinating conversation that had occupied him earlier. She was most relieved when Squire Wentworth appeared and bowed before her.

All in all, Lucy reflected later in the evening as she sat fanning herself after a spirited country dance, the ball was not the disaster she had feared. Thanks to their cousin Nigel, whose attention to Camilla had not gone unnoticed, her sister did not give the appearance of a woman scorned. In fact, Camilla had so far forgotten herself as to smile and even laugh occasionally—effectively, if unconsciously, spiking the gossips' guns. On the surface at least, she managed to appear indifferent to Mr. More's blatant pursuit of Mrs. William Lockhart.

Lucy only wished the lady's husband shared that indifference. She looked uneasily at William, who had not moved since he'd taken his stand by the punch bowl after the first dance. True, the punch was not potent stuff, but he seemed to be consuming it at an alarming rate. And unless she missed her guess, he'd partaken liberally of his famous "imported" brandy before he came. Now he was following Sophia and Carnaby More's progress in the set with narrowed eyes. The expression on his face was not enigmatic in the least. He looked murderous.

"May I join you, Miss Haydon?" Mr. Drury did not wait for the permission he'd requested but, after retrieving the fan Lucy had dropped when he startled her, sat down beside her. "I hope you're not dancing from choice and not because some calamity has happened to your ball gown. It's most becoming, by the by." He looked approvingly at her white crepe round dress which was spotted with white satin. "The last time I checked, it was entirely thorn-free. I trust there's been no recent change in its status."

"Perhaps I'm not dancing because so many gentlemen have come here mainly to converse, or so it would appear."

"Touché. It must seem inexcusable, I'll admit. But then I gather that there's not often this much excitement in the neighborhood."

"What are you talking about? What sort of excitement?"

"You mean you haven't heard? A knowing 'un like you? You do surprise me. The big news is that a company of customs' land-guards is being posted here to break up the local smuggling ring. The gentlemen I've been talking to seem quite concerned that their cellars are apt to be feeling the governmental squeeze. Really, Miss Haydon, it pains me to say so, but it does appear that your estimable father has quite failed to impart the proper moral stance to his flock in this one instance."

"Nonsense. I, for one, don't believe in your 'smuggling ring.' Oh, don't set in to lecture me. There's some free-trading

97

going on, of course, and that business we witnessed the other night may or may not have something to do with it. But it's all trifling stuff. Nothing to cause this kind of stir, certainly."

"Maybe not. But the government seems to think otherwise. They must believe the revenue involved is considerable and the smuggling well organized since they've consigned a naval blockade plus all these tidesmen to this locality. How do you feel about the business, Mr. Lockhart?"

William had left the punch bowl to stroll rather unsteadily over to join them. He had carried two cups, sipping the contents of one throughout the journey. "Thought you might be dry, Lucy. Saw you fanning. It's nothing but pap, but then I collect your father would approve." He offered her punch with an unsteady hand. A bit splashed on her dress. "Oops. Sorry, Lucy."

Mr. Drury tried to swallow his chuckle. "And here I thought your gown was actually going to make it through the evening unscathed," he said in an aside.

"I beg your pardon?" William put his own cup on a chair, as though to free his hands, and glared at Drury.

"Nothing, really. Just a private joke."

"Is that so? Well, if you ask me, sir, you London jackanapes are a bit too free with your private jokes and with the ladies around here." He shot a venomous look toward his wife and Mr. More, who had their heads together, oblivious to the other couples in their set. "Take a word of warning. It usually proves unhealthy for outsiders to tangle with Sussex men. And just because Lucy's brothers are away at sea, don't think she ain't protected."

"Oh, do sit down, William, and stop talking fustian." Lucy pulled out a chair so its back was toward the dance floor and then tugged William by the sleeve. He obediently sat down but continued to glare at Drury. "Mr. Drury was merely teasing me, William, about the gown I tore on the hedge going to the Tilney ball. He seems to regard me as a walking sartorial disaster."

"Well, he shouldn't, by God!" William's voice rose thickly. "A real gentleman pretends not to notice that sort of thing."

"You're right, of course. And I beg Miss Haydon's pardon for it," Drury said easily. "But to get back to our discussion,

98

Miss Haydon here thinks all this uproar over the free-trade is much ado about nothing. What do you say, Mr. Lockhart?"

"I say I don't know what the devil you're talking about, sir."

"Haven't you heard? It's the on-dit of the evening. The squire's just back from London and has been telling us that the excise people are in quite a taking over the smuggling in these parts. They're stationing a company of land-guards here."

"Oh really?" William, Lucy thought, was overdoing his casualness as he yawned with apparent boredom. "And just when is all this supposed to happen?"

"Lord knows." Drury shrugged. "Right away, Squire says. But then you know the government's 'right away.' Could be days, weeks—months even, I suppose."

"Well, it will be a damned waste of time no matter when they do it. They'll be no match for the Sussex men, you mark my word, sir."

"Oh, you think not?"

"I know it. Take this damned—beg pardon, Lucy—take this so-called blockade they've got out there now. It's laughable to a Sussex sailor. Why those lads can slip in and out amongst their cutters like child's play."

"They do say the blockade hasn't accomplished much so far."

"You're damned right it hasn't! Sorry, Lucy. And it won't, by God. There's been free-trading in these parts since—since the British painted their faces blue, by God. Lord, the stories my own grandfather used to tell. I don't doubt you've heard some of 'em, Lucy, from John and Paul." She nodded. "They didn't stop it then and they won't stop it now. Not with all their blockades and shore patrols and directives from London. 'Cause I'll tell you something for a fact, sir." He leaned drunkenly toward Drury. "If there's one thing that folk here in Sussex don't like, it's outside interference. And when it comes to that, we ain't all that partial to Londoners, if you take me meaning."

As if to emphasize that point, he twisted his chair around to afford a view of the dance floor again. The sets were breaking up. Sophia glanced their way, said something to her partner, and they started across the floor.

"So you finally remembered your husband's existence."

William's voice caused heads to turn curiously as he and Drury rose to their feet. "Look here, sir." He reached out to take hold of Carnaby More's lapel, perhaps as much to steady himself as to look the other in the eyes. "I don't know how it is in your rackety circles, but down here it ain't the thing to stand up with a lady more than twice."

"And *you* look, sir. My valet would take exception to your manhandling my coat this way." Carnaby's smile was dangerous and his eyes glinted as he pushed the other's hand away. People were beginning to edge closer, trying to appear casual about it but not wanting to miss any of the quarrel about to erupt. "As for the number of times I've stood up with your wife—are you sure, sir, in your condition, of the accuracy of your count?"

"By God, I'll not—"

"Oh really, William." Sophia moved quickly between the two would-be combatants and laid a hand possessively on her husband's sleeve. "While I do find your jealousy flattering, it's too absurd. You hate dancing. Now admit it. I consider myself fortunate to have coaxed you to stand up with me even once. So I'm most grateful to Mr. More. It's shameless of me, I know, but I've been dying for the opportunity to show off my new necklace."

"Oh, it's lovely," Lucy chimed in, as anxious as Sophia to avoid the quarrel. "I was admiring it when you first arrived."

"William gave it to me. I scolded him for being so extravagant. But the truth is, of course, that I was ecstatic." She beamed up at her husband.

"A beautiful woman has to have beautiful things," he muttered.

It wasn't just the punch, Lucy realized, that now caused William to look so besotted. She was admiring Sophia Lockhart's skill in banking down the fire when Carnaby More stirred the coals again.

"A beautiful woman shouldn't be hidden away in this godforsaken hole. A few baubles ain't going to make up for being buried alive when she should be moving in the first circles."

"And what business is that of yours, sir?" William brushed

Sophia aside and took a threatening step toward his rival. "I'll thank you to—"

"Oh, there you are, William," a hearty voice boomed. "I've been looking everywhere for you." Ada Tilney, apparently oblivious to anything other than her own objective, walked over to tug William by the arm. "Need you to settle an argument. Squire says his horse can outrun Trumpeter. Biggest pack of nonsense I ever heard. Want you to tell him so. He'll take your word even if he won't listen to me. There ain't anyone more knowing than you, William, when it comes to horse flesh. Even Squire admits that."

With one venomous backward glance at Carnaby More that held the promise of a continuation of their quarrel, William allowed himself to be led away. The disappointed crowd dispersed to form new sets. A gentleman arrived to claim Sophia's hand and Carnaby left to check on supper preparations.

"Whoooosh!" Drury let out a prolonged breath. "Top honors to your cousin, Miss Haydon. She did well. Now then, may I have the honor of this dance?"

"I suppose so."

"I find your enthusiasm overwhelming."

"Oh it's nothing personal. It's just that after all that, one hardly feels like dancing. But you're right. We should try and behave as normally as possible."

They had little to say to one another after taking their places in the set. Both were so intent, in fact, on looking across the room where William, Ada, and the squire were in animated, easy conversation that they had to be prompted when it was their turn to take part in the dance movement. This done, Mr. Drury asked abruptly, "Do you ride, Miss Haydon?"

"You really are hard up for conversation. There's always the weather, Mr. Drury."

He laughed. "I'm not making small talk. I really want to know. All that horse business put me in mind of it. I've missed riding since I've been here. And Carnaby stays—occupied. Won't you take pity and ride with me?"

"I've never heard that riding couldn't be managed alone."

"True, but I want your company."

Lucy looked up at him curiously. His expression was quite serious.

"Why, yes, I believe you do." She sounded quite surprised, then added in a more thoughtful tone, "What I'd very much like to know is why."

Chapter
Thirteen

*L*UCY HAD CONTINUED TO GIVE THE MATTER SERIOUS thought, so it came as no surprise the next afternoon when Drury suggested they ride along the beach. He had come leading a horse from Carnaby More's stable. And she had found it exhilarating to be mounted again.

"I've missed this," she confessed. "I used to ride a lot when my brothers were home. Our uncle Tilney let us have the run of his stables."

"I never heard that riding couldn't be managed alone." He grinned as he threw her own words back in her teeth.

Once they had made their precarious way down the cliffs, they gave their mounts free rein to gallop on the sea-packed sand. A brisk breeze was blowing inland, foaming the waves and sending the white clouds scurrying like sailboats in the sky. "I'll race you!" Lucy whooped, feeling like a child again as they took off neck and neck. But she soon found herself left far behind by a man and horse that had suddenly taken on the aspects of a centaur. "I kept the better animal." He grinned sheepishly as he reined in and she overtook him. Lucy got the definite impression that he had not intended to become so carried away.

"Fustian. You ride amazingly well."

"For a Londoner, you mean?"

"For anybody."

"Well that is high praise—from a resident of Sussex. We London types get short shrift here as a rule."

"Ah yes, William. I wondered how long it would take you to get around to him."

"Well, I must admit he interests me."

"No doubt. But before you begin to wheedle out of me whatever it is you need to know, let me ask you a thing or two."

They rode slowly side by side now. He looked wary. "Why do I feel I'm about to face the Inquisition?"

"A guilty conscience perhaps? No, never mind. What I chiefly want to know is, how long does Mr. More mean to stay here?"

He shrugged. "I'm not all that privy to his plans. But when we arrived here, you may recall, everyone seemed eager for him to settle permanently. Don't tell me you've changed your mind."

"Of course I have. You were there last night. If my cousin Ada hadn't whisked William away when she did, there could have been a very ugly scene."

"I quite agree. I can't but wonder why she bothered. Whatever happened to 'hell hath no fury like a woman scorned' or however the quotation goes?"

"Ada likes William. They've always been good friends. I explained all that."

"Oh yes, how could I have forgotten. 'Love wrecks everything' was, I believe, your theme."

She ignored his bantering tone. "Never mind all that. The point I wish to get across is that it was one thing for Mr. More to make my sister one of his flirts. From his point of view, at least, Camilla was fair game. But it's quite another matter to be dangling after Mrs. Lockhart. William is a proud man, Mr. Drury."

"So I noticed," he said dryly.

"And could prove dangerous. This time I think your friend's playing with fire."

"Carnaby can look after himself in that area. He's no stranger to irate husbands. It's not Mr. Lockhart who worries me. Mrs. Lockhart's the dangerous one. I wish I could be sure that this *is* merely one of Carnaby's flirts."

"And I wish he'd leave."

"And take me with him?"

"That brings me to my next question, Mr. Drury. What exactly are you doing here?"

"Good Lord. Surely that doesn't require explaining—again." Like a little boy reciting the lesson he'd just conned, he reeled off "Carnaby needed to come and didn't wish to rusticate alone. And since I was—uh—financially embarrassed, I was glad to tag along." He then added in a more normal tone, "There you have it, the lowering truth."

"Do I? I wonder. At least I have as much of it as I'm likely to get."

"You're bound and determined to make me into something mysterious, aren't you?" He allowed his horse to splash through the surf's edge. "A smuggler no less. Why not a pirate? Now there's a role I could revel in."

"I was wrong about the smuggling, I've since decided. But on the right track, I collect. Now I think I simply confused hounds with foxes. Take this ride we're on, for instance, and your desire for company."

"Well, what about it?" he asked to fill her pause. "I'm waiting with bated breath to learn my sinister purpose."

"First of all, you headed straight for the coast."

"Should I not have done? Seemed the ideal place for a good gallop. Not even to mention the view." He gestured out to sea.

"It's the ideal place if you've smuggling on your mind. And since it might be a bit too obvious if you, a stranger, were to be seen poking around all these coves, looking for concealed anchorages, you've brought me along. Now when someone sees you, the conclusion will be of course that you are courting me, not trying to break up the free-trade."

"By George, that's devilish clever of me. Especially in view of the crowds thronging this beach, watching my every move." He stared pointedly at a flock of plovers, intent upon their feeding.

"Oh, I know we haven't seen anybody yet. Having me along was merely a precaution."

"Having you along is a constant amazement."

"Besides, it's likely that we will eventually see someone. Or be seen. I've known all along that our destination is William's boat."

"Am I supposed to be astounded by your powers of deduction? If we continue traveling this direction along the seashore, yes, we're bound to reach the creek where we saw it anchored. Actually, I hadn't thought of it in terms of a 'destination,' though. I'll admit, however, that after last night's high drama, I'm curious to know if he's put out to sea."

"And if he has, I don't suppose you can believe that he's simply fishing."

"There's always that possibility."

"I for one don't believe for a moment that William Lockhart is involved in the local smuggling."

"Your loyalty does you credit, but other than the fact that he's your brothers' friend, why not?"

"He's a gentleman."

He laughed.

"Very well then, that may sound rather lame to a stranger. And I'll admit that the Lockhart family's always been rackety in many ways. Gambling, for instance."

"A most gentlemanly vice."

"Yes. I realize you're poking fun at me, but I still don't believe that a man of William's class would get involved with the free-trade."

"No? He does need the money."

"Oh, he needs it. There's no denying that. But he doesn't have it. You've seen the Place. It's falling down around his ears. If the free-trade's as lucrative as they say it is, you'd think he'd show a few signs of prosperity."

"Aren't you forgetting Sophia's sapphires? They had to cost him a small fortune."

"That's true," she admitted, "but perhaps he sold off something to buy them."

"What?"

"How should I know? His boat, perhaps. All I know is the necklace—and Mrs. Lockhart's clothes, of course—are the only signs of prosperity I've seen. Why I never even got paid for Louis's music lessons."

"Well now." He grinned. "I can see why they might have

been reluctant to cough up the blunt for that. He was pretty awful, you must admit. Besides, not paying tradesmen and tutors is another hallmark of the gentleman. One must stick to the appropriate forms of dishonesty."

"All right then. You've made your point. It was a mistake on my part to insist on class distinction. Especially to you."

"And just why to me?"

"Well, the only thing I find odder than a gentleman smuggler is a gentleman excise man."

"Good God! Do you possibly mean me?" He reined in to stare at her, then threw back his head and laughed heartily. She was a bit disconcerted by this reaction, having expected something more along the lines of "You've undone me."

"I don't suppose you're the common garden variety of excise man."

"Thank you for that much at least."

"You'd be more likely to be heading up the whole operation."

"Now that's more like it." He nudged his mount and they rode on slowly. "I'd no idea, Miss Haydon, that you held me in such high esteem. And as much as I hate to bring you down from one more of your famous high flights, I have to disillusion you again. I am not an excise man. Not even of high degree. Can you not simply accept the fact that my—admitted—interest in the free-trade stems from curiosity?"

"That seems a trifle thin."

"Why? No offense, but it's dashed dull in these parts, especially with Carnaby moping about nursing his thwarted passion. One has to keep occupied somehow." They were on Lockhart land now. Just ahead the creek spilled out into the ocean. "Now, look there. That blasts your theory, Miss Haydon. Lockhart didn't sell his boat to buy Sophia's necklace."

William Lockhart was not on his yawl, however. It was Bert who was swabbing down the deck and stared at them suspiciously as they rode by.

"He'd do better to be washing windows in the Place," Lucy remarked when they'd passed out of earshot.

"Shows where the Lockhart values lie, though, doesn't it? By George, now you've mentioned it, it *was* bright of me to bring you along so Bert'll believe I'm too besotted by your company to think suspicious thoughts, such as he's getting everything shipshape for the dark of the moon."

"Oh? And when might that be?"

"Tomorrow night, as a matter of fact."

"Fancy your knowing a thing like that."

"Just the sort of thing an excise man would know, am I right? Oh I say, your presence really is invaluable. This beach is becoming as crowded as Hyde Park during the fashionable hour."

William Lockhart's height made him easily recognizable from a distance. Lucy had taken it for granted that the female with him was his wife until the couples closed the gap between them and her cousin Ada called out a hearty "halloo."

As they stopped to greet one another, Lucy was once again struck by how well Ada looked on horseback. The tailored riding habit suited her far, far better than the ill-chosen frills her mother insisted she wear in the drawing room. The exercise had brought color to her cheeks and a sparkle to her eyes. In the ordinary way of things, she was almost handsome. But not when measured against Sophia Lockhart's beauty, of course.

There was nothing prepossessing about William's appearance, though. He was eyeing Jerrold Drury with ill-concealed hostility. At first, Lucy wondered if he was still inebriated, but she soon concluded that he was entirely sober, a condition that did little to lighten his disposition. He looked pale, despite his sailor's weathering. His eyes were bloodshot and the lines about them seemed to have multiplied since the previous evening. And if he did not have the grandfather of all headaches, then Lucy was a Frenchman. That he deserved that sort of retribution for the drinking bout he'd indulged in the night before didn't make her feel any easier in his company.

It had been Lucy's notion to ride on and put as much distance as possible between the two gentlemen, for it seemed obvious that William was longing to take up the quarrel where he'd left it off the evening before—that he was, in fact, spoiling for a fight. Ada, on the other hand, seemed bent upon improving the relationship between their escorts. As if determined to go the second mile in cordiality to make up for her companion's lack, she dismounted. It was Lucy's opinion that she'd have better luck trying to make boon companions of Napoleon and Wellington. But when Drury got off his horse, then reached up to help her down, she resigned herself to the inevitable. She did take pains to insert herself between William and Mr. Drury, though, as their foursome stood together, ringed by their impatient mounts.

Ada seemed to believe that some explanation for their presence was called for. "This is the animal Squire was hawking at the ball last night." She nodded at the large bay Lockhart had been riding. "William's trying out his paces for me."

"And what do you think?" Drury asked.

"A blood-cattle slug," William said contemptuously.

"Too bad. It's a handsome beast." The horse shook its head and whinnied, as if realizing he was the center of attention now.

"All show. Might do for most females. Not for Ada, though. She's a goer."

Ada tried to look modest at this compliment and failed entirely.

"Where's More?" William asked suddenly, challenging Drury across Lucy's head.

"I haven't the faintest idea." The other shrugged.

"Well, you can give him a message from me. Tell him to stay away from my wife."

"I will if you insist, but it seems a waste of time. You made that wish clear enough last night."

"Maybe and maybe not. Might not have taken me seriously. I was foxed."

"I think Carnaby took your meaning. Drunk or sober, you made your sentiments quite clear."

"Good. And did I also make it clear that I don't like you hanging around Lucy here?"

"Oh yes. You were eloquent upon that subject, too."

"William!" Ada protested. "Really! This is the outside of enough."

"No it ain't. John and Paul wouldn't put up with this sort of thing—" He gestured vaguely at Lucy and Drury.

"What sort of thing?" Lucy bristled.

"Now Lucy, don't you get on your high ropes, too." Ada sighed, walking over to pat her restless chestnut, who objected almost as much as Lucy to this interruption of their ride. "Really I don't know what's gotten into everyone of late."

"It's all of these newcomers around, poking their noses where they've no business," William said darkly.

"Are you referring only to Carnaby and myself or do you include all the riding officers and tidesmen as well?"

"What the devil do you mean by that?"

"Nothing. Just trying to clear up a point."

"Or make one? I don't think I like your insinuations, sir." He took a threatening step toward Drury. "And I'm damned sure I don't like you."

"A pity." Drury looked rather amused as Lucy edged herself more directly in front of him. "But then you haven't had the chance to get to know me properly. I'm told that I improve upon acquaintance." He reached over to take Lucy firmly by the arm and move her aside.

"I wondered if you were going to continue hiding behind her petticoats." Lockhart sneered.

"Do you think we should let the horses cool off this way, Ada?" Lucy gave her cousin a speaking look. But Ada, too, seemed to be waking up to the explosiveness of the situation.

"Lucy's right," she said with a manor-born authoritativeness. "Come along, William. Squire won't thank me for neglecting his animal, slug or not."

William was not to be as easily diverted this time as he had been at the ball. His blood was up. He was spoiling for a fight. "Don't worry about the cattle, Ada." His hamlike fists assumed the classic boxer's position and he walked slowly toward his foe. "My business won't take long."

He was right. What followed happened with such speed that later on Lucy had a great deal of trouble trying to reconstruct the sequence of events. In one instant she was thinking that William, a full head taller and much heavier than his intended victim, was bound to slaughter Drury and the next instant her childhood friend was stretched out upon the sand.

"Dear God, you've killed him!" she shrieked, all her previous fright and concern now perversely redirected. "You monster, look at what you've done!"

"Don't be goosish, Lucy. Get hold of yourself. It would take a lot more than this to kill William. I can only hope it's knocked a bit of sense into his thick head." Ada was helping her dazed escort to a sitting position, but when he attempted to rise, she held him firmly by the shoulders. "You're down for the count well and proper, William, and you might as well admit it. What's more, you had it coming. You've got no quarrel with Mr. Drury. It's that More fellow you really were lashing out at, and that's the long and short of it. Pity he wasn't here in person, for it's obvious you tangled with a wrong 'un. Here I was expecting you to mill him down the way you've done to every cove in these parts foolish enough to step in the ring with you, and damn if he doesn't feint you neat as anything with his right then poleax you with a left straight to the jaw."

"The sun was in my eyes," William said sullenly as he massaged his chin.

"Fustian. He outboxed you, William, and that's the long and short of it." Ada looked approvingly at Drury, who was massaging his knuckles and avoiding Lucy's indignant glare. "It's my guess you've spent some time in Cribb's Parlor," she said shrewdly.

"A little," he admitted. "But I've spent more time with Jackson."

"You mean you've actually stripped with Jackson?" William was looking impressed in spite of himself.

"I have no idea what you people are going on about," Lucy said coldly, "but if you are all right, William, and if the brawling is at an end, perhaps we might be going."

"Surely you've taken in that Drury here was taught how to box by Gentleman Jackson himself." William's voice was a trifle slurred as his jaw began to stiffen.

"Oh. Really."

"Don't be dense, Lucy. Jackson was champion of England, for God's sake. You must of heard your brothers talk of him."

"I can hardly be expected to remember all the male fustian John and Paul talked, now can I?"

"Don't mind her, Lockhart," Drury said soothingly. "She's disappointed that you didn't flatten me. Next time, perhaps, Miss Haydon."

"Not unless I get lucky," William said with surly magnanimity as he struggled to his feet. "But there's other ways of dealing with your kind than just bare knuckles. So I'll be watching. Step out of line with Lucy here and it'll be the worse for you."

"Really, William, you are being ridiculous." Ada was clearly exasperated. "Just because Camilla wound up wearing the willow doesn't mean that Lucy will. She's much too level-headed to let herself be swept off her feet by the first handsome care-for-nothing that comes along."

Drury choked and Lucy laughed, in spite of the fact that she longed to box the ears of both gentlemen.

"I tell you what," Drury said after he'd recovered, "why don't we ride back with you. Maybe your chaperonage will salvage Miss Haydon's reputation."

"Or vice versa." Lucy tossed her head. "For why it should look any more odd for us to be riding out alone than for you to be, passes my understanding."

She was immediately sorry for her words, for Ada turned a dark, painful red.

And later that afternoon, over tea, Lucy apologized for her thoughtless remark. Ada had walked down from the hall and had seemed relieved to find Lucy in the vicarage alone. "I didn't mean to imply that it was even the least bit improper for you and William to ride together. I was just trying to point out how absurd he was being for making such a fuss over me and Mr. Drury."

Ada waved the apology away. "No, I'm sure that seeing William and me together did look odd. I just didn't stop to think that anybody might get the wrong impression. But given our past history, I suppose it could start tongues to wagging. The thing is, I've forgotten all that business. That William and I were to have been married, I mean. It doesn't even seem real to me now. Can you understand it?"

Lucy nodded, more for encouragement than from candor. In truth she couldn't understand it at all.

"What does seem real now is that we were such great friends. I keep remembering all the things we did together as children— the riding and the hunting and the fishing—when John and Paul were home. We were always together, the lot of us. Mama used to throw fits over it." She chuckled at the memory. "Called me a regular hoyden. But now I keep thinking about how William was then—easygoing, amiable—a bit of a slow top, actually, compared to John, especially. Oh he'd flare up now and then— fight occasionally, the way boys will. But he was never a hot-head. And there was no malice in him. He's changed, Lucy." She gazed down sadly into her cup as though reading the tea leaves there. "That's why I went through all that horse cha-rade," she continued, "asking his opinion about the bay. As if I needed William Lockhart to tell me Squire was out to bam-boozle me. Cut my eyeteeth long ago. I just wanted to give him a chance to talk if he wanted to. Let him know he had a friend. Silly notion, actually. For of course he wouldn't. William's proud as Lucifer. Lord, I hate that woman!"

Lucy was startled by her cousin's sudden outburst. Her teacup halted in midair.

"Oh, I know you think I'm jealous. But that ain't it at all. I hate her for what she's done to William. She's changed him. Past all recognition. And well, I know it sounds foolish, said out loud this way, but I'm afraid."

"You are? Of what, Ada?"

"That's the strangest part. I haven't the slightest notion of what I'm afraid of. But all the same, I'm still afraid."

Chapter Fourteen

THERE'LL BE NO MOON TONIGHT. THROUGH A JUMBLE OF thoughts in Lucy's head next day, that one worked its way to the top and stayed.

The free-traders would be desperate to use every opportunity before the government troops arrived. And if St. Botolph's was involved, there'd likely be signals from the church tower this very night.

Lucy tried unsuccessfully to keep the motives for her own obsession with the local skulduggery at bay. They were a mixed lot, she realized. Perhaps the most acceptable motive was a desire to be one up on the London excise man, or whatever Drury was. To know what was going on before he did. He was an interloper. She was Sussex born and bred.

The least acceptable motive was, of course, by far the stronger, a need to know whether William Lockhart was involved. And here she entered a gray area in her thinking, for if he proved to be a smuggler, then what? Well, warn him, of course. For John and Paul's sake. For Ada. And for Louis. But if she did warn William that Drury was out to get him, what would that make her? An accessory? Someone out to cheat the law of its just retribution? Different rules for different classes, is that where she was coming from? Right and wrong, so simple to grasp when Papa leaned over the pulpit and exhorted his little flock, now seemed blurred and hazy. Perhaps it was best to believe she was motivated by simple curiosity.

Feeling like an old hand now in clandestine activity, Lucy spent most of the day making preparations. This time she most definitely was not venturing forth in her nightgown, though placing a sheet among the gravestones should the need arise for the ghost to walk again seemed a very good idea. But the clothing she wore should be dark, and warm, and allow for easy movement.

The situation of a clergyman's daughter was fraught with drawbacks. Any other establishment, she was sure, would provide some cast-off clothing. But in the Haydon household a garment was scarcely off one's back before it was handed over to the poor. Not one article of her brothers' outgrown clothing, ideal for her purposes, had outlasted their enlistment. After frowning over the problem for several minutes, she finally hit on just the thing and hoped it would not be missed. If discovered, she could always claim to be mending it. Lucy blushed with shame at the depths of duplicity to which she seemed willing to descend.

She was proud, though, of the foresight that prompted her to collect a quantity of soot, an action she did not attempt to explain when Emma came back into the kitchen and caught her scraping at the inside of the fireplace.

Now all she had to do was wait. But that proved to be something of a trial. Not only did Papa keep them sitting up well beyond their usual bedtime reading *Pilgrim's Progress* for the dozenth time, but the adventures of Christian so inspired the Reverend Mr. Haydon that he retired to his study to incorporate them into a homily for the Sunday after next. And as if that weren't enough, Camilla had to choose that particular evening to follow Pilgrim's example and leave the Slough of Despond, which resulted in a desire to stop by her sister's room and chat. Pleased though Lucy was to see her sister at least partially restored to her former self, it was hard to share her enthusiasm over the precious litter of kittens one of the stable cats up at the hall had just produced. Nor was she optimistic over the probability of Emma tolerating one of them.

"We've two cats already. Emma's always complaining about having them underfoot."

"But a kitten can be so cunning, chasing strings and balls."

"Go ahead and get it then." Yawning prodigiously, Lucy shoved her sister out of the room. "Then let it be its job to charm our Emma."

Even after all that, it seemed to take forever for the house to settle. Lucy, stretched out on her bed, nodded off and jerked herself back awake more than once while Camilla rattled around next door and Papa's footsteps were at last heard coming down the hall. Then she had to keep pinching herself until she judged it was now safe to make her preparations.

Finally, she leaned out her window and appraised the sky, not knowing whether to be glad or sorry that the stars were twinkling brightly. It certainly gave the world a more friendly look. But would the smugglers—or whoever—hold out for another cloudy night? Well, it was a bit late to stand here weighing the probabilities after she'd gone to all this trouble. The die was cast. Lucy turned away and crept silently out of the house.

She ran swiftly and silently across their garden toward the churchyard, glancing up now and again at the belfry as she went. No light flashed there. But what if the signaler was already up there, waiting. Or worse still, what if, like her, he was now speeding toward the church and they were destined to collide there. She stopped abruptly with a shudder, then pushed aside the thought and continued, warily, on her way.

She tiptoed up the marble steps and tried the door. The knob turned in her hand. If someone was in the tower, he hadn't locked the door behind him. The thought was comforting till it occurred to her he'd leave it open for his confederates. She eased the door ajar. The resulting creak caused her hair to stand on end and made her blood run cold. One would think the folk who wandered in and out of here in the dead of night would at least oil the hinges occasionally.

Lucy stood and listened. All was quiet as the grave inside—a dreadful simile. And then she imagined that someone might be creeping toward her from the road or through the graveyard. She quickly stepped inside.

Not till the door creaked closed behind her did Lucy realize just how benevolent the starshine had been. Here was total darkness. She screwed her eyes tight shut, then opened them again with scant improvement in her vision.

Well, she couldn't go on standing in the doorway, to be run over by a pack of cutthroats. But it passed all comprehension how a church she'd spent a large part of her life in could become such an alien place. Best to feel her way around the wall till she got her bearings.

Lucy was too busy exhorting her heart for its pea-goose behavior to make proper connection with her brain, which might have given her a warning. But as it was, she forgot all about the silver wall sconce until she swiped against it and sent it crashing.

The noise was horrendous. Lucy reached out and clutched a pew to keep from retreating to the cadence that her cowardly heart was beating. The crash surely must have roused the inhabitants of the graveyard, let alone any intruder who might be skulking in the church tower. She held her breath and did her best to listen. But it would have been hard to hear the church bells themselves above the drumming of her heart.

The attack came from entirely the wrong direction, from behind her as she was half turned toward the door. Lucy was

115

grabbed without warning and her arms pinioned while something hard and cold and ominous was pressed against her head. "One sound and you're a dead man," a low voice growled. An unnecessary warning, for she'd lost all power to scream.

She was being dragged now, backward. "Damn you, use your feet," the growl commanded as the arm shifted to support more of her dead weight, then immediately shifted once again. A hand began a rapid, intimate exploration that transferred her terror into indignation. "Stop that! For shame!" she snapped.

"It's you." Lack of volume in no way robbed the voice of any of its bitterness. "I might have known."

The pistol stopped pressing against her cranium. The hand took a more decorous position on her shoulder and was joined by its opposite member to give Lucy a sudden shake.

"You made me bite my tongue."

"Good. You deserve it. Though not as much as I do. It did occur to me that my stupid remark about the moon might bring you out. But I thought at least you'd wait till you saw a signal light."

"What made you think I wouldn't figure out that if I wanted to know what was going on, I'd have to be in the church before they came. You did."

"I suppose I was sap-skulled enough to keep the hope alive that one of these days you'll start behaving like a proper female. Not to mention a proper vicar's daughter."

"What do you think you're doing?" she yelped as she was propelled firmly toward the door.

"Sssh. Taking you home, obviously. I plan to stuff you inside and nail the door shut, if that's what it takes to keep you there."

"I've as much right to be here as you have," she whispered. "More in fact." But in spite of this voiced protest Lucy went without a struggle. Then catching Drury offguard as he reached out to open the sanctuary door, she jerked free and ran.

"What the devil!"

She had bolted halfway down the church aisle with Drury hot after her when a prolonged screeching sound stopped them in their tracks. It might have been the wailing of a banshee. But worse, it was the opening of the outside door.

Lucy forgot all about her former flight plan. Drury had been disqualified as Chief Pursuer. He was now an ally. She tiptoed back toward him as fast as she'd run away, but misjudged the distance and collided against him in the dark.

"*Oof.*"

She clapped a hand across his mouth and froze.

Chapter Fifteen

SILENCE. WAS THE SOMETHING—SOMEBODY—OUT THERE listening, too? If so he was almost bound to hear the renewed pounding of her heart. Then suddenly there were footsteps. Coming their way. Her hand clamped convulsively on Drury's arm. She forgot to breathe. The footsteps crossed the narthex. The door to the sanctuary opened for a moment, then shut again. The footsteps retreated, paused. They heard the door to the church tower open, close, then the more muffled sound of footsteps slowly mounting the corkscrew staircase of the belfry.

"You can let go my arm now," Drury breathed into her ear. "You've damn near paralyzed it. Not even to mention that it would have been inconvenient to try and use this pistol with you grafted onto my shooting arm."

"I'm sorry," she breathed back. "What are we going to do?"

"A very good question. Wait, I suppose. There's no hope of taking you home now. Our friend up there would be sure to spot us. Come on." He took her by the hand and started down the center aisle.

"I meant to hide in a pew," she offered helpfully.

"Well, don't let me change your plans. Go there if you want to. You won't be able to see our villains from there, of course."

Since he still held her tightly by the hand, the suggestion to go her own way rang rather hollow. "There's a step up here," he warned as they approached the chancel, for all the world as if it were his church, not hers. He did seem to have the eyes of a cat, though, she thought resentfully, a requirement no doubt for his form of work.

"Not up there, for heaven's sake," Lucy protested. He was actually starting to mount the curving steps, dragging her behind him. "We can't go in Papa's pulpit!"

"Why not?"

"It's not suitable."

"I disagree. It's the best hiding place around."

"I didn't mean that and you well know it."

"Sit down on the floor," he ordered when they'd entered the cramped pulpit. "You aren't here to preach, you know. Keep out of sight."

How like a man to put himself in charge, she fumed, but nonetheless sank down obediently on the wooden floor. There was one more thing to remember, along with dark clothes and soot: if she ever did this sort of thing again, she'd bring a cushion with her.

"There's no way of knowing how long that fellow will be up there, so listen closely, then take the vow of silence. God knows I didn't want you here, but since you are, there's nothing to do but make the best of it."

"If you plan to spend the rest of the night ringing a peal over me, I'm not going to know what it is that you have in mind, now am I?"

"What I have in mind is to look and listen."

"That's all?" She sounded incredulous.

"Yes. And keep your voice down."

"What had you planned to do before I happened along?"

"That was it. Look and listen."

"Well, you certainly didn't need to bring a pistol along for that!" Lucy didn't know whether to feel disgusted or relieved.

He sensed her ambivalence. "And what exactly did you expect me to do?"

"How should I know? Make an arrest, I suppose."

"Well, I'm sorry, Miss Haydon, if I don't live up to your ideal of proper derring-do. Which reminds me—you really are a distraction, you know—this won't jibe either with your heroic ideals, but wait a minute while I cover our retreat."

118

He made a move and she reached out a restraining hand. Since it closed on a well-developed thigh muscle, she promptly let go again. "Where do you think you're going?" Her whisper sounded panicked.

"What's the matter, Intrepid Miss Haydon? Scared to be alone? You came here by yourself, remember?"

"I came here planning to stay near the door where I could bolt whenever I needed to. You've got me holed up in here where I'll never get out. It will be like shooting fish in a barrel, for goodness' sake!"

"I'll just be a minute. I want to check whether the vestry door is open."

"I can save you the trip. It stays locked. Papa and Nigel have the keys."

"Why didn't it occur to you to filch one? A fine spy you've turned out to be."

"Even if I saw a need to, I could hardly pick my father's pocket."

"No? You disappoint me. I would have thought that sort of activity would be precisely your cup of tea. Well, we do need a back way out of here, even if I'm forced to pick the lock. Stay put. I'll just be a minute."

To Lucy, his minute became hours. She spent the first part of it on her knees feeling all around the walls of the pulpit, as if to ascertain that they weren't really closing in upon her. She spent the next while leaning back against the polished wood, trying to recall the details of last Sunday's sermon. When she failed completely in that edifying task, she took it as a sign that boded her no good.

The thing to do of course was to follow her own best judgment and position herself in the most favorable place for her own well-being. Let Drury perch up here if he wished—that is, if he had not already fallen asleep by the locked vestry door. That was it, of course! He'd no intention of returning. It was the graveyard all over again. He'd simply stuck her up here out of the way while he awaited developments in the most likely spot. Well, if he thought for one moment that she'd gone through all these elaborate preparations just to spend the night cowering in the pulpit, he much mistook the matter.

Careful to keep her head well down just in case the smugglers chose that moment to make their entrance, Lucy groped her way to the pulpit stairs and, still crouched below banister level, inched her way on down them. Then when something black and awful loomed up before her in the darkness, terror honed her instincts. She sprang and butted.

"Oof!"

By sheer good fortune she had caught the intruder in the stomach and had knocked the wind right out of him. Following up this advantage with a swift shove, she sent him reeling backward down the steps. She then tried to leap across her prone assailant but was caught by an ankle and dragged down. Lucy kicked out wildly with the other foot but encountered only air. Then a body hurled on top of hers and this time she was the origin of the *"Oof!"* Her outcry was of shorter duration than his had been, for a rough hand sealed off her mouth.

"Have you gone berserk?" a low, angry voice demanded. "These scuffles are getting monotonous, not to mention noisy. It'll be a miracle if that bat up there in the belfry hasn't heard us. Come on quick." Drury propelled her back up the pulpit stairs. They crouched down together, Lucy straining her ears until they ached, but the only sounds they heard were the familiar night noises from outside.

"Well, our belfry friend must have been chosen for his eyesight, not his hearing. I would have sworn that all that thrashing about could have been heard in Rye. Why in God's name did you attack me?"

"I wasn't attacking you. I mean to say, I thought you were one of them. I'd decided you weren't coming back, you see."

"I said I would, didn't I?"

"Yes, but when you were gone so long, I decided you'd just put me up here to be rid of me."

"Why didn't I think of that? Well, too late now. But I do assure you we have the best seat in the house for the upcoming performance. Now let's shut up. Our friends should be showing up any minute now."

If he was right, Lucy thought later on, then time was a lost concept for her. She might have been sitting here on the floor of Papa's pulpit all her life. She forced herself to think of wide

120

flowery meadows, the limitless sea, the spacious firmament on high. Her legs began to cramp. She tried to stretch them out, which proved a tactical mistake. They collided with the wood. She jerked her knees underneath her chin once more, but it was all too late. She felt herself grow clammy as her teeth began to chatter.

"Cold?"

"N-no."

"Then you've brought castanets along? Sounds like it."

Their cramped quarters allowed for only an inch or two of space between them. He closed the gap and pulled her close. "This is not to be mistaken for an amorous move on my part, you understand," he murmured into her hair. "It's either warm you up or have you warn off the enemy with your chattering teeth." His arms encircled her and held her close. She rested her head back against his shoulder. It was all she could do to repress what could have been a heart-felt sigh.

"Warm enough now?" he whispered sometime later. He certainly was, she noticed. She wondered if he might be sickening for something. He felt feverish.

"Actually I was never cold."

"Now you tell me," he groaned softly. "Much as I'd like to believe you deliberately maneuvered us into this position, Lucy, my conceit can't quite manage it. What was your problem then? Don't tell me that you're actually scared?"

"No. Well, a little perhaps. But that's not what set my teeth to chattering."

"What then?"

"It's this place. I can't stand being all closed in."

"You aren't closed in. There's no door or ceiling."

"But I can't see that, can I, here in the dark? Every time I move in the least there's a wall and I *feel* closed in. It's an awful feeling. I've been this way ever since I hid in the cupboard from Paul when we were children and he locked me in for a lark and then forgot me. It's silly I know, but it gave me the horrors. It was the only time Papa ever took the strap to Paul. I know I should have outgrown this long ago, but it seems I haven't."

"Poor little Lucy," Drury murmured. She looked up suspiciously to see if he was teasing but was unable to read his

121

expression in the dark. Then once again she had reason to wonder at his superior visual acuity as his lips unerringly found the target of her upturned mouth. All such thoughts were soon blotted out by the sensations that followed fast upon this contact.

She felt a lowering surge of regret when he pulled away, followed by a deep contentment when he merely shifted her to a more comfortable position upon his lap and resumed the lovemaking where he'd left it off. This new location enabled Lucy to cooperate more fully, to put her arms around him, to slide her hands up and entangle them in his thick, springy hair.

It was rather comforting to note that all the wonderful strange sensations coursing through her body had not completely shut off her mind. Lucy actually managed to entertain a thought: she would never fear enclosed places again.

Perhaps it was this bit of contact with some reality outside of the delightful pastime they were engaged in that made her conscious of the sounds before Drury heard them. (Later she would match this auditory acuity against his visual superiority and feel rather smug about it.) And with that consciousness came the realization that she'd been hearing stealthy noises for some time now. Had she actually ignored the squeaking of the outside door?

The tug Lucy gave to Drury's hair could in no way be mistaken for amorousness. It was just as well that his lips were silenced by her own. She felt him grow tense at the sound of a door closing and concluded it was now safe to draw away. She slipped silently from his lap.

At some point he'd removed the pistol from his belt when she'd complained of it. Now she felt him groping around the floor. Her blood ran cold as she suddenly identified the hard lump pressed against her hip as the weapon and handed it to him with a trembling hand.

The doors to the sanctuary squeaked open. "Have ye never heard of oil, Lucas?" a low voice growled. "I told ye afore to see to these doors." Lucy's mouth flew open as she heard their sexton's name.

There was a moment's silence, followed by the sound of flint on steel. The two cowering in the pulpit saw a faint, growing glow, like a hint of sunrise, as someone picked up the lantern and heavy footsteps started down the aisle.

"Look out!" There was a dull thud accompanied by low curses. "Ye clumsy ox, watch who you're bumping. Could've smashed the lot. Fine thing to have the church reeking of French brandy."

"Might bring more folk out of a Sunday." Someone sniggered and another voice guffawed.

The glow above the pulpit waxed steadily and then waned as the procession evidently passed beyond the pews and was now moving clumsily to the right. From the unsteadiness of their tread and their grunts and panting, the smugglers were burdened heavily indeed.

Metal rasped now on flagstone and the light steadied once again. A rapid succession of thuds followed, accompanied by whooshes of relief. Then came a *clang* that reverberated like a sounding temple gong.

"Lor' sakes, wot was that!" The horrified voice echoed Lucy's sentiments.

"My barker hit the brass," was the tense reply, and Lucy reached out and nudged Drury just in case he'd missed the revelation that these men were armed.

"What the hell were ye wavin' the damn thing around for?"

"Watch your mouth, Sam," a new voice chimed in. "You're in church, collect."

"Well, it's a thousand wonders the pistol didn't go off and bring the vicar running."

"Vicar's dead to the world by now."

"Been listening to his own sermons then, has he?" The wag of the group sniggered and Lucy felt Drury's shoulders begin to shake. She wasted a speaking look on him there in the darkness.

"Shut up, you lot, and give us a hand." This was the voice that had objected to the swearing. It carried the weight of authority.

The pulpit occupants now heard a heavy grating, punctuated by several grunts and huffs and the beginnings of another oath, which the blasphemous one managed this time to nip in the bud.

Drury's hand pressed hard on Lucy's shoulder. Its message was clear—*stay down*—as he slowly began to rise.

She was not about to obey such a directive. She hadn't come this far to stay cowering down behind an ecclesiastical barricade. She held her breath and stood up soundlessly.

As her eyes rose over the pulpit's edge, they widened to enormous size and she reached out convulsively to clutch Drury's sleeve. The grating sound increased to a teeth-aching pitch. The smugglers were opening up Sir Sham!

Chapter Sixteen

IT TOOK ALL FIVE OF THEM TO SHIFT THE HEAVY MARBLE LID of the false crusader's tomb. Strenuous though the task appeared to be, they'd obviously had a lot of practice, for rather than attempting to remove the heavy cover altogether, they pivoted it until it left a large enough opening for their purposes. Lucy was grateful for their skill. Not only was Sir Sham safe from being dropped, so far they'd even avoided finger smudges on the brass effigy that it was her task to shine.

Drury's hand was on her shoulder once again, pressing down insistently. She reached up and plucked it off. The two of them were no more visible than he alone would be. Besides, there was really little danger. The arc of lantern light was confined to the area around the tomb. The rest of the church, including the pulpit, lay in deep shadow.

This state of affairs seemed to prey on the mind of one of the smugglers, who paused frequently in his task of prizing the lids off a stack of wooden crates to look apprehensively over his shoulder.

"Wot's the matter, Tom," the clown of the group jeered. "Think sumthin' from the graveyard's coming in to claim this tomb now we've opened it up for tenants?"

"Happen it'd be a step up from those common-type graves at

that," another chimed in. The laughter at this sally seemed rather forced.

"You can laugh all you like," the nervous one replied, "but you didn't see it. Tell them, Sam. It was there all right. Plain as anything."

The joker snorted. "Reckon some of you must've tapped a keg when I wasn't looking. There's no such thing as ghosts."

"You wouldn't be saying that if you'd seen wot we did. It was there. Plain as anything. Hovering over the grave." His tone was sepulchral, eerie enough to cause the scalp of the ghost herself to prickle. Now some of the scoffers were throwing anxious glances back over their shoulders. Lucy concentrated upon holding perfectly still. "It floated there for a bit, didn't it, Sam? And then it moaned—ever so low and pitiful, like it didn't want to have to go back down, don't you see, and then it did. It sank down, ever so slow, down, down into the grave."

"Maybe it would like Sir Sham's spot better at that. Ain't like he was using it." This time the jest rang hollow as the empty tomb.

Now that the shock of discovering their cache had worn off, Lucy was busy trying to recognize the smugglers. This posed a problem. They all wore large-brimmed floppy hats pulled down low upon their foreheads, effectively screening their blackened faces from the elevated angle of the pulpit. She relied more on voices than anything. Lucas Wyse, their sexton, had been easy enough. He was the wit who'd slandered Papa's sermons. She seethed with indignation. And he must have been the one in the bell tower. She was also sure of the blacksmith. Sam, the short fat man, was one of Nigel's tenants. She wasn't positive of the younger, nervous one's identity, but thought him likely one of the miller's numerous brood. The authoritative voice had been easy enough to recognize. It belonged to Bert from Lockhart Place.

This identification process had not been necessary to relieve her mind of its greatest fear. For from her first glimpse of the smugglers, she'd known that William Lockhart was not a member of the band. No amount of soot or concealing garments could have disguised his towering height. Still, it was a relief to make such positive identifications. Even Drury would now be convinced of William's innocence.

"Quit your jawing and hurry up there." Bert looked up from his task of pulling straw-wrapped bottles out of the crates to exhort his troops. "Mr. William said to do our business quick and get on out."

Lucy's blood ran cold at what she'd just heard. She prayed that Drury had missed it. Her relief had been short-lived.

"Folk round here are already getting too suspicious," Bert continued. "Mr. William thinks the spook you saw was flesh and blood. Lord Tilney most likely. Never can tell when he'll take the notion to work on that history of his. If he'd stay abed of nights, we really wouldn't need old Lucas here up in the tower."

"That why Lockhart don't take the risk of coming here hisself?"

"*Mr.* Lockhart to you, Tom, and watch your mouth. Mr. William takes more risk than any of us, sailing right under the noses of the law the way he does."

"That's right, Tom," the blacksmith's voice chimed in. " 'Tweren't for Mr. Lockhart you wouldn't have all that blunt buried under your floorboards, now would you?" He was lighting a pipe and sending up huge billows of smoke.

"And I'll tell ye another thing." The burly blacksmith talked around his puffing as he handed the wrapped bottles to the small sexton, who'd climbed down into the sarcophagus. "There's no other I know of who could sail up Little Creek in the dark without going aground. That channel's not got so much as a hairsbreadth to spare."

The others were murmuring agreement.

"Still, it ain't right, asking us to use the church this way," the young one protested.

"I suppose you know of a better place than Sir Sham to store old Lord Simcox's special brandy? Constant temperature—dark—good as any wine cellar."

"Don't seem right though."

"That's as may be. Just bear in mind that this lot"—he held up a bottle for emphasis—"fetches a better price than the rest of the cargo put together. And wot's more, its price keeps ris-

126

ing. Every time his lordship gives one of his toffish friends a taste, it's a brand-new customer for us. Now this lot here, for instance, will fetch a higher price than the stuff we shifted out of old Sir Sham last week. Supply and demand. That's wot the free-trade's all about. And there's more demand than we can supply. At these prices, I reckon this brandy deserves the extra trouble and attention. Besides, old Sir Sham here don't mind." There was general chuckling.

The sexton in the sarcophagus began to cough. "Belay it with that pipe, will you, Ned? If there really was a corpse down here, you'd cure him like bacon."

"Ain't right to smoke in the church anyhow," the boy called Tom said piously.

"And who says it ain't? They do it all the time. Why the air gets down right blue with the stuff, it does." As if in illustration, the blacksmith puffed all the harder. Clouds of smoke billowed all around them.

"Don't be daft. That's incense. That's holy stuff."

"Smoke's smoke."

Lucy was in complete agreement. Smoke was smoke and the clouds of it being created by the pipe, for all the world as if the blacksmith was fanning his forge with a pair of bellows, were rising rapidly and, caught by drafts of air, swirled ever higher. A sneeze was tickling her nose, building momentum. She warded it off by covering her nostrils and mouth with the loose sleeve of the clerical robe she wore.

The smoke was settling all around them now, in thick, stifling clouds. She held her breath. Then, just before she'd have to breathe or perish, the smoke and the tickling sensation both abated. She removed the black material from her face and filled her lungs.

"Ker-choo!"

The sound echoed and reechoed in the cavernous church, followed by the splintering of glass on the flagstone floor.

"Lor', wot was that!" Lucas Wyse came leaping out of the marble tomb. The smugglers stared in the direction of the sound.

"Come from the pulpit, it did. There's sumthin' up there!"

The words had scarcely left the speaker's mouth before

Drury was jerking Lucy after him down the pulpit steps, dashing past the altar, sprinting toward the vestry.

Lantern light and the trampling of feet pursued them. "God save us, it's the vicar!" the sexton gasped as Lucy's robe fanned out behind her. This revelation momentarily halted the pursuers. Drury took advantage of the lull to slam the inside vestry door and wedge it with a chair. Then he went tearing through the exit he'd previously prized open, tugging Lucy after him like a kite that at any moment must surely soar into the air.

She tried to turn toward home, but her arm was nearly wrenched from her shoulder as Drury jerked her in the direction of the hall. He didn't slow down their furious pace till they'd reached the thorn hedge.

"Where's the opening in this blasted thing?"

She showed him and they squeezed through the prickly foliage, then collapsed behind it, gasping with exhaustion and, in Lucy's case, holding her painful side.

"Why are we here?" she asked when she'd finally caught her breath.

"It was the first hiding place I could think of in the opposite direction the smugglers are likely to take. If they actually mean to pursue us, they went toward the vicarage, since they're convinced that you're the vicar." He choked suddenly. "My God, I hadn't realized up till then what you've got on. Well, I did tell you to wear black, no need to look offended. Anyhow—I don't really expect those fellows to follow us. They didn't strike me as the murderous types, though you never know. It's my guess that they've taken to their heels before we can round up reinforcements. Better not to chance it, though. We'll just sit here for a bit till we're sure the coast is clear. Then I'll take you home."

Lucy strained her ears. All around them there was a cacophony of night noises. Surely the crickets alone were enough to drown out the sound of stealthy pursuit. Overhead all but a few of the stars had disappeared. Clouds were drawn over the rest like heavy window curtains shutting out the comfort of candlelight. An owl hooted quite near by. Lucy shivered.

"Don't worry. They're miles away by now." Drury spoke in the same low voice that had become habitual. He was sitting a few feet away as if to emphasize that it was only the confines of the pulpit that had forced their intimacy.

"You'll be going after William now, I collect."

"Now? Good Lord, no. I'm going home to bed. He can wait till morning."

She sat with her chin resting on her knees while the tears stung her eyes and she struggled not to shed them. For what at first had seemed merely an adventure, a storybook affair, had taken on a grim reality. From the time she'd first spied the church-tower signal, it was the mystery of the thing that had intrigued her most, a puzzle to be solved. Now it all boiled down to human lives destroyed.

The law was the law, of course. Made to be obeyed. And William Lockhart had done what he had done with his eyes wide open, knowing well the consequences of discovery. What were the consequences, anyhow? she wondered. Not hanging, surely? Prison or deportation was more likely. Poor William would find hanging more merciful than those alternatives.

"Let's go." Drury rose to his feet and reached out a hand to help her up. He let go of hers as soon as he'd accomplished that bit of chivalry. Lucy wondered if she weren't weighing on his conscience.

As they squeezed back through the hedge, her robe caught fast. She heard him suppress a chuckle as he worked to get her loose. "No harm done this time," he pronounced when she was finally thorn free.

He turned with her toward the vicarage. "There's no need to see me home. I'll be all right."

"Probably. But those scoundrels could still be waiting around."

It wasn't the need for stealth that accounted for the silence that lay heavy between them. They approached the church and stood straining their ears a moment before they crossed the graveyard to the vicarage.

He took her to the window, for all the world as if he were escorting her conventionally to her door.

"Good night," she said, just as formally.

"Thank you, Miss Haydon, for a most enjoyable evening,"

129

he replied with mock seriousness. "You've certainly made the company of other females seem tame."

"No doubt." She recalled their pulpit intimacy with a surge of shame.

"Oh that, too." His mind-reading talent had become uncanny. "But actually I was referring to our other activities. I simply meant that except for your deplorable tendency to sneeze at even a whiff of smoke, you're the perfect confederate. We must go spying together again sometime, Miss Haydon."

"That we will not!" Her whisper choked as she hitched up her robe, preparing to climb in the window. "I want no more of it, thank you very much."

"Lucy." He turned her gently around, then touched her face and brushed at the tears with his fingertips. His lips met hers once more with the same familiarity, yet with a difference. The passionate insistence was now missing, displaced by a tenderness she was sure would break her heart.

Back in her room, Lucy moved as silently as possible, pouring water from the pitcher into the washbowl and soaping away the soot as best she could there in the darkness. What Emma would say when she saw the towel, which was bound to be smudged, didn't bear thinking on. She stuffed Papa's robe out of sight in the cupboard and then took out her cloak.

She hesitated for a moment before leaving the house. But surely Drury was halfway home by now and all the smugglers had long since taken to their heels. A sigh escaped her lips as she crawled through the window once again. Doors might never have been invented for all the good they had done her lately.

As she trudged down the roadway in the dark, Lucy had new cause to regret the fact that her father did not keep a stable. How glorious it would have been to saddle up and go galloping to the rescue. Oh well, be practical. The sound of horses' hooves would have roused the sleeping household.

She stared up at the sky. The stars were all gone now. And what was delaying the dawn? Surely it should have arrived ages ago. A raindrop hit her upturned cheek. Another splashed her nose. That was all that had been missing from this disastrous evening. It really was the outside of enough. Lucy pulled the hood of her cloak over her head and trudged on. The rain fell harder.

She had begun to think she'd passed the gatehouse in the dark, for never had the walk to Lockhart Place seemed so long. But then, just as she was contemplating turning back, she spied its dim outlines in the distance.

It was only as she turned off the open road toward the overgrowth crowding in on the carriage drive that she thought of Bert. She quickly dealt with the prickle of fear the thought brought with it. Bert would be too concerned with saving his own skin to remain here repelling boarders. She pushed open the creaking gate and walked bravely between its posts just as a dark form materialized from the gatehouse. Lucy screamed.

"I've been here for ages," a conversational voice replied. "What kept you?"

Chapter Seventeen

"YOU SAID YOU WERE GOING HOME TO BED!" LUCY accused.

"I know. I meant to. But then it occurred to me that you might get the quixotic notion to send Lockhart haring off to France before I could get to him. But gentleman that I am, I thought I'd not rouse him out of bed unnecessarily."

"How very considerate."

"Oh, that's the kind of fellow that I am. So I waited here to see if you'd show up. I'd just washed the soot off and decided I could finally get some sleep myself when here you came, trudging through the rain. Well, Miss Haydon, shall we go disturb the gentleman together?"

But it appeared that would prove unnecessary. Lockhart Place was ablaze with lights as they approached. "Someone

131

seems to have taken the trouble to warn Lockhart. I'm afraid our bird has flown."

"If that's so, thank God," Lucy breathed reverently.

"Wait a minute. Let's look first." Drury reached out and stopped her from going up the steps to the front door.

Well, why not. She might as well add "peeping Tom" to her growing list of sins.

They peered first into the long windows of the withdrawing room. No one was there. Lucy's eyes focused on the pianoforte before they turned away. Had she ever been a respectable music mistress?

When they came to the library windows, Drury squeezed between the boxwoods ahead of her. Her heart sank as she heard his softly breathed "Ahhh." On tiptoe she peered across his shoulder. The master of Lockhart Place was at home all right. The wing chair almost obscured him, but there was no mistaking the long, top-booted legs or the large hand that reached out for the glass on the candle stand beside him.

Knocking would have been obscene, Lucy conceded, as Drury tried the front door, found it unlocked, and opened it. Best not to rouse the rest of the household. Let them sleep peacefully while they could. She tried to dodge the thought that she would have to stay behind and break the news of his arrest to William's wife and stepson. She didn't think she could face that. But then she knew she'd have to. Mama would never sidestep a duty, no matter how painful it proved to be.

William looked up as they paused in the library doorway, but betrayed no surprise, as if predawn visits from his neighbors were not unusual in the least. Nor did he appear to think it the least bit odd that they were dripping wet or that a Bond Street gentleman was dressed in a laborer's dark smock. The evidence of an all-night drinking bout was plain to see. An empty bottle lay on the floor beside his chair. Another, almost depleted, shared the candle stand.

"I ain't foxed, if that's what you're thinking." He had watched them take in the scene. "Though God knows I've tried," he added. As they approached his chair, William seemed to wake up to the peculiar circumstance of their being there. "Lucy," he said, "I tried to tell you to stay away from this man.

132

Should've known to save my breath, though." He rubbed his eyes wearily. "There's no reasoning with women. God knows why I've always put 'em on pedestals. Don't belong there. Got no moral sense at all."

"Oh William." Lucy was close to tears again. And the last thing she wanted was to go all weepy. "I'm not with *him*." Drury gave her an enigmatic look at this disassociation. "I tried to get here before he did. I'd meant to warn you he was onto you. I was going to tell you to run for it, to take the *Seagull* and cross the channel. But he was waiting in the gatehouse." Here they came now. It needed only this. The tears were welling up and spilling over. "Oh William, why did you do it?"

He looked bemused. "What are you going on about, Lucy?"

"It's no use playing innocent, William. We were there in the church when your men hid the brandy in Sir Sham's tomb. They talked about you. You're the ringleader. You've been using the *Seagull* in the free-trade. Oh, William, why?"

"Money."

"If you needed money so badly, your friends would have helped you. Papa hasn't much, of course, but Nigel, I'm sure, would have tided you over."

He gave her a weary look. "Ain't a question of 'tiding over,' Lucy. It's a question of needing to live like a gentleman again. Just look around you." He gestured vaguely at the peeling plaster, the threadbare carpet. "Place is falling down around us. And that ain't the half of it. A beautiful woman needs beautiful things. Clothes. Fripperies. Jewelry to set her off. I promised her all that. She thought I was rich, you see. And the free-trade was the only way I knew of to make money in a hurry. But then it wasn't enough. Not near enough to match More's fortune."

"What are you talking about?" Drury spoke sharply.

"I'm talking about what I could give Sophie compared to what More could give her, of course." He looked as if Drury might be more than a bit dull-witted. "And it was no contest. He won. Hands down."

"Won? How? Explain yourself, man." Drury took a threatening step nearer and Lucy put out a restraining hand.

"What's there to explain? Sophia's run off with Carnaby

More. But then you knew that already. Ain't that why you're here?"

"Where have they gone?"

"To Italy. She left a note. More was to come and get her as soon as I sailed to pick up my cargo." He laughed suddenly as the joke struck him. "And after all the trips I've made, this is the one that's done for me. And I didn't even need to make it. The reason for it's gone." His voice broke. His shoulders began to shake. Tears coursed down his cheeks. Drury shook off Lucy's hand and went to stand over him.

"Did they take the boy with them?"

When William continued to blubber, Drury reached over and shook him by the lapels.

"Stop it!" Lucy protested. "How can you be so heartless?"

"Get hold of yourself, man. I asked you a question. Did they take the boy?"

The shaking seemed to work. William stopped crying with one last shuddering sob. He looked at Drury in disgust. "I just said they've eloped to romantic Italy, didn't I? Of course they didn't take Louis with them. Think Sophie wanted him along on her honeymoon? No, along with the note she left me the boy."

"Thank God." Drury crossed over to a companion wing chair and collapsed upon it.

"Thank God!" Lucy was incensed by this shortsighted reaction. She stood by William protectively and glared at Drury for his lack of sensitivity. "Do you actually believe that being spared from exposure to his mother's scandalous mode of living is preferable to being abandoned by her and having his stepfather arrested for smuggling? I for one can't see it. What's to become of the child now?"

"Oh, I've had my instructions about that." William was seeing the joke of the thing again. "Didn't think she left a note out of consideration for me, now did you? That was the real purpose of it."

"What do you mean, William," Lucy prodded. He seemed to consider the subject closed.

"You don't think she would have left me a farewell note unless she had to, do you? Last thing she wanted was for me to find out she was gone for good and who she'd gone with one minute before I would finally put two and two together for myself. Kept saying I mustn't try to follow them—that she wouldn't come back with me even if I caught up with 'em. She's afraid I'll kill More," he said confidentially to Drury.

"Anyhow, Sophie didn't leave the note out of consideration for my feelings. There was no 'I'm sorry, William,' in the damned thing, I'll tell you that much. Just a lot of 'you tricked me into marriage'; that sort of business by way of justifying what she'd done."

"Tricked her! What a shabby thing to say." Lucy was indignant.

"Oh that part's true enough. Made her think I was a nabob. Not that I ever said so. But I went out of my way to give that impression. I had to have her, you understand. And she was dangling after a rich husband. Made no bones about it. She'd made one bad marriage—Roger Aldington didn't have a feather to fly with. His family cut him off when he married Sophie, don't you see. Happened I'd just won big at faro when I met her. Spent it all on her. Talked a lot about my estate in Sussex. Oh, she's right. No mistake. I did deceive her. All's fair in love and war, they say." He gave a bitter chuckle.

"But what's to become of Louis?" Lucy prompted. "You said Sophia left instructions."

"I'm to send the lad up to London to his uncle."

Drury stared at William in openmouthed disbelief, then collapsed back limply in his chair. His shoulders began to shake with helpless laughter. "Just like that," he said.

"How can you possibly find this amusing!" Lucy snapped. Had she ever imagined herself in love with this callous, unfeeling minion of the law?

"I—I'm sorry." He waved a helpless hand at her as he tried to control himself. "It's just too damned absurd. When I think of all I've—we've—been through." He doubled up again, then finally wiped his eyes. "When I think of all the unnecessary conniving—spying—I've done to bring the thing about and then Carnaby carries her off and sh-she simply leaves a note behind, 'Send the boy to London.' All of this high drama. And I could just have stayed there for all I've accomplished."

"Do you know that you are making no sense whatsoever?" Lucy addressed him coldly. "I can't speak for William, but I, for one, haven't the slightest notion of what you're talking about."

"I—I'm sorry. Truly." He made an effort to get hold of himself. "You see, I'm Louis's uncle."

"Louis's uncle!" She was appalled as the full import of what he'd said just struck her. "Louis's uncle is here to haul his stepfather off to prison? That's—that's—obscene!" She sank down upon a library reading chair and stared at Drury with horror.

"You're actually Sir Clive Aldington?" William seemed to lose some of his torpor with this new revelation. "Well, I would've thought being an excise man was beneath your touch."

"I'm not an excise man. That was her idea entirely." He nodded at Lucy. "My only reason for trying to catch you out was to get some leverage so I could persuade Sophia to let me have the boy."

"Blackmail us, you mean."

"Not to wrap the thing up in clean linen, yes."

"Could have simply asked for him, you know."

"That I didn't know! My father tried it and Sophia turned him down flat. After he'd offered her a handsome settlement, too."

"I know." William sighed. "She really enjoyed doing it. Had it in for your father, don't you know, for disinheriting your brother when he married her. Gave her a lot of satisfaction to fling his offer back in his teeth. She'd met me then, you see. Believed I was King Midas and that she could well afford the gesture. Then by the time she learned how things really stood with me, your father had died. You were off in the army, weren't you?"

"That's right. I sold out then and came home."

"Never occurred to Sophia that you'd want the boy. She was sure you wouldn't, in fact. Didn't seem likely. A bachelor and all."

"My father left instructions that I was to do whatever I could to look after Roger's son. It preyed on his conscience that he'd cut my brother off, you see. Father was proud as Lucifer. Had an awful temper to boot. He couldn't abide the thought of an Aldington married to an actress. He'd have come round, though. Only Roger died of the fever and it was too late. Then Father wanted to make it all right through the boy."

"So he left it for you to do. I understand all that," William said, "but not why you decided to pretend you were an excise man. Last thing I'd choose, I can tell you."

"I didn't," Drury repeated patiently. "That was simply Miss Haydon's latest theory to explain my odd behavior. You see, she'd figured out that I was using her as an entrée to Lockhart Place. And at first she thought I was smitten with Sophia—right, Lucy?" When she made no response, he continued. "Then she realized I was really after you, so it was only logical to think I was a customs official of some kind."

"But you actually came to Sussex to get Louis?" Lucy had found her voice. But the night had been far too long, too eventful. She wasn't up to comprehending this new development.

"That's right. When Carnaby mentioned that he owned an estate down here, I saw it as a heaven-sent opportunity to come to Sussex and check on my nephew with no one the wiser. For even though I'll admit to being prejudiced against Sophia myself—not because she was an actress but for marrying again before my brother was cold yet in his grave—still I wasn't prepared to take a small boy from his mother just because I don't happen to approve of her. I wanted to learn firsthand how he was faring and what his life was like. Besides," he added, "I don't suppose she'd have let me see him if she'd known who I was.

"Then, after I'd been down here awhile, it became pretty apparent that you were involved in all the smuggling that's going on. And I didn't like the idea of Roger's son being mixed up in that sort of thing. I decided it behooved me to catch you before the authorities did. And, yes, I meant to threaten to turn you in unless Sophia gave Louis to me. Blackmail you, as you've just said. It was all a pretty circuitous means to an end, I'll grant you, but it seemed a sure one. It's turned out to be much ado about nothing, though."

"So what are you going to do now?" Lucy forced herself to ask. "About William and the other smugglers, I mean."

"Why what any red-blooded Sussex man—or woman, when it comes to that—would do. Turn a blind eye, of course. It's finished now anyhow. Isn't that right, Lockhart?"

"Aye. There's no point in it now. Or in anything, comes to that." He reached for the bottle by his elbow but Drury was quicker.

"You're going to need to keep a cool head." He carried the bottle to the library table, then came back to stand over William Lockhart once again. "It's reasonable to assume, you know, that there are other folk besides Miss Haydon and myself who have suspicions about your recent fishing trips. I think it would be a good idea if you came to London with Louis and me right now. And stayed there till the real excise men are through nosing around. In the state you're in, I wouldn't put it past you to confess."

"Oh I ain't so far gone as all of that." William's smile was twisted, but it was a smile, nonetheless.

"Still," Drury insisted, "it would be prudent to make yourself scarce for a while. And leaving for London's the most natural thing in the world. Man, deserted by wife, makes arrangements for her little boy. Damn fine way to turn suspicion into sympathy."

He ignored Lucy's scandalized reaction to this Machiavellian notion and pulled William to his feet. "Hurry up and get your things together, Lockhart, while I go break the news to Louis. Lucy"—he turned her way, rather apologetically—"it will soon be daylight. You'd best go home. You'll be all right alone, won't you?" He barely waited for her nod before he was hurrying William toward the stairs. She picked up her damp cloak from the chair seat where she'd dropped it and put it back on.

At least it had stopped raining. Lucy stood on the steps of Lockhart Place and looked up at the low-lying clouds, now breaking apart with the sunrise. For the first time she realized how tired she was. It took all her concentration to put one foot in front of the other as she trudged down the long, rutted carriage drive. And once she'd reached the road and walked on awhile, she felt a deep resentment for the few extra steps it took to make way for a group of horsemen. They looked at her curiously. She stared dully back. They must be the new company of land-guards that had been the catalyst to all the recent turmoil. Well, they'd come too late. For the time being, at least, smuggling around here was over. And she herself was partly responsible for its demise. The knowledge gave her little satisfaction.

Lucy forced herself to turn into St. Botolph's before going home to bed. She was apprehensive about what she might find there. But the smugglers hadn't been so panicked as to leave Sir Sham open or pieces of the shattered bottle lying on the floor.

Lucy carefully avoided the pulpit with her eyes as she turned toward the little chapel. Suddenly she sneezed. The smugglers had not been able to wipe out all traces of their nocturnal visit. The blacksmith's pipe smoke still contaminated the air, over-laid with a strong reek of brandy.

Lucy walked over and stood gazing down at the brass effigy. The armored knight lay in calm repose, hands folded piously, eyes closed to all the drama that had swirled around him. Only the fact that the top of the tomb was slightly askew, scarcely no-ticeable unless one stared hard, betrayed the fact that it had been used as a smugglers' cache. "You needn't look so pious." Lucy spoke aloud to the false crusader. "If you did but realize it, you're tarnished."

She'd have to polish him soon, she thought. That is, if she ever took up such routine living again. Right now what she needed most was deep, obliterating sleep. But she continued to stand there, staring down at the sculptured features.

What was it that William had called Jerrold Drury? Sir Clive? Sir Clive Aldington. She had a much better name for that particular knight—or baronet—whatever. From now on, if she ever thought of him at all, a circumstance she took a solemn vow to fight against with all her willpower, he, too, in her mind at least, would now be dubbed "Sir Sham."

Chapter Eighteen

Mrs. Haydon arrived home that day at noon, bearing messages to each member of the family from Eleanor and the Reverend Mr. Landseer, as well as a fund of stories about the cunning things little Jane had done and said and the adorableness of Baby Edward. And if she was amazed to find the elder of her daughters still abed at such an hour, after ascertaining that Lucy was not sickening for something, Mrs. Haydon tactfully let the matter drop.

During the next few days the vicarage seemed inundated with morning callers. It was natural enough for the local matrons to wish to welcome Mrs. Haydon home and hear all the details of Eleanor's confinement. But outweighing those worthy motives was the treat of finding fresh ears to regale with all the recent happenings in the neighborhood.

It was after Lady Tilney had called on two consecutive days, and overstayed her limit on both occasions, that Mrs. Haydon sent for Lucy.

She looked up from the stocking she was darning as her daughter entered the withdrawing room. "Don't you have some handwork to do, Lucinda dear? I think it time that you and I had a comfortable coze." And though Mrs. Haydon gave rather a speaking look at the neglected shirt Lucy pulled out of the worktable, once again this admirable lady kept her thoughts inside her head.

There was scant resemblance between Mrs. Haydon and her younger daughters. She'd laid little claim to beauty even in her youth. Now she was plump and comfortable looking, with a round, placid face and brown hair fading into gray. Only her eyes seemed out of keeping with her bland appearance. They gazed at the world with a shrewd intelligence.

Now Lucy had the uncomfortable feeling that her mother, glancing up from the Reverend Haydon's stocking, was looking straight through her when she said, "It's wonderful how much has been happening since I've been away, Lucinda. Perhaps you'd care to tell me all about it."

"I doubt I could add much to Aunt Tilney's account." Lucy bent over Papa's shirt, trying to sound casual. "She always seems to get the news before anyone else does. I collect she's told you about the move afoot to put a stop to smuggling?"

The gray eyes impaled her. "Don't dissemble, Lucinda. It does not speak well for your character. But since you choose to be evasive, perhaps I should prompt you. First of all, let's discuss your sister. Lady Tilney says that the young man who ran off with William Lockhart's wife—a shocking piece of information, by the by, that I would have expected to learn from my own daughters."

"But, Mama, you've always discouraged us from gossip-mongering," Lucy said virtuously, and got a second piercing look.

"Apprising the vicar's wife of actual events in the parish is hardly gossipmongering, Lucinda. But at the moment it is not poor William I'm concerned with, but our own Camilla. According to Lady Tilney, for a while everyone believed Mr. More was in love with her. They spent much more time in one another's company, I'm told, than was at all proper. Then, just as quickly, Mr. More dropped Camilla and, according to Lady Tilney, broke her heart.

"But with all due respect to her ladyship . . ." Mrs. Haydon snipped off her wool, folded the white stocking, and drew another from the worktable. "We're both well acquainted with your aunt's tendency to exaggerate. I used to think of you, Lucinda, as quite levelheaded. Now I would like to hear your version of the affair."

Lucy's narrative began haltingly enough, but under her mother's skillful prodding, the story soon came pouring out. "I fear Mr. More did break Camilla's heart, Mama." She sighed at the conclusion of her slightly expurgated version of the evening

141

party at the hall. "And it was entirely my own fault. Most likely he would never have noticed Camilla if I had not schemed so to bring her to his attention. You see, I completely misjudged him, Mama." Her voice quivered with self-reproach. "He did not look at all like my notion of a rake."

"Rakes seldom do, m'dear. That's undoubtedly why they're so successful."

"Then, too"—Lucy's confession was coming in a rush now—"I collect that what really made me so determined to bring Camilla to Mr. More's notice was the fact that our aunt was so—blatant—about hiding her away. It just didn't seem fair, Mama. Here all the eligible females in the district were vying for Mr. More's attention and the one with the most right to it was plucking a harp behind a bank of flowers. You won't like my saying so, Mama, but at times being a vicar's daughter is the outside of enough."

Lucy braced herself for a scold and got a sympathetic nod instead. Thus encouraged, she continued. "And the thing is, I kept thinking, Mama, that if only you had been there, you would not have allowed Camilla to be so hidden. And I knew that she would never thrust herself forward. So I did it for her. And made a proper mull of things."

"It could have been much worse, dear."

"It's hard to see how, if you'll forgive my saying so. Our Camilla was in raptures at first. I've never seen her so happy. Mr. More might as well have been Prince Charming. Then when he dropped her, she had to bear all the humiliation on top of the hurt. What could have been much worse?"

"The possibility that if Mrs. Lockhart had not come along he might have married her—though I'll admit it seems a bit unlikely. For with that type of man, someone always does come along. But it's obvious that he and Camilla would not have dealt at all well together.

"Camilla's unhappy experience may prove a small price to pay for a lesson in gauging a man's true worth. So don't be too hard on yourself, Lucinda. I also must share some of the blame, for I've been remiss, I now realize. I can see that I should have taken you into my confidence long ago. I intend Camilla to marry your cousin Nigel."

"Camilla and Nigel!" Lucy gasped. "You can't be serious!" She reddened as her mother raised her eyebrows.

"I would hardly be otherwise where my daughter's welfare is concerned. Why else would I have arranged that Camilla assist him in his work?"

"But I thought that was Papa's doing."

"Your father's mind stays fixed on higher matters, Lucinda, than settling the futures of his daughters." There was not the slightest trace of irony in Mrs. Haydon's voice.

"But our aunt Tilney will never approve of Nigel's marrying Camilla. She expects him to make a brilliant match."

"Of course she does. But then Lady Tilney will have little to say in the matter. You may not realize it, Lucinda, but once Nigel has made up his mind to a thing, he really can be most stubborn in spite of the bumbling impression that he gives. Besides"—Mrs. Haydon smiled down at her neat darning—"though it's too much to expect that she will be, Lady Tilney should be quite pleased with the match. Few daughters-in-law would have Camilla's sweet disposition or would tolerate all the interference her ladyship is bound to inflict upon Nigel's household."

"You're right again, Mama." Lucy laughed. "Do you know, I think Camilla almost likes the old behemoth."

"That is no way to speak of your aunt, Lucinda," Mrs. Haydon said reprovingly, but her eyes still laughed.

They stitched companionably for a bit longer, Lucy hard at work trying to picture her little sister as mistress of Tilney Hall. Even if the notion did strike her as farfetched, she in no way questioned her mother's infallibility in such matters.

"It was odd, was it not," Mrs. Haydon broke the silence, "that Mr. More's friend turned out to be little Louis Aldington's uncle. Your aunt takes a rather dim view of his deception. She feels that you are well rid of him."

"*I'm* well rid of him!" Lucy sputtered. "How dare she say such a thing! Mr. Drury—Sir Sha—whatever-his-name-really-is has nothing to do with me. I'm not rid of him any more than anyone else is."

"Oh? Your aunt gave me to understand that you were a great

deal in his company. Indeed, I collect that you and he caused almost as much talk as Camilla and Mr. More did."

"If that is so, it only goes to prove how little our neighbors have to occupy them. I can assure you, the two cases were not at all alike."

"No need for you to get so worked up, Lucinda dear. At any rate I can't be sorry that Sir Clive has taken charge of Louis. I always felt that he was a very unhappy child. And it does speak well of his uncle to have gone to so much trouble to gain custody. Yes, I quite look forward to meeting your 'Mr. Drury.'"

"He isn't *my* Mr. Drury. For that matter, he isn't anyone's Mr. Drury. And when the gossipmongers were telling you so much, I'm amazed they did not tell you that he left, too. He's taken Louis to London. So you won't be meeting him."

Much to Lucy's annoyance, her mother merely smiled and changed the subject. "Did you know that our sexton has resigned?"

"He has?" Lucy pricked her finger.

"Yes. Your father is quite puzzled over the matter. It seems that Mr. Wyse failed to show up at the church for two days, so your father assumed he was ill and went to see him. Lucas was quite well but most peculiar. When your father asked why he'd stayed away, he mumbled something about taking it for granted he'd been dismissed. But for the life of him"—Mrs. Haydon chuckled—"your father couldn't recall what Lucas had done, or hadn't done, this time that was bad enough to cause him to think the vicar would finally put his foot down. He had always been so incompetent that it was hard to settle on any one thing. But then your father has lately suspected him of drinking while on duty. Edward actually smelled brandy in the sanctuary! So undoubtedly that was it.

"I'm amazed, though, that Edward did not try to persuade him to come back. It would have been just like him. But I suspect that through the years Lucas Wyse had been a bit too much even for your father's Christian forbearance.

"I had suggested young Tom Mapp for the position. He seemed a conscientious youth and his family needs the money. I must say, I was very disappointed in the lad, for he turned the position down with some absurd excuse about the churchyard being haunted."

"How ridiculous," Lucy murmured, keeping her eyes lowered to her sewing. She was rather relieved when Emma appeared at just that moment and took her mother away to solve some problem that had arisen in the kitchen.

Chapter
Nineteen

SINCE SHE'D BEEN HOME, MRS. HAYDON HAD NEVER REferred to the fact that upon her return she'd discovered Lucy in bed at noon. But this must have preyed upon her mind, for she seemed determined to keep her daughter occupied. Each day she presented Lucy with a long list of tasks that could only be accomplished by constant diligence. And if her prime motivation was to cure her daughter of this new tendency toward sloth, it also had the secondary effect of allowing Lucy no time to fall into the mopes.

On the morning that "polish Sir Sham" headed her list, Lucy sighed heavily and put the hated task off as long as possible, preferring to weed the flower beds, make a new supply of bark mixture, and call on ailing Mrs. Green rather than stir up all the memories that working on the brass effigy was bound to evoke.

But by late afternoon the time of reckoning had come, and Lucy approached the sarcophagus with her polish and cloth and a baleful expression.

Her first act was to check the marble slab's alignment. It was still the least bit askew. No one had been back to disturb it. Just how long would that state of affairs continue, she wondered. Surely for as long as the land-guard patrolled the neighborhood. And perhaps with a new and, one could hope, more conscientious sexton, Sir Sham might keep his guilty secret for years to come. She applied a glob of polish to his chain mail and rubbed vigorously.

The creak of the outer door still had the power to make her hair rise and her heart leap to her throat on cue. Stop it! she chided. All that business is over and done with. And the minute you finish with Sir Sham you're going to oil that door. She listened as the footsteps crossed the narthex. Nigel, of course. Lucy went back to her polishing. But as the steps drew nearer, she looked over her shoulder and froze.

"Hoping to gloss over his secret sins?" Drury inquired as he picked up the polishing cloth that Lucy had just dropped and began to buff the enigmatic knight.

She had never seen him look so elegant. His maroon tailcoat with silver buttons, his long, tight-fitting dove-gray pantaloons, the tall beaver hat he'd placed on the floor, all seemed to proclaim his revealed status. Just as the thorn-ripped, berry-stained frock she'd put on to do the polishing proclaimed her own.

"What are you doing back here?" she finally managed to ask in a voice grown unrecognizable.

"Oh come now." He paused to admire the sheen he'd just created. "You knew that I'd be back."

"I knew nothing of the sort." She was glad to note that her speech mechanism was beginning to work properly once more.

"You didn't? Oh well then. I got the impression from your mother just now that I was expected. My mistake, no doubt. I say, could you let this go awhile? It's not that this place doesn't hold certain fond memories for me"—he glanced significantly toward the pulpit—"but I still find it all a bit inhibiting. Could we walk somewhere?"

"I suppose so."

"Do I detect a lack of eagerness? Really, Miss Haydon, after all we've been through together, I expected a more cordial reception."

"It's just that I'm supposed to finish him." She nodded toward Sir Sham.

"He can wait. He's most adaptable." Drury took Lucy's hand. She quickly withdrew it. His look was quizzical.

"It's out of line," Lucy remarked by way of easing some of the tension between them.

"Oh, you mean Sir Sham here." He squinted at the tomb. "For a moment I was afraid you referred to me. I collect that means the cognac's still in there."

"I fear so. I keep worrying that Nigel will notice and have it opened up. The shock of it all would upset Papa terribly."

"Hmmm," Drury said thoughtfully. "I was considering sneaking in here the first moonless night and helping myself. No? Oh, well then. It's obvious you never tasted the stuff or you wouldn't be quite so high principled. Anyhow, I think I can fix this." He studied the sarcophagus through narrowed eyes. A well-placed kick moved the heavy marble lid the fraction of an inch required. "Can we go now?"

Outside the church Drury gestured toward the sea and Lucy nodded. They crossed the down in silence. Then it behooved him to take her hand again in order to safely navigate the steep path that gave access to the beach. And once that hazard had been overcome, he found it necessary to put an arm around her in order to guide her across the barrier bank of treacherous shingle. He did not remove it, though, when they reached the well-packed sand. And Lucy felt it would be hypocritical to protest at this late date even when he continued to hold her close after they'd sat down upon an upturned fishing boat.

A fine breeze was blowing inland. They watched the billowing sails of a distant cutter on patrol. "Pity we can't let them know they're wasting their time," Drury said. "I'd hoped they'd be gone by now. William's aching to come home. London holds very few charms for him these days."

"I trust he's learned his lesson." She watched the cutter fade out of sight. "You know, it's still hard for me to realize that you're actually not an excise man. You certainly had a flare for it."

"You also seemed to think I'd a flare for the free-trade. I'm not sure whether to feel flattered or insulted."

"Instead you turned out to be a soldier." She studied him curiously.

"Ex-soldier. Cavalry to be exact."

"I might have known. I've seen you ride. And on top of everything else, you're a baronet, they say."

"How is it, Lucy love, that you make my title sound more disgraceful than the free-trade?"

"I don't mean to. It's just that you've made me feel like such a gudgeon."

"I assure you that's not the way I wish to make you feel." He tenderly removed her bonnet and secured it with a stone, then brushed back the hair that was blowing in her eyes. She quickly averted her face as he leaned toward her and asked rather breathlessly, "How does Louis like it in London?"

He pulled back and sighed heavily. "Not very well, actually. We both agree that we'd rather live down here. Oh, did I mention that I've bought Dighton House?"

"Mr. More's estate?" She gaped up at him. "Whatever for?"

"For all sorts of reasons. For one thing, I owe Carnaby a great deal. And nabob or not, he'll need all his resources to support Sophia in the style she's determined to become accustomed to. Besides, he can hardly bring her back here to live, now can he? Even Carnaby could not outface the neighborhood to that extent.

"And then of course there's Louis. A boy can't really fly a kite properly in London. Besides, the city doesn't provide the moral climate that the country does. I prefer to bring him up where the gentry are rum runners, the churches serve as smugglers' caches, where vicars' daughters haunt the graveyards at night—wailing like banshees."

"That will do!" Lucy snapped. "You needn't keep harping on that theme. I'm well acquainted with your attitude toward us by now."

"I wonder if you really are," he murmured, bending toward her once again. This time she planted her palms firmly against his chest and shoved. He had to catch himself to keep from toppling backward off the boat.

"Mr. Drury—oh blast! I can't even get your name right!"

"Drury's fine. It's one of several I was inflicted with at my christening. I much prefer it to Clive, actually."

"Sir Clive," she continued, "I think it most ungentlemanly for you to presume that just because—under the most peculiar circumstances, you must agree—when I was frightened out of my wits in the churchyard—and later on when we were in peril

148

for our lives there in the pulpit—just because I allowed you to take certain liberties—and even reciprocated"–she felt the color rushing to her face—"I have given you a carte blanche to continue that same familiarity. In spite of my rackety behavior, sir, I am not Sophia Lockhart."

"And I'm not Carnaby More." He sighed. "Really, that particular Lothario has a lot to answer for. Tell me honestly, Lucy, if he had not treated your sister so shabbily, would you be so suspicious of my motives?"

"Mr. More has nothing at all to say in the matter and I don't condemn your motives. When a female acts as I have done, of course she invites a certain type of conduct. And what's more she would be a complete hypocrite to lay all the blame at the gentleman's door."

"How charitable. And just how sure are you about your own motives, Miss Haydon? Besides the gothic ones of being scared to death—a condition that I trust won't always be a necessary prelude to our lovemaking—are you trying to make me believe that you don't care for me at all? Forgive my conceit, but I'll not believe it. Damn it, Lucy, look at me." He cupped his hand underneath her chin and tilted her face toward his. His eyes met hers with a searching, intense look. He finally seemed satisfied with what he saw there. "That's all right then." He smiled. "And if you weren't such a complete pea-goose you'd know I feel the same.

"No need to say it." He brushed aside the protest forming on her lips. "I realize I put up quite a fight against my growing feelings for you. God knows, as I collect I told you, I had no desire to become leg-shackled. Any more than I wanted the responsibility for Louis. Now I couldn't bear the thought of losing either of you. By the by, the boy's besotted over you, too. I hope you don't object to a ready-made family. Do you?"

Since she'd just been struck speechless, he continued thoughtfully. "You know, I think I always knew from the moment you rang the peal over me there in the library that I'd been well and truly poleaxed. And in retrospect I don't think it was just that you were so devastatingly beautiful, with your cheeks flushed in anger and your eyes snapping—"

"Fustian!" Lucy had found her voice. "I am certainly not beautiful."

"Of course you are. Though it's to your credit you don't realize it. Your own ideals of beauty are your slightly insipid sister—oh, all right then, I beg your pardon. I should not have said that. But as I was trying to point out, your ideals of beauty are your sister Camilla and Sophia the Cyprian. Should I not have said that either? Oh very well then, you're right. She is Louis's mother. I must learn not to speak of her in such terms. But anyhow, believe me, those two diamonds of the first water can't hold a candle to you, love.

"But before we wandered off the subject into those pointless comparisons, I was trying to explain that it was not your beauty that enslaved me as much as your flair for fashion. You may find this hard to believe, but I'd never before known a female who wore hedge thorns in her dress."

"It really is odious of you to keep recalling things like that."

He ignored the interruption. "I'm not sure, though, if the thorn gown lives up to your graveyard-haunting ensemble. And you were most fetching in your ministerial robe."

It was a mistake to glare up at him, for this time she was not quick enough to turn away. And having succumbed that far, it seemed rather pointless to try and push him away, not even when one kiss led to another and then another, till finally he eased her down off the boat and onto the sand where they lay in one another's arms quite shamelessly.

It was only when Lucy began to feel a certain dampness about her feet that she wriggled free and discovered that the rising tide had already soaked Drury's shoes and the bottoms of his pantaloons and had been lapping at her leather slippers. "Oh my heavens!" She stood up and began shaking her skirt vigorously.

"Here, let me." Using his snowy handkerchief for a brush, Drury began to flick the sand from the back of her gown. "Now it's your turn to play valet." He passed the linen to her and she ministered to his maroon superfine.

"Do you think we'll pass muster?" he asked as they began walking toward the cliff. "Your mother asked me to come have a cup of tea after everything was settled between us. And it's my

150

opinion that the lady doesn't miss much of what goes on. Two remaining grains of sand and she'll know exactly what we've been up to."

Lucy stopped to stare at him. "When we've settled *what* between us?"

"Come, Lucy love, don't be so dense. You know perfectly well what we've just settled."

"I most certainly do not. We've settled nothing that I know of."

"Well, Miss Haydon, if after what just transpired you don't intend to marry me, forgive my saying so but that would make you the very type of female you've just stoutly denied being. No offense, but Sophia Lockhart does spring to mind."

"You slow top, you haven't asked me!"

"By George." He snapped his fingers. "I knew I'd forgotten something. But could we back up a bit? This shingle is a damned uncomfortable spot to go down on one knee. Ah, this is better." They'd retreated to the sand where he struck the classic pose and then reached out to take her hand. "Since I'm madly in love with you, Miss Haydon, and wish to spend the rest of my life being driven to distraction, will you marry me?"

Lucy was momentarily diverted from answering. She was struggling with a puzzling thought. "But how on earth could Mama possibly have known that things were going to be settled between us?"

"The same way she knows that Lord Tilney will marry your sister, I suppose."

He rose and carefully brushed the sand from one knee of his pantaloons. "May I take your indifference to my offer for a 'yes,' then? Thank goodness that's finally settled. Shall we go now and ask your mother about Cousin Ada and William Lockhart? Who knows, perhaps there's even some hope for them there in her crystal ball."

*A Season for
Scandal*

Chapter One

"**YOU LOOK LIKE THE VERY DEVIL!**"

The Earl of Rexford glared at his only son, Lord Dalton.

Though many would have quarreled with the earl's assessment—Lord Dalton was generally considered one of the handsomest men in London—the fact that his extraordinarily blue eyes were bloodshot, his black hair was tousled, his unshaved cheeks were a trifle pallid, gave some credence to Lord Rexford's words.

"B'gad, Pierce"—he stamped the stick he carried upon the floor for emphasis, causing his suffering son to wince—"it's a disgrace to still be in your dressing gown at noon. When are you going to put a period to your carousing and set up your nursery?"

Lord Dalton sighed and collapsed in a wing-back chair that flanked an Adam fireplace. He waved a languid hand at its duplicate on the other side of the marble hearth. "Do sit down, Papa. If I'm to be harangued, let's at least be comfortable."

The older man yielded up his stick, gloves, beaver, and the greatcoat he'd worn against the February weather to the footman who had been lurking in the background since admitting him to his son's Mount Street residence. The servant thereupon disappeared, soon to return with a pot of strong, hot tea.

"Do you know, sir," Dalton remarked pleasantly after a sip of the restoring brew, "I suspect there are other ways to start a conversation than with inquiries about my matrimonial intentions, but damned if you've hit on an alternative for the last ten years."

"Can you blame me?" Lord Rexford's eyebrows were bushy,

155

gray, and formidable when he frowned. "Neither of us is getting any younger."

"True. But since I'm not quite thirty yet, and you're only— err—fifty-something, I fail to see the need of all this urgency. As I think I've remarked each time we've had this conversation, if you're so concerned about the succession, why don't you remarry? I'm sure you're quite capable of producing other brats. Just look at you."

It was true that the Earl of Rexford did not look his fifty-seven years. And while not nearly as tall and never as good-looking as his only son, who owed both traits to his late mother's family, he was, by other standards, a fine figure of a man. He had retained his hair, a becoming iron-gray, and his waistline had expanded very little. He did require spectacles for reading, but since he was not addicted to that habit, it caused him little inconvenience. He could still spot the fox or the hare on the hunting field as quickly as the next cove.

His son acknowledged all this with an admiring look. "You really are looking quite fit, sir. Must be all that clean living and country air. I'll bet a monkey that all the Sussex widows are in hot pursuit. So why haven't you remarried?" He'd dropped his bantering tone and was frankly curious.

His father, who had momentarily ceased to glare, resumed it. "You can seriously question why I haven't brought another female into my house? My God, Pierce; I never thought you lacked for common sense!"

Lord Dalton, who had four sisters still at home and two more now comfortably settled on nearby estates, acknowledged the hit. "I do see what you mean, sir."

"And as for starting up a nursery again—" Rexford shuddered. "I'd ask for much better odds than six to one for producing another male."

"Ah, breakfast." Lord Dalton welcomed the interruption as the footman reappeared with a heavily laden tray and set it down on a circular table at his elbow. "Never mind, Jack." He waved away the ministering servant. "We can manage."

There was an interlude while Lord Rexford heaped his plate with boiled eggs, ham, and Sally Lunn, while his slightly queasy son settled for a light wig. Then, "What brings you to

156

London, sir?" Dalton inquired politely. "That is, besides your parental duty to periodically rake me over the coals."

"That's it," his lordship responded thickly as he chewed.

"Oh, come now." His son looked dubious. "You surely can't be serious. You wouldn't leave the hunting field on so feeble a pretext. For I can assure you, you've no need to vex yourself on my account. I do intend to wed—eventually."

"*Eventually* won't cut it, Pierce. Now's the time. Started to write you a letter about it, but knowing you as I do, I judged you'd just glance at the thing, then pitch it in the fire. So I've made the trip here in person to tell you that—By the by"—another thought intruded—"do you have a voucher for Almack's?"

"Certainly." Lord Dalton looked slightly offended. While admittance to the Assembly Rooms in King Street, St. James, was jealously guarded by a cabal of patronesses who saw to it that only the crème de la crème of society attended, there could be no question of Lord Dalton's bona fides. "Not that I ever go there," he added. "For a more tedious way to waste an evening, I can't imagine."

"Well, you're going to start going. And to Fremantle House when you're asked there."

It had never fallen to the Earl of Rexford's lot to order troops of soldiers into battle. But if the occasion had arisen, and he'd used the same tone he'd just employed, outgunned, outmanned companies would have unquestioningly moved forward into the very teeth of the enemy.

Lord Dalton was, however, made of sterner stuff. "Now why would I do a damn fool thing like that? For if there's any place likely to be an even bigger bore than Almack's, it's an establishment presided over by James Fremantle."

"I mean to tell you why if you'll keep your comments to yourself long enough to listen. Didn't I say I've come to London for that very purpose?" He placed his teacup on the hearth beside him and inched forward in his chair to give an urgency to what he was about to utter.

"Did I ever tell you about the Percival sisters, Pierce?" The question was rhetorical; Lord Rexford did not yield the floor. "It was the Season of '98, I collect. No, make that 1797.

Twenty-one years ago now. Fancy that." He did pause now to shake his head sadly and wonder at the passage of so much time.

"What about the sisters, sir?" his son prodded.

"Why, they took the town by storm. That's what about 'em. Four of them, there were. And all glorious. Nobody had ever seen four such lovely girls all in one package, as it were. And they hadn't a feather amongst 'em to fly with. Their father was a country parson, well connected, but poor as his own church mice. God knows how he raised the blunt for all of 'em to make their bows, but somehow he managed. And it paid off handsomely. Every last one of 'em married a fortune.

"Oh, did I mention that there was a pair of twins? The middle girls they were and alike as two peas in a pod." His face took on a dreamy quality. "I was in love with one of them."

His son, whose attention had wandered for a bit, was now all ears. "Oh, really? With just one, sir?"

"Of course just one!" his father snapped. "What do you take me for?"

"Well, you did say they were exactly alike. I just wondered how you told 'em apart, that's all. Are you quite sure they never pulled a switch on you? I've heard of twins getting up to that sort of thing. In point of fact, a friend of mine—"

"Devil take your friend!" his father interrupted. "Twins ain't the point here, you ninnyhammer."

"Well, then, what is?"

"The point is, these famous beauties now have three daughters who are about to make their bows." The earl looked expectantly at his offspring.

"Don't tell me. Triplets!"

"Don't be impertinent. Dammit all, I'm trying to get it through your skull that this is the chance of a lifetime. And I'm—yes, by gad—*ordering* you to bestir yourself before the other beaux in town snap up the three of them. By gad, sir, I expect you to marry one of these girls."

"Even if they turn out to be antidotes?"

"They won't. The thing's impossible."

"Well, now, sir, I beg to differ. I've seen some perfect horrors whose mamas were, by all accounts, quite presentable in their salad days."

"Well you can rest easy on that score. Friend of mine saw Caro's daughter a few years back in Vienna. Turned out that Caro's husband's a diplomat. Surprised me no end. Never would have thought he had it in him. The daughter was only a schoolroom miss at the time, of course, but Cobb swore she'd outshine her mother. Not that I think that's possible. Bound to be an exaggeration. But still—"

"Caro? That was your twin, I take it."

"You might say that. Anyhow, it's her daughter I want you to marry."

"Sight unseen? Isn't that a bit rash? She could be a shrew or a sapskull, you know."

"Impossible."

"If you say so. By the by, did my mother know of—Caro?"

His father looked indignant. "Of course not. Wouldn't of been the thing to speak of it."

"Sorry."

This wasn't the time to ponder over his parents' marriage. They had always seemed content enough as he remembered. But their wedding had been arranged, he knew. A tradition his father seemed determined to continue.

"Isn't there a bit of incongruity here, though? I mean to say, you've sat here telling me that you still regret letting the love of your life get away. And yet you want me to dangle after some chit you've picked out for me sight unseen. Where's my chance for a love match?"

"Well, if you've not managed the thing during these last ten years, I'd say it ain't likely to happen."

Lord Dalton's expression acknowledged the hit, and his father pushed home his advantage. "Besides, if you can't manage to fall head over heels with this particular diamond-of-the-first-water—well, there's something the matter with you, lad."

"If you say so."

Lord Dalton was feeling cornered. He made one last feeble attempt to fight his way out. "It still doesn't make sense to exert myself just because of a pack of sisters who were all the rage

159

before The Flood. Why can't I do my own choosing in my own time, sir? I still can't share your sense of urgency."

The Earl of Rexford sighed. He'd anticipated this kind of opposition from his heir. Reluctantly he flung down his trump.

"Didn't want to have to say so, Pierce, but you leave me no choice. Went to see that London quack of mine yesterday. And not to put too fine a point on it—well, he told me I'd only a short time to live. Said I'd best be putting my affairs in order. And having you married, right and tight, Pierce, is the most pressing affair I can think of."

Chapter Two

THE HONORABLE JENNY BLYTHE PAUSED ON THE threshold of her aunt's withdrawing room and struggled to hide her shock. When she had last seen her cousin, Lady Claire had been a plump, pretty child of ten. Now—and there was no other word for it—Claire was obese.

Jenny had just arrived. Her boxes were in the process of being removed from the traveling coach that had brought her to Grosvenor Square. Lady Fremantle's butler had informed her that whereas her ladyship and her cousin Sylvia were out shopping, her other cousin could be found practicing the pianoforte. Jenny had followed the sound of Mozart to its source.

In spite of the jolt her cousin's size had given her, she was forcibly struck by Claire's considerable musical skill. Consequently when Claire glanced up from her playing, the look that she encountered was fortunately admiring.

Claire's eyes in their turn widened. Well, now the shoe's on the other foot, Jenny thought, with wry amusement. "Bravo!" she said aloud. "That was marvelous."

"Jenny!" Lady Claire jumped up to give her cousin a welcoming hug. Jenny could not help but compare the embrace with being smothered by a bolster.

The cousins parted to gaze at each other affectionately. Though separated by too much distance to see each other often, they had been tireless correspondents. Jenny had always believed that there was little about Claire's life she did not know. Now she began to wonder.

But not for long. Her attention was suddenly distracted. "Well, well, well," she breathed as she gazed upward over her cousin's head. "There it is. The famous portrait. Well, well, well."

Followed by Claire, Jenny walked over to an ornate marble fireplace that occupied the center of a pale green, silk-covered wall. There above the mantle, dominating the drawing room, was an enormous painting.

Four young women, astonishingly beautiful, were artistically posed within a sylvan glade. They were draped in filmy gauze, each with a shoulder bare; the effect was vaguely reminiscent of Ancient Greece. One stroked a harp. Another, seated, held a flute carelessly on her lap. One bent studiously over a tambour frame, while the fourth appeared to be sketching the profile of the sister with the harp.

The two cousins stood silently for several moments, studying every aspect of the portrait. At last Jenny heaved a heartfelt sigh. "I hate to admit it, Claire, but they actually surpass all that I've ever heard. I always took the whole business with a grain of salt, you see."

"Did you really? I never did."

"Of course the artist—Romney, isn't it?—could have exaggerated."

"I really doubt it."

"But just what are they supposed to represent?"

"The Muses, I believe."

"Impossible. There were nine of them."

"The Graces, then?"

"Wrong number again. They were only three. Still, though, perhaps Sylvia's and my mother only count as one." She moved closer and studied the identical twins, whom the artist had treated as the focal point. "Yes, *Graces* most probably explains it."

"What they were were beauties." There was a tinge of bitterness in Claire's tone. "They didn't have to be anything else. By the by, our cousin Sylvia looks just like them."

"Well, so do you."

It was true. In a sense. Though almost obscured by cushions of fat, there were the same perfect features, the cornflower-blue eyes. Claire's hair was the identical softly curling blond of the portrait beauties. Her skin was fully as petal-fine.

"Oh, yes," she said wryly. "You could say that. You could even say that I'm twice the beauty they are. Three or four times even."

"Well, you're certainly closer to the ideal than I am," Jenny pointed out.

"That's not true. Why, you're"—Claire appeared to grope for the proper adjective—"stunning."

Her cousin laughed. "That's very good. Most people are stunned when they first see me."

"That's not what I meant at all and you know it. I'd give anything to look like you. You're so—"

"*Junoesque?* That's the word bookish folk use to describe me. Most, however, settle for Long Meg.

"No, let's face it, cousin, I've missed the famous Percival look by several miles. And I don't just refer to altitude. You're all so English-fair. And—well, just give me a tambourine and I could easily pass for your average gypsy."

The two cousins stared at the painting a little longer, and then, as if on cue, they began to giggle. The giggles increased to near-hysterical laughter.

"This really is absurd, you know," Jenny said as she wiped her streaming eyes. "What could those ninnys have been thinking of all those years ago? Fancy deciding that their daughters would make their come-outs together and repeat their triumph. Didn't it occur to the widgeons that some of us just might possibly look like our fathers?"

"I think they took it as some sort of sign when the three first-born were so close in age and female."

They looked at each other once again, then back at the

beauties—and were for the second time convulsed with laughter. "Well, thank God for Cousin Sylvia," Jenny choked. "She, at least, will uphold the family honor."

"You know," Claire remarked a bit later as she reclined on a Grecian couch in her cousin's bedchamber while Jenny arranged her toilet articles on the dressing table, "all that laughing has done me a world of good, but it actually isn't at all funny." She helped herself to another chocolate from the open box beside her. "In fact, I'd give all I own not to have to go through with this business."

"The come-out? Now you're being absurd. You simply have to forget all that nonsense about comparing us to our mothers."

"Easy enough to say. But will anyone let us? I've been here for two whole days and Aunt Lydia still has a fit of the vapors every time she claps eyes on me. She keeps moaning, 'How could my sister allow her only daughter to get so fat?' "

"Well, that's Aunt Lydia's problem. I, for one, am quite willing to put up with all sorts of nonsense in order to enjoy the freedom of a London holiday. It's obvious that you don't have a gaggle of younger brothers and sisters to look after the way I have or you'd welcome the chance to spread your wings and see something of the world."

"I wish I did have a gaggle of sisters." Claire swallowed her chocolate and popped in another. "Then Mama would not have to be quite so disappointed in me."

Jenny paused in her search for a mislaid hairbrush to give her cousin an anxious look. She was disturbed by Claire's obvious unhappiness and appalled by her ravenous chocolate consumption. It was all she could do not to point out the obvious: If Claire was unhappy with her size, her behavior could only make things worse.

Instead, she gave her cousin an affectionate look and went to sit beside her. "Come now"—she patted the plump hand—"you're making a Cheltenham tragedy out of something that could really be fun."

"For you, perhaps. You've no reason to dread the come-out. Once people get over the fact that you're not cut from the same pattern card as the previous generation, why, you'll have no end

163

of gentlemen dangling after you. You're every bit as pretty as the famous Percivals, you know."

"What a rapper," her cousin said, laughing. "But I do appreciate your loyalty."

"No, it's true. You have much more—more . . ."

"Height?"

"No, peagoose," the other said, giggling. "I think *character* is the word I'm groping for. You look more . . . interesting. Oh, you'll have no trouble at all in catching a husband, Jenny."

"No, that's where you're wrong. I know from sad experience that gentlemen are not comfortable with a female who towers above them. And as for flirting—well, that's quite beyond me. Batting one's eyelashes down at the top of a man's head can never have the same effect as batting them up at him.

"But never mind. I don't have my heart set on catching a husband. What I really want to do is see the metropolis—the Tower, the museums, Westminster Abbey—Oh, all of it. I can hardly wait."

"Well," Claire observed glumly, "we'll need escorts for most of that."

"That shouldn't present a problem. If our cousin is half as lovely as you say, we'll just stake her out like a Judas goat and have her admirers squire all of us here and there."

"Oh, you are a goose!" Claire laughed, carefully choosing another of the rapidly diminishing chocolates and, after an exploratory nibble, returning it to the box to take another. "Let's just hope our cousin Sylvia is generous with her beaux."

"By the by, what's she like? Besides the obvious, I mean to say. What's Sylvia really like? Good heavens, that sounds like Shakespeare's verse, doesn't it? 'Who is Sylvia? What is she? That all our swains commend her'?"

Claire looked thoughtful as she closed the chocolate box on the one remaining piece. "I don't think I can really say. For we haven't become at all acquainted. We've never sat down for a coze or anything like that.

"I will say one thing, she was quite embarrassed over the fuss our aunt made over her. I'd arrived first, don't you see"—Claire grimaced—"and I'm sure Aunt Lydia was braced for the worst. So Cousin Sylvia proved to be an answer to prayer. Aunt all but fawned over her, and I collect that made our cousin quite uncomfortable. For my sake, that is. But that's just a feeling. As I said, we've never actually talked together or anything like that. She's very—quiet."

"Shy, perhaps?"

"Oh, I shouldn't think so. I cannot imagine what she could find to be shy about. But somehow I got the impression—But, no, that's fanciful. I've nothing really to go on."

"Come on," Jenny prodded. "Out with it. What's your impression?"

"Well, no. The more I think on it, it's too absurd."

"Oh, do tell. I don't plan to carve your words in stone, you know. We can agree later that you're most likely mistaken, but what is your impression?"

"Well, if I didn't know better—for there's not the least doubt in my mind that our cousin Sylvia will be the belle of every ball that she attends . . . But if it were not for that, I'd say that she is dreading the come-out almost as much as I am."

"Indeed?" Jenny's eyebrows rose in surprise. "Would you care to elaborate? Just what gives you—?" She cut off her words at the sound of approaching voices while Claire quickly stuffed her chocolate box behind the cushion of the couch. A light tap on the door preceded its opening. A modish-looking woman and a petite young beauty entered the room.

Thanks to a talented modiste, an abigail with a flair for hair arrangement, and her own good figure, Lady Fremantle still held considerable claim to beauty. She was, however, cast entirely in the shade by the young woman who trailed after her. For Lady Sylvia Kinnard, so her cousin Jenny thought, might have just stepped out of the Romney portrait.

Jenny wrested her attention away from Sylvia and stood to greet her aunt. This action had the effect of freezing Lady Fremantle in her tracks. The dowager looked appalled. She threw her hands up in the air. "Don't tell me you are my other niece!" she gasped. "Heaven preserve us! You *are* a Long Meg!"

Chapter Three

DINNER WAS, TO SAY THE LEAST, A STRAINED AFFAIR. Jenny, who kept country hours at home, had thought she'd never last till seven. She took her seat in the sumptuous dining room and gazed ravenously around her at the bounty. Harricot of mutton, neck of venison, a sauté of sweetbreads and mushrooms dominated the first remove. It was all she could do to force herself to take genteel portions of the dishes next to her, and she ate her first few bites of venison and sweet peas with unalloyed pleasure. But then she noticed the plate of biscuits and the glass of water being set before her cousin Claire and her appetite deserted.

Lady Fremantle, seated at the foot of the table pulling apart a pheasant with apparent relish, saw her distressed look. "I have persuaded Claire to eat as little as possible between now and her debut into Society. Granted, a week is not much time to undo the damage of what I can only term unbridled gluttony, but it is a beginning."

"Surely," Jenny protested as Claire's face flamed red, "she needs more than biscuits and water."

"I am merely following the regime that served Lord Byron so well when he began to put on undesirable weight," her aunt replied in a tone that pronounced the matter closed.

"I hardly consider Byron a proper model to be followed in this household," her stepson remarked dryly from his place at the table's head. Jenny hoped that he would follow up this observation by overruling her aunt's decision, but he did not.

It was not in Lord Fremantle's nature to lock horns with his stepmama. He had been only five when she had captivated his widowed father at the famous come-out. The new Lady Fre-

166

mantle had not been the maternal sort and had left the rearing of the lonely little boy to those hired to do so. She had never been unkind, however, and his lordship, after he came of age, was reasonably content to have her run his household.

He was a quiet, self-contained young man, uninterested in the social milieu of his stepmama. This suited Lady Fremantle well, since she had no desire to be supplanted by a daughter-in-law and had managed, in fact, to dampen the aspirations of several ambitious mamas who would have thrown their daughters at his head for his considerable fortune. And since he was not blessed with romantic, Byronic good looks, being instead thirtyish, with thinning, mouse-colored hair, pale blue eyes, and a countenance neither displeasing nor noticeable, the daughters themselves made no great push in his direction.

Despite his general disapproval of the social scene, Lord Fremantle had raised no objection to sponsoring his stepcousins' come-out. Nor was he lacking in social skills himself, as he now demonstrated by diverting the attention away from his humiliated cousin Claire. "And how did you leave your family, Cousin Jenny?"

"On the whole, quite well," she replied, a little too heartily to cover the general embarrassment. "Of course, with a brood like ours, there's always something amiss, you realize. Just before I left, Charles, our seven-year-old, fell out of the apple tree and sprained his wrist rather badly. But he was so proud of the sling he wore that it took away the pain. He went around for the rest of the day being a casualty of Waterloo."

Lord Fremantle chuckled dutifully, and Lady Sylvia, who had hardly spoken throughout the meal, was also moved to help ease the tension. "Just how many brothers and sisters do you have, cousin? Oh, dear. I really should know that, shouldn't I?" She looked embarrassed. "But living abroad, and all . . ."

"Oh, no need to apologize. I own I sometimes lose track myself. But at last count there were eight of us."

"And what your mama could be thinking of to have another I cannot imagine," Lady Fremantle chimed in crossly. "She could not have chosen a worse time to become enceinte—again."

It was on the tip of Jenny's tongue to observe that surely her papa must share the blame, but she bit the words back as perhaps too indelicate. "Mama was most sorry not to be able to come to London with me," she substituted. "But our doctor told her it would be quite unwise."

"Well, she would have been of little use in her condition anyhow," her ladyship grumbled as she helped herself to fruit and cheese. "But I must say it was the outside of enough. When we planned your come-out years ago, it was agreed that all four of the Percival sisters would take part. We had hoped to make it a re-creation, as it were, of our own Season. And how it should have come about that I, the only childless one of the four, should have full charge—not that I'm not pleased to do so," she added as her nieces exchanged furtive glances. "But I had looked forward to a reunion with my sisters." She sighed theatrically. "It's been years now since we were together. Really, Jenny, it was too bad of your mother to be so inconsiderate. And as for your mother, Claire, I suppose it's understandable that she would not wish to come to London."

Jenny had thought it impossible for her cousin to look more miserable. But at her aunt's tactless remark, Claire appeared ready to sink right through the floor. Lord Fremantle cleared his throat, apparently about to change the subject, but her ladyship plowed on.

"As for Louisa"—she turned to Sylvia—"I really cannot see why she did not come with you. She has not the slightest excuse for failing to do so. And I should have thought that nothing in the world would have prevented her—" Her words were superseded by her shock as Lady Sylvia suddenly burst into tears, jumped to her feet, muttered, "Pray excuse me," and fled the room.

The remaining diners sat in stunned silence. Lady Fremantle recovered first. "Well, really!" she exclaimed.

"Perhaps I should go after her," Jenny offered.

"It might be wise to give her some moments to collect herself," Lord Fremantle reflected. "I expect that the long journey, plus the excitement of a London Season, are proving to be a great strain on her nerves."

"Well she's too sensitive by half if she took offense at anything I said." Lady Fremantle helped herself to tart.

At the conclusion of the meal, Claire pleaded the headache and fled to her room, and to her hoard of chocolates, her cousin feared. This left only Jenny to spend a dutiful hour and a half in the withdrawing room with her aunt, after which she got no argument when she proposed an early night.

But once she'd made her escape, she was in a quandary over which of her distressed cousins needed her the most. Well, at least she knew what to do for Claire, whereas her cousin Sylvia was an enigma. So, making sure her aunt was nowhere in sight, she stole down the back stairs to the kitchen.

Jenny found the servants grouped around the table at their own supper and was much embarrassed when they all sprang to their feet. "Oh, pray don't let me disturb you. I was feeling rather peckish, you see." Her face grew pink as she recalled the bounty of the dining table—which had been followed later on by a laden tea tray. "I'll just help myself to a little something." She had spied the joint and turkey, flanked by an array of vegetables, laid out on the dresser.

She was joined, however, by Mrs. O'Hara, the cook, who was surprisingly young and slim for such a culinary artist. "I'm sure you're welcome to whatever you see, miss," she said in a low voice. "But if it's Lady Claire you're concerned with, His Lordship has already seen to that. I sent up a tray just a bit ago. But His Lordship did ask, miss, that we not mention the fact to Her Ladyship."

"My lips are sealed," Jenny whispered back. "How very kind of his lordship."

"He is a most considerate gentleman," the cook replied as she carved off a thick slice of beef and placed it between two pieces of bread, then wrapped it in a napkin. "Best take this along for yourself, miss. As an excuse like. We didn't see the need to let the entire staff know, you see, that we were going against Her Ladyship's precise orders."

"Oh, yes, I do see," Jenny replied conspiratorially. Then she added in a louder voice, "Thank you very much, Mrs. O'Hara. This will be the very thing to help me sleep well."

She stole back up the stairs, feeling rather like one of the spies she often represented in her younger brothers' games, and tapped softly on Claire's bedchamber door.

There was a long delay, during which she thought she heard the rattle of dishes. "It's me, Jenny," she hissed through the heavy paneling.

"You should have said so," Claire said reproachfully after she'd unbolted the door, then relocked it. "I thought you were Aunt Lydia."

"Sorry. I should have realized. I went to fetch you supper, but Cook told me that our cousin James had seen to it already."

She watched with fascination as Claire knelt to pull a heavy tray out from under the bed ruffle. It made her wonder what else might be concealed there.

"Wasn't this kind of our cousin?" Claire's eyes moistened as she sat down on the couch with the tray in her lap. "And brave. I don't know how he has the courage to go against Aunt Lydia's orders."

"Well, it is his house." Jenny pulled the dressing-table chair nearer her cousin. "Besides, our aunt will most probably never know. I do believe that the servants are very much in his lordship's pocket."

"Even so, it was exceedingly good of him. I would not have expected such kindness."

Jenny looked at her cousin thoughtfully while Claire gnawed at a chicken wing. She rather suspected that kindness had been a short commodity in that young lady's life.

"Won't you have something?" Claire inquired politely as she helped herself to pickled beets. "There's certainly enough here for the both of us."

That was true, Jenny observed, as she politely declined the offer. The quantity was certainly not lacking. But she also noticed that someone seemed to have selected the food quite carefully. Lean meats and vegetables predominated, with fruit and cheese to follow. Certainly a far more wholesome diet than the ubiquitous chocolates.

"Tell me, Claire ... what did you make of our cousin Sylvia's outburst?" Jenny asked when the other had devoured the last crumb.

"I don't know what to make of it." Claire wiped the chicken grease from her fingers with a linen serviette. "But I was right,

170

was I not? She doesn't want to be here in the least. I can't begin to imagine why, but there it is."

"Do you think we should go see about her?"

"I think that *you* should go see about her."

"She's your cousin, too."

"Yes, but I scarcely know her."

"Well, you're as well acquainted as I am."

"But you're much better at that sort of thing than I am, Jenny. Comes of having all those younger siblings, I don't doubt."

Jenny gave an exasperated sigh and stood up. "Fustian. My own mother says that I'm totally devoid of tact. But somebody ought to look in on the girl. And better me than our aunt—speaking of tact.

"Well, good night, Claire. Sweet dreams." She leaned over and gave her cousin's plump cheek a peck.

"Do tell our cousin that I'm worried, too. I truly am, you know. It's just that I wouldn't know what I should say."

"Well, fools rush in. I'll see you in the morning, Claire."

But when Jenny tapped softly on Lady Sylvia's door, there was no reply. She opened the door a crack and saw by the moonlight streaming in the window that her cousin had already gone to bed. "Cousin Sylvia, are you asleep?" she called softly.

The only answer was a slow, rhythmic breathing.

There was no good reason for it, but even though Jenny gently closed the door again, she was quite convinced that her cousin Sylvia was wide awake.

Chapter Four

"I'LL TAKE THAT ONE."

The Honorable Jenny Blythe, accompanied by her cousins and chaperoned by Lady Fremantle and her stepson, stood in the ballroom doorway scanning the members of the ton packed together for a Wednesday night Assembly at Almack's. Her eyes had settled upon a distinguished, rather bored-looking gentleman who towered above the crush. Both her cousins, who had been viewing the Assembly Room with approximately the same enthusiasm they might exhibit if mounting the platform steps to the guillotine, giggled. "It doesn't work like that, peagoose," Claire whispered. "*They* pick us."

"Really? Well, what a poor arrangement."

"This is no time for funning, Jenny," her aunt scolded in an aside. At the same time, aware that they were rapidly becoming the center of everyone's attention as one clique after another spied them to turn and nudge and whisper to their neighbors, she managed to keep a fixed smile upon her face. "You must learn to curb your unfortunate tendency toward levity. It's most unbecoming. And as for the gentleman you've just singled out, no need to set your cap in that direction. That's Lord Dalton. The most sought-after bachelor in town. He's eluded all pursuit for ages. Indeed, miss, you aim too high."

"Well, a person of my stature has to aim high, Aunt," Jenny replied, sotto voce, with a perfectly straight face. "Never mind what the rest of the world sees in Lord Dalton. I'm attracted by the fact that he's the tallest man in the room."

Claire and Sylvia laughed again, bringing on another well-hidden scold. As she nodded to first one acquaintance and then another, Lady Fremantle's ostrich feathers bobbed above a cluster of curls that were definitely unmatronlike. Her smile never wavered while she whispered to her nieces, "Get control of yourselves, young ladies. I cannot stress sufficiently the importance of this evening."

Actually she had no further need to do so. She had done nothing else for the past week as she endeavored to prepare her nieces for their entrée into society. And, all things considered, she had done her best. No one could do more. She barely suppressed a shudder as she heard, or imagined, the gasps and titters elicited by the sight of her two outsized protégées.

Well, at least no one could say they were not dressed suitably. She had Sylvia to thank for that, her ladyship conceded.

Indeed, Lady Sylvia had demonstrated a decided flair for

172

fashion. She had overridden her aunt's determination to deck out her cousins in gowns becoming to the paragons in the Romney portrait. She had insisted upon a simple round dress for Claire, Urling's net over a soft gray slip. And with a firmness that amazed her relatives and made them wonder if they'd only imagined her still-unexplained flood of tears and sudden exit from the dining table, she had vetoed the lace flounces festooned with bouquets of roses and bluebells that the French modiste had insisted upon, substituting for them a tiny, twisted rouleau of satin and pearls.

Even the strong-minded Jenny had listened meekly to Sylvia's advice. She was wearing a white crepe gown with a three-quarter-length apron, which, coupled with the several bands of silk tassels that finished off the skirt, distracted the eye from the exaggerated length of the current high-waisted fashion.

Every eye seemed fixed upon the second-generation Percivals. Lord Dalton was no exception. From across the room he experienced a surprising twinge of disappointment. He could have sworn that he hadn't taken his father's raptures seriously, but there it was again, that familiar sense of letdown he always felt when someone had promised to produce the "perfect girl" for him.

"Oh, I say," a voice at his elbow remarked. He looked down to see young Reginald York-Jones, a fellow member of White's Club for Gentlemen and Lord Rexford's godson, staring in the same direction. "That can't possibly be the Percival offspring, can it?"

"Must be. They're with Fremantle, their stepcousin."

"Well, that's what I get for being bear-led by my father," York-Jones sighed. "Had a letter from the old fossil practically ordering me to dance attendance."

"You too, eh?" Dalton grinned.

"Oh, lord, yes. He made it sound like multiples of Venus were bound to appear. *Oddities* would be more like it."

"Oh, you're coming it a bit strong, aren't you? Granted they don't live up to their advance publicity, but except for being such a Long Meg, the dark one's not bad."

"Easy enough for you to say." The diminutive York-Jones

looked up—and up—at his lordship. "You've no need to be put off by trees. And I suppose you'll also add that except for looking like a fleecy cloud bank, the other one—Oh, my word!" He broke off with a sharp intake of breath as Lady Sylvia Kinnard moved out from behind her corpulent cousin to be presented to the Almack's patronesses. "Now that's more the thing, I'd say."

Lord Dalton silently echoed the other's sentiments as he, too, stared at the vision that had suddenly materialized. Lady Sylvia seemed ethereal, gowned in white lace over white satin. The high waistline accented her perfect bust. Her creamy throat was bare, as were her shoulders, except for the tiniest of puffed sleeves decorated with knots of pale blue ribbon. Satin cockleshells of the same blue color accented a narrow lace flounce that allowed the merest glimpse of her trim, ribbon-laced ankles and white satin shoes. Her hair was dressed in the French fashion, swept up to the crown and entwined with tiny white roses. Soft golden curls escaped to frame her face.

"She's—an—angel" the Honorable Reginald stuttered. "Looks like my hoary sire didn't exaggerate after all."

"Mine did," Lord Dalton drawled. "He led me to expect three of those. Excuse me, Reggie." He moved purposefully off to find a patroness who could introduce him to this vision.

Lord Dalton was not accustomed to being second best. But it took time to disengage Lady Cowper, the most amiable of the seven ladies in authority, from a whispered conversation concerning the latest royal scandal. Then the patroness would keep pausing to speak to this person and that as they made their way across the ballroom. So by the time they reached the chairs where Lady Fremantle had seated her charges, two other chaperons were there before them with swains in tow. Lady Sylvia was instantly engaged for the cotillion. Sizing up the situation, literally, Lady Cowper quickly presented Lord Dalton to the Honorable Jenny Blythe, leaving Lady Claire to the much shorter foot-guard captain.

"See, what did I tell you about our own Judas goat?" Jenny whispered to Claire as they rose to join their partners.

After they'd taken their places in the forming set, Jenny stole a glance at her partner, noting as she did so that it was refreshing to look upward for a change. This pleasant reflection soon turned to pique. His eyes were fixed upon her cousin Sylvia across the room. Squelching the urge to administer a swift kick, she cleared her throat delicately when the dance demanded their participation. Lord Dalton danced easily and gracefully for a gentleman of his stature, she observed. As a matter of fact, so did she. But she did not think for one minute that he noticed. After they'd completed the figure, they went back to their original occupations. He stared at Lady Sylvia; she looked at him.

But she could find nothing to read in his expression. He seemed almost scientifically detached as he silently watched her cousin's every move. Well, two can play that game, Jenny decided, and matched his silence with her own. But since he was unaware of her forbearance, this ploy left much to be desired. She went on the attack.

"It's your turn to say something now, Mr. Darcy. I talked about the dance, and you ought to make some kind of remark on the size of the room or the number of couples."

"Eh?" He shifted his attention, but looked at her without interest. "I think you're a bit confused, Miss Blythe. I'm Dalton, not—err—Darcy."

"Not really confused, your lordship. Actually I was quoting from a favorite book of mine—where the heroine also had a partner who wouldn't bother to do the polite."

"Oh, I see." He smiled frostily. "And did the gentleman in question grow immediately loquacious?"

"Sufficiently to make it through the set, as I recall."

"Well, then, I can do no less. How's this? Tell me about your cousin."

"With pleasure. Besides being blessed with amiability, Claire is remarkably talented. Musically, I mean. She plays the pianoforte skillfully, but her real forte is singing. She has a voice like an angel."

"Claire? I thought her name was Sylvia." He looked momentarily puzzled. "Oh. I see."

She threw up her hands in mock surprise and seized the opportunity to bat her eyelids upward. (It was disappointing to discover that this felt quite as silly as the other way around.)

"Oh, stupid me! I had no idea that you meant my *other* cousin— the one you've been watching like a hawk all evening. Well, then. Actually I don't know Sylvia very well at all. She has always lived abroad, you see. But I can say that she is very"—she felt a necessity to stress the word—"*nice*. And she's rather quiet. Shy, I suspect."

"Hardly a family trait, I take it?"

Jenny chose to ignore the hit. She continued her summation. "And she's breathtakingly lovely. But then you may have noticed that. However, I think you're a bit—old, for her."

He looked down his nose. "Hardly, I collect. I'm not yet thirty."

"Oh, no? Well, you could have fooled me. But then I expect that London gentlemen are rather more world-weary than our country types."

"Town-bronze may not necessarily be a virtue, Miss Blythe, but I never heard that it made one old before his time. As for your cousin's and my relative ages, I've always heard it was advantageous in a marriage for a man to be more mature."

"You do jump ahead, don't you?" She looked at him curiously. "Shouldn't you at least meet my cousin before posting the banns?"

"I was merely being hypothetical. Trying to refute your premise that I was too ancient for your cousin."

"Oh, well," Jenny sighed. "You waste your time, for I didn't really mean it. I was going to say that you're too *tall* for her, but I thought that observation would come better from another source."

"I see. And I am, I collect, just right for you."

"In inches, yes. Though it doesn't appear we'd suit in any other way."

"Nor in that." He was finding this pert miss a bit tiresome. "At least I've no desire to sire a whole new race of giants."

They were separated again by the demands of the dance. This was just as well, for as much as Jenny longed to wither his lordship with a scathing setdown, nothing sprang to mind. He, on the other hand, had no such handicap. "May I give you a word of advice, Miss Blythe?" he asked when they came back together.

"Why seek permission? It's obvious that you're about to."

"Here goes then. You've come to town much heralded, because of your famous mother and aunts. And since you're not at all in the style of those fabled creatures, it's obvious that you've decided to make yourself noticed by your clever tongue."

"I can assure your lordship"—Jenny's black eyes took on a dangerous glint—"that since the age of twelve I've never had to work at being noticed. That distinction was accorded me automatically."

"And I can assure you, Miss Blythe, that you cannot hope to succeed in London Society by impertinence. What might get you favorable notice in provincial Society will be more likely to disgust the more jaded members of the ton. We've seen it all, you see, Miss Blythe. And your attempts to be noticed can never hope to rival those of a Lady Caroline Lamb, for instance. So perhaps instead of aping the heroine of your favorite novel, who sounds rather tiresome, by the by, you would do better to emulate your cousin. The quiet—or shy—one, I mean."

"And you, sir, should consider taking orders. Then your bent for sermonizing would have a captive audience. I, at least, am now let off the hook."

The orchestra's final note had faded away. Jenny's eyes blazed as she returned a token curtsy to his perfunctory bow.

Chapter Five

LADY CLAIRE WAS FULLY AS RELIEVED AS HER COUSIN THAT the dance was coming to a close. Though her partner, the reluctant military man, was more at pains than Lord Dalton to do the polite, his attention had also kept straying toward Lady Sylvia. He, too, had some difficulty in disguising his relief when the set at last was ended.

Settled once again in her chair beneath the orchestra balcony, Claire was wondering if it might not be possible to slip away to the cloakroom while her aunt was engaged in a rehash of past glories with a bored contemporary. Just as she saw her chance and had halfway risen, a deep voice asked, "May I have the honor of this dance, Lady Claire?"

"Oh." She switched her gaze from Lady Fremantle to find her stepcousin looming solemnly over her. You don't really have to do this, you know, she longed to say, but quickly changed her mind. It would no doubt distress Lord Fremantle to have his motives questioned. She gave him a timid smile instead and took the arm he offered.

She did not entirely abandon her impulse toward plain speaking, however. "I've had no opportunity to thank you for your kindness, Lord Fremantle," she told him when they'd reached a point in the country dance that called for no participation on their part.

"Eh?" He obviously had no notion of what she meant.

She lowered her voice so the neighboring couples might not hear. "I was given to understand that you were responsible for having my meals served in my room."

"Oh, that. Well, yes." He looked embarrassed. "You mustn't think, Lady Claire, that I'm in the habit of countermanding your aunt's orders. It's only on rare occasions that I think she lacks good judgment. And then I find it's simpler to have a quiet word with the servants rather than a head-on confrontation with my stepmama. For I've learned she soon gets over these little crochets."

Claire sighed. "I don't think she will soon get over her shock at the sight of me. It's understandable that she'd wish to reduce me as quickly as possible."

"Not at the expense of your health." His lordship frowned. "May I speak frankly, Lady Claire?"

"Of course, Lord Fremantle."

"At the risk of giving you the wrong impression—for I can sincerely say that I've never personally had the slightest cause to complain of my stepmama's treatment—you must not take her criticisms too much to heart. She is, in certain respects, a very shallow woman."

At this moment they were swept apart by the dance. Claire felt almost lighthearted as she was led through a figure by another gentleman who concluded that the Beauty's daughter, while several stone too heavy for his liking, seemed a jolly enough sort.

When she once more joined her partner, Claire was loath to let the subject die. "How old were you," she asked, "when your father remarried?"

"Five."

"That must have been a difficult time for you."

He seemed to think it over seriously. "No, not really," he concluded. "Though I collect it might have been otherwise had I been a girl."

"Oh, really? Why?"

"Well, for one thing, I would have had to look forward to all of this." His eyes swept the ballroom with disapproval. "I must say, Lady Claire, that you ladies have my utmost admiration for your courage. I'd as lief ride into battle, I do believe, as to be flung into Society, willy-nilly, in this fashion. It's rather like the Persian slave bazaar, wouldn't you say?"

She laughed. "There is a certain similarity now you mention it. Still"—she sobered up—"it wouldn't be quite so bad if one didn't have quite so much to live up to."

"The fabulous Percival sisters?"

"Well, your mother does tend to go on and on about her come-out, doesn't she?"

"Indeed I was raised upon the story. It quite eclipsed Cinderella and The Sleeping Beauty, I must say. I collect," Lord Fremantle considered, "that on the whole it was a very good thing my stepmama never had a daughter."

"Well, at least she has my cousin Sylvia. This evening appears to be a triumph for her." Claire had not failed to notice the line of suitors who besieged the Beauty for every dance.

"That's true." Lord Fremantle followed her gaze. Lady Sylvia had just joined hands with Lord Dalton and the two were going down the set. "She has hitherto seemed refreshingly unconscious of her great beauty. I've admired her for it. I hope that this evening—and my stepmama—will not spoil her."

For some unaccountable reason, Lady Claire's spirits had

began to plummet once again. She thought it a good thing on the whole that the dance had now concluded.

Lord Dalton's frame of mind was not much better. He took note of Lady Sylvia's mechanical smile as he thanked her for the dance. And even though she readily agreed to stand up with him again later in the evening, he could detect nothing beyond social civility in her acquiescence. He was more than a trifle out of sorts as he went to lounge against the wall. His masklike expression effectively concealed a mood that came close to a fit of the sulks.

Lord Dalton was not at all accustomed to female indifference. Indeed, his chief problem with the fairer sex had been the need to ward off too much attention. Take the Beauty's forward cousin, for instance.

Dalton inwardly cursed himself. Why he'd allowed that tree-like chit to irritate him was beyond his understanding. A chilly setdown was more his style. No, not even that. He was wont to squelch pretensions with a haughty stare, coupled, if the occasion seemed to warrant extreme measures, with the elevation of an eyebrow. And yet he'd given that tiresome young woman a scold that he'd not even have wasted on his bothersome sisters. He felt his dignity had been diminished by the exchange. Dammit, her remark about sermonizing had hit home.

Still, though, he realized he would not ordinarily give a second thought to their conversation. It was not the Percival sisters' offspring, per se, that were ruffling his feathers. It was the situation. Though well aware of his duty (he shuddered inwardly at the ominous word), he had felt no sense of urgency about marriage until his father's visit. Indeed, few men were more content than his lordship with the bachelor existence. True, the age of thirty loomed rather large. But even that milestone had aroused no panic in his breast. His father's announcement had, however, been a facer.

Even though they'd never been particularly close, Dalton did have, he now realized, a considerable affection for his parent. And if it was his father's wish to see his son settled before he shuffled off this mortal coil, then, by George, he'd do it. And since his had always been of an "in for a penny, in for a pound" disposition, he was determined to marry his father's choice. He just wished that Lady Sylvia were more receptive. Dammit, marriage was bad enough. He was in no mood to woo—

"Good God, Dalton! You here at Almack's!" A drawling voice at his elbow interrupted his lordship's reverie. "I'd as soon expect to see our Prinny walk the high wire."

Dalton turned to find Mr. Roderick Chalgrove eyeing him with a languidly bored expression, seemingly the only expression of which Mr. Chalgrove was capable.

He was a handsome man, of medium height, fair, with shrewd gray eyes framed by dark, heavy lashes. His sartorial elegance and jaded manner were aped by many a young aspirant to fashion. The dandy had been on the town as long as Dalton. They belonged to the same clubs and ignored the same invitations. They had known each other far too long to even consider whether they were friends.

"Chalgrove." Dalton acknowledged the other's greeting with a mocking bow. "I'd say it was stranger to find you here than me. Looking over the latest crop of husband-hopefuls are you?"

"Why, yes, as a matter of fact." The dandy extracted an enameled snuffbox from the recesses of his coat, placed some of the contents upon his wrist, and inhaled delicately. (Several young men nearby covertly eyed this maneuver and vowed to practice the elegant gestures later on in the privacy of their rooms.) "I'm here by royal command you could say. My uncle's, not Farmer George's."

Mr. Chalgrove did not need to explain that his uncle was the one piper who could call the tune in his care-for-nothing nephew's life anytime he wished. Dalton was well aware that Chalgrove was heir to the uncle's immense fortune.

"Don't tell me," his lordship groaned. "The Percival sisters."

"*Et tu*, then?"

"Oh, lord, yes. Seems my father was badly smitten a quarter of a century ago."

"So was that entire generation, it appears. Well, let's get this over with and be off for White's. Where are the heirs apparent—or whatever you might term them?"

Dalton scanned the ballroom. "Hmm," he said. "Don't see

the trio. Perhaps they're at the refreshment table." Recalling Lady Claire's proportions, this seemed a reasonable likelihood. "Come on."

"I think you're mistaken," Chalgrove observed as he followed his lordship through the crush. "Nobody would willingly fight this mob for stale cake and lemonade."

"Oh, yes, but don't forget, there's also bread and butter." Dalton grinned over his shoulder. "Tallyho!" he whispered as he spied their quarry. Lady Sylvia was concealed from view by a bevy of beaux while she sipped the lemonade that they'd vied with one another to serve her. But the Honorable Jenny and Lady Claire stood facing in their direction.

"Where?" Chalgrove raised his quizzing glass and raked the company. All eyes, with the exception of the enthralled group around Lady Sylvia, were fixed upon him.

"There are two of them," Dalton murmured. "With Fremantle. And for God's sake, keep your voice down."

The glass moved in that direction and stopped, transfixed. Its scrutiny seemed to go on and on while the onlookers held their breath. The objects of so much attention hardly knew which way to look. Jenny, whose good humor had been quite restored since her encounter with Lord Dalton, was now beset with a mounting rage.

At last Mr. Chalgrove lowered his glass. An almost audible sigh escaped the watchers. But then the dandy whipped out a snowy handkerchief and polished the lens assiduously. He then reapplied the glass to his eye as though not really believing its previous evidence. The renewed scrutiny began at Jenny's feet, then traveled slowly up her considerable height, while an onlooker smothered a titter. Satisfied, Mr. Chalgrove then transferred his attention to Lady Claire and the glass traveled slowly from side to side. At the conclusion of this examination his seemingly nerveless fingers dropped the quizzing glass. It swung like a pendulum from its ribbon.

"Dalton, are you quite sure that these are the famous Beauties' daughters?" he inquired in a shocked and carrying tone. "Looks more like a cursed freak show to me. Come on. Let's go to White's."

There was a stunned silence. Claire's plump cheeks flamed bricky red. Jenny's turned white with fury.

"You can go to the devil, Chalgrove," Dalton growled under his breath.

"I take it you're not coming with me then?" The other smiled. "Well, suit yourself." And he turned to leave.

As he sauntered toward the doorway, Jenny hurried past him, seemingly intent upon accosting her aunt who had just entered the refreshment room. And at that very moment she somehow stumbled, sending the contents of the brimming cup of lemonade she carried down the front of Mr. Chalgrove's satin knee smalls.

The onlookers, who by that time were as synchronized as a Greek chorus, gasped even louder.

"Oh, dear, oh, dear." Jenny gazed with counterfeit consternation at Chalgrove's furious face. "How dreadfully clumsy of me. I do beg pardon, sir."

The gasps had turned to titters, and then to stifled laughter as rivulets of lemonade ran down Chalgrove's well-shaped legs to puddle by his dancing pumps. He shot the Honorable Jenny a venomous look, then whirled abruptly, and left the room. The laughter grew braver behind the dandy's back.

Lord Dalton did not join in the merriment, however. The look he bent on Jenny was grave. "I fear you've made a powerful enemy, Miss Blythe."

"Surely your mathematics are at fault, your lordship," Jenny answered, with an angelic smile. "It totals *two* enemies by my arithmetic."

Chapter Six

*L*ADY SYLVIA, WHO HAD BEEN POLITELY ATTENDING A young gentleman's conversation, was one of the few people in his vicinity who had missed Mr. Chalgrove's "freak" remark. She had, however, witnessed Jenny's "accident" with her lemonade and was horrified that people seemed amused by the victim's soaking. So when she spied the snuffbox he'd dropped during the altercation, she snatched it up and hurried after him.

Mr. Chalgrove had a good head start and for once in his life neglected to be languid. He had, therefore, reached Almack's outer doorway when Sylvia caught sight of him. "Sir . . . Oh, sir," she called. "Could you wait a minute, please? I think you dropped this."

Chalgrove turned, his face dark with fury, prepared to vent his rage on whoever had had the temerity to accost him. But his scathing remark died aborning as he saw a vision in white hurrying toward him with an outstretched hand. Sylvia's face was sympathetic as she offered him the exquisitely enameled box. "I collect this is yours, sir, is it not? It must have rolled beneath the chair during the accident with the lemonade."

If Mr. Chalgrove had been asked an hour ago about his attitude toward women, he would not have hesitated to admit that as a class he held them in low esteem. But there was something about this lovely innocent before him—with her look of unfeigned concern—that gave him second thoughts. He was not too far gone, however, to pick up on her words.

" 'Accident'?" he sneered.

The lovely eyes widened. "Why, of course. My cousin is not by nature clumsy, sir. But in a crush like that"—she gestured

184

back toward the crowded rooms—"accidents will happen." She studied his soaked smalls thoughtfully, with no desire at all to titter. "I do hope the stain will come out of your breeches. Thank goodness it's lemonade, not claret. If you will instruct your valet to make a paste of honey and soft soap and then dissolve it in a strong whiskey—or I collect gin will do in a pinch—then rub it into the stain with a soft brush, it should be good as new. Oh, but tell your man he mustn't squeeze or wring the material. He should simply let it drip. And indoors, not outdoors."

Mr. Chalgrove could not quite believe his ears. And had anyone besides the doorman been within earshot, his reputation for caustic wit would have suffered to the point of total extinction. All he could find to say to this naive miss—who honestly believed he would concern himself in such a domestic matter—was a choked, "Thank you."

"I mustn't keep you standing here." Sylvia handed over the snuffbox. "This is an exquisite enamel. You would not wish to lose it, I'm sure."

Again Mr. Chalgrove's riposte was another "Thank you" as he was leveled with the sweetest smile of his experience. And when Lady Sylvia had turned away and was hurrying back toward the Assembly Rooms, he continued to watch her with a stunned look upon his face until she was completely out of sight.

An unrepentant Jenny had returned to the ballroom, where she was immediately beset by would-be partners. More than one person had felt the sting of Mr. Chalgrove's tongue and were happy to see him discomforted in turn.

At the conclusion of the boulanger she looked around the floor for Claire. She spied Lord Fremantle, making his bow to some unknown lady, and his mother, who was still gossiping with her acquaintances. Since Claire was with neither member of the family, Jenny thought it best to go in search of her.

At first glance, the cloakroom seemed deserted. But as Jenny turned away, a decorative screen caught her eye. Sure enough, her cousin was seated behind it, nibbling a chocolate daintily, determined to make it last as long as possible.

Jenny had been quick to discover that eating was her cousin's

185

antidote for distress. "Oh, Claire," she chided. "Surely you didn't take anything that odious mushroom said to heart."

"Well he was half right, wasn't he? I, at any rate, am a freak. If you don't believe me, just ask our aunt. Or better still, my mother."

"Do you know something, Claire?" Jenny studied her cousin thoughtfully. "Self-pity does not become you. What you are is a young woman who is by no means sylphlike, but who is nonetheless extraordinarily talented and also pretty when not self-conscious. And who makes friends easily under the same condition. I cannot believe that you would react so—so—"

"Spinelessly?"

"Exactly."

"Yes, I collect I should have behaved like you and baptized him with my lemonade." Claire giggled suddenly. "Oh, Jenny, how could you? I expected all seven patronesses to converge upon you at once and march you straight out the door, never to darken these hallowed halls again."

"For an unavoidable accident?" Jenny protested, with an evil grin. "Why even Lady Jersey could not be so cruel."

"I see. An 'accident.' "

"Oh, yes, indeed. But a gloriously cathartic one. If you really had joined me in that libation to the God of Civility, I can assure you that instead of hurt feelings—" She broke off her comment as they heard voices.

"Really, Frances. You are rapidly becoming a bore."

Jenny had no difficulty in recognizing Lord Dalton's voice. She reached out a hand to stop her cousin from rising. The last thing she wanted was another confrontation with that gentleman. But then, almost immediately, she regretted the impulse. Anything would have been better than to eavesdrop upon a distasteful quarrel.

The unseen lady was obviously in the grip of a fury. "Oh, I'm boring you now, am I? You certainly were not bored when you took advantage of me and climbed into my bed."

" 'Took advantage,' Frances?" The voice was incredulous. "The only inconvenience was to me. As I recall I had to cool my heels for quite a while waiting my turn."

There was a resounding slap, and the listening cousins winced.

"Well, I deserved that," his lordship was heard to drawl. "I hope you feel the better for it."

"You are a low-life cad, sir."

"Oh, I agree. I'm certainly not proud of cuckolding your husband. So let me suggest that you start showing him more attention. It could do wonders for your marriage."

"Oh, so it's Gerald you're concerned with, is it?" she said, with a sneer. "My husband is quite well entertained by his opera dancer, thank you. As you're quite well aware of. No, you aren't concerned with either me or him. I watched you make a cake of yourself over that whey-faced Percival brat. Why, the girl's a schoolroom miss. Half your age."

Lord Dalton found himself weary of these frequent references to his antiquity. "Half my age? I think not, Frances. I'd only give myself about a dozen years seniority to Lady Sylvia. Which is not a bad thing for a husband."

" 'Husband'?" she hissed. "You're bamming me. You wouldn't actually marry that—that—"

"Beauty? I fully intend to."

The cousins behind the screen clutched each other at this revelation and were hard-pressed not to gasp aloud.

"And I don't know why this should come as a shock to you. You knew it had to happen sooner or later."

"I knew that you were a heartless swine."

"If you say so."

"I pity the woman—or child—that does wed you. And I wish you to the devil, Dalton."

There was a swish of satin, then the cloakroom door slammed viciously.

The two cousins had turned to stone. They stared, wide-eyed at each other. Then Jenny saw Claire's eyes grow even larger, more horrified. She whirled to see Lord Dalton standing with folded arms on their side of the screen staring at them. "Something told me that we had an audience for our little scene."

Jenny, for possibly the first time in her life, was at a total loss for words. It was Lady Claire who rose to the occasion. She thrust a packet toward him. "Will you have a chocolate, sir?" she asked politely.

The buzz of conversation died abruptly when Roderick Chalgrove made his appearance at White's. He stood in the gaming-room doorway and surveyed the assembled gentlemen with cool disdain. He didn't need the sudden silence to tell him that he had been the subject of their conversation.

Indeed he was often the subject of conversation in this, the oldest and most exclusive of the gentlemen's clubs in London. Since the great George Brummell had fallen out of favor with the Regent and departed for the continent to escape his debts, Chalgrove had stepped forward to fill the gap he'd left. Of course, no one could ever hope to be the arbiter of fashion that Brummell was; still, Chalgrove had succeeded to the point that his dress and deportment were aped by White's younger members. And he and his cronies had taken over the bow-window area, once the exclusive territory of the Brummell clique, as their particular preserve. Ordinary members, then and now, never dared to trespass.

Play had been slow throughout this evening as gambling gave precedence to gossip. First, those few members, either fresh from the country or simply shockingly uninformed, who had not heard of the Percival sisters or their daughters, had to be filled in on those details. Then Chalgrove's "freak show" comment had been passed around from the whist to the baccarat to the faro tables to be chewed on and swallowed. The majority of the membership found the remark witty. The remainder had found it rag-mannered at best, cruel at worst. Opinion was also divided as to whether the tall Percival daughter had doused Chalgrove accidentally or on purpose. The only area of agreement was that Chalgrove's humiliation was long overdue.

The members were not nearly brave enough to nudge one another or smile as the dandy made his way across the room. If all eyes tended to focus on the pristine whiteness of the evening's second pair of knee smalls, he chose to ignore the fact with a lofty disdain. Reggie York-Jones came closest to referring to the incident as he invited Chalgrove to join the play. "Didn't actually expect to see you here tonight." His impish grin died aborning, however, as Mr. Chalgrove made him the target of his famous look. "It being so late and all, I mean to say," the small man stammered.

"Late?" Chalgrove registered surprise. He swiveled in his chair to consult the mantle clock. "A mere half-past two o'clock is late?"

As a matter of fact, he was himself a bit startled by the passage of time. He had not realized that he had sat in his room for quite so long before deciding to outface his fellow members, most of whom had good reason to be delighted by the Almack's incident. "I can assure you, York-Jones, that there's ample time to fleece you before daybreak."

There was something feral in his look and tone that made Lord Dalton, who had been on the point of leaving, decide to stay awhile. He gave the dandy a questioning look as he cut the cards. Chalgrove's answering smile was enigmatic.

Cards were played for lower stakes at White's than at Brook's, a club famous for deep play. Even so, when dawn brought St. James Street slowly to life, the Honorable Reginald York-Jones found himself in debt to Mr. Roderick Chalgrove for the considerable sum of one thousand pounds.

"Oh, lord," he groaned at settling-up time. "My pockets are to let right now, Chalgrove. Have to give you my vowel, I'm afraid."

"Sorry, Reggie. I don't think I can accept it."

The other players paused in the act of polishing off the dregs of the brandy to stare at Chalgrove.

"Now see here," York-Jones sputtered. "I'm good for your blasted thousand pounds. Never welched on a wager in my life. It's just that my quarterly allowance ain't due for two weeks yet."

Dalton looked from one to the other. York-Jones's face was rapidly reddening at the insult. Chalgrove was counting his winnings, quite unconcerned by the shocked stares of the other players.

"I can let you have the blunt, Reggie," Dalton said. "That is," he added dryly, "if Chalgrove here will hold *my* vowel till the bank opens."

"Oh, that won't be necessary." Mr. Chalgrove waved away

189

the suggestion. "There seems to be some misunderstanding. I know that Reggie's good for it. I just don't happen to want his money. I've a much better way for him to discharge his debt."

The smile he bent upon the Honorable Reginald did little to alleviate that young gentleman's discomfort.

Chapter Seven

AS THE HOUR FOR MORNING CALLS DREW NEAR, LADY Fremantle grew more and more agitated. "No one will come," she moaned for the thousandth time. "We're ruined. You'll see." The words were directed at the Honorable Jenny.

Since their departure from Almack's the evening before, her ladyship had harped on this one theme. They had barely settled themselves in the crested carriage when she had burst into noisy tears. "You've ruined us," she had wailed at Jenny. "Oh, how could you? Don't you know that Mr. Chalgrove can make or break us with Society?"

"No, ma'am, I didn't know. The fact certainly doesn't speak well for Society, does it?"

"Don't give me any more examples of your impertinence," her ladyship had stormed. "If you wished to ruin your own chances—well, that's one thing. But to ruin your cousins' as well—that's unforgivable!"

"Now, now, Mama," Fremantle had said soothingly. "I collect you're blowing the incident out of all proportion. I grant you that Mr. Chalgrove is something of an ape-leader. But even he must know that accidents will happen."

" 'Accidents'!" Her ladyship was unmollified.

"Accidents," her stepson repeated firmly. "And even if Mr. Chalgrove is so small-minded as to think otherwise, I'm convinced it will not be the general opinion. I think the evening went very well, actually. In fact, I can safely say that my cousins' debut into society was a success."

Her ladyship sniffed. But the tears had ceased to flow. "Lord Dalton did stand up twice with Sylvia, did he not? And Lady Jersey herself whispered to me that his lordship appeared quite taken. And certainly his consequence is at least the equal of Mr. Chalgrove's. Or larger. Most definitely, larger. For if their fortunes are about the same—well, there's the title to be considered." She was cheered for just a moment, but then as the carriage turned into Grosvenor Square, she succumbed to the dismals once again. "Still, they're thick as thieves. So if Mr. Chalgrove chooses to cut us, I'm certain that Lord Dalton will follow his lead."

Good, was Jenny's private thought. But she was already too much in her aunt's disfavor to dare speak it aloud.

If she had hoped that the dawn of a new day would bring Lady Fremantle a new perspective, Jenny was doomed to disappointment. She bit her lip to keep from saying, For heaven's sake, do sit still, as her aunt crossed the drawing room for the third time in so many minutes to stare out the window at the street below. "No one is coming," she sighed. "What did I tell you?"

"Well, at least Lord Dalton's sure to come." Claire looked up from the tambouring she was engaged in to speak soothingly.

Her well-meant remark brought on a fresh outburst. "What a goosish thing to say. How can you, of all people, possibly hope to know what Lord Dalton would do?"

Claire reddened as Jenny shot her a warning look. "I d-don't, of course. It's just that you did say he stood up with Sylvia twice. And so I thought—"

"You thought!" her aunt replied witheringly.

Sylvia, who had been reading, or at least holding a copy of *La Belle Assemblee* upon her lap, closed it to try to act as peacemaker. "I cannot speak for Lord Dalton, either," she said mildly. "But I'm certain that your friends will call on us, Aunt. I do believe you've underestimated your own consequence in dwelling upon Mr. Chalgrove's. Why, several of the young gentlemen told me last night that their fathers had expressly asked them to meet us, merely because they have such fond memories of you and your sisters."

"That is true." Lady Fremantle preened herself a bit. "The Percivals still count for something in our generation. But still"—she quickly reverted to her former gloom—"the young men of today aren't like their fathers. They don't think for themselves. Mark my words, it will only take one word from that odious Mr. Chalgrove to ruin us."

If this was so, it soon became obvious that Mr. Chalgrove had not yet delivered that fatal word. For shortly after Lady Fremantle's prophetic utterance, a steady stream of young gentlemen came calling. Lady Sylvia was the magnet that drew them, as Lord Dalton discovered to his chagrin when he, too, entered the withdrawing room.

Although it was almost three o'clock he had struggled from his bed only a short while earlier. His eyes were bloodshot. He suffered from the headache. Calling on a green young girl, no matter how beautiful, was the last thing on earth he wished to do. To say the least, his mood was far from sunny. Nor did it brighten when he stood in the doorway and observed the gaggle of swains clustered around Lady Sylvia. It suffered a total eclipse when he noted that the only available place to sit was on a sofa next to the Honorable Jenny Blythe. Lady Claire, who was diligently tambouring, somewhat removed from the crush around her cousin, looked alarmed when he did so.

"Well, you certainly look like a dire warning against dissipation," was Jenny's word of greeting. "Have a late evening, did you?"

"You do delight in going for the jugular, don't you, Miss Blythe?"

"Not at all. In fact, I've taken your preachment very much to heart. What I really wished to say is that you look like the very devil. I was using restraint, you see."

" 'Restraint'? I doubt you know the meaning of the word. Did you, for instance, restrain yourself from telling Lady Sylvia of the cloakroom conversation you overheard?"

"Now who's dealing in plain speaking? To be equally as blunt, I'm hoping that won't be necessary, Lord Dalton."

"Oh? And why not, if I dare ask."

"My hope is that in the cold light of day you'll realize yourself how unsuitable you are for my young cousin. And then I won't be obliged to repeat what I overheard."

"Blackmail, Miss Blythe?"

"If you so choose to label it."

"I see no need to wrap your tactics in clean linen. I also refuse to be victimized. Say anything you wish—to anyone you wish—Miss Blythe. Eavesdropping is a waste of time otherwise, is it not?"

"I was certainly not eavesdropping," she said, bristling. "I'll have you know that my cousin and I were already in the cloakroom before you and your—whatever—staged your little scene."

"Concealed behind a screen. That's surely odd behavior."

"Where else should we tie our garters?"

"You could have coughed, you know."

"We could do no such thing. You and your *friend* were well into your row before you ever entered." She tried to modify her heated tone as her aunt frowned in their direction. "Isn't your proper fifteen minutes up?" she whispered pointedly.

"That won't work, Miss Blythe. I'll not leave till I speak to your cousin." He rose to his feet. "I think I can now beat my way through the throng. Good day, Miss Blythe."

"I was hoping you'd be reasonable," she sighed. "You should know, Lord Dalton, that I intend to do everything in my power to throw a rub in your way."

"And you should know, Miss Blythe, that you are sadly overmatched."

He'd never spoken a truer word, Jenny thought glumly as she watched him edge the would-be suitors away from Sylvia. Jenny was too far away to hear what was being said, although she strained her ears to do so. She wondered what Dalton might be like when he exerted himself to please, a condition she would never experience firsthand, she realized.

She was overmatched all right. He was rich, handsome— Here Jenny firmly put a stop to the catalog of Dalton's assets and dwelled on the one important fact. He was bound to be a total disaster as a husband. Especially for someone as seemingly gentle and sensitive as her cousin Sylvia. And it was all very well to announce that she planned to put a rub in his way, but how? Sylvia might or might not be put off by an account of the cloakroom scene. That men had mistresses was a fact of life. How Dalton had got rid of his would probably lose a great deal in the telling. You really needed to be there to appreciate the nastiness.

Well, one ploy would be to see to it that Sylvia was not left alone with his disagreeable lordship. And it was futile to expect any help from her aunt in achieving this end. Jenny had rejected the idea of telling Lady Fremantle about the cloakroom incident. She would simply be ecstatic over Dalton's declared intentions, never mind the reflection upon his character. She was already in transports over the mere possibility of such a match and was certain to throw the two together as much as possible. No, if there was to be any chaperoning done, she, Jenny, would have to do it. And from the way Dalton was smiling down at Sylvia, he was on the point of suggesting some kind of tête-à-tête. She had best move fast.

"Oh, Mr. West," she called in a carrying voice to one of the young gentlemen who had been supplanted by Lord Dalton. "My cousins and I plan to spend the next several days seeing the sights of London. We particularly long to view the Elgin Marbles. Can you suggest a time when we might best avoid the crush?"

Mr. West could do better than that. He could personally escort the ladies to Burlington House tomorrow.

"Claire? Sylvia? Would that suit?" Jenny studiously ignored the glare that Lady Fremantle sent her way. "Oh, good, then. That's settled."

There was a sudden competition among the other gentlemen present to offer themselves as guides to the metropolis. Jenny, who had spent hours pouring over the guidebook she had purchased for five shillings, began to tick off the places that the three of them most longed to see. If the young gentlemen were somewhat daunted by the prospect of having to drag along her cousins in order to spend time with Lady Sylvia, they were too well-bred to show it. Perhaps it was the formidable prospect of Lord Dalton as a rival that made them eager to pay any price for a few hours spent in the company of the nonpareil. Jenny was swamped with eager volunteers. She made quick arrangements for visits to Westminster Abbey, St. Paul's, the Tower, the Guildhall, the British Museum.

"Well, that should certainly keep us occupied for a while." She smiled politely, rejecting one gentleman's suggestion that they really should visit the museum more than once. "I do believe I've scheduled all the free time we'll have available for weeks now."

"You most certainly have," her aunt replied icily.

"And a deadly boring job you've made of it." Lord Dalton forced a smile—while eyeing her with a look that left no doubt he knew what she was up to. "As an antidote to all those educational excursions, may I suggest a spectacle at Astley's Amphitheatre? I shall be pleased to take you three ladies there."

"Oh, I don't think so." Jenny's smile was just as false. "It's kind of your lordship to concern yourself, but a spectacle seems so—childish."

" 'Childish'!" Lady Fremantle sputtered. "It is no such thing. Why, *everybody* goes there. Sylvia, you are sure to like it above all things. My nieces will be delighted to accept your kind invitation, Lord Dalton."

"Good. That's settled then." He rose to go, favoring Lady Sylvia with a charming smile, then bowing slightly to Jenny, a mocking gleam in his narrowed eyes.

Chapter Eight

"WELL, WE CERTAINLY DID NOT LACK FOR CALLERS," Jenny said brightly when the final visitor had gone. "It appears that your worries were unfounded, Aunt. Mr. Chalgrove has not sent us to Coventry. Indeed, I think things went very well."

" *'Well'!* " Her ladyship unleashed the wrath that had been building within her breast for the past hour or more. " *'Well,'* you say. Of all the brass-faced, forward exhibitions! How dare you monopolize all of your cousin's time that way? I'm sure that Sylvia is capable of making her own plans. And I'm also certain that Lord Dalton—quite the biggest catch in London, as if you didn't know—was on the point of asking if he might drive her in the park when you cut him off with your silly arrangements."

"Well, he did make it onto our list," Jenny replied mildly.

"No thanks to you! And you've given him no opportunity to spend time alone with Sylvia. Which was obviously his only reason for coming here. You should have allowed *her* to decide."

"But I don't mind in the least," Sylvia interposed. "Indeed, I think Jenny's plans are famous. I'd much rather that we all went places together than ride alone with Lord Dalton. I'm sure I'd never think of a thing to say to him."

"You wouldn't need to," Lady Fremantle snapped. "He has enough address for both of you. And you'd do well, miss, to recall just why you're here. Your objective is to get a husband, not visit every fusty place listed in that odious guidebook. And if Lord Dalton makes any alternative suggestions to the regimen your cousin has entangled you in, you are to accept his invitations. Do you understand? Not wish to ride with Lord Dalton indeed! What your mother would have to say to such foolishness I cannot imagine. But I can assure you that when we sisters made our come-outs we kept our eyes wide open—to recognize the best chances when we saw them."

"I'm sure that you did, Aunt Lydia."

There was no insolence in Sylvia's tone, but there was something about it that caused Jenny to stare at her cousin curiously. There was no time to search for nuances, however, for Lady Fremantle's wrath descended once again upon her head.

"I can only conclude, miss, that you are jealous of your cousin's popularity since you chose to interfere with her opportunities in this flagrant manner. In the future you are to make no more arrangements without first discussing them with me."

At this point Claire, who had endured as much misery as she

could bear for one afternoon, mumbled a quick "Pray excuse me," and fled before her aunt could direct any part of the scold her way. Her mind was upon the lovely box of chocolates hidden in her room. She felt that she had certainly earned one of the delicious confections. Or two, perhaps. She was hurrying toward her bedchamber when her attention was caught by the sound of someone playing the pianoforte very skillfully.

Claire loved music above all things. The chocolates could wait. She followed the sound to its source. Her stepcousin was seated at the instrument in the smaller gold withdrawing room playing Mozart with half-closed eyes. He appeared, in fact, to have been transported to some other sphere. It was some moments before he sensed Claire's presence in the doorway and stopped abruptly.

"Oh, I do beg pardon, Cousin Claire. I'd no idea that you were standing there. Did you wish to see me?"

"Oh, no," she breathed, then looked embarrassed. "What I mean to say is, please don't stop. I heard you playing. And it's so beautiful. I'd no idea you played at all, Cousin James, let alone so marvelously. Please, do go on. Mozart is my particular favorite."

He flushed with pleasure and then continued. She left her position by the door to stand where she could watch his fingers on the keyboard. When the last note had faded away, she stood enthralled; her eyes were misty.

"Oh, thank you," she breathed. "That was lovely. I play that piece myself, but not half so well."

He laughed dismissively. "Now you're flattering me, cousin. I'm the merest amateur."

"Oh, no, you are not," she replied earnestly. "That is to say, of course you are in the sense that you don't perform for money. But if you were not Lord Fremantle"—her gaze took in the elegant room as if to suggest all that his title implied—"you could easily play professionally."

"Not really," he replied candidly. "Oh, I'd like to think I could, with assiduous practice, acquire the necessary skill. But the very thought of facing a hall full of people would give me the horrors."

She nodded sympathetically. "I know exactly what you

mean. My mother was always pushing me to perform for her friends. But she finally gave it up. My fingers would turn to sticks from terror, and my throat would tighten till I could merely squeak. But it's a great pity that you should suffer in the same way. For you should be heard. You have the gift of taking a person right out of herself with your playing. It's easy to forget—everything—while listening. You should never stop." She smiled.

He picked up on her wistfulness. "Has the day been trying then? Jackson tells me that the house was fairly awash with callers. After my stepmother's dire predictions, I thought everyone would be in raptures."

"Well, Aunt Lydia was pleased by the number of gentlemen who visited. All to see Sylvia, of course."

Lord Fremantle gave her a sharp look, but there was no sign of resentment on her countenance. She appeared merely to accept this as fact.

"But then she turned positively livid at Jenny's behavior." Claire went on to tell him how her cousin had recruited Sylvia's suitors to serve as guides for all three of them. "It was obvious that Aunt Lydia longed to throttle her, but could think of no graceful way to put a stop to her maneuvers."

"But I don't really understand what was so terrible. My cousin may have been a trifle forward, but surely not so forward as to give offense."

"Well, Aunt Lydia accused her of using Sylvia's popularity to secure escorts for herself and me. But that wasn't it at all. Oh, Jenny did joke earlier about using Sylvia for a Judas goat to attract gentlemen. But it was only a joke."

"And a poor one, I'd say." Fremantle frowned.

"The truth is, Jenny was trying to put off Lord Dalton. To block him from a serious pursuit of Sylvia."

"I don't understand. Does Cousin Jenny want Dalton for herself? I remember she did make that remark at Almack's about choosing him, but I thought she was merely funning."

"Oh, she was. In truth, she doesn't like him above half. That's it, you see. She knows he's not at all suitable for Sylvia. Whereas Aunt Lydia is quite determined to throw her at his head."

"I'm surprised to hear myself say so"—Fremantle smiled crookedly—"but I'm in complete agreement with my step-mama. Dalton is, and has been for donkey's years, the matrimonial prize of London. I do not approve of throwing Sylvia at his head, of course. That's bound to disgust him, I should think. Far too many mamas have tried that already. Perhaps Mama should be grateful to Jenny for making Sylvia appear not quite so desperate."

"Is Lord Dalton so very rich, then?" Claire asked curiously.

"A regular nabob."

"Well, I still don't think he's right for Sylvia." She wrinkled her nose in distaste.

"Why ever not? Except for a disparity in years—Dalton's my age. We were in school together, actually, though in different sets, of course. But as I was saying, except for an age difference, I don't see why they shouldn't suit."

"Oh, I don't object to that at all. I think Sylvia might actually like someone a bit older. She's rather biddable. At least for the most part. I will say she has her own ideas on certain things, though. She vetoed the gown our aunt had chosen for Jenny's come-out. She said it was entirely unsuitable for her type. And neither Aunt Lydia nor that odious modiste could budge her."

Fremantle's lips twitched. "That does show remarkable resolution. But I doubt that Dalton would try to run over her roughshod. I must say I'm surprised, Cousin Claire, by your aversion to the man. Ever since I've known him, Dalton has been everyone's beau ideal. Just what is it you object to?"

The question was a poser. Even if the cloakroom incident were not entirely too delicate to relate to a member of the opposite sex, Jenny had sworn her to secrecy. "It's just that I've heard that Lord Dalton is a man of poor character," she offered rather lamely.

He looked amazed. "You heard that? Well, it's news to me. Someone must have been jealous to blacken his name like that. If I were you, I'd discount it as slander. I can assure you, he's entirely honorable."

"Even in his dealings with women?" So much then for propriety.

Fremantle looked uncomfortable. "I don't pretend to keep

abreast of such. But I don't doubt that he has—has had throughout the years—certain liaisons. But you mustn't make too much of this. While I can't say I approve of . . . certain conduct, I fear that if you eliminate every suitor who has had dalliances, the marriage rate would decline shockingly.

"No, really, cousin, I think you refine too much on malicious gossip. I will vouch for Dalton. If he should become enamored of our cousin Sylvia, there's no reason to be otherwise than pleased. Frankly, I'm more concerned that she will get her hopes dashed. It has happened to more than one young Beauty, I understand."

"Well, perhaps you're right," Claire said doubtfully. "At any rate, that's quite enough about Lord Dalton. Would you please play something else? There's still a bit of time before we need dress for dinner."

He was more than willing to oblige. She stood, enthralled, while he played a long medley of Irish airs. "Oh, that was marvelous," she breathed when he'd finished.

"As much as you love music, you must take advantage of your visit and hear some of the truly great performers. Do you like opera, Cousin Claire?"

"I've never been."

"You haven't?" He was amazed. "Well, we must rectify that. I'll speak to my stepmama. We'll make up a party as soon as possible."

"Oh, I'd like that above all things." Her eyes shone with pleasure.

"It's settled then. Now I expect we had better dress for dinner. If her ladyship is up in the boughs already, it would never do to upset her further by being late."

Claire hurried to her room, her thoughts filled with the coming treat. For the first time she was actually looking forward to an event in London. She dressed for dinner with unusual care. And it was only as she closed her bedchamber door behind her that she realized she'd forgotten all about her chocolates.

Chapter Nine

THE NEXT SEVERAL DAYS WERE TAKEN UP WITH A FLURRY of activities. Besides the outings Jenny had arranged, the cousins were deluged with invitations. But all this was prelude. Lady Fremantle was determined that her own ball should be the most talked of party of the Season.

She had a finger in every pie of preparation. Mrs. O'Hara had threatened to quit if her ladyship changed the menu one more time. The orchestra leader had been driven to exclaim that he was quite capable of choosing suitable music without her help. Had the Prince Regent ever complained? The butler informed her stiffly that there was no need to order more wine; their own cellar was more than adequate for the occasion. The footmen threatened to walk out in a body if her ladyship issued one more order only to countermand it an hour later.

But no aspect had received greater attention than the guest list. Every eligible male in town had been asked. Lady Fremantle had even scoured the country estates for possible suitors. When Jenny, who along with her cousins had been addressing cards till her hand ached, wondered at this, the curt answer was, "I think you and Claire might be most comfortable with some country squire."

"Well, you're probably right." Jenny refused to be offended. "A regular bumpkin would be preferable to this bit of town bronze." She wrinkled her nose with distaste at the next name on her list. "Why on earth are you inviting Mr. Chalgrove?"

"Everybody invites Mr. Chalgrove. His presence assures a function's success. He seldom accepts, of course. And after what you did, he certainly won't accept our invitation." The memory still rankled.

"Why ask him then?"

"Didn't I just explain?" Lady Fremantle's nerves were reaching the raw stage. "Everyone invites Mr. Chalgrove."

"Oh, I see." The three young ladies exchanged looks across the library table and tried hard to keep from smiling.

No amount of planning could control the weather. The day began with a downpour that later moderated but refused to go away. An awning was erected from the portico to the street, but Lady Fremantle was convinced that no one would show up to use it.

She was wrong, of course, a circumstance that surprised no one but her. By then her nieces had grown accustomed to the fact that she took the gloomiest view of all occasions. Indeed, it seemed that no one had disregarded her invitation. The number of guests soon swelled into a veritable crush, that uncomfortable state of affairs every hostess longs for.

The first indication that Lady Fremantle's ball was to be an unqualified success was the arrival of Lord Dalton, more elegant even than usual in white satin knee breeches and a white waistcoat, topped off by a black coat with very long tails.

While not quite as elusive as Mr. Chalgrove, he was known to avoid those gatherings where he was certain to be bored. But not only had he accepted the invitation to Fremantle House, he was among the earlier arrivals. Lord Dalton, as his former tutors could have testified, was not backward. He wanted no repetition of the Almack's fiasco. This time he not only secured the first dance with Sylvia, he engaged her for his supper partner as well.

Then, when Mr. Chalgrove arrived only minutes later, Lady Fremantle was beside herself. She was trying to decide whether to apologize for her niece's clumsiness at Almack's or to pretend it had never happened, when Mr. Chalgrove quickly put a period to her effusive greeting. With a curt nod to Fremantle, who along with his stepmama was receiving guests, he passed on into the ballroom. Mr. Chalgrove was closely trailed by the Honorable Reginald York-Jones who tried, quite unsuccessfully, to ape his mentor's air of world-weariness.

Unlike Dalton, Mr. Chalgrove seemed content merely to watch the dancing. He positioned himself near the doorway and eyed proceedings through his quizzing glass. The glass seemed to rest overly long upon Lady Sylvia, who was dancing a cotillion with Lord Dalton. Dressed in pale blue, she had never looked more lovely. When he at last forced his gaze away, he had no trouble at all locating the Honorable Jenny Blythe. She had no need to resort to the ostrich plumes that topped the coiffures of so many of the ladies present in order to stand out above the crowd. Even Mr. Chalgrove had to acknowledge that she looked quite elegant. The British net she wore over rose satin effectively set off her dark hair and sparkling eyes.

"Now." As the cotillion ended, Chalgrove gave the diminutive gentleman beside him the briefest of nods.

"Now? Right, then. Seems a deuced easy way to cancel a—" He caught Chalgrove's frown and broke off what he was about to say. "See you a bit later."

Mr. York-Jones began to elbow his way through the crush—no easy matter for a gentleman his size—to eventually wind up where Jenny had found a seat in one of the rout chairs that ringed the wall. "Will you grant me the honor of this dance, Miss Blythe?"

Jenny interrupted a conversation with the young woman beside her to turn and gaze into the eyes of a small, personable young man. He seemed to be having a great deal of difficulty containing his mirth. She immediately saw the joke and laughed back at the irrepressible pixie. "You are aware then that the next dance is a waltz?"

"Oh, yes, indeed."

"Then if you're game, I am."

She stood, feeling rather like a spyglass unfolding, and took the arm he proffered.

When they were positioned on the dance floor and he'd clasped her waist and hand, his eyes were on an exact level with her décolletage. A thought struck her. "You came with Mr. Chalgrove, did you not?"

The music cut off his reply, but no confirmation was needed. She'd caught a glimpse of Mr. Chalgrove leveling his glass their way. Lord Dalton stood frowning there beside him.

A miniature whirlwind seemed to have sprung up for the purpose of sweeping her into the dance. Jenny soon discovered that her partner possessed extraordinary skill, despite—or perhaps because of—his size. And she had taught too many little brothers and sisters how to waltz to be disconcerted by a partner whom she dwarfed. As they circled the ballroom, weaving skillfully in and out of the mass of spinning couples, Mr. York-Jones twinkled up at her, and she laughed back. All eyes appeared fixed upon them. Jenny was enjoying herself immensely.

"If you'd hoped to make her look ridiculous, I don't think it's working," Dalton remarked dryly to his crony. He had just admitted, grudgingly, to himself that the tall, willowy waltzer looked magnificent.

The other shrugged. "Well, it was worth a try. It's always difficult to give a setdown to a female. You never have the slightest notion of how the creatures will react."

"Aren't you being a bit petty, old fellow?"

"Undoubtedly. But one must find amusement in these tiresome gatherings any way one can."

"Well, you could always dance."

"Do you know, that odd notion had just occurred to me. Do excuse me, will you, Dalton."

With an exaggerated bow, Chalgrove left his station by the wall and worked his way around the perimeter of the ballroom. Dalton's face betrayed none of his uneasiness as the dandy approached Lady Sylvia, who was fanning herself after the exertions of the waltz. But he did not miss the shy smile she gave Mr. Chalgrove as he led her into the dance.

Lady Fremantle was none too pleased. She had been quite content to have her stepson engage Claire's hand for the initial dance. He was a conscientious young man and could be counted upon to do his duty by his cousins. But standing up with Lady Claire a second time went well beyond the call of duty. Particularly since it was no secret that Lord Fremantle loathed dancing. It was bound to cause a bit of tittle-tattle. Her ladyship decided to nip it in the bud.

Her eyes scanned the gentlemen scattered here and there about the ballroom who were unpartnered. They settled on a callow, spotted youth. She bore down upon him with a determined smile and ushered him across the ballroom, murmuring instructions in his ear as she did so.

"My dear James." She accosted her stepson just as he and Claire were moving toward the dance floor. "I cannot allow you to monopolize your cousin in this fashion. Mr. Brett has been longing for a dance." Her smile seemed permanently etched. "Lady Claire, may I present the Honorable Wesley Brett? Hurry, m'dears, before the sets are all made up. Now come along, James. You mustn't shirk your hostly duties." He trailed obediently behind her.

Two of her ladyship's bosom bows had watched the incident with interest. They gave each other knowing looks and began to whisper behind their fans.

Miss Blythe and Mr. York-Jones were well pleased with each other. They both shared a lively sense of the absurd, as they discovered when recovering from their spirited waltz. They found two empty chairs near the orchestra and sipped fruit punch thirstily while York-Jones kept Jenny in stitches with his comments about this or that person on the floor. As he spied Jenny's next partner bearing down upon them, he quickly asked to take her in to supper.

"I'd be delighted." She smiled down at him. "That is, if you are following your own inclinations and not Mr. Chalgrove's orders."

"Both, actually."

"Oh, well." She shrugged. "If a mere disparity in size can give that gentleman amusement, who am I to begrudge him his entertainment? It all seems rather odd, though. But then I expect he is. Odd, I mean."

"Oh, no, not really." York-Jones was ready to leap to the defense of one of his idols, but he was not given the opportunity. Jenny's next partner had arrived and was offering his arm.

If he'd any plans to resume his advocacy at supper, they were thwarted, for Miss Blythe seemed determined to take refreshments with her cousins. She had seized upon Lady Claire and the spotty youth who had dutifully asked to be her supper partner, and the four had joined the crowd making its way to the supper room together. Lord Dalton did not look best pleased when he reappeared with Lady Sylvia's supper plate to find Miss Blythe seated by his vacant chair. His spirits felt no lift when Mr. Chalgrove joined their group a bit later. "You still here?" was his less-than-cordial greeting.

"Can't tear myself away, as you see." Uninvited, he insinuated a chair between Lady Sylvia and York-Jones. "And since you seem the most scintillating group among all this scintillating company—well, even at the peril of my knee smalls"—he gazed speculatively toward Jenny—"I was determined to join you."

"Oh, I think you're at a safe enough distance, sir." There was a tinge of regret in Jenny's tone.

"I am relieved." He took a sip of champagne, his only supper. "But don't let me interrupt the merriment. Far be it from me to cast a pall. What were you speaking of when I so rudely interrupted?"

"Mr. York-Jones was telling us about Lord Alvanley." Sylvia spoke in a conspiratorial voice, directing his attention toward a group of the more mature guests gathered around their hostess. "He has had us in stitches."

"Oh?" Chalgrove stifled a yawn. "And which oft-told tale was it? The apricot tart? Really, Reggie, must you bore the ladies?"

"They may be 'oft-told' in your circles," Sylvia retorted, "but I can assure you, we were not the least bit bored. Quite the contrary, in fact. He was telling us that Lord Alvanley had a friend who hated staying in the country because the quiet got on his nerves. So Alvanley hired a hackney coach to drive underneath the friend's window all night long." She laughed—and looked enchanting as she did so.

"You're right, of course. That is a wonderful story. I stand corrected," Chalgrove said humbly. Lord Dalton gave him a suspicious look.

"Yes," York-Jones chimed in. "And I was just about to add that he had the boots call out the time and the weather on the hour." The others, excluding Mr. Chalgrove, joined his laughter.

That gentleman was surveying the assembled guests thoughtfully, too absorbed even to employ his quizzing glass.

"Lady Fremantle has achieved a sort of social miracle," he observed dryly. "Why, there are husbands and wives here together who I daresay haven't spoken in ages—some of whom no longer make a pretense of living together. It certainly speaks volumes for her ladyship's reputation as a hostess.

"No, let me amend that, somewhat," he mused on. "I suspect this in a sense a reunion for all those of a certain age. A harking back, as it were, to the glory days. For as our elders are all too fond of telling us, there was never a Season like the one in 1797 when the famous Percival sisters made their entrée into Society. Oh, by the by, Lady Claire, I seem to have missed your father in the crush. Surely he's here somewhere? After all, he was one of the fortunate foursome who managed to capture a Percival prize. I know he wouldn't miss this for the world."

There was a long, uncomfortable pause. Lord Dalton's face was granite. Mr. York-Jones seemed not to know which way to look. Lady Claire had blushed an unbecoming red. She was forced to swallow before she could answer. "My father is abroad, sir."

"Indeed?" Mr. Chalgrove's eyebrows rose. "Was he called away suddenly then? I could have sworn I saw him in Pall Mall only yesterday. But then, of course, I may have been mistaken. For," he added slyly, "I understand that he rarely wanders far from Russel Street these days."

"I think you're confusing my father with someone else, sir." Claire appeared close to tears. "His direction is Berkeley Square."

Jenny was trying, unsuccessfully, to think of a way to divert the conversation when Sylvia was suddenly stricken. She slumped in her chair, moaned pathetically, and weakly fanned herself. All eyes turned toward her. "Are you all right?" Jenny asked anxiously.

Sylvia's quivering smile was brave. "I'm just feeling a bit faint, that's all."

The gentlemen were all consternation, offering to fetch glasses of water and/or brandy; sal volatile and/or burned feathers; Lady Fremantle and/or her abigail.

"Thank you so very much." Sylvia's voice was weak. "But that won't be at all necessary. If I lie down a few moments, I'm sure to be myself again. These little—upsets—never last long. Cousin Claire, forgive my selfishness in dragging you away. But would you mind very much coming with me? You always seem to know exactly how to rub my temples when I have these little spells."

It was difficult to say whether Lady Claire looked more mystified or relieved as she rose to accompany her cousin. Lady Sylvia's expression was much easier to decipher. The look she bent on Mr. Chalgrove was censorious in the extreme.

Chapter Ten

MR. RODERICK CHALGROVE COMMITTED A SOCIAL SOLE-cism by calling at Fremantle House the following morning. When he asked to see Lady Sylvia, the butler, at his most starchy, was in the very act of telling him that her ladyship was not in the habit of receiving guests on the day following an all-night ball, when Sylvia herself came down the stairs and overheard. "Oh, Jackson, I will see Mr. Chalgrove," she called. Making no attempt to hide his disapproval, the majordomo opened the front door wide.

Lady Sylvia ushered Mr. Chalgrove into the smallest of her aunt's three withdrawing rooms and ordered tea. Jackson served them himself, exuding disapproval. After the butler had left them, Chalgrove smiled ruefully. "I'm certainly in your butler's black book. But I had to see how you were feeling after your fit of the vapors last night."

Mr. Chalgrove had spoken the simple truth. After he had finally gone to bed he had tossed and turned for the little that remained of the night, going over and over the scene that had led up to Sylvia's seizure. Every time he began to drift toward sleep, her parting look came back to haunt him and force him wide awake once more.

"Did I understand you right, Lady Sylvia? You're prone to frequent fainting spells?"

Sylvia looked embarrassed. "Why, no. As a matter of fact, I've never swooned in my life. It was simply the only way I could think of to get you to hush."

"Indeed?" He was, for an instant, his usual toplofty self. "Was I that boring?"

Her look was impatient. "You know perfectly well what I'm referring to, Mr. Chalgrove. You were upsetting my cousin Claire dreadfully, referring to her father in that manner. My cousin Jenny says you did it deliberately to hurt her. But I'll not believe that."

Now it was his turn to feel uncomfortable. "I merely spoke the truth," he said defensively. "I did see her father in Pall Mall."

"Then you should have stopped to think before you said so."

There was a long pause. The tea tray lay untouched between them. Mr. Chalgrove came close to squirming before her reproachful gaze. He caught himself wondering whether his mother, if she had lived beyond his birth, might have acted in just this way. He felt five years old of a sudden.

Then, remembering who he was, Mr. Chalgrove rallied. But an icy setdown, intended to put this schoolroom miss in her proper place, died on his lips. For some hidden reason he couldn't search for at the moment, he found her large, trusting eyes devastating. He tried to bluff.

"Lady Sylvia, I'm noted for my scorching tongue. They say I can level strong men with a single sentence. Indeed I've actually been called out on two occasions for rather witty remarks at which certain gentlemen took umbrage. But for the life of me, I don't see what was so terrible about mentioning I'd seen your cousin's father. If Lord Hazlett chose to dodge his sister-in-law's ball, I for one would hardly blame him."

"My cousin Claire would. As you should have realized."

"I should? Why in heaven's name should I have that sort of insight?"

"Oh, come now. You, like everyone else in town, have been

aware of all the foolish talk about the famous Percival sisters. And how everyone expected their daughters to repeat their triumph. Don't tell me you have not."

It was apparent to Mr. Chalgrove that no one had repeated his freak show remark to her. His relief surprised him. "Why, yes. I've heard a bit of talk," he admitted cautiously.

"Well, the whole idea is patently absurd." Sylvia picked up the teapot and poured. He watched apprehensively as the liquid splashed with her indignation. "We are different people entirely. My cousin Jenny, for example, looks nothing like the Percivals. I happen to think she looks much, much better." Her look was challenging as she thrust a porcelain cup toward him. "She's tall and striking. She makes the Percivals look . . . insipid. And as for my cousin Claire—well, you must see that her weight could be the subject of cruel jests. Her mother—whom I consider a *monster* even if she is my aunt—has made no secret of the fact that her daughter is an embarrassment. She would not even come to London for Claire's come-out. Now you have made it appear that her father feels the same. It was a cruel, even if unintentional, thing to do. I repeat, sir, you should have stopped to think."

"I can only say, Lady Claire, that I'm sorry." Chalgrove spoke softly. He was amazed to realize his words were true. They sat in silence, sipping their tea for a moment. Then he was overcome by curiosity.

"But what about you, Lady Sylvia? You've pointed out that your cousins don't measure up to the Percival standard. That leaves only you to uphold the family tradition, as it were. Well, it's obvious that you more than make up for any—err— variations—in the other two. I studied the famous Romney portrait carefully last night. And in my opinion you far outshine your mother and your aunts. So I'd say the Percival legend lives on."

If such a lovely face could ever contrive to look fierce, Lady Sylvia's achieved it. Mr. Chalgrove was startled out of his last vestige of aplomb as he stared at her.

"I, sir, am *not* a Percival." She tossed her head defiantly. "Nor have I any desire to be one. I, Mr. Chalgrove, am Lady Sylvia *Kinnard*."

Lord Dalton arrived at Grosvenor Square just as Jackson was ushering Mr. Chalgrove out the door. His lordship drew his watch from his pocket and looked pointedly at it. "For a high stickler in the world of fashion, aren't you a bit previous, Chalgrove?"

"Mine wasn't a social call," was the other's enigmatic answer.

"Can't tell you how relieved I am to hear that. It would be a pity if you and I turned out to be rivals for the same lady's hand."

"Oh? And just which of the young ladies would that be, Dalton?"

"After your tasteless remark at Almack's, that doesn't even deserve an answer."

"Touché! But the idea of you pursuing *any* female with an eye toward matrimony is staggering."

"The time comes for us all sooner or later. Even you are bound to succumb."

"Oh, no. I'm immune to that particular disease." The dandy tilted his high-crowned hat at a rakish angle.

"Well, let's hope the immunity doesn't lose its effect in the near future. It could prove awkward."

"Are you threatening me, Dalton?"

"What an absurd notion. I'm just pointing out that this is not the time for you to abandon your role of London's leading misogynist. Good day, Chalgrove."

The gentlemen bowed to each other politely. Both frowned as they went their separate ways.

Lord Dalton's intent was to engage Lady Sylvia for a drive in the park later that afternoon. Since he did not plan to linger any longer than it took to issue an invitation, he left his rig in the street with his tiger in charge. Right after the front door had closed behind his lordship, Jenny, trailed by one of Lady Fremantle's maids, returned from a ribbon-buying excursion. She stopped short to admire the high-perch phaeton. Lord Dalton emerged a few moments later to find that his equipage had disappeared.

He was on the portico—leaning against a Corinthian column

with fire in his eyes—when his rig rounded the corner. His tiger, dressed in scarlet livery resplendent with silver buttons, was contriving to look six feet tall as he skillfully maneuvered the perfectly matched pair of bays under the admiring eye of the Honorable Jenny who was seated beside him. The effect was spoiled by an involuntary jerk of the reins as he spied his seething master. He carefully eased the carriage to a halt in the precise spot where Lord Dalton had left it. The tiger's eyes were wide with apprehension as Dalton, slowly, deliberately, came down the marble steps.

"I wasn't wanting Your Lordship's cattle to cool off too much," the tiger volunteered in an attempt to avert the tongue-lashing that was coming.

"I think you can rely on me to see that my horses don't suffer. I did say I'd be right back you may recall. And even if you chose to disregard that—purely from concern for my cattle, of course—can you explain why you decided to take on a passenger?"

"Oh, for heaven's sake!" Jenny intervened, smiling pleasantly. "No need to fly up into the boughs, Lord Dalton. None of this is Jasper's fault."

"I can't explain why that fact fails to surprise me, Miss Blythe."

She ignored the sarcasm. "I've never ridden in a high-perch phaeton, you see. And I can't imagine that there's a more handsome equipage in London. No, in the world."

"No need to overdo it, Miss Blythe. I don't intend to skin my tiger alive. Only to see to it that he doesn't come near my rig for at least a fortnight."

"Now lookee 'ere, sir," the tiger wailed. "That ain't fair, that ain't. I didn't let 'er *drive*."

"That's the truth; he didn't," Jenny offered helpfully. "And I really begged him to let me hold the ribbons. I've never seen such mettlesome bays, Lord Dalton. Or so beautiful a pair. Why, it's like seeing double. I did quite long to drive them. And I not only begged, but wheedled. But Jasper was adamant."

The tiger, though unfamiliar with the word, translated the intent and nodded vigorously. "I said as 'ow she'd have to get Your Lordship's permission," he observed virtuously.

"That's true. So now I'm asking it. When may I drive your phaeton, Lord Dalton?"

"When hell freezes over, Miss Blythe." He held out a gloved hand to help her from the rig. She chose to ignore it, but spoiled the effect by catching her toe in the hem of her pelisse. He caught her as she tumbled.

"That was graceful," he offered as he still held on to her.

"Blast! That thing is high."

"That's why they call it a *high-perch* phaeton," he said witheringly. "And speaking of heights—" It was an odd experience to hold a lady in his arms almost at eye level.

"You do so at your own peril," she retorted, extracting herself from his support, a maneuver that took a surprising effort of will.

"You're prickly about that, aren't you? Damned silly, if you ask me. There are many advantages to being tall."

"For a man, certainly. Well, for a woman, too," she conceded. "Except that every advantage seems to be offset by the fact that ladies are expected to be inferior in every way, including stature. But my size is without doubt an asset when it comes to driving. And, I can assure you, I'm a complete hand."

His look spoke volumes.

"Spare me your skepticism. It's true. But I totally lack the power to persuade you to let me demonstrate. Whereas were I five-feet-nothing and could gaze up at you adoringly, I'm sure you wouldn't hesitate to put the ribbons in my hands. With you giving me the benefit of your *superior skill*, of course. Which I really wouldn't need since I drive quite as well as you, sir."

"In a pig's eye, you do. But never mind that. If it's any comfort, size has nothing to say in the matter. I don't intend to entrust my rig to Lady Sylvia, either."

"I can't imagine that she'd wish you to do so."

"Which is, undoubtedly, a great part of her appeal." He grinned evilly and vaulted up onto the maroon-colored leather seat. "Good day, Miss Blythe." He tipped his curly-brimmed beaver in exaggerated courtesy as he sprang his horses.

"Well, isn't he the regular red-hot tearer," Miss Blythe observed disgustedly to the world at large as his lordship shaved the corner on two wheels.

Chapter
Eleven

INSIDE, JENNY WENT IN SEARCH OF HER COUSINS. SHE FOUND Sylvia in her bedchamber being helped into a becoming walking dress by her abigail. "Our aunt wants me to go with her to pay a call on Lady Jersey. I think she wishes to revel in last night's triumph." Sylvia sounded rather less than delighted at the prospect.

"Well, there's no point in your staying here, since Lord Dalton has already called," Jenny observed, sitting down on the canopied bed. "For, according to Aunt Lydia, if you have him in your pocket, there's no more to be desired. And as much as I hate to agree, she may have a point. Have you seen his high-perch phaeton?"

This produced a chuckle. "You really are awful, Jenny. But you'll not persuade me you're mercenary."

"Not when it comes to jewels, perhaps. But, oh, those bays! You must see them."

"I collect I shall—at five this afternoon—for he's asked to drive me in the park." The abigail withdrew, and Sylvia turned away from the cheval glass. "I was coming to find you before I left to see if you'd go with me."

"Whatever for? You certainly don't need a chaperon to ride in an open carriage with a gentleman."

"Oh, I know that. But I should prefer it."

"Well, our aunt would not. Nor would Lord Dalton. Not that I care a fig for his feelings in the matter. It's yours I don't understand, Sylvia. Have you taken a dislike to Lord Dalton?"

"Oh, no. Nothing like that. It's just—" She hesitated, as if finding it too difficult to put feelings into words. "It's just that I don't wish to be on intimate terms with anyone just yet."

"Well, that is unfortunate, since it's the purpose of this whole come-out exercise."

"I know. But there's no need to rush matters that I can see. Please say you'll come, Jenny. It sounds silly, I know, but it's quite important to me."

There was no ignoring her intensity. Jenny capitulated. "Oh, very well then. But if either our aunt or Lord Dalton murders me, my blood will be on your head."

They were interrupted by their aunt who was, as always, the very picture of fashion in a lavender pelisse with black braided frogs and a matching bonnet. Jenny had to admit that she was still quite stunning, despite her years. It was just as well, she thought, that her own comfortable and countrified parent could not see her. She liked her mother the way she was, despite the fact that she no doubt now looked to be the older sister.

"Oh, good. There you are, Jenny. I had planned to leave word that Sylvia and I are going out and that you and Claire can play hostess to any callers who may come merely to congratulate us on last night's success. It will be good training for you both. And do try and persuade your cousin to be more sociable. Since she has destroyed her beauty through gluttony, she should work particularly hard on her conversation. Come along, Sylvia. We must hurry if you're to be back and changed by five."

Jenny sighed—and waited long enough for the pair to be out of sight. She then went in search of the butler. "Oh, Jackson, if anyone should call, we aren't at home." Perhaps it was only her imagination that he gave her a questioning look. After all, good butlers did not ask for explanations. She also hoped that good butlers did not report everything to their mistresses. It did seem a colossal waste of time for Claire and her to entertain Sylvia's admirers, who invariably made up the majority of their callers. It would be pleasant to have a few moments to themselves.

Jenny went first to her cousin's bedchamber, hoping to pass the good news of their reprieve on to Claire before she fortified herself for the ordeal with chocolates. Although, come to think on it, it did seem that Claire was not as heavy as she had been. Still, it was hard to see how the cracker-water regimen could be helping since regular meals were being smuggled in to her.

Claire was not to be found in her bedchamber. Jenny went

from there to the next likely place. Sure enough, she heard piano music as she approached the gold withdrawing room.

It was not her cousin Claire who was playing so beautifully, but Lord Fremantle. Claire was there, however, leaning on the pianoforte with a rapt expression on her face. Jenny looked at them thoughtfully as a startling idea struck her. She was turning to tiptoe away when Claire glanced up and spied her.

"Oh, Jenny! How famous! Do come in. Have you heard our cousin play? He's truly marvelous, isn't he?"

"Why, yes, he is," Jenny heartily agreed. "Do you mind an audience, Cousin?"

"Well . . ." he smiled. "I truly would mind an 'audience,' but I'm certainly glad to have you listen if you're sure you won't be bored."

Jenny was certainly not bored. Although her own compulsory music lessons had borne very little other fruit, she had developed an appreciation for the talents of others. "Oh, that was lovely," she breathed when he'd finished.

"Yes, wasn't it?" Claire turned toward her eagerly. "Did you know that Cousin James has promised to take us to the opera? I can hardly wait."

"How kind of you, Cousin. And did you know that our Claire has an exquisite voice herself?" Jenny felt rather like an overly eager mama with a daughter to launch. She did hope that she didn't sound it.

Lord Fremantle's response was all that she might have wished for. His face beamed with pleasure. "Why, no. You should have told me," he said to Claire. "Can I persuade you to demonstrate? Do you perhaps know 'Robin Adair'?"

Claire did indeed know it, and after he had played it through once by way of prelude, she began to sing in her clear, true soprano. Jenny sat through a verse and then slipped quietly away. The musicians were far too engrossed to notice her departure.

Lord Dalton did not bother to look pleased that Sylvia had included Jenny in their ride. In fact, Jenny suspected that it was on the tip of his tongue to tell her to stay home, but even Lord Dalton, she collected, would not be that lost to propriety. She returned a sweet smile for the darkling look he gave her.

Nor did he allow her to climb up into his phaeton unassisted, though he did look sorely tempted. But after he'd taken rather longer than necessary in seeing that Sylvia was comfortably settled, he turned and held out a gloved hand. "Do watch your step. I trust you're better at going up than down."

"Oh, don't worry. I've no intention of flinging myself at you again."

"Oh, no? Well, appearances say otherwise."

She might have known, she fumed, as she squeezed in next to Sylvia—who showed little inclination to scoot over, though there was ample room next to his lordship to allow it. The conceited ape believed she was in hot pursuit of him. Oh, well, let him think it. It must be reflex with him at this point, thanks to all the bird-witted females that London seemed to attract.

Lord Dalton appeared completely engrossed by his driving as he skillfully threaded his bays through the heavy traffic. Sylvia was not one to chatter at the best of times. Now she seemed to be put off entirely by his lordship's failure to make conversation. Jenny endured the silence as long as her nature would allow, but as Dalton steered his pair into the park entrance, she leaned across her cousin to inquire, "Have you been in some sort of brawl, sir?"

"A brawl?" He frowned, puzzled. "I don't know what— Oh." He touched his face gingerly. The skin below his left eye was puffed, beginning to discolor.

"Should I not have called attention to the fact that you've recently been battered?"

"Hardly *battered*, Miss Blythe. In fact, you should see the other cove."

"You've left him bruised and bleeding in some mews, then?"

"Nothing quite so dramatic. I did manage a leveler that took him to the mat. But only momentarily."

"How tame. Whatever happened to pistols at dawn for settling quarrels?"

"No quarrel, Miss Blythe. Sorry to disappoint."

"You came to blows then purely for the fun of it?" Her tone was sarcastic.

"Exactly."

"Well, if you don't choose to explain, I certainly will change the subject."

"Good."

"Surely, Jenny," Sylvia said, "you must by now realize that his lordship has been to visit Gentleman Jackson's."

"And who, pray tell, is Gentleman Jackson?"

"You really are from another planet, aren't you?" Dalton observed.

"Gentleman Jackson has a boxing establishment on Bond Street," Sylvia supplied. "Did you strip with Jackson himself, sir?"

"Yes, as a matter of fact, I did." His lordship was thawing.

"That's quite an honor, I understand."

"Why?" Jenny's tone conveyed her lack of appreciation.

"Because"—Dalton assumed the patient expression of a tutor with a backward child—"he's a pugilist. A former champion of England, no less."

"And you knocked him down? He must be well past it, then."

Sylvia tried, unsuccessfully, to stifle a giggle with a white kid glove.

Dalton whipped up his horses—as if eager to get the ride over with as soon as possible.

Chapter
Twelve

HE WAS SOON FORCED TO SLOW DOWN, HOWEVER, FOR THE park teemed with activity. It almost seemed as if all fashionable London was abroad, to see and to be seen. As they proceeded down Rotten Row, they were constantly nodding and waving to acquaintances in curricles, gigs, landaus, and phaetons, as well as passing or being passed by men and women on horseback.

"Oh, how I long to ride," Jenny sighed as they approached an elegant lady in a slate-colored riding habit, accompanied by a corpulent middle-aged gentleman who seemed several stones too heavy for his horse. The gentleman doffed his hat as they drew abreast, but the lady gave Lord Dalton a pointed stare, then cut him dead.

Without hearing the woman's voice, Jenny had no way of actually knowing, but she would have bet a monkey that this was the lady from the cloakroom at Almack's. "A friend of yours, Lord Dalton?" she inquired innocently.

"Obviously not." His lordship's mood was not improving.

Sylvia tactfully changed the subject. "I didn't know that you enjoy riding, Jenny. Perhaps our cousin could mount you."

"No. I hinted, but it seems that Fremantle doesn't keep riding horses in London. I gather he's not fond of the exercise."

"There's always Tattersall's," Lord Dalton offered. "You could hire a mount, you know."

"Not on my allowance."

"Well, now, Miss Blythe, if you're expecting me to offer to mount you, you're in for a disappointment. I've far too much respect for my horses to risk them with a green'un accustomed to empty country lanes. Riding in London is another matter entirely, I assure you. So save your hints for Fremantle."

"I was not hinting." Jenny glared around Sylvia. "I would not dream of doing such a thing. Not only would it be presumptuous, it would also be a waste of time. For as you should recall, I've already experienced your 'generosity' with your cattle. But I can assure you, sir, that I'm an accomplished rider as well as an able whip."

"Indeed? Do remind me to put your name up for the Four-in-Hand Club."

Jenny glanced at her cousin to see how she was taking all this bickering. If she'd hoped that Sylvia might be developing a disgust for his irascible lordship, she was doomed to disappointment. Her cousin appeared oblivious to anything that had been said. Her attention was riveted upon an approaching group of horsemen. She was pale as death. She might have seen a ghost.

The four mounted gentlemen were passing the phaeton, absorbed with their own conversation, when one of them, dressed in the uniform of the Household Brigade, reined in suddenly. "Lady Sylvia!" he exclaimed.

Dalton obligingly pulled his bays to a halt. The young officer rode up beside them while his companions proceeded slowly on down the Row. "I had heard you were in London." The soldier smiled. "But I had despaired of seeing you."

Jenny studied the newcomer with unabashed interest. He was exceedingly handsome, with dark brown hair and eyes and a brave military mustache. And, needless to say, the dashing uniform he wore did nothing to dim his luster. There was no way to account for the effect he was having on Sylvia. She was clearly agitated and made the introductions with difficulty. "May I present Captain St. Laurent?" Her voice shook slightly. "We became acquainted in Vienna. Captain, this is my cousin, Miss Blythe, and our friend, Lord Dalton."

The introductions were acknowledged and Sylvia, doing her obvious best to sound offhand, turned to her companions. "Would you please excuse me to have a private word with Captain St. Laurent? I can't tell you how I long to hear the news from home."

"Of course." Dalton did not look best pleased, but he jumped down and assisted her from the carriage, while the handsome captain dismounted. He then guided the phaeton off the carriage drive and onto the grass, while Sylvia and her friend walked out of earshot, the captain leading his horse by the bridle.

"If you don't wish to keep your horses standing, this would be an excellent time to show me what it would be like to drive a high-perch phaeton."

"I don't mind letting my horses stand."

"But wouldn't it be considerate to allow Sylvia time alone with her friend? They obviously have a great deal to say to each other." She looked back over her shoulder to where the twosome stood. The usually reticent Sylvia seemed to be talking a mile a minute while she gazed earnestly up into the captain's face. The soldier had released his horse. It was cropping the dried grass nearby. "I think it would be tactful to drive on."

"I'm not noted for my tact, Miss Blythe."

"How you amaze me. The captain's a handsome fellow, isn't he?" A wide smile brightened her face.

"You're really enjoying this, aren't you?"

"Frankly, yes. I dare say this is the first time in your heart-breaking career that you've been left to cool your heels while your lady enjoyed a tête-à-tête with another gentleman."

"Never mind all that. Who is he, anyhow?"

"I haven't the slightest idea."

That was not strictly true. She did have her suspicions. Ever since Claire had first intimated to her that Sylvia seemed reluctant to make an entrée into Society, they'd often speculated about the cause. Their favorite theory had been that Sylvia was already in love with someone. This incident gave some real substance to their surmise. St. Laurent certainly looked like a likely candidate. It was easy to imagine any female losing her heart to him.

Dalton was imagining just that. And while the possibility didn't cause him any painful heartburnings, he did find the situation irritating. It was ironic, at the very least, after maneuvering for years to avoid the marriage trap set for him by love-smitten and/or mercenary females and their mamas, that once he'd finally decided to take the fatal step, he should find the going so confounded rough.

He was sorely tempted to give up on Lady Sylvia. Except for her astonishing beauty, he did not find much about her to interest him. But she was his father's choice. And pleasing his dying father was now his lordship's main concern. Besides, the man who had just floored the former boxing champion of all England was highly competitive. He did not approve of being second best.

"Well, well. It is true then, that one sees everyone one knows on Rotten Row whether one wishes it or not."

Jenny's disgusted tone pulled Dalton out of his reverie. He glanced over his shoulder, in the direction she was looking, and saw Chalgrove cantering their way. He reined in by Sylvia and the captain and dismounted. "Were we speaking of tact?" Jenny inquired of no one in particular. "So much for privacy."

"One doesn't come to Hyde Park for privacy. You can't fault Chalgrove for his sociability."

"Oh, you're quite wrong there, Lord Dalton. I can fault Mr. Chalgrove for anything."

"You still haven't forgiven him I see. Small wonder, perhaps. But tell me, Miss Blythe. Have you met anyone in London you do approve of?"

"A few."

"Would you care to enumerate? I'm agog to know who these paragons might be."

"Well, my cousin Fremantle, for one."

"Hmm. We've been acquainted for years, but I'll confess I don't know him all that well."

"No, you wouldn't. He lacks your—dash."

" 'Dash'? Well, since you were at an obvious loss for words I won't belabor the point. Indeed, I confess I expected worse. But I was going on to say I don't doubt that Fremantle possesses sterling qualities. Who else has made your list?"

"There's Mr. York-Jones for another. I don't know about 'sterling qualities,' though. I suspect he's too much under Mr. Chalgrove's thumb to possess many of those. But he is delightfully amusing. I like him prodigiously."

"And I understand he's quite smitten."

"With me? Fustian."

"No, I have it on the best authority. Everyone's remarking on it."

"*Snickering* on it, more likely."

"Well you aren't the conventional couple, you must agree."

"We aren't any kind of 'couple.' But I am thinking seriously of him for Cousin Sylvia. I think they'd deal well together. Tell me, is he as rich as you are?"

"Near enough." Dalton refused to rise to the bait.

It appeared that Mr. Chalgrove had brought the reunion to a halt. He now escorted Sylvia back to the phaeton.

Dalton greeted him with a sardonic smile. "Ah, the ubiquitous Mr. Chalgrove. And to think I only used to see you at White's—or perhaps Brook's—when we're both in funds. What brings you to the park today?"

"Why, the beautiful weather." Chalgrove looked upward at the glowering skies that threatened a downpour at any moment. "And of course the need for exercise."

"It's beyond my ken," Jenny offered to no one in particular, "why certain persons refer to riding as 'exercise.' Surely the horse does all the work."

"Miss Blythe puts me in my place as usual." Chalgrove's smile was patently artificial. "You're looking especially charming today. That cherry color becomes you. But perhaps I should also complement Lady Sylvia. Your aunt informs me that she chooses all your clothes."

It was on the tip of Jenny's tongue to inform him that she'd brought this particular pelisse from home when she realized how childish that would sound. She must stop allowing every word he uttered to make her hackles rise. She returned a smile fully as false as his. "My cousin and I *both* thank you," she replied.

"If you slide over a bit, Miss Blythe, I'll hand Lady Sylvia up."

It seemed awkward not to comply and make Sylvia clamber over her. Jenny slid.

And it seemed to her that petite Sylvia was taking up altogether too much room on the carriage seat, for Jenny was jammed, shoulder and thigh, up against his lordship, a fact that did not seem to please that gentleman overly much.

And what was worse, as she had ample time to discover on the long ride home, the proximity was more than a bit unsettling to her own sensibilities.

Chapter Thirteen

THE FOLLOWING MORNING JENNY WATCHED FROM AN UPstairs window as her cousin Sylvia, enveloped in a heavy cloak against the bitter chill, hurried down the street. The weather did not seem conducive to exercise. Nor was Sylvia in the habit of taking early walks. And, what was more, Sylvia had ventured forth alone.

But it wasn't the fact that her aunt would fly into the boughs at the mere thought of such impropriety that caused Jenny to snatch her own cloak and hurry out-of-doors. She fully admitted to herself that she was consumed with curiosity.

Sylvia was nowhere in sight as she hurried along Charles Street. But as she rounded the corner she saw her up ahead, still walking at a prodigious clip. I should be ashamed of myself, Jenny scolded silently, for spying on my cousin. But her conscience refused to respond properly.

Jenny kept a considerable distance between herself and Sylvia, in the meantime picking spots to duck out of sight in case her cousin suddenly turned around. She also tried to think what she might say if she were discovered skulking along behind her cousin. Oh, Sylvia, I didn't see you up ahead, sounded rather lame.

Every instinct told her that this exercise had something to do with the handsome captain they had met yesterday in the park. For it was totally unlike her conventional cousin to set out alone this way. It had to mean an assignation. Jenny slowed her pace on Mount Street as she realized that the destination must be the circulating library. A "chance encounter" in such a place would be above reproach.

She dawdled outside, thinking regretfully of the books she might have returned if she had only known. But after having given ample time for Sylvia perhaps to consider it coincidence if she were spied entering the place, she strolled nonchalantly inside.

She went directly to the watercolor table, as though intent upon a purchase. Sylvia must not suspect she was being followed. Jenny glanced furtively about the room, where a sprinkling of customers were browsing among the items for sale. Her cousin wasn't there. She must have gone on into the library proper. Jenny chose a box of paints to account for her presence, then discovered that in her haste she'd forgotten her reticule. "Oh, blast!" she muttered.

"Tsk, tsk. Out of funds?" a sympathetic voice murmured behind her. She clutched her heart.

"Mr. Chalgrove!" she said crossly. "You startled me out of my wits."

"Oh? Jumpy, are we?" The gentleman smiled mockingly. He was looking unusually dapper in a rust-colored coat and pale lemon, tight-fitting pantaloons with matching buttons marching up the sides of his muscular legs. But Jenny was in no mood to appreciate sartorial splendor.

" 'Jumpy'? Not in the least," she retorted. "It's just that you slipped up behind me. What was it Lord Dalton called you? *Ubiquitous?*"

"Oh, there's no secret as to why I'm here, Miss Blythe. In fact, I can safely say that my objective is the same as yours."

"Indeed? I'd no idea that you are a watercolorist, Mr. Chalgrove."

"I'm not. You and I share another interest entirely."

"I haven't the faintest notion of what that might possibly be."

"Oh, I think you have, Miss Blythe. We both seem to share a penchant for spying."

The look she gave him was intended to be withering. He merely laughed. "It's a pity females aren't addicted to quizzing glasses. They are no end helpful when it comes to setdown looks." To prove his point he leveled his glass at her and imitated her expression.

"I know you have a reputation for wit, sir, but your humor eludes me."

"Then I beg pardon." He bowed mockingly. "And to atone for my sins I'll save you a bit of bother. Your cousin is in the next room, pulling volume after volume off the shelves . . . as though intent upon selecting a book for herself. Captain St. Laurent, who was here some fifteen minutes before her and kept consulting his watch nervously all that time, is going through the same book-hunting charade. But actually, they're in earnest conversation."

"Indeed? Well, I'm amazed that you aren't behind them eavesdropping."

"I would be if there were places for concealment within earshot."

"You, sir, are shameless."

"And you, Miss Blythe, are not entirely above reproach."

225

"You are also presumptuous. Sylvia and I are actually together. She simply came on ahead when I had to run back home a moment."

"To get your reticule, perhaps?"

"My reasons are not your concern, sir. Nor is it any business of yours if my cousin should chance to encounter an old family friend."

"That's true. Nor is it my concern that this is no chance encounter. You see, I happened to hear her ask the captain—quite urgently—to meet her here. And since it seemed unlike Lady Sylvia to behave so . . . oddly, I was motivated to discover what was going on. Though I must confess I'm still no wiser. Except that they're obviously much more than mere acquaintances. Perhaps you might enlighten me."

"I've already told you. He's a dear family friend."

"In other words, this business is as mysterious to you as it is to me. I suspected as much when you came skulking in here." He pulled his watch from its pocket and consulted it. "Well, now, Miss Blythe. I think we should be going."

" 'We' will do nothing of the sort."

"Well, I don't intend to embarrass her ladyship with my presence. I merely wished to satisfy my curiosity, not put her to the blush. And I really think it would be considerate of you to do the same. I don't think we should count on their being inside the library much longer. It could be noticed by the other book lovers. So shall I pay for that box of watercolors you're clutching?"

"That isn't necessary." Jenny put the box back down on the table. She hated to admit that he had a point, but she certainly didn't wish to be discovered by her cousin. Chalgrove opened the outer door for her with a flourish and they stepped outside.

"You don't need to escort me, sir," she said pointedly as they set out together.

"We are going in the same direction," he answered reasonably. "I could, of course, fall several paces behind you. But it seems a bit absurd. Could we not call a truce, Miss Blythe?"

"Why ever should we?"

He sighed. "Yours is certainly an unforgiving nature. I long ago repented of my sinful remark at Almack's."

"Good. But that's no reason we should become bosom bows."

"I don't ask for that. But is it necessary to be at daggers drawn?"

"Mr. Chalgrove"—she stopped in the middle of the walkway—"you are, they tell me, greatly admired by the fashionable world. And I understand that it's necessary to have your good opinion—or at least not to incur your ill opinion—if one is to be accepted by that fashionable world. Well, I must tell you, sir, that I don't give a fig about that world. And I certainly will not believe that you give a fig for my good opinion."

"But that's where you're wrong, my dear lady. I do care. Quite a few figs in fact."

"Whatever for?" she demanded.

"That's simple enough to answer. You're Lady Sylvia's cousin. She admires you greatly. And I greatly fear that I'm falling in love with her."

He tipped his beaver and gave a courtly bow. She stood rooted and gazed after him, mouth agape, as he strolled jauntily on down Mount Street.

Chapter Fourteen

JENNY HAD BEEN SO PREOCCUPIED WITH SYLVIA'S AFFAIRS that she had paid little mind to Claire. But as she went into her cousin's bedchamber to borrow a pair of eardrops for the opera, it occurred to her that Claire was looking quite nice indeed.

She was seated at her dressing table while the abigail made a final adjustment to her coiffure. And though far from slender, Claire had surely lost some weight, Jenny concluded as she observed her closely. The change was most evident in her face, which had lost a great deal of its puffiness. The skillful maid was helping the cause along by ignoring the current fashion that called for ringlets before the ears, broadening the face even further. She had swept Claire's lustrous blond locks upward to the crown and tied the gathered curls with a ribbon. The effect was charming. But the biggest change was in Claire's expression. She seemed alight.

"Oh, you do look nice," Jenny blurted out.

Claire rose and regarded herself in the looking glass. "It is a nice gown, isn't it?" she said, turning this way and that. "Sylvia does have excellent taste, does she not? She seems to know exactly what a fat person should and shouldn't wear."

"Oh, for goodness sake, Claire! Can't you learn to accept a simple compliment? I said *you* look nice. I wasn't speaking of Sylvia's taste in gowns. And I certainly was not making any reference to your weight. You know, you really can be most exasperating."

"Well, then, thank you, Cousin." Claire dropped an exaggerated curtsy. "Now, is that better?"

"Much, thank you." Jenny smiled. "I've come to borrow your pearl eardrops. That is, if you don't mind."

"As a matter of fact, I do." Claire was studying Jenny's cream-colored gown thoughtfully. "I think my garnets would suit better." She rummaged in her jewelry box, produced them, and held one up to her cousin's ear. "Oh, yes. I was right. These will be the very thing. See?" She laughed. "I haven't watched our cousin Sylvia in action for all this time and learned nothing."

"Heaven help me," Jenny groaned as she fastened the jewels in her ears and stood back to survey the results. "I'm sure you're right. But how I'm going to survive two arbiters of fashion is beyond me. I'll never be allowed to leave the house."

"You goosecap. It's just that I wish this evening to be absolutely perfect. In every detail. Oh, Jenny, I can't tell you how excited I am. I've longed all my life to attend the opera. Isn't it famous of Cousin James to take us?"

"Oh, yes, indeed." Jenny refrained from saying that at least a half-dozen other gentlemen had made the same offer. She, too, wanted Claire's evening to be perfect.

* * *

It had been Lord Fremantle's intent to limit the opera evening to a family party. His stepmama was having none of that, however. First and foremost, Lord Dalton must be included for Sylvia. Mr. York-Jones would do for Jenny. Their disparate heights did make them an absurd-looking couple, but they seemed to get on well together and York-Jones could be depended upon to enliven the dullest of parties. What's more, his antecedents were impeccable. His father had fallen head over heels in love with her in '97. And, she mused on, Sir Bertram Philpott, the spotty young man from Almack's, would do nicely for Claire. That left Lord Fremantle, of course, to be her escort. If her stepson found any fault with these arrangements, he kept it strictly to himself.

Jenny, however, was not so biddable. On the way to the Haymarket she managed to put a flea in York-Jones's ear. So when they took their places in a box overlooking the stage of the opera house, she somehow managed to commandeer Sir Bertram—while York-Jones firmly attached himself to Lady Fremantle. This left the two music lovers together to enjoy the performance.

She was only sorry that the twosome were relegated to the back of the box along with herself and her overawed escort. Fremantle had at least seen to it that Claire sat behind petite Sylvia, and she declared, with shining eyes, that she had a wonderful view of the stage. Lord Dalton had then obligingly offered her his seat, but under the influence of Jenny's glare had not insisted when Claire politely refused the trade.

Jenny took advantage of the opera glasses that her host provided to drink in the grandeur of the building. It had been redone by Nash and Repton only a few years previously and was a tribute to their superior taste and style. She quickly counted five tiers of boxes, surmounted by a gallery, then turned to admire the proportions of the enormous stage with the orchestra recessed in front of it. She noted the painted horse and chariot galloping on clouds within the dome and the intricate plaster work that ringed this ceiling painting. After admiring the rich red curtains and the candelabra that extended in rows above the boxes, she then felt free to peruse the audience.

She was marveling at all the finery—the plumes, the jewels,

the gowns that surely even Paris could not surpass—when her glass ceased its pilgrimage with a sudden jerk, then leaped back to confirm what it had just glimpsed.

Sure enough, there sat Mr. Chalgrove in the same tier, almost opposite them, across the wide expanse of auditorium. And it came as no surprise that he was surveying their party through his quizzing glass. She quickly lowered her own glass, feeling a bit foolish. But she had already identified his partner. It was the haughty beauty from the park, the lady who had cut Lord Dalton dead.

The orchestra struck up the overture just then, but failed to capture Jenny's attention. She kept thinking about Mr. Chalgrove across the way. There was no use pretending that his presence here was mere coincidence. It was obvious that he was following Sylvia. Jenny was not at all pleased with this further evidence of his devotion. She soon succumbed to the magic taking place onstage, however, and by the first interval was almost as enraptured as Claire.

The party then decided to leave their box and stretch their legs a bit. Jenny was surprised to find Lord Dalton at her elbow. Sylvia had joined Sir Bertram and was concerned with setting the awkward young man at ease, which Jenny, in her preoccupation, had failed to do. "Enjoying yourself, Miss Blythe?" Dalton inquired politely as they strolled behind the other two down the crowded corridor.

"Why, yes, as a matter of fact," she answered. "And you?"

"Let's just say that I find *Figaro* less of a dead bore than most operas. And I've had other things as well to intrigue me."

"Indeed? I trust you plan to elaborate."

"Most assuredly. I've become somewhat accustomed to your high-handedness. And I'm well aware that you bear-lead your cousins shamelessly—"

"I do no such thing!" she interrupted.

"Shamelessly. You put even the most scheming mamas I have met—and believe me, I've met quite a few of them—to the blush. So I was most admiring of the way you sorted out our party, commandeering young Bertram and palming York-Jones off onto your aunt. All in aid of seeing to it that Fremantle and your cousin Claire could be together. Am I right?"

"Absolutely. And I'm not the least bit ashamed of it."

"I didn't suppose you would be."

"Fremantle arranged this outing for Claire's benefit. They are both talented musicians. It was only fair that they enjoy the performance together."

"Oh, I heartily concur. But what surprises me is that you failed to separate Lady Sylvia and myself. Don't tell me it proved too much for your generalship. I'll be sorely disappointed. Why, there are all sorts of possibilities. You could have attached yourself to me, leaving Lady Sylvia to deal with Sir Bertram. Which she's doing famously, isn't she?" He looked admiringly at the couple ahead. The young man had emerged from his shell and was talking a mile a minute. "Look at her. She appears to be hanging on that young pup's every word."

"She doesn't 'appear to be,' she is. I told you that Sylvia is nice."

"All the more puzzling why you didn't try and come between us this evening."

"To be quite candid—"

"Are you ever otherwise?"

"To be candid, I thought parting you two might well be the final straw where my aunt's good nature was concerned. But more to the point, I wasn't sure it was advisable."

"My God!" He came to a sudden halt. A gentleman behind bumped into him and apologized. "Don't tell me I've gained your approval?"

"Well . . ." she temporized, "let's just say you're the lesser evil. I think you're to be preferred over your chief rival."

" 'Chief rival'?" He looked puzzled for a moment. "Oh, you mean Chalgrove."

"I'm afraid so."

"It's odd. He was never in the petticoat line before, but he does appear to be smitten. He's certainly developed the habit of turning up everywhere we go."

"Then you know he's here tonight."

"Oh, yes, indeed. And I also know who's with him." He looked grim. "I've been expecting a visit momentarily. That's the sort of thing Chalgrove has always delighted in—throwing

231

the cat among the pigeons, as it were. Heretofore he's never needed a reason to make mischief. God knows the lengths he may go to in order to put me out of the running." He grinned suddenly. "This should prove interesting."

"I don't see anything amusing in the situation. I certainly don't wish my cousin to become entangled with him."

"I hope this doesn't mean you're about to sponsor me in the lists. Something tells me that could be fatal. Or perhaps I just have a natural aversion to becoming one of your pawns."

"I wouldn't dream of pushing your suit." She grimaced with distaste. "Just because I find you preferable to Mr. Chalgrove doesn't mean I think you'd be ideal husband material. Of course"—she brightened up—"if you two become rivals and go to any lengths to cut each other out, there's always the chance Sylvia may form a disgust of you both."

"How charming of you to point the possibility out." He dropped his bantering tone and turned serious. "I shouldn't wonder if we're neither one in the running, though. I'll own I'm more than a bit curious about the military cove she met in the park when we took our drive. She seemed most upset by the encounter. I wonder if he's the rival I should fear, not Chalgrove. What do you think, Miss Blythe?"

Sylvia and Sir Bertram turned at that moment to join them, and Jenny was prevented from having to reply. Which was just as well, for she hadn't the slightest notion of how to answer Dalton. She, too, was convinced that there was a romantic involvement between Sylvia and the military stranger. She was also convinced that the handsome soldier had to be in some way unsuitable or Sylvia would not be tearing herself apart over him, as was so obviously the case.

Lord Dalton and Sir Bertram changed places as they strolled back to their box. Jenny was too preoccupied to do the polite, and Sir Bertram lost all his newly acquired vivaciousness. At the second interval, Dalton's prediction came true. Mr. Chalgrove arrived at the Fremantle box just as the party had risen to leave it. Jenny gazed curiously but, she hoped, covertly at the lady with him. Though well beyond the first blush of youth, she was certainly handsome, fairly tall, although not in Jenny's class, with titian hair, and hazel eyes bordering on green. She was beautifully and expensively dressed and fairly blazed with diamonds. Jenny wondered if the elaborate necklace that she wore was intended to draw attention away from—or to—her rather daring décolletage.

There was no need to present Lady Warrington to Lord and Lady Fremantle or Lord Dalton, to whom Lady Warrington gave only the briefest of nods. But she declared herself in raptures at finally meeting the three cousins. "I can't tell you how I've longed to know the celebrated Percival progeny. I can assure you, London talks of little else."

I don't doubt it for a minute, Jenny thought darkly. And I'll wager that Lord Dalton's castaway is about to tell us exactly what they're saying.

"Now let me sort you out," Lady Warrington continued. "You're one of the twins' daughters, am I not right?" She smiled falsely at Jenny, who merely nodded. "But surely the resemblance is slight? At least I can't recall it being said that the Percivals were above the average. Oh, dear. I did not mean— What a rackety thing to say." Her laugh was brittle. "I referred only to stature, needless to say. You must have inherited your height from your father."

"No, ma'am. My father, like the Percivals, is little above the average. I'm the family anomaly." Jenny's smile was fully as false as her ladyship's.

"Now, then, let me see." Lady Warrington turned her attention to Claire. "You're Lord Hazlett's daughter, then. I find it so charming the way he quite dotes on the little ones. But then I collect it's quite typical of gentlemen who come to fatherhood late in life. It's pride in their own prowess that makes them so foolish over their offspring I've no doubt."

Lady Fremantle gave a little gasp. Lord Fremantle did not change expression, but moved a bit closer to Lady Claire. Dalton could have been contemplating murder, while Mr. Chalgrove, for possibly the first time in his life, looked out of countenance.

"I—I beg pardon," Claire stammered, "but I've really no notion of what you're talking about."

Jenny, all too aware of the currents swirling around them, quickly intervened. "I think you've confused me and my

233

cousin, Lady Warrington. It's *my* father who has the young children. And, yes, he is extremely foolish over them. But I'm not at all sure that age is a factor. He actually dotes on us older ones as well."

"My mistake." Lady Warrington looked well satisfied with the effect she was creating. But she had been saving her best for last. "And I'm particularly delighted to meet you at last, Lady Sylvia. All London seems to be at your feet. Why, I understand you've even managed to enslave Dalton here. How odd to hear he's lost his heart when it was the consensus that he didn't have one. But then, when one has been on the town as long as he has and played the field so tirelessly, I suppose he was finally bound to settle down—from sheer fatigue." Her laugh appeared to taunt him. He stared back at her with folded arms, his face expressionless. "But it is quite plain, Lady Sylvia," she continued, "that you're destined to perpetuate the legend of the beautiful Percival sisters . . . who cast all those poor, unfortunate debutantes of their Season in the shade."

"Oh, come now, Lady Warrington, I'm sure that you exaggerate." Jenny smiled. "I know the Percivals had a reputation for beauty, but I'll not believe that they could cast *you* in the shade."

There was a pregnant silence. Then the Honorable York-Jones snickered. Two bright spots, not accounted for by the rouge pot, burned on Lady Warrington's cheeks. "If you are implying that I was present at that come-out, I can assure you I was in leading strings at the time."

"Oh, dear. Really? Well then I have made a faux pas, haven't I? You must forgive me. The mistake is understandable. It's not that you look so very old, Lady Warrington, it's just that our aunt here looks so very young. It totally confuses one's perspective."

"Well, Emily, m'dear," Mr. Chalgrove murmured, "the orchestra is tuning up. I do believe we should be going and leave the field in Miss Blythe's possession." And with a rueful backward look at Lady Sylvia, who returned it with one of deep reproach, he whisked Lady Warrington from the box.

"What a perfectly odious female." Lord Fremantle seemed to speak for them all.

"Yes, but our Miss Blythe certainly spiked her guns." York-Jones grinned appreciatively.

"Indeed she did!" Lady Fremantle nodded with satisfaction, setting the purple plumes that adorned her hair into vigorous motion. "I may have reproved you in the past for your unruly tongue, Jenny, but this time I must applaud you. Lady Warrington richly deserved the setdown. I only regret it wasn't worse."

Jenny smiled rather weakly. While it was certainly refreshing to be in her aunt's good graces for a change, she could almost wish she might recall the words she'd spoken. She glanced at Lord Dalton, whose granite face, she was quite sure, masked a seething fury. She suspected that losing him was punishment enough for the spiteful Emily Warrington. It had been quite superfluous to drive another stake into that lady's heart.

Chapter Fifteen

THE COUSINS COULD BY THIS TIME HAVE WRITTEN THEIR own tourist's guide to London. Jenny's sight-seeing program had been quite a success, from the Tower of London to an exhibition in the Royal Academy. The various young men whom she'd recruited on the day after their introduction to Almack's had, for the most part, proved delightful escorts. Now it was the turn of Lord Dalton and Astley's Royal Circus.

Jenny thought he'd made an odd choice and called up to him to say so. He merely shrugged and waited a moment to answer as he guided his barouche between a loaded cart that had stopped without any warning and an oncoming yellow-and-black hackney.

Others might find it rather eccentric for his lordship to serve as his own coachman, with his tiger as postillion, but Jenny could not find it in her heart to blame him. Not only did it spare him the necessity of entertaining three females, the carriage itself must be a joy to drive. It was fit for royalty. She was almost inclined to nod and wave at the pedestrians that stared their way as they tooled down Piccadilly.

"I had thought you needed a rest after all that culture," Dalton said over his shoulder once he'd completed his deft maneuver through the traffic.

The cousins were soon delighted with his choice. After they'd taken their places on the second tier, which afforded the best possible view of the extravaganza, Claire declared that the amphitheater was almost as elegant as the opera house, high praise indeed from her.

Lord Dalton, mindful of his role as tour guide, informed them that the stage was the largest in England, a necessity for the grand spectacles performed there. Astley's was also particularly proud of its lighting. A magnificent glass chandelier was suspended over the circular arena and contained no less than fifty patent lamps.

The audience was certainly more diverse than at the opera. People of all classes were crowded into the huge theater. And there were, of course, a large number of children, transformed into jumping jacks with anticipation. Their excitement seemed contagious, for the crowd as a whole was boisterous though good-natured.

"Oh, this does look like fun!" Jenny leaned across Sylvia to smile gratefully at Lord Dalton. It was only later on that the genuineness of his returning smile seemed surprising.

She soon forgot all else as the performance began with an exhibition of trick riding. Equestrians dashed around the ring performing death-defying acrobatics while the audience gasped and cheered. Then, as a change of pace, a lovely young lady draped in transparent gauze danced like a second Taglioni on the back of a white circus horse. Jenny stole another glance at Dalton. His eyes were glued upon the performer. No wonder he prefers this to opera, she thought.

Lord Dalton's party were soon holding their sides, convulsed with laughter at the antics of the celebrated clown, John Ducrow, who did a series of somersaults on horseback before drinking the

236

contents of a bottle, because he'd been told to "pour it into a tumbler." There was a pause between acts and Jenny was looking forward to the next event, advertised as the "Wild Horse of Tartary," an equestrian drama based on a Byron poem, when Claire suddenly clutched her arm.

"Look down there," she hissed.

Jenny obediently leaned over the balcony to gaze downward into the pit. She fully expected to see Mr. Chalgrove, though the circus hardly seemed his cup of tea. Her eyes scanned the crowd, back and forth, but she saw nothing to account for her cousin's distress. "What is it, Claire?" she whispered.

"There in the front row. Don't you see him?"

Jenny followed Claire's stare, riveted upon an area opposite the recessed stage and just behind a low barrier that framed the ring. She appeared to be looking at a man and two small children. The man, whose thinning hair was the most evident thing about him from their vantage point, had his arm around a female toddler who was standing on the bench beside him so that she could see. A slightly older boy, dressed in a short coat and pantaloons, was leaning rather perilously over the rail. As Jenny watched, the man, obviously a gentleman from the cut of his dark blue coat, pulled the lad back to safety.

"I still don't see what—"

Claire cut her off. "It's Papa," she choked.

Jenny hadn't seen her uncle for years. Certainly Lord Hazlett had had more hair. "Are you sure?" she whispered back.

"Of course I'm sure!" Claire snapped. "I should certainly know my own father."

"From this angle?" Jenny received a withering glare.

Sylvia looked curiously toward her cousins. But as she opened her mouth to speak, she was cut off by a tremendous clap of thunder. This was followed by a rapid succession of fiery streaks of lightning, then a deafening crescendo of thunder. Rain and hail came down in torrents amid what the broadsides had described as the carnage of battle, with wheeling, rearing horses and riders, shouts and bloodcurdling screams, and the clash of sword on sword.

As far as Jenny was concerned, the spectacle was a total waste. She was far too engaged in watching Claire watch the gentleman and his charges below them. The little girl had clapped her hands upon her ears and, apparently, was crying. Lord Hazlett appeared to be trying to comfort her. The lad was made of sterner stuff. He stamped and shouted and cheered with the rest of the audience while the battle raged.

Claire's distress was patent. In order to relieve it, Jenny wracked her brain for acceptable reasons that could account for Hazlett's presence in London and his failure to get in touch with his daughter. Perhaps he doesn't know she's here. She quickly dismissed that thought as highly unlikely.

As for the children with him— Well, there were all sorts of explanations for that, she told herself, trying to hold the worst of her imagination at bay. They could be the children of a friend. Or a servant, when it came to that. Lord Hazlett was fond of children, as she recalled. He'd been most avuncular with her and her siblings on his long-ago visit to their home.

But the odious Lady Warrington's insinuations came back to haunt her. And what was it that Chalgrove had said at their aunt's ball? Surely he, too, had made sly references to Lord Hazlett.

The amphitheater spectacle seemed to be working its way toward a happy ending. The music had softened from its previous blaring frenzy to sweet, melodic strains. Below them, the gentleman with the thinning hair gathered his charges, apparently wishing to whisk them away in advance of the crowd. As he turned slightly to envelop the small girl in a cloak suggestive of Red Riding Hood, Jenny saw his face clearly. She could no longer doubt that it was, indeed, her uncle. As his party began to ease its way out past the knees of the other spectators, Claire stood up suddenly and headed for the exit. "We'll be right back," Jenny whispered hurriedly to Sylvia and followed her.

Claire raced down the stairs and out into the street with Jenny at her heels. They were just in time to see Lord Hazlett lift the children into a waiting carriage and give the coachman a signal to drive on.

"I have to know where he's taking them." Claire sounded desperate. "Do you understand, Jenny? I *have* to know."

Jenny nodded and looked frantically around for a hackney. There was none in sight. "I could go fetch Dalton," she offered.

"I don't want anyone else to know about this. Oh, Jenny, they'll soon be out of sight."

Desperate times call for desperate measures. Jenny turned toward the queue of carriages just beginning to form in anticipation of the end of the performance. Sure enough, Lord Dalton's barouche was second in line. "Come on!" She dragged Claire by the hand. Jack was holding the mettlesome horses by a bridle and talking to them soothingly as the two young women came rushing up. "Get in," Jenny ordered Claire, then turned toward the tiger. "We want you to follow that carriage. It's a matter of life or death."

Jack looked alarmed. "Where's 'is Lordship?" he demanded.

"He's staying till the end of the performance. Now hurry up. We can be back by the time the place empties."

"Lor', miss, it would be as good as me life if I was to drive 'is Lordship's rig without 'is by your leave. Why, 'e 'ardly lets me—"

"Oh, do hurry," Claire wailed, and Jenny reacted. "Well, I can't stand here arguing."

Before the tiger realized what was happening, Jenny had climbed up upon the box and was snaking his lordship's whip out over the horses' heads, where it exploded in an ear-splitting crack.

"Now see 'ere, miss!" the tiger yelled. He made the mistake of releasing the bridle and starting toward her. The horses sprang around the gig in front and out into the street as if pursued by devils. Jack instinctively made a flying leap and landed on the boot as the barouche sped by.

"Oh, do be quiet or else jump off!" Jenny shouted at him as the young man continued to voice his protest at maximum lung power. "We aren't going to harm his lordship's precious carriage."

The tiger might have found this reassuring if at that very moment they hadn't been sideswiped by a curricle coming in the opposite direction.

"You bleedin' nincompoop!" Jack screeched.

"That wasn't my fault!" Jenny shouted indignantly. "That driver was obviously castaway."

"I was yellin' at 'im, not you," the tiger bellowed. " 'e almost knocked me off me perch. Which would 'ave saved 'is Lordship the trouble of murdering me—which 'e's plainly going to do."

As they turned off Westminster Bridge Road, Jenny slowed her team. Lord Hazlett's carriage was in full sight now, proceeding at a sedate pace, illuminated more by the full moon than by the flickering streetlamps.

Jenny kept her distance. Though she didn't think her uncle would know her from Adam's off-ox, she had no doubt that the sight of a young lady in evening dress—tooling a barouche down The Strand—would rivet his attention. No need to take the chance.

When it became obvious that they were headed to Covent Garden, Jack was heard from once again. "Might just as well 'ave jumped off Westminster Bridge and been done with it," he offered to the world at large.

"Don't be absurd," Jenny scoffed. "We'll be perfectly safe."

She would not allow herself to think of the shocking escapade she was engaged in. She did, however, close some of the gap between her and the carriage she was following. From the glimpse she'd had, Lord Hazlett's burly coachman looked far abler to cope with footpads than their diminutive tiger.

She was more relieved than she cared to admit—even to herself—when they turned into Russel Street. Her newly acquired knowledge of London told her that they were around the corner from Bow Street, the home of the metropolitan law enforcers. The same comforting thought had occurred to Jack. "I 'opes them Runners is in earshot," he offered.

The carriage ahead was slowing up. It came to a complete halt before a row of modest houses. Jenny drove several yards on past it and then pulled to a stop in the shadows. She turned around to look down on Claire. "What do we do now?" she asked.

Chapter Sixteen

"L ET'S WAIT HERE TILL HE COMES OUT."
Jenny opened her mouth to debate the wisdom of this course of action, but one look at Claire's miserable face stopped her cold. "If that's what you want," she answered.

Jack was not so compliant. He kept muttering to himself. "Never mind what could 'appen to a cove with two dotty females parked on a dark street in the middle of the night; it ain't even a circumstance compared to what 'is Lordship's gonna do to me. Being given the sack without a proper reference will be the least of it."

"Oh, do be quiet!" Jenny snapped, her nerves rubbed raw. "If Lord Dalton discharges you, I'll ask my father to take you on."

"And where is 'e, miss?"

"Birmingham."

"I'd as lief be dead, then," the tiger muttered glumly.

Time seemed at a standstill. Except for a carriage or two that rattled by, Russel Street was quiet. And cold. Perched upon the box, Jenny thought longingly of the many-caped greatcoats that other coach drivers seemed to favor. Her evening cloak was patently inadequate. As surely Claire's was. "Don't you think we should go?" she asked diffidently.

"He's bound to come out soon," was the taut reply.

But when the last light had flickered out in the last window, Jenny had no choice. "Claire, he isn't coming out. We really must go now. I fear I've kept the horses standing far too long as it is."

"I know." Claire sounded close to tears. "Sylvia and Lord Dalton must be thinking we're never coming back for them."

"Claire," Jenny answered patiently, "we've been gone for ages. They won't still be waiting at the amphitheater."

Lord Dalton was, in fact, waiting outside of Fremantle House when Jenny drove slowly up the street. He had taken the greatly perturbed Lady Sylvia home in a hackney coach and had been pacing rapidly up and down in order to keep warm. He was, however, now leaning against a portico column with folded arms and a face like thunder as Jenny pulled his team to a decorous halt.

"You go on in," she said, speaking softly to Claire. "I'll handle this."

"No, it's all my fault. I'll stay."

"No, you won't. You're on the verge of tears—and the last thing Dalton needs right now is a weepy female. Besides, he can't eat me, can he?"

Jenny soon decided that Lord Dalton was capable of doing just that. He didn't spare a glance for Claire as she hurried past him. His eyes were boring straight through her.

Jack had leaped down from the boot and was holding the horses. Lord Dalton, arms still folded, murderous look still firmly in place, stood by his rig and stared up at the "coachman." "Did you enjoy your trip, Miss Blythe?" he inquired with counterfeit pleasantness.

"Not particularly. And I'm well aware that I owe you an apology."

"For leaving us stranded? For upsetting your cousin, who thought you had been kidnaped? A circumstance I myself felt highly unlikely, by the by. An apology seems most magnanimous of you."

Jenny sighed. She might as well get the worst over with. "Yes, and for scratching your carriage."

"Oh, my God!" Dalton stepped back to survey the damage. "Well, I collect I'm fortunate to even get the thing back at all," he said bitterly. "It could be in complete splinters."

"Oh, I say, guv," Jack piped up, still clinging to the bridle, "that ain't really fair, you know, considering you ain't ever seen Miss Blythe drive. She handles the ribbons a fair treat, she does. For a female."

Dalton turned his withering gaze upon his tiger. "I think

242

you'd do well to keep out of this, Jack. I'll deal with you later for your part in this night's fiasco."

"I just thought you ought to know that this 'ere scratch weren't Miss Blythe's fault." Jack stuck stubbornly to his guns. "Some nob in 'is cups swerved right into 'er. I doubt if you yourself could 'ave dodged 'im."

His lordship's look was a scornful contradiction, but Jenny was touched. "Why, thank you, Jack," she said warmly. "And, remember what I said about employment. You could grow to like Birmingham."

"Oh? So, Miss Blythe, you aren't content just to steal my equipage. You plan to steal my tiger as well?"

"Only if you're sapskull enough to discharge him. Now if your lordship will excuse me, it's been a very trying evening." She began to climb down from the box. He put up a hand, reluctantly, to help her.

She winced as she surveyed the ugly scar on the pristine newness of his coach body. "Send me the bill for that, Lord Dalton."

"Damn the bill. It's your blasted effrontery that I'm incensed over. I realize that for some unfathomable reason, my rigs hold a great fascination for you. But why you had to pick this particular time to prove your prowess as a whip is beyond me. Do you have any idea of how next to impossible it is to secure a hackney once Astley's has let out?"

Jenny ignored the question. She was chewing over a part of the preamble to it. "Proving my prowess as a whip?" She glared. "Did you truly think that was what this was all about?"

"God knows what this was all about. A pleasure jaunt, perhaps?"

" 'A pleasure jaunt'! Well, that really is the outside of enough," she said wearily, all the starch suddenly draining out of her. "I know you don't think very highly of me, Lord Dalton, but I did think you'd realize that I would never have taken your rig so—cavalierly—if it hadn't been an emergency."

"Then suppose you tell me about it." He was studying her face and his tone had softened.

"Really, I'd rather not."

243

"Come, Miss Blythe. I do think you owe me that much. And whatever it is, I can assure you, I'm not a gabble-grinder."

She hesitated a moment longer and then capitulated. "Oh, very well then. You probably know all about this already, judging from the mischief-making hints your friends have dropped. The thing is, you see, Claire saw her father at the circus tonight with two small children. And"—Jenny swallowed—"she wanted to follow and see where they went. We couldn't get a hackney, either. And she was frantic, so . . ." She gestured eloquently toward his coach.

"Oh, my God. You drove all the way to Covent Garden with just him?" He nodded toward Jack, who looked offended.

"So you do know."

"Yes, and I wish you'd come to get me. I could have taken you or, better still, saved you the trip. For I'm afraid it's common knowledge that Lord Hazlett keeps a mistress and that they have two children. I am sorry that Lady Claire had to discover it. She's bound to be upset." He grimaced at his understatement.

"She's devastated. Now I really must go see about her. And I truly am sorry for all the inconveniences I've caused you. And I will pay for the damage. I insist."

"No, you'll do nothing of the kind." Lord Dalton smiled a twisted smile. "I'd far liefer hold a grudge. If you and I should ever sheathe our daggers, I'd feel totally at a loss. Good night, Miss Blythe." To her surprise he reached for her gloved hand and brought it lightly to his lips. "Go drink a tisane. If you don't get a case of the grippe from all this exposure, it will be a miracle."

He watched her inside and remained staring thoughtfully at the front door for several seconds after it had closed.

Jack watched him watch. The tiger's eyes were bright with interest.

Sylvia was waiting in Jenny's bedchamber. She was in her nightclothes, settled on the couch with a candle on the stand beside her and a book in her hand that she'd been quite unable to read. She jumped up when Jenny entered.

"Where have you been?" she demanded in a whisper. "I've been beside myself with worry."

"I am sorry." Jenny shed her cloak and came over to sit wearily beside her cousin. Oh, dear, she thought, I can't possibly go through all this again. I'm far too tired. But she knew that she owed an explanation to Sylvia for the anxious evening she'd spent.

Sylvia listened intently without interruption, her face mirroring her compassion for her cousin Claire. Then she sat silently for a bit, lost in thought, and when she spoke her voice was bitter. "He knew it all along," she said.

"Lord Dalton? Why, yes, he did."

She shook her head impatiently. "No, not Dalton. Mr. Chalgrove. He knew all along that our uncle has another family. And he tried to fling it in Claire's teeth. That was—cruel."

She jumped up suddenly and hurried from the room.

Jenny undressed and crawled wearily into bed, where the events of the evening whirled in her brain like so many speeding horses in the ring at Astley's Circus. And just before she finally fell asleep she suddenly recalled Sylvia's odd reaction. Mr. Chalgrove indeed! It was beyond her just what Mr. Chalgrove had to say to anything. Still, maybe it was true that every cloud has its silver lining. If this miserable evening had made the scales fall from Sylvia's eyes and she now saw that odious coxcomb clearly, at least that was one small outcome to the good.

Chapter Seventeen

ANOTHER FORTUNATE CIRCUMSTANCE, AS JENNY DISCOVered the following day, was that neither Fremantle nor his stepmama was aware that the cousins had not come home together the night before. Her ladyship had been invited to dinner, followed by cards, and Lord Fremantle had spent a rare evening at his club. Jenny breathed a prayer of thanksgiving for this deliverance as she went in search of Claire.

She found her cousin at the pianoforte, lightly strumming the keys. "Are you all right?" she asked.

"Certainly," was the bland reply. "Why shouldn't I be?" She stopped playing to dig a chocolate out of her pocket and pop it into her mouth.

Jenny tried, none too successfully, to keep the concern out of her voice. "There's no reason not to be, actually. But last night you did seem upset, so I was worried."

"Well, it was a shock," Claire admitted, "but now I've had time to accustom myself to the idea. And really"—she began to play again—"there's nothing at all unusual in the situation. I expect that most gentlemen, if the truth be known, have their love nests. That is the proper term, is it not?"

"Well, it's certainly one of them," Jenny said dryly.

"Why, just look at the Regent. He's certainly never lacked for mistresses. Though if he's had any out-of-wedlock children, I've not heard of it. But the royal dukes have."

"Well, the Duke of Clarence, certainly."

"So it was silly of me to make so much of the situation. And I'm sorry to have put you through all that last night. Was Lord Dalton furious?"

"No, not really. At least not for long."

"So all's well that ends well." Claire spoke a bit too heartily, but Jenny inwardly applauded the effort. "So now let's just forget about it, shall we?"

"Consider it forgotten."

Jenny left Claire to her playing and went off to write an expurgated version of her London adventures to her family and then to settle in for a long session with a Gothic novel. Just as she'd reached the climax and a chain-clanking specter was set to do its worst, she was interrupted by a very young and nervous maid who announced that her ladyship was ready to receive callers and expected her nieces to join her. "I've informed Lady Sylvia, miss, but I can't find Lady Claire anywhere."

"Oh?" Jenny reluctantly closed her book. "Have you tried the drawing room?"

"Yes, miss. And she's not at the pianoforte."

"Well, never mind. I'll find her."

Some sixth sense was making Jenny quite uneasy. The unease grew when she checked Claire's wardrobe and found that her cloak was missing. As she emerged from her cousin's chamber, the maid was just coming to find her. "Oh, miss"—the girl's eyes were saucerlike—"Edward the footman just told me he saw Lady Claire go out by herself and flag down a hackney coach, cool as ever you please."

"Oh, my word." Jenny thought swiftly. "Listen, Jill, if she asks, you must tell my aunt that Lady Claire and I have gone to the circulating library and will be back shortly."

"Oh, but miss—"

"Just do it!" Jenny snapped, and ran to snatch her own cloak and reticule.

She thought it best to take the servants' stairs and emerged onto the street from the lower level. How Claire had managed to find a hackney so easily was more than she could imagine. Now there was not one in sight. Lord Dalton's phaeton was standing in front of Fremantle House, however. Jack had momentarily abandoned his post to wheedle a cup of tea from the kitchen.

"Oh, why not," Jenny muttered to herself, and sprinted toward the rig. At that instant Jack emerged, tea in hand. But the fact that he froze in horror gave her the advantage. She was established in the driver's seat before he reacted. He did not give up easily, however. Tea splashing from the cup, he chased her down the street, whooping, "Oh, no, please! Not again! Do come back, miss! 'is Lordship'll skin me alive this time for sure."

"I'm sorry, Jack," she called. "Just tell Lord Dalton I'll be right back. I've gone to fetch my cousin."

At the entrance to Russel Street Claire paid off her driver and walked slowly down it. She earned a few curious glances; such a well-dressed young lady, all alone, was obviously out of place here. She hesitated in front of the house that her father had entered the night before. It was a modest, unpretentious dwelling, but from the newly painted shutters to the tiny, well-tended patch of garden, a lot of care had been lovingly lavished upon it.

Claire almost lost her courage. Indeed had she told the hackney driver to wait (her first inclination), she would have fled. She now toyed with the idea of returning to a main thoroughfare in hopes of finding another. Such a course of action seemed craven, though. She had come this far. She squared her shoulders and started up the gravel walk.

Since the woman who answered the door was drying her hands on the apron she wore, Claire took it for granted she was a servant of some sort. She was a pleasant-looking female of young middle age, with a round face under her crisp white cap. Very bright, very blue large eyes were her only claim to beauty. She gave Claire a cordial, if somewhat puzzled, smile.

For the first time it occurred to Claire that she hadn't the faintest notion whom to ask for. The sound of children's voices in the background did little to calm her agitation.

"Might I—I see your mistress?" she stammered.

The woman laughed at that. "Lord save us, I'm the only one that's here. Maid and mistress all in one packet you could say. I think perhaps you're at the wrong house, m'dear."

"No, I don't believe so. I'm Lord Hazlett's daughter."

The woman looked as if she'd just been struck. But she quickly rallied and said quietly, "You'll want to come in then, won't you?"

She ushered Claire into a tiny parlor, made to appear even smaller by the profusion of toys littering every surface. A cozy fire burned in the fireplace. There were bookcases on each side of it, filled with well-thumbed volumes. The chairs and sofa were worn, but comfortable. Underneath all the clutter of blocks and dolls and balls and soldiers the place was shiny clean. And despite that clutter, or perhaps because of it, the small room seemed inviting. Claire could not prevent herself from comparing it with the spacious elegance of her own house. It was hard to imagine the lord of that manor here in this humble setting. She thought it better not to try.

"Let me fetch some tea."

"Oh, no, please," Claire said, now wishing she had never

invaded this woman's privacy, hating herself for the distress she must be causing. "You shouldn't go to any trouble on my account."

"Oh, it's no trouble at all, Lady Claire. It will only take a moment." She lifted a toy donkey cart off a wing chair and indicated that Claire should sit there. "Do excuse the mess." She looked helplessly around her, a proud housewife caught in an awkward moment. "I tell Hazlett that it's sinful to have so many toys, but he will keep bringing them." Her cheeks flamed at what she'd just said and she hurried from the room.

Claire sat with folded hands, staring at the fire, resisting the urge to bolt. She hadn't thought beyond her own need to come here. Now how was she to explain such an unforgivable action? It somehow made it all seem worse that the mistress of the house knew her name.

It very slowly penetrated her consciousness that the babble of childish voices she'd first heard upon entering had stopped. Claire looked around to see two pairs of enormous eyes staring at her.

They stood in the doorway, the two tots from the circus. The little boy was about four, she judged, and his sister couldn't be older than two. Her thumb was planted firmly in her mouth as she regarded the newcomer solemnly.

"Gwenny's afraid of strangers," the little boy announced.

"But you're not, are you?"

"Of course not," was the scornful answer.

"And what's your name?"

"Will." He was inching closer, his sister following.

Will for William. He had her father's name.

When their mother returned a few moments later carrying a tray laden with a teapot, cups, and assorted biscuits, Claire was seated on the floor with the two children, helping to construct a castle of the blocks. "I saw my father and the children at Astley's Circus," she explained in a rush. "And I had to see them. I somehow knew, you see, though no one told me. And— well, I've always longed for brothers and sisters. My cousin Jenny is oldest of an enormous brood, and I did so envy her. Your children are adorable Mrs.— Oh, dear," she broke off in consternation. "I don't even know your name."

"It's Mrs. Rogers." She carefully placed the tea tray on the worn carpet next to Claire and sat down beside it. "I was a widow when I met your father—Now stop it, Will," she broke off as Gwenny demolished the castle, and William let out a roar. "Don't hit your little sister."

"Never mind, we'll build it back," Claire interposed diplomatically, and quickly began stacking blocks.

As Will became absorbed once more in the project, she said in a low voice, "He looks so very much like Father."

Mrs. Rogers brightened. "Oh, do you think so? So do I, but Hazlett pooh-poohs the notion."

"He's just being modest. I know how he's always longed for a son. And it was easy to tell, even at the circus, that he dotes on little Gwenny." Claire tried hard to keep any traces of jealousy from her voice.

"Well, men always dote on their daughters, don't they, dear? They may say they want sons, but it's the daughters who twist their heartstrings. You should hear him rave on and on about you."

"About me?" Claire tried to force a smile and failed. "I'm afraid you exaggerate, Mrs. Rogers. There's nothing about me to rave about."

"Well, if that's so, no one's told Hazlett," Mrs. Rogers replied firmly. "He never tires of talking about how talented you are. A regular prodigy you were, to hear him tell it. Oh, there's nothing like the firstborn, you know. No other child can ever quite measure up. I know that from my own family. The sun rose and set in my oldest brother. But I am hoping that little Gwenny may have a bit of your musical ability. She does sing along with her papa already," she said proudly, "though of course it's early days to really tell if there's talent there. She can never hope to be the beauty you are, though. Looks too much like me for that, I fear."

"Thank goodness she doesn't look like me. I wouldn't wish that on her."

Mrs. Rogers gazed at Claire in astonishment. "Why, I do believe you're serious. Don't you know what a nonpareil you are?"

"That's ridiculous. What I am is . . . fat."

"Well . . ." Mrs. Rogers looked her over judiciously. "You certainly aren't one of the skin-and-bones type—which gentlemen don't care for all that much in my experience. And everything else about you is perfection—your hair, your eyes, your complexion. Surely you must know that."

"Well," Claire said doubtfully, "I think I probably have lost a bit of weight just lately. My aunt has had me on a special diet, you see." She chuckled suddenly and told Mrs. Rogers how Lord Fremantle had had her meals smuggled to her room.

Mrs. Rogers laughed and clapped her hands. "Oh, your cousin sounds like such a nice gentleman."

"Oh, yes, indeed, he certainly is," Claire responded enthusiastically.

The gentleman in question had returned to his house a bit before to find Lord Dalton on his doorstep dressing down his tiger. Lord Fremantle handed the reins of his curricle to his own servant and went to see what the altercation was all about. At the same moment the front door opened and the butler joined the group.

"Is there a problem, Dalton?" his lordship inquired politely.

"Not really." Dalton sighed. "It's just that this mutton-headed lad of mine has developed the habit of allowing my rigs to be taken out from underneath his nose. But I beg pardon, Fremantle. I shouldn't have chosen your front doorway to strip the young rascal's hide off."

Fremantle looked horrified. "My word! You mean that your phaeton's been stolen?"

"Not stolen—borrowed."

On the step above, Jackson cleared his throat. "I think, m'lord—at least Edward tells me—that Lady Claire departed in a hackney coach a bit ago and now Miss Jenny has—err—borrowed His Lordship's carriage to go fetch her."

"How . . . odd!" Lord Fremantle was not given to hyperbole. His face, however, reflected his astonishment.

"I think I've a very good notion of where they're off to," Dalton said grimly.

"You have?" Fremantle turned to the butler. "No need for

you to catch your death out here in the cold, Jackson." His tone was dismissive.

As soon as the reluctant butler was out of earshot, Dalton quickly filled Fremantle in on the details of the night before. "I don't doubt for a minute that Jenny believes her cousin's gone to Russel Street," he finished. It was an indication of both states of mind that neither gentleman noticed his free use of Miss Blythe's name. "If you'll lend me your rig, I'll go fetch them."

"I think that's more my responsibility."

"Of course," Dalton said hastily. "But you won't object if I come along? I have a vested interest. In my rig, that is. Besides, my poor excuse for a tiger knows the exact direction."

They were proceeding down Old Bond Street at a pace that Lord Fremantle considered a rapid clip and Lord Dalton found so sedate that it set his teeth on edge when they became aware of an altercation up head.

"Oh, my prophetic soul!" was Dalton's Shakespearean reaction.

"Lor' save us; she's struck again!" Jack offered more prosaically.

The Piccadilly intersection had become a tangle of carts, carriages, and cursing, shouting passengers and drivers. Above it all, tall and stately on the box of the high-perch phaeton, sat Miss Jenny Blythe, the haughty target for most of the invective that dinned the air.

Lord Fremantle pulled his horses to a halt, and Lord Dalton leaped down from the passenger seat onto the pavement. "You go on, Fremantle. I'll tend to this," he called over his shoulder. "Stay with his lordship, Jack. He'll need you to locate the house for him."

There must have been something about the cut of Dalton's five-caped greatcoat, the tilt of his curly beaver over his brow, his gleaming boots, his soft leather gloves, the cane he carried, but most of all, the expression on his aristocratic face that bespoke authority. At any rate the crowd parted before him like Red Sea rushes. He halted by the step of his property and gazed up into the face of his nemesis.

"How now, Miss Blythe?" he queried.

Chapter Eighteen

A T FIRST, LADY FREMANTLE WAS NOT PARTICULARLY DIS-pleased that two of her nieces weren't present to help her receive visitors. She had more or less washed her hands of the Honorable Jenny and Lady Claire. Their lack of social success was more than compensated for by Sylvia's.

Lady Fremantle looked with satisfaction at her favorite niece, now surrounded with a bevy of admirers. She was, indeed, a pretty child. And modest with it. Even the most censorious of Lady Fremantle's friends could find no fault with Sylvia. The come-out had been a success after all. Oh, not the triumph of twenty years ago, of course, but her ladyship could not, in all honesty, wish for that.

"Mr. Chalgrove seems most reluctant to leave," a friend remarked as she rose to go. "I'm sure he was here before I was."

"He's probably waiting to speak with Lord Dalton." Lady Fremantle looked smug. "His lordship visits us every day now. And he and Chalgrove are particular friends, you know."

Chalgrove was not waiting for Dalton. What he wished was a private word with Lady Sylvia. He seized his opportunity when the gentlemen surrounding her rose and took their leave of Lady Fremantle.

"Is there something wrong?" He inched his chair closer and spoke in a low voice.

Her glare took him aback. He would not have dreamed that Sylvia was capable of such hostility. "My cousin Claire knows everything now. I do hope her misery makes you happy, Mr. Chalgrove."

He turned quite pale. "I've no notion of what you're talking about," he protested.

"Oh, have you not?" Her lip curled with scorn. "You were dropping hints about her father's other family right here at our own ball. Can you deny it?"

"No," he replied. None of Chalgrove's acquaintances would have believed he could look so stricken. "But at the time I—"

"I should have listened when they told me what you were like," she interrupted, her low voice bitter. "They said you actually enjoy exposing other people's scandals for the unfeeling to snicker over. But I could not believe it of you till I heard of my uncle's situation and then remembered what you'd said. Well, enjoy your little laugh, Mr. Chalgrove. And if anything of that nature ever happens to me, at least I'll know that *someone* gets pleasure from my humiliation. Now I think you'd better go. And I should prefer not to see you again, Mr. Chalgrove."

Chalgrove brushed past the butler, who had hastily leaped to open the outer door at the sight of his face. "The devil take her," he muttered between clenched teeth as he made his way, with angry strides, toward his club. Who would have thought that sweet, gentle Sylvia could turn on one like that? Her eyes had actually snapped, he now recalled. "Dalton's in for a rude surprise," he said, chuckling bitterly. "He'll think he's captured an angel for himself; instead he'll get a shrew."

Mr. Chalgrove slowed his steps. He suddenly realized he did not wish to go to White's after all. For he was not sure just how long he could nurse this anger he was feeling. And instinct told him that once he'd let it go, he was due for the worst fit of the dismals of his life.

Lady Claire had proceeded on foot a little way down Russel Street when Lord Fremantle's carriage pulled up beside her. She gaped in astonishment.

"How did you know?" she asked as he handed her up.

"That's rather an odd story. Can it wait just a bit?" He clucked at his horses.

"I collect you need to give me a scold first," she sighed.

"Well, yes, as a matter of fact, I must," he replied gently. "Cousin Claire, it's not at all the thing for you to go traipsing around London alone. Particularly in this part of town. Why did you not tell me that you needed to come here? I would have brought you."

She looked up at him in wonderment. "You would actually do that? I didn't suppose that you'd approve."

"My approving or not approving has nothing to say in the matter. If you felt you needed to come here, then I would have brought you," he answered simply.

"Oh, cousin, you are so kind." Her eyes filled with tears. She impulsively laid a hand upon his sleeve, then quickly removed it.

They rode a moment in silence. Claire realized she was feeling a wonderful sense of peace. How much of it was due to her recent visit and how much to the solid presence beside her wasn't a ratio she could sort out. "You knew about my father's—other family—didn't you?"

He looked uncomfortable. "Well, yes. I had heard about the liaison."

"Can you understand that I just had to see for myself?"

"No, I really can't," he replied seriously. "You see, I can scarcely remember my own father, so I've no notion of what such a revelation would be like."

"Well, at first it was a terrible shock," she admitted candidly. "Rather like being kicked in the stomach, I collect. And I felt betrayed. I confess I was really bitter at my father."

"I should think that would be a perfectly normal reaction."

"But then, over and above everything else, I kept thinking, I have a little half-brother and sister that I've never met. And that seemed—intolerable.

"And, oh, Cousin James, they are the most cunning children. Little Will is so bright—and bossy. But the baby refuses to be bear-led. We actually played together on the floor. And it was delightful. I do wish"—her face grew wistful—"that they were truly my brother and sister. I hated being an only child, you see."

"Yes, I can understand that."

"Of course you can." She smiled up at him. "But do you know," she went on seriously, "what has been the strangest thing of all? I actually liked Mrs. Rogers."

"Did you indeed?" His voice was noncommittal, his eyes fastened on the road.

"Yes, I did. And I was quite prepared to hold her in contempt. That sort of woman. You know the terms you hear. Light-skirt. Cyprian. But she's nothing at all like that. She's nice and soft-spoken and a very good mother. And—well, it's obvious that she loves my father. But do you know what the strangest thing is about her?"

"No, what?" He guided his team carefully around a farmer's cart loaded with straw.

"She's plain. No, *plain* is not the right word at all, for she has the kindest face—that really lights up when she smiles, eyes and all. But she really has no claim in the least to beauty. She's not terribly young now, of course, but I can't believe she ever could have done."

"Well, is that so very strange, my dear?" Lord Fremantle looked puzzled. "Most of the world's population falls into that category. Otherwise your family would not have created the sensation that it did."

"I realize that. But I should have thought a— mistress"—she choked a bit over the word—"would have to be ravishing. In order to pull a man away from his wife and family, I mean. Especially—" She left the words unsaid.

"When the wife is a celebrated beauty?" he supplied. "Well, I'm certainly no authority on the subject, but there are other qualities besides beauty that cause a man to fall in love."

"I was always taught that it was the only thing worth having for a female."

"I know you were."

"But I also know my parents were never happy. They quarreled incessantly when I was small. And then Papa began to stay away longer and longer. That's why I dreaded this come-out so much," she blurted out. "I know everyone thinks of the Percival sisters as Cinderellas. But in my mama's case, it doesn't fit at all. Or perhaps," she said reflectively, "Mama did get what she wanted out of life. Papa's very wealthy, you know. Perhaps he was the only one disappointed. And I should be glad, I collect, that now he has found happiness."

"Oh, should you indeed, Claire?" He smiled down at her. "You don't think that's carrying Christian forebearance too far, then?"

She'd never known her serious cousin to tease before and she giggled in response. "I did sound dreadfully sanctimonious, didn't I? All right then. I'm not *glad*, exactly. But I can truly say that I'm no longer bitter."

"And that's quite good enough," he pronounced firmly. "I'd rather hate it if you were suddenly elevated to sainthood."

"Well, I am mostly pleased about the children. Though I'll go ahead and admit to being a little jealous as well, since you seem to see right through my hypocrisy. For I can't help but envy their relationship with my father. He used to be my father, too, you see."

"Claire," Fremantle said earnestly, "you mustn't make too much of the fact that your father hasn't been to see you since you've been in London. I think he was merely trying to save you embarrassment. He is the object of a great deal of gossip, of course."

"That *could* be the reason." She sounded doubtful. "And I wonder if my mother really believes he's out of the country. Do you suppose she knows the situation?"

"Well, it would amaze me if someone hasn't informed her by now," he answered dryly. He didn't add that his stepmama would be a prime candidate. "That could explain why she didn't wish to come to London."

"In part, perhaps." She did not sound convinced. "Of course, Mama could have written Papa to stay away during my come-out," she mused. "By the by, I asked Mrs. Rogers not to tell him I'd visited. It would only upset him, I'm sure."

"That was wise of you, Claire. And considerate."

"Do you know that Mrs. Rogers says he talks of me constantly? And that he's—proud of me?"

"That's hardly amazing."

"Of course, she might have made it up. I told you that she's kind."

"That will do, Claire!" He frowned down at her. "I do, as a rule, despise conceit. But, damme, the other extreme is equally bad—or worse. Your father has every reason to be proud of you. You are not only extremely talented, you have a lovely character. And though I confess I'm glad that you don't seem to prize it, you must surely know that you are beautiful."

Her eyes widened in amazement. "That's what Mrs. Rogers said."

"Blast Mrs. Rogers! It's what *I* say."

Lord Fremantle actually whipped up his team.

Chapter
Nineteen

JENNY WAS NOT ABOUT TO ADMIT EVEN TO HERSELF JUST how glad she was to see Lord Dalton. She watched, with respect mingled with resentment, as he dispersed the crowd.

"Well, I could have done that, too, with a full purse," she observed acidly as he climbed up on the driver's side and picked up the reins. "Don't you think bribery is rather contemptible?"

"Would you rather they mobbed you?"

"They wouldn't do that."

"Maybe not. But there was talk of fetching the Runners."

"I wish they had done. Then I might have explained that none of this was my fault."

"That's not what the cart owner says. He says you came flying into the crossing, which caused his animal to rear and upset his cart."

"Fustian. And your paying him off was tantamount to admitting my guilt."

"Exactly."

"You really are an odious man, you know." She made the observation with scientific detachment as she gazed at his classic profile.

"Not at all. In fact, I'm amazed at the forebearance I'm developing. My foes won't even recognize me, I've become so mellowed."

"What are you doing?" she asked as he turned right onto St.

Martin's Lane. "I thought you knew I was going to Covent Garden. It's that way." She pointed back over her shoulder.

"Thank you for that guide to my city," he said sarcastically. "Fremantle's fetching your cousin. I don't think it requires a regiment."

"No, I was quite prepared to do it myself."

"And a right proper mess you were making of it, too."

"That was not my fault, as I've been— Why are we stopping here?" she asked as he pulled his horses over.

"Well, Miss Blythe, if you are going to make it a habit to help yourself to my rigs at will, I think it's high time you learned to drive. And I, God help me, am about to teach you."

"I'm not planning to ever touch one of your precious carriages again. Nor would I have done so today except that it was the first thing to hand."

"Bit of luck then, I'd say, that His Royal Highness didn't happen to be calling."

"Besides, I know how to drive."

"So you've demonstrated. Now quit arguing and climb over me before I change my mind."

She did actually follow his instructions. It was due entirely to the circumstance that one of the horses decided to step forward that she landed in his lap.

"Clumsy," he muttered, extracting the ostrich feather that adorned her bonnet from his mouth.

"Can I help it if you don't hold your horses?"

The seat exchange and reins transfer having been accomplished, "Now let's see you crack that whip," his lordship ordered.

"There hardly seems any necessity for that. You surely can't wish me to spring 'em."

"What I wish to do— No, correct that. What I *feel compelled* to do is to teach you to drive this rig. And in the event you need to employ that whip you'd better learn how."

"Do you have to sit so close?" she asked crossly.

"Yes. I have considerable affection for my team. I want to be in a position to rescue them."

"Well, give me room to operate." She plucked the whip from its holder.

He obligingly scooted over a few inches. His eyes were fixed critically upon her.

The long whip snaked and cracked. The look she shot him was smugly satisfied.

"Watch out!" he shouted, lunging to snatch the reins and steer the team out of the path of an oncoming coach. "Watch where you're going!" he snarled, as Miss Blythe's face flamed red at the expletive hurled their way by the irate coachman.

"Well, what do you expect," she snapped back, "with you telling me what to do? I *said* it was folly to crack the whip."

"The only folly involved was your looking for my approval instead of watching the street."

"You must admit I handled the whip well."

"It was . . . all right."

" 'All right'?" She glared at him indignantly, and his gloved hands landed once more atop hers on the reins.

"That's really not at all necessary." The truth was, his proximity, as always, was most unsettling. Whether she found it more irritating than pleasurable was best left unexplored.

They drove in silence for a bit, Jenny doing her best to concentrate. "By the by, where are we going?" she finally inquired.

"We'll drive down the Strand," he replied, with martyred resignation. "You might as well experience the thick of traffic."

She could have managed quite nicely without him. It wasn't the other vehicles crowding the thoroughfare that presented a problem. It was knowing that his confidence in her ability was nil, that he sat tense and ready to take over at any given moment. They had proceeded up the Strand for some little distance without incident, Jenny stopping and starting her team as the necessity arose and with considerable aplomb, or so she thought. She was on the verge of saying that he surely could relax now, when he suddenly froze beside her. "Oh, dear God," he breathed.

"Now really! There's no need for that. You're making an absolute nervous wreck of me." She glared up at him to discover that his attention was not on her at all. His gaze was riveted on the upper reaches of a tall mercantile establishment. She followed the direction of it and her blood ran cold. "Oh, dear God!" she echoed.

From a five-storey height, the building dominated its row. It was a handsome edifice, built of ancient brick. An arched entryway was a full storey tall, flanked by demicolumns and surmounted by the company's coat of arms, executed in marble, taking up the full height of another storey. Not content with that much adornment, the architect had continued upward with more marble, more half columns, this time framing windows and forming niches for classical statuary. And above it all, at a dizzying height, there stood the stone figure of a goddess upon a marble ledge. A marble arch curved gracefully behind her at shoulder height, sloping down to culminate in two short ledges, a continuation of the one the goddess stood on. Behind her, with an oeil-de-boeuf for balance on each side, was a large, open, arched window. A small tot had just crawled out it and was peering delightedly around the goddess's head.

Dalton leaped from the high-perch phaeton and sprinted across the street, oblivious to the traffic.

"Hey, you! You, there!" Jenny screeched at a crossing sweep who was pushing his broom idly back and forth. "Come hold these horses."

The lad was quick to respond, motivated as much by the elegance of her equipage as the urgency in her voice. "Pay you when I get back," she said, and began to run after his lordship.

"Cor!" the street urchin breathed as he located the source of Jenny's panic. In the short interval of time it had taken to engage the sweep, the tot had decided to explore further. He was settled on his small posterior now and, making delighted gurgling noises, was scooting his way down the marble arch.

Jenny, her pelisse hiked up to a scandalous altitude, took the steps of the staircase two at a time. She arrived panting to see Lord Dalton, who had already shed both his coats, pull off his Hessians.

"Oh, do be careful," she breathed as he stepped up upon the windowsill.

She had not expected an answer, of course, but she noted with an increase of alarm that his lordship appeared incapable of making one. He was every bit as white as the polished marble. He stood statuelike, a rival to the goddess, for just one second, then he climbed out the window and, with a death grip upon the sill, lowered himself onto the ledge.

The toddler had suddenly become aware of his predicament and was giving tongue. The howls did little for his lordship's equilibrium. They did, however, alert the youngster's mother to his disappearance. She came popping out a closed door, into the hallway, and looked frantically around. "Earnest, where are you?" she called. For answer there was an increase in the volume of the howls coming from outside.

Jenny pulled her head in to deal with this new development. "It's all right. His lordship will fetch him," she said soothingly as she tried to prevent the young mother from looking out. In this she was completely unsuccessful. The woman did lean out, did look, and went into strong hysterics. Jenny jerked her away from the sill and administered a sharp slap.

It was effective. The woman collapsed upon the floor, rocking back and forth with near-silent sobs. "Sorry," Jenny muttered. "But your caterwauling will send them both—" She choked on the sentence and leaned out the window once again.

His lordship, she saw, had reached the child and was now speaking soothingly to him. Jenny held her breath as he carefully eased himself down to a sitting position, his legs dangling off into space. "What's your name, lad?" he asked conversationally.

"E'nest," was the choked reply.

"Well, Earnest, I'm going to carry you back up to the window. But you're going to have to help. You must hold on tight and not wiggle. Think you can manage that?" The child nodded. "All right, then. Here goes."

Slowly, carefully, Dalton lifted the youngster while Jenny ceased to breathe. Earnest's little arms came together around his lordship's neck in a stranglehold. "Not quite so tight, boy," he managed to croak.

Oh, please, God, Jenny prayed silently, as, pressing his back against the wall, Dalton struggled slowly to his feet. One arm clasped the child; the other hand pressed against the brick for purchase. It seemed to take forever, but at last he stood. Stood and swayed sufficiently to send up a concerted gasp from the crowd of spectators that had spied the elevated drama and were huddled, necks craned, below.

People were gathering inside as well. A gentleman from the office she'd just vacated was ministering to the stricken mother. Others tried to crowd round Jenny at the window till she told them in no uncertain terms for God's sake to stand back.

Slowly, slowly, slowly, Lord Dalton inched his stocking feet across the narrow marble ledge, pressing back against the arch as he did so. Jenny, leaning far out the window to her own peril, strung together soft words of encouragement. "Fine. Good. Famous. You're doing great. Just don't look down. You're almost there. About three more steps now and you can reach the statue."

The three steps seemed to take three hours to her way of thinking. But at last he was there, beneath the window. "Can you peel the little beggar off me?" he managed to gasp.

"I think so." She leaned out even further. "But your hand's in my way. Move it off the wall and brace against the statue.

She waited for him to comply. Nothing happened. "Dalton!"

"I . . . don't think I can do that," came the muffled reply.

"Do it! Now!" Jenny employed the same tone she'd used with the hysterical mother.

The wet palm left the marble and grabbed the goddess's shoulder in a vise.

Earnest didn't want to leave the secure shoulder he was plastered on. As Jenny grabbed his arms she used all the persuasion at her command to make him turn loose the two handfuls of cambric that he clutched. Dalton seemed to have nothing to say in the matter. With closed eyes, he was clinging to the marble goddess.

The tot's mother, however, managed to rise to the occasion. She appeared in the window beside Jenny. "Do what the nice lady says, Earnest," she wheedled. And with a howl that sent the pigeons flying, the child suddenly turned loose. He did, but not Dalton.

"Let the boy loose," Jenny hissed. And as he obediently released his hold on Earnest to transfer that hand to the marble arch, she plucked the screaming child inside.

Earnest was placed in his mother's arms—who now felt free to reindulge in her hysterics. The other people rallied around to comfort and congratulate, leaving Jenny alone to focus her attention upon Lord Dalton.

"You can come in now," she told him.

"I . . . don't . . . think . . . so," he replied.

"Of course you can," she said heartily. "The bad part's over. You can't possibly take a tumble. The statue's a buffer. Come on now."

"Sorry. Can't move," he mumbled.

Oh, dear God; he really is frozen there, she realized. Once more to her peril Jenny leaned far out to pat his head reassuringly. "Come on. Just one more effort, Dalton. You can do it. I won't let you fall."

"That's about as damned silly a statement as I've ever heard."

She giggled. In spite of every circumstance, Jenny giggled. It occurred to her that she might be no better in a crisis than Earnest's mother. "You're right, you know," she managed to tell him. "But do turn around and get yourself back in here. I don't know about you, but I really need a cup of tea."

Her matter-of-fact tone evidently did the trick. He began to rotate slowly while the spectators held their breaths. He completed the rotation by embracing the stone goddess like a lover. He shinnied halfway up her, then, with his legs locked tightly around her, reached out to grasp the window ledge. Dalton heaved himself up and over, whereupon he slid down onto the floor and put his head between his knees.

It took some persuasion on Jenny's part to prevail upon the knot of people to go away and leave them alone. Earnest's mother was profuse in her thanks, kneeling down at his lordship's level, still sobbing intermittently. As she poured out her gratitude, she kept a tight grip on Earnest, who was now struggling to get out of her arms. The only response from Lord Dalton was a dismissing wave of the hand.

"Please, leave him alone," Jenny asked. "And, no, I'd best not tell you his name. He's extremely modest, you see, and hates having a fuss made over him."

"If you say so." Earnest's mother's tone was frosty. She had obviously not forgiven the slap. She rose to her feet, however,

264

though she appeared to feel that something was lacking. The look she gave the prostrated Dalton was clearly dissatisfied.

After Jenny explained that she felt quite faint and wished to just sit quietly a moment and regain her equilibrium, the people ringed above her and Dalton did at last disperse. She turned then to his lordship, whose head still rested on his knees. "I think that was the bravest thing I've ever seen," she said.

He did raise his head then to stare straight at her. It was the mother of all baleful looks. "You're really enjoying this, aren't you?"

"Of course not!" She was indignant. Then native honesty took over. "Well, I collect I am rather pleased to discover that you're human after all."

" 'Human'!" The look actually increased its intensity. "Why not go ahead and say it. When it comes to heights, I'm a quivering jelly." His head now rested back against the wall. "Always have been."

"Oh, that was perfectly obvious from the very first. That was what made your action so heroic."

" 'Heroic'!" His lip curled.

"Exactly. I meant what I said, even if you don't believe me. I thought that forcing yourself out on that narrow ledge when you obviously couldn't bear to do so was really brave. And did you notice that as long as Earnest's welfare was uppermost in your mind you were all right? It was only when you'd turned him safely over to me that you—err—fell apart."

" 'Fell apart.' You do have a way with words, Miss Blythe, that goes a long way to restore a cove's manhood. Dammit," he said musingly, "why did that blasted brat have to choose the one way to imperil his life that would totally unnerve me? He might just as easily have tumbled off Westminster Bridge. I swim like a fish, you know."

"Yes, but have you thought of the height of that selfsame bridge?" She tried to keep a straight face, then snickered.

"Damn you," he said pleasantly. "Actually, that would have been no problem. After I'd gotten sick and dizzy on the ledge and *fallen* in the water, I'd have gotten us both out with ease."

"Yes, I can see that. And how are you with burning buildings?"

"Oh, first rate."

"I can picture you now, dashing through a wall of flames."

"Why do I feel that you'll never let me hear the end of this?"

"Because you're a silly ass," she replied seriously. "I've more respect for you now than I would have dreamed possible. Oh, I've heard all those stories of what a Nonesuch you are. A fearless pugilist. A champion cricket player. A neck-or-nothing rider. York-Jones raves on ad nauseum. But to make yourself do something that's so against the grain. That's *really* bravery. Whereas getting knocked around by Gentleman Jackson in the ring is merely stupid."

"Thank you for that analogy. What I should have done, of course, was step aside and let you pull Master Earnest off the ledge."

"You think I could have done so?"

"In a tick. No doubt about it. You'd have probably skipped along the ledge, la-de-dah, la-de-dah," he finished bitterly.

She sighed. "I do tend to give that impression, don't I? It's a kind of curse. Comes along with my height. It's silly to even try to appear fragile and fluttery, given my size. But as for what you just said, no, I don't think I could have done what you did. If there was no one around more capable, I'd like to think I would have tried. But I doubt that I could have gotten down and picked him up as you did." She shuddered suddenly. "It's one thing to joke about it. But that was truly the worst moment of my life. I think I'll have nightmares from here on out." Her eyes filled with sudden tears.

He put an arm around her shoulder and gave her a shake. "Hold on, Jenny. Don't go to pieces on me now. I'd really prefer that you keep on needling me. Remember what you were just saying. Tears aren't your style." He brushed a vagrant drop of water off her cheeks, then bent over to kiss the spot tenderly. It was no journey at all from there to her lips.

Later on, they could both attribute the next few minutes to nervous reaction. A spontaneous antidote to the harrowing experience that they'd been through. But for whatever reason, they found themselves kissing—passionately, ardently, frantically, desperately, and lengthily.

Only the sound of footsteps approaching up the stairs brought them to their senses. Jenny untangled herself, reluctantly, and rose unsteadily to her feet. Dalton tossed her bonnet, which had somehow become dislodged in the melee, up to her. She was smoothing the skirt of her pelisse, and he was pulling on his Hessians, when the approaching matron reached their floor.

The stout woman, puffing with the exertion of the climb, paused at the head of the stairs to catch her breath. Her mouth pursed in disapproval as she looked from one sheepish face to the other red one. Her sniff was eloquent as she continued her journey on down the corridor.

Jenny hoped she would soon learn to curb this deplorable tendency for giggling she was developing. At the moment it was well beyond control. "H-how's your manhood now?" she managed to utter between spasms.

"About two-thirds restored, I'd say." He grinned back as he offered her his arm.

" 'Two-thirds'? Is that all? Oh, I'd certainly give you higher marks than that."

They both struggled for composure as they proceeded arm in arm down the stairs and out into the street.

Chapter Twenty

PERHAPS IT WAS A GUILTY CONSCIENCE THAT CAUSED JENNY to dread an interview with her aunt. Lady Fremantle was indisposed. She hadn't left her bedchamber the entire day. Jenny came into her presence with unaccustomed meekness and took a seat beside her bed.

There was no doubt that Lady Fremantle was displeased. The very fact that she'd demanded an interview before her abigail had done everything in her power to restore at least a reminder of her former beauty spoke to that. She sat propped up in bed, still in her nightgown and nightcap, sipping her tea while a plate of almond cakes remained untouched. The eye she fastened upon her eldest niece was baleful. Jenny braced herself.

"I'm most displeased with Sylvia."

"I beg your pardon?" Jenny's eyes widened in astonishment. That was the last thing she would have expected her aunt to say.

"You heard me, Jenny. I've no desire to keep repeating myself."

"Yes, ma'am. It's just that you amaze me. What could she possibly have done?"

"It's what she *hasn't* done that's the problem. Do you realize that neither Lord Dalton nor Mr. Chalgrove has made an appearance here in a week?"

"I—err—really hadn't noticed." That was half true at any rate. Jenny was well aware that Dalton had not called at Fremantle House since he'd plucked little Earnest from off the ledge.

"Well, you should have done." Lady Fremantle's cup met its saucer with a peevish click. "Here they were, the two most eligible bachelors in all of London, dancing daily attendance upon Sylvia. All of my friends were remarking on it. Having *either* dangling after her would have been a triumph. But *both*!" For a moment her ladyship allowed herself to look triumphant before her face refell. "But now it has all come to nothing."

"Perhaps there's an explanation," Jenny offered. "They could be otherwise engaged. Or out of town."

"Both at the same time?" her ladyship snapped.

"Well, it could happen."

"The point is, if there is a reasonable explanation, Sylvia knows nothing of it. At least she *says* she knows no reason for it. Really, that girl is most exasperating. To have been blessed with all that beauty and not know how to use it! Why, any one of my sisters or myself would have had those gentlemen down on their knees in a fortnight. Really, I could shake her!"

"Well, perhaps they simply wouldn't suit," Jenny offered diffidently.

"Not suit!" Lady Fremantle's tone implied that her niece was bird-witted. "Each of those gentlemen is worth upward of twenty thousand pounds per annum. Of course they'd suit!"

"Yes, I do see what you mean," Jenny murmured. What she

really didn't see was what her aunt expected her to do about it. She wasn't left long to wonder.

"I want you to have a talk with Sylvia. Find out exactly what's going on. Why, I shouldn't wonder if one—or both—of the gentlemen haven't already offered for her and the silly peagoose has turned them down. Really"—Lady Fremantle straightened her nightcap with a jerk—"I don't know what's wrong with you young women of today. It's nothing like my time, I can tell you."

"No, ma'am. I'm sure it isn't."

"And another thing." Her ladyship looked martyred. "As though I weren't distressed enough, now Fremantle is insisting that I arrange a musical evening and have Claire sing."

"Why, I think that's a famous notion."

"You do? Well, I'm not at all convinced. I don't know that it's a good idea to seem to be pushing Claire forward. Now I grant you that her appearance has improved—and I give myself full credit for doing what her mother should have done before foisting the girl off on me—but she's still far too plump to be considered a Beauty."

"But surely the point is, Aunt, that Claire sings like an angel."

"The point is to find a suitable husband for her. And, frankly, I'm not at all certain that she has the poise to carry off a performance. She's no good at all in company. Just sits there like a lump." Her ladyship shook her head. "No, I think it's a terrible notion and will no doubt end in disaster. But Fremantle insists. I vow I've never known him to be so stubborn over a thing. I wish you to speak to him as well."

Jenny was thinking furiously. "Do you know, Aunt, a musical evening might be a very good notion at that. You could include Mr. Chalgrove and Lord Dalton in your invitations and give Sylvia a chance to mend her fences as it were. That is, if such a course of action is really necessary. And since the evening is in Claire's honor, they need not think that you are throwing Sylvia at their heads."

"Hmm." Lady Fremantle took a bite of almond cake and chewed it thoughtfully. "You may have a point," she observed thickly. "Just let me think on it a bit. In the meantime, you have a word with Sylvia."

But Sylvia was not to be found. She had slipped out of the house and was, at the moment, driving in the park with Captain St. Laurent.

She had been reluctant to do so. "Surely you aren't ashamed to be seen with me?" His handsome face looked hurt, and she'd hastened to deny it. "It just doesn't seem a good idea for us to be seen together. It might lead to questions."

"Who cares? We're old family friends, are we not? And I don't mind admitting that I'd like to meet your influential friends. There's my career to be considered. You do see that, don't you?"

She nodded. And tried not to look self-conscious as they drove through the park in his hired rig. The equipage was certainly not what she'd grown accustomed to. She tried not to make comparisons with Dalton and Chalgrove, for she knew it had set him back more than he could afford. She therefore did her best to make it appear that she was enjoying herself. But if the truth were known, she was hard put not to flinch every time they approached another carriage.

They did earn several curious looks and nods from mere acquaintances. But Sylvia had just begun to think that they might actually leave Hyde Park without seeing anyone whom she knew well when she saw a familiar-looking curricle approaching. Her heart sank a bit as she spied the Honorable Reggie York-Jones holding the reins. It plummeted even farther when she discovered that it was Lady Warrington with him.

Reggie had been much in that lady's company of late. He was under no illusion as to why. He was on intimate terms with Lord Dalton, and it was common knowledge that Lady Warrington was wearing the willow for that gentleman. Indeed, she did seem to spend most of their time together pumping him about Dalton's activities. He frankly found it all a bore. But he was most anxious to become a man about town, and, being seen in Lady Warrington's company boosted that ambition, so he put up with it.

"Oh, look," she cooed in his ear as their curricle approached the rented rig. "I can hardly believe my eyes. That's Lady Sylvia Kinnard on that shabby gig. But who is the Adonis with her? Oh, do stop, Reggie, dear."

Sylvia tried not to sound uneasy as she made the introductions. But the truth was, Lady Warrington's overdone cordiality filled her with apprehension. She was well aware that the lady had no cause to like her. She found her open flirtation with the captain most suspect. "A family friend and a newcomer to the metropolis. Shame on you, Lady Sylvia, for keeping this military hero hidden. I shall see to it, sir, that you no longer remain her ladyship's exclusive property. After all, she has enough gentlemen at her feet." Here she was unable to keep a note of spite from creeping in. "I shall personally see to it that you begin to circulate, Captain St. Laurent."

"What a charming lady," the captain exclaimed after the gig and curricle had gone their separate ways. "And such a Beauty."

When Sylvia didn't answer, he gave her a searching look. "Oh, come now. Surely you're not jealous."

"Of course not. I just wonder what she's up to, that's all."

"That doesn't sound at all like you, Sylvia. Surely you can't begrudge me the chance to make a bit of a splash on my own? After all, as the lady said, you've all of London at your feet."

"N-no. Of course I don't. Just be on your guard, that's all."

"Oh, don't worry, m'dear." He flipped his reins to urge his sluggish cattle out into the traffic of Park Lane. "I'm the soul of discretion. You surely must know that by now."

For his part, Reginald York-Jones couldn't see why Lady Warrington was so elated over meeting Captain St. Laurent. If the truth were known, the fellow had struck him as something of a mushroom. Not quite the thing, somehow. Didn't seem up to Lady Sylvia's standards. But then, of course, he was a handsome fellow. And females valued that sort of thing. Still, Reggie thought, it wouldn't hurt to make some inquiries. He knew two or three chaps in the captain's regiment. Made sense to find out a bit about the fellow.

But after he'd taken Lady Warrington home and returned to his rooms in Bird Street, a new development pushed Captain St.

Laurent completely from his nonretentive mind. Among the letters and invitations awaiting him on a silver tray was a missive with the Earl of Rexford's seal pressed into the wax. Reggie tore it open and perused it three times before he actually comprehended what he'd read. "Now that's deuced odd," he muttered to himself.

Chapter
Twenty-one

TWO BRIGHT SPOTS GLOWED IN CLAIRE'S CHEEKS. EXCEPT for this telltale evidence, she seemed the soul of calm. Both cousins had come to her room to supervise her toilette, a bit of attention that the abigail, putting the last touches on a Grecian coiffure, could have done without.

"We want you to wear these. For luck, you know." Jenny handed the abigail her single-strand pearl necklace and Sylvia's pearl eardrops. "Not that you need luck," she hurried on to explain.

"No," Sylvia added, "we simply like the notion of being a part of your triumph."

Claire managed a wan smile. "You two are being marvelous. And I do appreciate your support, believe me. But I don't think you need worry. I passed being frightened ages ago. I've proceeded on to numb. Now hadn't you best be going? Guests should arrive at any moment and Aunt will have your heads if you aren't there to help receive. There's one thing about being the featured attraction of the evening. I am spared that."

Lord Fremantle, also intent upon Claire's well-being, stopped Jenny for a private word as she and Sylvia left the room.

"I have a favor to ask, Cousin Jenny."

"Certainly. Anything." She suspected that underneath his

usual calm exterior he was more nervous than Claire. She liked him for it immensely.

"I've asked Lord Hazlett here tonight—" he began.

"You've *what*?"

"Sssssh" Her voice had risen inadvertently. "I thought it important to Claire that she be on good terms with her father. But I don't wish her to have added pressure during her performance. So could you see to his lordship, Cousin Jenny, and keep him out of sight until Claire has performed?"

Just how she was to accomplish such a feat was beyond imagining. Hide him behind a potted palm? Give him a loo mask? She kept all such reservations to herself, however, and managed an encouraging smile. "Why, yes, of course, Cousin James. I'll be happy to do so."

"Where is Fremantle?" Her aunt was fuming when Jenny joined her and Sylvia by the drawing-room door. "People will begin arriving at any moment."

"He's on his way. He just wanted to wish Claire luck."

"Having palpitations is she? Well, never mind. I've seen to it that we also have professional musicians on hand."

The sound of the doorbell cut off the retort Jenny longed to make.

Reginald York-Jones was among the first arrivals. Jenny thought he looked rather tired and drawn. And for some reason he did not meet her eyes. "Are you feeling quite the thing?" she inquired solicitously.

"Oh, yes. Never better, in fact," he told the jet lozenges that trimmed her bustline.

She was kept from wondering about his odd behavior by the sight of Lord Dalton, who was bending over her aunt's hand. This would be their first encounter since the rescue of Earnest with its curious aftermath. She hoped she'd not do anything foolish like blushing when he approached. Her voice, at any rate, didn't quiver when her turn came and she said for his ears alone, "I need to have a private word with you."

"Yes, I expect you do," he said dryly.

"Oh, don't be an ass. It's not what you're no doubt thinking."

"I don't see how you could possibly know what I'm thinking." He then was forced to move along and greet Sylvia.

Even though she managed to smile at him, there seemed some restraint on that young lady's part. Lord Dalton, with difficulty, suppressed a sigh. He was in for a long evening, it seemed.

Lord Hazlett arrived late. On purpose. Lady Fremantle had already taken her place upon the temporary platform erected at one end of the drawing room and was preparing the fifty or so assembled guests for the musical treat ahead. Jenny, still lurking in the hall, turned to greet him. "Uncle, I'd almost given you up."

"I thought it might be more ... politic to just slip in unobserved."

They didn't quite succeed in this, however. Lady Fremantle saw them taking their places in the very back of the rows of rout chairs and was momentarily thrown into confusion. She managed to recover her aplomb, however, and, before any of the guests were moved to wonder at her odd reaction, went on praising the harpist and baritone that they were privileged to hear. "My niece will also sing for you," she added, apparently as an afterthought.

The harpist began. And as far as Jenny was concerned, played interminably. Then came the baritone. Jenny squirmed impatiently throughout his solo. She even grew oblivious to her uncle's presence in her anxiety for Claire. Lord Dalton was looking at her from the row just in front of hers and across the center aisle. Her nervousness must be showing, she concluded as she tried to compose her features. Dalton looked away.

When the polite applause for the baritone had faded, Lady Fremantle rose from her position in the front row of chairs and turned toward her guests. "My niece, Lady Claire, will now sing for you," she announced, then shot a darkling look toward the young lady's father. Without realizing she was doing so, Jenny clutched her uncle's hand.

It was obvious to those who knew her best, that Claire was nervous. The red spots in her cheeks glowed brightly and the gloved hands, clasped together at her waist, trembled ever so slightly. But even as Jenny's grip on her uncle's hand became viselike, she could not help noticing with pride how very nice Claire looked. The blue net gown she wore, chosen of course by

Sylvia, was most becoming. And no one could now consider her more than "pleasingly plump."

Lord Fremantle had set aside his aversion to public performance and agreed to accompany Lady Claire. Indeed, that had been the only way to persuade her to perform. Now he played an introduction and smiled encouragingly. As the smile lit his usually grave face, Claire visibly relaxed. And so did Jenny.

Fremantle had chosen her music carefully. Claire began with a ballad, lovely, but undemanding. The applause was enthusiastic. She looked abashed at first and then seemed pleased. The next selection, an aria, was chosen with an eye to showing off her range and artistry. She sang as though inspired; every note was clear and true.

The applause was thunderous. The dangling prisms in the huge crystal chandelier above them danced in rhythm with it. The ovation would have been tumultuous under any circumstance, Jenny was certain, but it lost nothing from the fact that Lord Hazlett so completely forgot himself as to leap to his feet and lead it. His "Bravo" resounded above all the rest.

Claire could not fail to see him. She appeared thunderstruck at first, but then she smiled shyly in her father's direction. Jenny felt her eyes begin to moisten. You peagoose, she chided herself, and went on clapping.

"Your cousin was a triumph." At the end of the concert, when the other guests were collected around Claire, Lord Dalton spoke at Jenny's elbow.

"Yes, I see she even kept you awake. Listen, I have to talk to you."

"So you said. Here I am."

"Not here. Privately. Come on. Let's slip away while no one's noticing us."

She closed the library door behind them, then turned to face him. The often rehearsed words came out in a rush. "I think we ought to clear up something right away. There's no need for you to avoid Sylvia on my account. If you think I've said one word about that—trivial incident—after you'd saved Earnest, you much mistake the matter. I wouldn't dream of such a thing. Nor would I overblow it. We were neither one ourselves. It is best forgotten. And, I assure you, for my part, it would have been

275

already . . . but for the fact that you've become—well, conspicuous by your absence. My aunt has commented on it. And while Sylvia would never speak of her feelings, I'm sure she must be wondering why you are avoiding her."

There was a long, intense moment of silence. Lord Dalton, lounging back against the bookcase with an elbow resting on a shelf, stared at her. Only her height seemed to prevent his looking down his nose.

" *'Trivial incident'?* " he asked.

"I beg your pardon?"

"You said you hadn't told your cousin about the *trivial incident*. Is that truly what you considered it?"

"Well, naturally."

"You mean that it's *natural* for you to sit passionately kissing on a dirty landing in a business establishment while interested onlookers mill back and forth? You do shock me, Miss Blythe."

Her cheeks flamed. "That was a shabby thing to say. And no *'onlookers'* milled back and forth. There was only one odious woman."

"I stand corrected. Just one spectator *would* trivialize the incident, of course."

"I do wish you'd quit harping on that phrase!" she snapped. "You seem to completely fail to take my point. It's Sylvia who's at issue here."

"Obviously." His face was enigmatic.

"I do not wish you to feel any constraint there on my account. I am not laying any claims upon your affection because of an unguarded moment, Lord Dalton. And I hold myself more to blame than you for the incident."

"*Trivial* incident," he corrected.

"For what happened. Do I make myself clear?"

"Abundantly."

"Well, then," she said crossly, "I don't know why you are being so odiously starchy. I thought you'd be relieved. To speak plainly, I haven't seen you behave like this since you lectured me at Almack's. I did think, m'lord, that we'd progressed beyond that."

"Oh, yes. I'd say we'd progressed *a great deal* beyond that."

"Quit echoing everything I say. I do beg pardon if I've offended you—though I don't see how I could have done. I have never before felt constrained to stand on points with you, and certainly didn't see a need to begin now."

"No need whatsoever."

"Then will you speak to Sylvia?"

" 'Speak to Sylvia?' " His eyebrows shot up. "Are you suggesting that I go down on one knee, Miss Blythe?"

"I'm suggesting nothing beyond this one simple thing—that I've tried, with little success I fear, to make you understand." She deliberately dragged out her words. "There-is-no-need-to-shun-Sylvia-on-my-account. Now is that clear?"

"Perfectly, Miss Blythe. Don't you think we should join the others before someone wrongly concludes that another *trivial incident* is taking place?"

He moved to open the library door . . . and gave a mocking bow as she swept by him with an angry glare.

Lord Dalton was in no mood to stay for the lavish supper that would conclude the evening's entertainment. He was striding toward Mount Street in something approaching high dudgeon when he heard footsteps hurrying behind him. "Dalton! Wait up!" Reggie York-Jones called.

Dalton was not overjoyed. His tone was less than cordial. "Never knew you to leave a party before the refreshments, Reggie."

"Well, I had to talk to you, didn't I? And I saw you streak out of there as if your tailcoat was on fire."

"Can't it wait?" Dalton sighed.

"Well, no, it can't, I'm afraid." Reggie struggled with himself and then lost. "Look here, old fellow. I'm supposed to pump you subtly and find out some things for your father. But I'm no good at that sort of havey-cavey business. Seems best to just come right out and ask you. But, I say, do we have to go on standing here?"

After they had settled in front of a crackling fire in his lordship's parlor with a bottle of claret between them, Dalton, who was sprawled in a wing chair opposite Reggie's with his feet stretched to the blaze, inquired, "Now do I have this straight? My father wrote asking you to worm some information out of me?"

"No, no. That is to say, he didn't write. He asked me."

Dalton sat up straight. "Papa's here in London? And he didn't want me to know?" He looked stricken. "Oh, God, he must be worse. I collect he came up to consult with his doctor."

"Well, no. At least he may have done that, too. But he mainly came up to see Harriet Wilson."

"He did *what*? I'll not believe it."

Harriet Wilson was the most fashionable courtesan in London. Her clientele was made up exclusively of the pink of the ton. The Dukes of Wellington and Argyll, among others, were her regular visitors.

That Reggie was well aware of this was reflected in the smug expression that now suffused his boyish face. "You'd best believe it. Harry—by the by, that's what she asked me to call her, don't you know—Harry doesn't see just anybody. But your father's a particular favorite of hers, she said.

"Now wait just a minute, York-Jones. You aren't going to tell me that Papa—in his condition— actually went to bed with Harriet Wilson."

"Why, no, I'm not."

"I should think not."

"No, for he asked her as a particular favor to take me in his place." The young man turned suddenly pink. "Initiate me, as it were."

"I see," Dalton said dryly.

"That was deuced nice of him, you must admit, for Harriet would never as a usual thing—err— entertain the likes of me. She prefers her gentlemen well established, she said. But I don't know what you mean about your papa's condition. He—ah— went with Harriet's sister Fanny, you see. And afterward, when we all had a late supper together, she went on and on about how exhausted she was. And how your papa put all the young men to shame. Harriet—*Harry*, I mean to say, laughed and said that she took all the credit. That she'd been governess to him for years and had certainly taught him a trick or two."

Lord Dalton was suddenly looking dangerous. "She said that, did she? Oh, you must have been a jolly little group."

278

"Oh, we were. The best," York-Jones replied enthusiastically. "I'd always been in awe of your father, Dalton. Don't mind saying that even though he is my godfather, he always made me quiver in me boots. But he really is a right 'un, I must say."

"A regular life of the party, I take it."

"Oh, yes. Last thing I would have expected, like I said. Treated me just like a son."

"Not exactly." The tone was even dryer.

"You don't mean to say! You surely ain't implying that Lord Rexford never took *you* to Harry's."

"Not even once."

"Well, I'm dashed."

There was a pregnant silence. Both men seemed rocked by recent revelations.

"Well," Reggie was finally moved to say, "I collect that makes it even more important for me to find out what his lordship wants to know."

"Which is?"

"How your suit is prospering. Those are his words, not mine. Seems he has his heart set on your marrying Caro Percival's daughter. I told him that as far as I knew you were going about the business in first-rate fashion. But he wants me to find out whether you've gone down on one knee yet. And if you've not, just when you plan to. What shall I tell him?" He paused expectantly.

It was on the tip of Dalton's tongue to tell his esteemed parent to go to the devil, but he bit back the words and rose to his feet instead. "Go home, Reggie."

"Oh, but you have to give me an answer, Dalton." York-Jones was obviously distressed. "I mean to say, I can't let his lordship down. Not after Harriet Wilson. Surely you must see that."

"Hmm. Well, yes, I suppose you are rather on the spot." He stood a moment in frowning thought. "Very well, then. You can tell my father that I mean to make an offer of marriage at the first opportunity."

"Oh, I say!" The young man leaped to his feet and began pumping Dalton's arm up and down. "That really is famous, by Jove. And to think I get to be the first to wish you happy!"

"A bit premature, but thank you all the same. Now go home, Reggie. I have a call to make first thing in the morning."

Chapter
Twenty-two

"MY GOD!"

Lord Dalton had at last located Mr. Chalgrove. He had gone first to White's, then to Boodle's, and on to Brook's. The last place he'd expected to find him was in his own rooms. Nor in his wildest dreams would he have expected to find this pattern card for aspiring Corinthians looking so disheveled. At nine o'clock in the evening he was still wearing his nightclothes and dressing gown. He was unshaven and, so Dalton suspected, unwashed. He was seated, gazing morosely at the fire with a wine decanter at his elbow. Dalton noticed—with a measure of relief—that it appeared to be untouched. "I say, are you sickening for something?" he asked.

"No, of course not." The dandy didn't bother to turn his head and look at his visitor. "I just happen to prefer my own company at the moment. Go away."

"I'll do nothing of the sort. I've come to take you to Almack's. Hurry up and get ready. We don't have all that much time."

At least he got his host's full attention. The gaze was stony. "Whatever put such a maggot in your head, Dalton? I've no intention of going to Almack's. Tonight or any night. Ever. Going to Almack's was the biggest mistake of my life."

"Hmm." Lord Dalton, towering above the seated man, studied him carefully. "Well, I see that I was right. You are well and truly smitten. Get dressed, Roderick. You are going. For I badly need you to get me off the hook."

"Oh, and just what hook is that? Not that I intend to move a muscle, mind you."

"The matrimonial hook. As you, and everyone else in town, are aware of, I've been pursuing Lady Sylvia for weeks now with an eye toward marriage. But now I've discovered that there's no need for such drastic action. It was all my dear father's idea, you see. His dying request. Or so he put it. But this morning I visited his London quack and found out that the old fraud is healthy as a horse and will probably outlive me. So I don't intend to become a Tenant for Life just to please his lying lordship. But the problem is, it wouldn't be the thing just to drop Lady Sylvia. So that's where you come in, my dear fellow."

Mr. Chalgrove's attention had been rapt. But his expression was not encouraging. "It's a bit difficult for me to imagine why," he drawled.

"That should be obvious. There's no question that you have a *tendre* for the girl. In fact, you look ready to die of it. You know, if my own case weren't so desperate, I'd actually be enjoying this. But the thing is, Chalgrove, I need you to get in there ahead of me and offer for Lady Sylvia. That would fix everything right and tight. No one could think the worse of the girl for accepting you. You're almost as good a catch as I am."

" 'Almost'?" Chalgrove's eyebrows rose. Despite his unkempt appearance he managed to look himself again.

"Almost," Lord Dalton repeated firmly. "Your fortune may be as good. Or better? And I will admit that females seem to find you handsome, though God knows why. But you mustn't forget my title. In the female mind that always tips the scale. Aside from all that," he said musingly, "I've had the impression that this little gudgeon"—he ignored Chalgrove's dangerous frown—"actually prefers you over me. Which is another reason for my not going down on one knee. I'd hate like the very devil to wind up leg-shackled to someone with so little taste."

"Never fear. You won't be."

"Ah, that's the spirit. Come now. Get into your evening clothes and it's on to Almack's."

"Skip your cursed exhortation to the troops, Dalton. You miss my point entirely. Lady Sylvia's not going to marry you *or* me. She's in love with someone else."

That was a leveler. Uninvited, Dalton pulled up a chair and collapsed in it. "I'll not believe it."

"Well, you'd better. She's been meeting the fellow on the sly. Some military cove she knew on the continent.

"So you were never really on the hook, old man. She's played us both for fools. You can go down on one knee till it gets rheumatism and she still won't have you. So go on"—he waved dismissively—"get out of here, make your offer, and leave me in peace."

Dalton was thinking furiously. "Don't expect me to be that rash. She wouldn't be the first female to let love go chase itself when a title and fortune got dangled before her. Take my word for it, 'all for love's' more honored in the breach than the observance."

"Not Lady Sylvia!"

"No need to look so murderous. Your loyalty does you credit. But will you answer me two things?" Without waiting for Chalgrove's permission, he proceeded. "First, how did you learn of her attachment to this fellow?"

"From Emily Warrington."

Dalton's lip curled. "And you believed that malicious doxy? I say, Chalgrove, you are losing your touch. Now for the second question. Are you in love with Lady Sylvia?"

"That's none of your damn business."

"So I was right. You are then." Dalton seemed satisfied with his probing. "Come on. Get dressed. You've wasted enough of my time already."

"But you don't understand, Dalton." Chalgrove's customary haughty expression had been exchanged for abject misery. "She told me that she never wants to see me again."

"Did she, by Jove?" Dalton visibly brightened. "Well, that *is* good news. Sounds like she may actually be in love with you."

"Have you lost your senses?"

"Not at all. You see, the trouble with you women-hating coves is that you never gain any experience of the way the feminine mind works. Then, when you finally do get smitten, you're completely out of your depth."

He got up, walked to the mantle, and pulled the bell rope.

"Just what do you think you're doing?"

"Calling your man. We're going to Almack's even if I have to hold you down while your valet dresses you."

The young ladies of Grosvenor Square were only slightly less reluctant to visit Almack's than Mr. Chalgrove. But Lady Fremantle met their demurs with a rush of indignation. "Not go? Of course you will go! Do you realize that the Season is nearly over and not one of you has had an offer? I vow I'll never be able to show my face in Society again. I'll be forced to take up residence in the country, and if there is one thing I cannot abide, it's the country. And what is more, my sisters are bound to blame me for the fact that the three of you have not found husbands. Though who could have made a greater push than I have, I'd like to know? And without one of them so much as lifting a finger! Why, just look at what I've done for you alone, Claire. You certainly are not the same hopeless case you were before I took you under my wing, now are you?"

"No, ma'am." Claire's face remained composed, but her eyes twinkled as they met her tall cousin's.

Except for claiming credit, for once my aunt is right, Jenny mused. Claire has changed. Almost beyond recognition. And not primarily in appearance, though she has slimmed down a great deal. The real change comes from within. She seems confident. And happy. The reunion with her father has done wonders for her.

She was snapped out of her reverie by her aunt's summation. "We will indeed go to Almack's tonight. And the three of you shall be at pains to make yourselves agreeable to any eligible gentlemen present or I shall be most displeased."

The contrast to their first visit to the Assembly Rooms was striking. The cousins were no longer a curiosity. Indeed, they had quite a few friends among the assembled ton. It was no longer necessary for the patronesses to steer eligible young men their way. None of them lacked for partners. Claire, particularly, was experiencing a change of fortune. Several gentlemen present revised their earlier impressions of her appearance and recalled the sizable fortune that came with this only child. And, noting the absence of those two formidable rivals, Lord Dalton and Mr. Chalgrove, other gentlemen, who had been too intimidated at other times, now vied for the chance to stand up with the trio's beauty, Lady Sylvia.

Jenny did not quite achieve the popularity of the other two. She had her admirers, but her height and her insightful wit put off the more faint of heart. York-Jones, however, was not among their number. One night with Harriet Wilson had made him feel equal to anything. During a rather long lull in the course of a country dance, he proposed.

No sooner were the fatal words out of his mouth than Jenny was swept away from him. "Well?" he asked when they were once more reunited.

"Well, what?"

"You know," he whispered frowning. "Will you?"

She sighed and looked down at him with tender exasperation. "I was sure that I'd misheard you. Nobody, Reggie, would actually make an offer during a country dance. And at Almack's of all places."

"Well, I didn't know when else I might see you privately."

"And you might not get up the nerve again?" she ventured.

His denial was spoiled slightly by his blush.

Once more, they were involved in the dance figure. "Whatever put such a maggot in your brain?" she asked when they came together.

"It's not a maggot. I've been thinking of it all along. And Lord Rexford himself said it was time I married."

"Lord Rexford? Dalton's father?"

The small man nodded.

"What does he have to say to anything?"

"He's my godfather, didn't you know?"

The dance came to an end. As he escorted his partner back to her chair, York-Jones whispered, "You don't have to give me an answer now. Just promise you'll think about it."

"Oh, there's no need for thought. I can give you my answer now. It's no. Despite the great Lord Rexford, you're far too young to think of marriage to anyone. And as for marrying me, the fact is, I do happen to love you. Like a brother. And what's more, I have the perfect young lady in mind for you, my little sister Elizabeth. She'll make her bow in three years time. And if I may be permitted to boast, I collect she may cast even our cousin Sylvia in the shade. And, no, she is not a Long Meg like me."

"Oh, I say," he protested.

"No, you don't say. But what you will do is wait for Elizabeth." Jenny could not believe just how much she sounded like her aunt.

Lord Dalton and Mr. Chalgrove created their usual sensation when they made their appearance. Mr. Chalgrove resisted all efforts to be paired with a dancing partner. "We came only for the refreshments," he told a patroness solemnly. "Who could resist the lure of weak lemonade and stale cake?"

Lord Dalton was, however, more conforming. He whisked Lady Sylvia out from under a prospective partner's nose and took the floor with her.

As he watched the handsome couple dance, Chalgrove concentrated upon keeping his face a blank. His success was only moderate, evidently. "I wouldn't give a penny for your thoughts," a brittle voice spoke at his elbow. "I can't begin to tell you how wearied I've become from watching all the men in this town make cakes of themselves over that Kinnard chit." He turned to find Lady Warrington there beside him.

"Jealousy doesn't become you, Emily," he drawled. "It's frightfully bad ton, you know."

"Oh, I'm not jealous in the least, I can assure you. It's just that I find all of this second-generation Percival lore tedious to the extreme. Tedious *and* ridiculous. Did you know that— But, no. I do have the most delicious *on-dit* to tell, but I promised Lady Jersey she should hear it first. Do come along, though, Chalgrove. This is a bit of gossip you won't want to miss." She took his arm.

The dancers left the floor. Lord Dalton escorted Lady Sylvia to a chair next to Claire and Jenny and, with the Honorable Reggie York-Jones and Lord Fremantle, went for refreshments. Lady Warrington, with Chalgrove still in tow, drew Lady Jersey and the entourage around her to one side. She took care to position her group within easy earshot of the cousins.

After the gentlemen had returned bearing tepid lemonade,

the conversation lagged. Lady Sylvia, who rarely had much to say in any case, seemed all too conscious of Mr. Chalgrove's proximity. Lord Dalton was too engaged in assessing this reaction to contribute much in the way of small talk. Lord Fremantle appeared uncharacteristically blue-deviled. He had seldom strung three words together throughout the evening. Claire watched him anxiously. And the usually garrulous York-Jones was at a loss whether to be cast down or relieved over his rejected marriage offer. After a few failed attempts to get a conversation going, Jenny had given up, and, without much interest, was watching the dancing.

Then the name "Percival," spoken in a mocking tone, caught all their attention. It was impossible thereafter to miss a word of what Lady Warrington was telling the group collected around her, lured by the prospect of hearing the "juiciest scandal to come this way for years."

"The entire business is enough to send me into the whoops just to think on it," she was saying. "The *fabulous* Percivals. Almack's own version of the Cinderella story. Here came these penniless beauties out of the Irish—or was it the Welsh?—cinders. And each captivated a handsome prince. Am I not right? Isn't that how the story goes? And were they not, then, to live happily ever after in the best fairy-tale tradition? Well, my dears"—she looked around the group in a conspiratorial manner and lowered her voice; it seemed to lose none of its histrionic carrying power, however—"so much for happy endings. I have it on good authority that every one of those marriages ended in disaster.

"Well, to be fair," she qualified, with a straight face, though her eyes sparked mischief, "I should except our own dear Lady Fremantle. After all, her spouse was considerate enough to die in two years time and leave her a very wealthy woman. Her case, I'll grant, carried on the fairy-tale tradition."

The group around her tittered appreciatively. Lord Fremantle's head turned angrily, but Claire had laid a restraining hand upon his sleeve.

"And of course everyone in town knows all about Lord Hazlett's mistress and little bastards. So much for *that* Percival's happy marriage. And as for the one in the north—the Long

286

Meg's mother—I understand that the poor dear breeds more often than the gamekeeper's rabbits. But, then, you must know all that. It's the latest scandal I wished to tell you."

Jenny heard Sylvia's sudden intake of breath and looked her way. She had gone white as chalk. Jenny just stopped herself from reaching out to take her hand. Such an impulsive action would only call attention to her cousin's distress.

"A friend of mine just let the cat out of the bag," Lady Warrington was saying, with obvious relish. "Vienna has been abuzz with the scandal. It has quite eclipsed all political matters. Everything pales beside the news that the fourth Percival—our own dear Lady Sylvia's mother—has thrown her cap over the windmill, deserted her husband—whom she's been cuck-olding for years, so they say—and has run off to Paris with a cavalry officer who's at least ten years younger than she . . . and has left a wife and two little ones behind. Now I ask you, is that not the last ironic touch? Indeed if that does not write finis to all of this absurd Percival nonsense, then, my dears, I for one cannot imagine what it will take."

Lady Warrington paused to enjoy the sensation she'd cre-ated. Her audience was looking appropriately shocked and began stealing glances at the Percival daughters, trying to as-certain whether they'd overheard. Mr. Chalgrove broke the silence.

"Emily, dear." His tone was solicitous. "You must allow me to summon your carriage."

"Whatever for? I've certainly no intention of leaving yet."

"But my dear lady, you surely cannot contemplate staying here a moment longer with the front of that lovely gown of yours soaked with lemonade."

Lady Warrington glanced hastily down at her modish Urling's lace creation. "Have you taken leave of your senses, Chalgrove? There's no lemonade on my gown."

He raised his quizzing glass and peered closer. "By Jove, you're right." His voice was redolent of surprise. "Well, now, that's easily remedied." And he slowly, deliberately, to the ac-companiment of an entire chorus of shocked gasps, emptied the contents of the glass he held down her ladyship's décolletage.

Chalgrove took no notice of the ringing slap across his

cheek. Instead, he turned toward Jenny, bowing gracefully, and raised his empty glass in a salute. "My gratitude, Miss Blythe," he called out to her. "Now, thanks to you, I've at last discovered a proper use for this insipid, undrinkable concoction."

Chapter
Twenty-three

L ADY CLAIRE FOLLOWED THE STRAINS OF MUSIC TO THEIR source. The melody was somber, as befitted the mood of Fremantle House.

Lord Fremantle glanced up from the keyboard as she entered the room. His smile was rather forced. "I hope my music didn't disturb you. I've been trying to play softly. Is anyone else up?"

"Your playing could never disturb me." She came to stand by the pianoforte. "And I'm the only one up. Or at least the only one to have left her room. Please don't let me interrupt you. We do need music."

"How is Cousin Sylvia taking all of this?" He continued to play softly.

"It's difficult to say. Last night she told us that she had known about her mother's affair before she came here. She had wished to stay home with her father, but he'd insisted that she make her come-out. He wanted her to behave as if nothing had happened. It was his opinion that the scandal wouldn't reach London. At least not until the Season was over. But Sylvia has been braced since her arrival for the ax to fall at any moment. Especially when Captain St. Laurent arrived in London. She was terrified that he'd let the cat out of the bag. He had given her his word that he wouldn't mention it, but that odious Lady Warrington wormed it out of him."

"She would." Lord Fremantle forgot himself and struck a dissonant chord.

"Sylvia has been convinced that the scandal would make her ineligible for a brilliant marriage. That's why she never encouraged any of her suitors. She felt it would be dishonest to do so."

"That's absurd, of course. No right-thinking man would give a fig."

She smiled at him. "Yes, but one gets the impression that right-thinking men are rather scarce in London."

"Oh, come now. Aren't you a bit hard on us males?"

"Never on you, Cousin James. But tell me. I was thinking of having a talk with Sylvia later in the day. Do you think I should? She is so very reserved, she might feel it an intrusion. Then, too, Jenny is much better than I at this sort of thing. We both look up to her."

"And rightly so. But not in this instance," his lordship said firmly. "You are the very one to talk to her, Claire."

"I'll do it then if you think I should," she said resolutely.

He played on softly for a few moments, then asked casually, "I collect that you will all be leaving soon, then?"

"Yes. I do think last night put a period to our Season." She smiled wryly. "Poor Aunt Fremantle is utterly prostrated by the whole business, you know." She laughed suddenly. "She even went so far as to blame Jenny for the fact that Mr. Chalgrove has been barred from Almack's for life. Aunt says that he never would have thought of such a shocking thing without her example."

Fremantle laughed, too. "Oh, I don't know. He's an inventive man, I collect. And the choices are limited. One cannot, after all, challenge a female to a duel or give her a leveler. Though I must say that for the one and only time in my life I quite longed to."

"You? Well, that just goes to show the lengths you've been driven to by our invasion of your orderly life." She couldn't quite bring herself to look at him. "I collect you'll be relieved to see the last of your troublesome cousins."

"Quite the contrary," he said huskily. "I shall hate it above all things. I don't think I've ever spent such a happy time. In fact, I know I haven't.

"And what about you, Claire? Will you be glad to leave? I know you didn't wish to come, but has it been so bad for you?"

289

"Oh, no. In fact, it's been the most marvelous thing that has ever happened to me."

"Yes, there's no denying your success." His smile was forced. "I watched you last night, you know, with all the young gentlemen flocking around you. I can't believe that any Percival sister was ever more sought after."

"You exaggerate. But no matter. For the point is, that although I never in my wildest dreams expected such a thing to happen, I've fallen in love."

Lord Fremantle looked as if he'd just received a mortal blow. But he managed to keep his voice steady. "Well, then, I, of course, am happy for you. And who is the fortunate fellow? If you don't mind saying, that is."

"Why, you, of course."

"I b-beg your pardon?"

"Oh, I know it's a shocking thing to say, James. And I realize your regard for me is—cousinly. But I did want you to know. For I feel that even though you are such a tower of strength to everyone around you"—tears filled her eyes—"and no one could have been kinder to me than you have been, I do believe that in many ways you undervalue yourself . . . prodigiously. So in the teeth of maidenly modesty, I had to tell you that you are— and always shall be—my beau ideal.

"Now I know I've embarrassed you terribly. And you must not concern yourself that I shall ever regret such plain speaking. For thanks to you, I am not that same quaking, self-loathing creature that I was. I shall be all right. Truly."

"Are you certain that you aren't confusing gratitude—a *misplaced* gratitude at that—for love? You were always beautiful, Claire. You just didn't realize it."

"I do know you truly thought so. Which made you a candidate for a straightjacket of course. But it meant everything to me that you saw more than—or should I say *less* than"—she grimaced—"just the surface."

"I was very little ahead of the others in realizing what a superior person you are. Your kindness. Your talent. Your sense of humor. All these things eclipse even your physical beauty. You do realize that you can have any man in London, don't you?"

"Not unless *you* offer for me."

"Are you serious?" He looked unbelieving. "You'd actually settle for a dull dog like me?"

"No, I'd not '*settle*.' I wish to marry you above all things. And if you don't feel the same—well, I won't kill myself or eat myself obese or enter a convent or anything else of the kind. But I won't ever marry. You may be sure of that. For no one—*no* one—can ever hope to measure up to you, James."

"I'd—I'd—no idea. Oh, Claire, my dearest Claire. I don't doubt that I've been in love with you from the moment we first met. But it never occurred to me that you felt the same."

"Oh, James, you peagoose. I said that you were hopeless. Now it's shocking enough that I've actually proposed to you. Oh, please, my darling, don't make me kiss you as well. I'd never be able to face myself in the glass again after such rackety behavior."

Lord Fremantle needed no more prodding. He jumped up from the pianoforte and folded her in his arms.

Lady Fremantle's majordomo had been fully engaged in turning away morning callers. "Her Ladyship and the young ladies are not at home," he announced time after time to the would-be gossipmongers who were dying to assess the full damage caused by the scandal that had broken at Almack's. London had seen nothing like it for years. No one would soon forget this Season. But the curious had to content themselves with the satisfaction of being able to report at their next port of call that toplofty Lydia Fremantle was too humiliated to show her face.

Mr. Chalgrove was not so easily put off, however. He pushed past Jackson impatiently, and, over the butler's protests, handed him his greatcoat, hat, and cane. He was running up the stairs as Jenny was coming down them. "Where is she?" he demanded.

Her eyebrows rose, but for once she bridled her tongue. "The first door on the right," she told him.

"Come in." A listless voice answered his preemptive knock. Lady Sylvia was seated on the window seat, her legs tucked up underneath her skirts, looking out at the leaden skies that so aptly reflected her frame of mind. She glanced with disinterest over her shoulder. Then her eyes widened with shock.

Chalgrove closed the door softly behind him and leaned against it. "Will you marry me?" he asked.

She pretended not to have heard the question. "I'm truly sorry, Mr. Chalgrove, that you were barred from Almack's on my account. I wish there was some way I could make amends."

He strode across the room to sit beside her and clasp both her hands in his. "There is. Marry me. Then we can both not go to Almack's together."

She managed a smile. "I must confess I'm glad that I never have to see that odious place again. But please don't feel sorry for me, Mr. Chalgrove—" Her voice broke. "I don't think I could bear that."

"I don't feel sorry for you," he said impatiently. "Oh, well, dammit . . . I do feel bad that you're obviously miserable, but that's because I love you and has nothing to do with those tabbies who are chewing us up right now while they drink their scandal broth. Those people are beneath contempt, my darling. And you should not mind them in the least."

Her steady gaze seemed to pierce right through him. "That's an odd speech for you to make, sir. It was my impression that you, above all people, savored a good scandal. And that you would never be able to tolerate becoming an object of sport yourself. You've been used to being the conveyer of gossip, never its subject."

He reddened. "Sylvia, I've done a lot of shabby things in my lifetime. But none, believe me, that I regret so deeply as hurting your cousin. I know you have every right to hold me in contempt. I know that I'm not nearly good enough for you. But I will try and change. Oh, I realize that people who make that sort of statement rarely do, but, honestly, my darling, I have the highest hopes in my case. You see, I'd always thought it quite impossible for me to fall in love. And—well, now that I've managed that without so much as trying, I can't help but feel that all things are possible. Will you marry me?"

She gazed at him with wonder. "You really do love me?"

"With all my heart. Tell me. Am I going about this proposal business all wrong? I've never given it the slightest thought you see. I'm quite a high-stickler in other things. But in affairs of the heart I'm a complete novice. Stands to reason, for when I think on it, I just discovered lately that I have one. But I'm quite willing to go down on one knee, my dearest Sylvia, or do anything else that's required."

"Oh, no, that isn't at all necessary, Roderick. Your proposal is imminently satisfactory."

"So—will you marry me?"

"You're certain that you won't at some later date mind about my mother?"

"Your mother has nothing to say to anything. Will you marry me?"

"Of course. It's what I've wished ever since I returned your snuffbox."

Had anyone been alert enough to interpret it, the cessation of melody in the drawing room might have served as a clue that some passionate lovemaking was taking place there. But there was no such signal in Lady Sylvia's bedchamber, particularly since no one besides Jenny and the butler was even aware that Mr. Chalgrove was on the premises. Therefore, the unwitting chambermaid who walked into the room carrying a scuttle filled with coal was not really to blame for the fact that, when she saw Lady Sylvia on the lap of some strange gentleman, kissing him as though that activity might never stop, she let the heavily laden scuttle drop through nerveless fingers. The resulting reverberating crash earned only the merest glance from Mr. Chalgrove. A master of aplomb, he carried on thereafter as before.

Jackson the butler stood, he thought, in grave danger of losing his position. For the second time, in defiance of her ladyship's order, a young gentleman had brushed on past him.

"You're a bit late," Jenny observed when Lord Dalton strode into the library where she sat reading. "Mr. Chalgrove arrived ten minutes ago."

"I know. I've been lurking, waiting for him to show up. By the by, where is he?"

"As far as I know, in Sylvia's bedchamber."

"Why, that sly dog!" He grinned.

She gave him a hard look. "Well, I must say you don't seem too upset by the fact your rival has stolen a march on you."

"Oh, I'm not." He pulled up a chair beside her and collapsed on it. "*Relieved* is the mot juste."

"Aren't you the same fellow who openly declared your intention of marrying my cousin Sylvia?"

"One and the same. But the situation's quite different now. I'm under no compulsion to wed. Thank God."

"I collect that out of loyalty to my cousin I should now take offense at your relief. But my curiosity has the upper hand. Just why were you under a compulsion—and what happened to it?"

"Well"—he stretched out his legs and yawned lazily—"for the first time in my life I was trying to please my parent. And let my case be a lesson to you, Miss Blythe. Never, never try and please a parent. It's a complete waste of everybody's time."

He went on then to explain his father's feigned illness and how he'd discovered he'd been hoodwinked. "So I no longer need to hurry toward the altar. The old fraud will probably outlive me. That is," he added quietly to himself, "if his increase in exercise doesn't bring on a seizure."

"I beg your pardon?"

"Never mind."

"Well, that explains a lot. I did think that for an acknowledged rake you weren't very skillful in your courtship. Still, if your heart wasn't in it . . ."

"If you're trying to insult me, you're wasting your time. I'm at peace with the world just now."

"I must say you look it. But just suppose that Sylvia and Mr. Chalgrove don't make a match of it, what then?"

"Don't be so negative." He frowned. "I have every confidence in Chalgrove. He's a most determined fellow. Always gets his way in the end. Does that upset you? I realize he's no favorite of yours. As I recall, you even preferred *me* to him. Which sinks the poor cove past all redemption."

"I grant you I did feel that way in the beginning. But after he doused Lady Warrington with lemonade, it's amazing how Mr. Chalgrove's stock has risen." She grinned wickedly, and he laughed. "And as much as I'd like to see you squirm, I also expect his suit will prosper. There seems to be something in the air today. I strongly suspect that my cousins, Lady Claire and Lord

294

Fremantle, are now betrothed. At least I saw them kissing shamelessly by the pianoforte."

"Did you, by Jove!"

"Isn't it famous? Aunt will need sal volatile."

"Hmm. Them in the drawing room and the other pair upstairs. That would appear to leave only us."

"Oh, well now, I don't like to boast—though of course I will when I go home—but I, too, have had a most flattering proposal."

She had his full attention. He sat bolt upright and glared. "Not that pup York-Jones."

"Why, yes, as a matter of fact."

"I'll kill him!"

"Why on earth would you do a shatter-brained thing like that?"

"Because I intend to marry you myself."

"You do?" She choked, then rallied. "In that case it's fortunate that I turned young Reggie down."

"Quite fortunate. Saves me a murder."

"But I don't understand." And, indeed, she did look dazed. "Didn't you just tell me, only minutes ago, that you didn't intend getting married?"

"No. You weren't paying close attention, a habit I trust you'll rectify once we're wed. I said I didn't *have* to marry. That's not at all same thing as marrying to please myself, which I intend doing as soon as possible after we post the banns."

Jenny was beginning to collect her wits a bit. "And, when, may I ask, did you reach this startling conclusion? That we should wed, I mean."

"That's entirely the wrong question. For I couldn't get around to that stage till Lady Sylvia was disposed of. I would have hated to cause her any humiliation by appearing to jilt her. Far better that she jilt me. The question you should ask is when did I realize I was in love with you." There was a pregnant pause. "Well?"

"I'm sorry. I'm too busy trying to comprehend that you *are* in love with me. I haven't gotten around yet to wondering when it happened."

"Well, I'll tell you anyway. I've spent a great deal of time trying to puzzle the whole thing out, you see. For I don't mind saying, it took me by surprise."

"So I'd imagine."

"I collect I should have suspected when I kept thinking of another Percival daughter all the while I was actually pursuing Lady Sylvia. But since what I was thinking wasn't necessarily complimentary, I overlooked the symptom. I should have known, though. Then of course the clincher came when you coaxed me in off the ledge that infamous day. What a helpmeet to have, I told myself. No crisis too great. No hero too small. That's Miss Blythe for you."

She was regarding him suspiciously. "Surely you don't wish to wed me because I'm the only one who knows your guilty secret—that you're afraid of heights?"

His look was censorious. "I'll ignore that suggestion as unworthy of you.

"Of course, to be perfectly candid"—he grinned suddenly— "it wasn't the coaxing off the ledge part that was the clincher. It was the bit that followed on the floor of the landing that really cooked my goose. By the by, would you mind standing up for just a moment?"

"Not at all," she replied politely, and did so.

He took her in his arms. "I just wondered what it would be like to kiss a girl this tall while we're standing up. Should be a novel experience. I generally have to do a lot of stooping, don't you know. Well, here goes."

After a long, breathless interval he released her. "There now"—he grinned triumphantly—"that should take care of my fear of heights."

"Lord Dalton," she managed to gasp, "I do not intend to marry simply to prevent you from getting a crick in your neck."

"Seems a good enough reason to me. But let's try the sofa there for a change of pace. It could be even more satisfactory."

It was. So very satisfactory, in fact, that they remained oblivious when first Lady Claire and Lord Fremantle and then, a bit later, Lady Sylvia and Mr. Chalgrove came looking for Jenny to tell her their happy news. At least they were almost oblivious.

"I say," Dalton observed after they'd finally forced themselves apart. "Why do I keep having the feeling we're being watched?"

"A guilty conscience, perhaps?"

"My conscience is clear. My intentions are entirely honorable. You're the one with the problem. I can't recall that you've ever said yes to my proposal."

"Yes."

This brief declaration called for another spate of lovemaking. At its conclusion, while Jenny smoothed out her crumpled gown to the best of her ability, Dalton found himself staring at the Romney portrait. "It must have been those Percival sisters that I felt watching us," he said. "I say, do you realize, my love, that your generation has outdone them?"

"You must be funning."

"No, I'm dead serious. It's true. Though it's undoubtedly immodest of me to say so, Fremantle, Chalgrove, and I are far superior catches to the ones they made."

"Don't be absurd." But she did look a bit smug as she played with the idea.

He had walked over to the mantle and was studying the portrait seriously. "Well," he concluded, "I must admit I can see what all the fuss and feathers were about. And, by Jove"—he reached up to touch the lady with the harp—"your mother's the loveliest of the lot."

"Thank you, but that's not my mother. Mama's holding the flute. She couldn't play a note, of course."

"But I thought the flute one was Caro."

"It is."

"Your mother is Caro? It can't be. Are you quite sure?"

"Of course I'm sure. I ought to know my own mother, for heaven's sake. Other people were always confusing the twins, of course.

"But whatever is the matter?" she asked anxiously. "You look as if you'd seen a ghost."

"My God!" he choked, and sat down suddenly. "What a rotten, miserable turn of events that is. Dammit, Jenny, this really is the outside of enough. I've just discovered that I'll be marrying to please my father after all."

WINTERBOURNE

by Susan Carroll

In the harsh, turbulent Middle Ages, sweet, timid Lady Melyssan is content to be alone. But in a desperate move to resist the advances of the dreaded king, she claims to be married to his worst enemy, Lord Jaufre de Macy, the legendary Dark Knight.

When she seeks temporary shelter in Jaufre's abandoned castle, Winterbourne, she is unprepared for the fierce, angry warrior who arrives to confront her. He is a man as rough and unforgiving as the Welsh borderlands he rules. But neither Jaufre's dark heart nor Melyssan's innocent one can resist the love that is their destiny.